A
MILLION
WORLDS
WITH
YOU

A MILLION WORLDS WITH YOU

—A FIREBIRD NOVEL—

CLAUDIA GRAY

An Imprint of HarperCollins*Publishers*

HarperTeen is an imprint of HarperCollins Publishers.

Library of Congress Control Number: 2016941453
ISBN 978-0-06-227903-3

Typography by Torborg Davern
18 19 20 21   PC/LSCH   10 9 8 7 6 5 4 3
❖
First paperback edition, 2017

A
MILLION
WORLDS
WITH
YOU

1

I CAN'T BREATHE. I CAN'T THINK. ALL I CAN DO IS HANG ON to this cable and stare down at the river at least four hundred feet below me. Nothing stands between me and death but a few nylon ropes, clutched in hands that are already slick with sweat.

Traveling to other dimensions can be scary—but I've never been thrown into anything as terrifying as this.

Panic clouds my thoughts and turns everything surreal. My brain refuses to accept that this is actually happening—even as the truth stretches my arms and pulls my muscles. Every pound of my body weight cramps my fingers and tells me how immediate my situation is. The city lights from the ground below seem so distant they might as well be stars. But still my mind cries, *This is just a nightmare. You're seeing things. This can't be real—*

But the Firebird locket hanging around my neck still

radiates heat from my journey into another world. What I'm seeing—the mortal danger I'm in—is definitely real.

Then I realize that I'm dangling from a hovership, one projecting holographic advertisements upward into the dusky sky. My eyes finally focus on one detail from the metropolis beneath me long enough to recognize St. Paul's Cathedral—and, beyond it, a futuristic skyscraper that has never existed in my version of London.

The Londonverse. I'm back in the Londonverse, the first alternate dimension I ever traveled to.

Apparently it's also going to be the dimension I die in.

"Marguerite!" I turn my head to see my Aunt Susannah, who's hanging out of one of the hovership's passenger windows. Her dyed-blond hair whips around her face, blown by the same strong gusts that tear at my gray dress, exposing me to the world below. Not that I care who sees my butt while I'm on the verge of death. Aunt Susannah's eyes are wide, and dark lines of mascara streak down her cheeks with tears. Other passengers crowd around her, pressing their faces to the hovership windows, eyes wide as they stare at the girl who's about to die.

Okay, I think, trying to slow my breaths. *All I have to do is climb back in. It's not that far. Up four feet, over twenty?*

But it's not that easy. I don't have the upper body strength to climb the rope on its own, and the nearest metal strut is out of reach. How did I even get here? This universe's Marguerite must have tumbled from one of the hovership windows and grabbed a rope to save herself, which is why

I'm now dangling hundreds of feet above the city of London. . . .

Panic seizes me again. Every inch between me and the river seems to elongate. Dizziness courses through me. My muscles go weak. And my grip on the ropes trembles, bringing me closer to death.

Oh, God, no no no. I have to pull this together. If I don't save her, we're both doomed.

Because if you're in another dimension when your host dies, then, at the exact same instant, you die.

I could just get the hell out of this universe. My parents' invention, the Firebird, gives me the ability to travel to a new dimension at any moment. Now seems like a really good time to check out some other reality—any other reality. But to use the Firebird, I'd have to hit the controls and leap out. Both of my hands are currently busy gripping this rope to keep me from plunging to my death. Kind of a catch-22 here. The hovership flies so far up that by the time I fell all the way down, my body would be traveling at a velocity that would make hitting the water as instantly fatal as smashing onto concrete.

"Marguerite!" another voice calls out. In astonishment I look over and see Paul.

What is he doing on this hovership? We didn't even know each other in this universe!

I don't care why he's here. I only care that he is. My love for Paul Markov is one of the few constants in the multiverse. He would do anything, even risk his own life, if it meant he could keep me safe. If anyone can get me out of this, he can.

Normally I get myself out of my own perilous situations, but this, today? This is bad.

"Paul!" I shout back. "Please, help me!"

"They're landing as fast as they can," he calls to me. The wind ruffles his dark hair, and he edges out onto the metal frames for the hovership's projectors with total assurance; he must go rock-climbing in this universe too, because the height doesn't faze him. "Just hang on."

Sure enough, I can hear the changing key of the engines. The propellers send new winds to buffet me. London below comes slightly closer, though it's still mostly a blur of lights and murky twilight colors—dark blues and grays and blacks. My adrenaline-flooded brain refuses to make sense of the shapes below me any longer; I might as well be staring down at artwork by Jackson Pollock with its squiggles and blots and spills.

I imagine a Pollock painting with a huge red splotch in the center. Blood red. Nothing else will remain of me if I let go of this cable.

My fingers hurt so much. My shoulders. My back. No matter how badly I want to hold on, I won't be able to manage much longer. Within minutes, I will fall to my death.

Sweat beads along my face despite the chilly winds blowing around me. I can taste the salt as it trickles into my open, panting mouth. As I try to readjust my grip, people on the hovership scream. One of my black shoes slips from my foot and tumbles out of sight.

"Marguerite, no!" Aunt Susannah sounds like she's been screaming. "You don't have to do this, sweetheart. Don't let go! We'll make it right, whatever's bothering you, I swear it. Just hold on!"

I want to shriek back, *Does it look like I need any more encouragement to hold on?* But then I realize what my aunt just said. *You don't have to do this.*

She thinks I'm attempting suicide. And since I can't figure out any other way this world's Marguerite could've wound up in this situation, I think—I think Aunt Susannah is right.

But it wasn't this world's Marguerite who tried to kill herself. It was the other one. The wicked version of me who's working on behalf of Triad, even now. She attacked me at home and escaped into this dimension, but only in this instant—as I gulp in desperate breaths and hang on with the last of my strength—do I realize what her plan really is.

She's trying to kill me.

She's trying to kill every me, in every world, everywhere.

2

I LEARNED OF MY DARKER SELF A FEW DAYS AGO, WHEN I first visited her dimension. But I only realized how dangerous she was when I tried to go home earlier today—only hours before I wound up dangling above London—and she followed me there.

By *follow*, I mean *possess*.

I had just leaped back into my own body after a mad chase to save Paul Markov, who is—

—what can I call him? Throughout the multiverse, our fates are entwined in ways both beautiful and tragic. We have seen worlds where we rejected each other, hurt each other, hated each other—and the knowledge of how terrible our romance could turn devastated us both.

But I've got bigger problems than my love life.

The moment I returned to my own dimension, I opened my eyes to see Theo standing above me. He looked haggard and pale—proof of the terrible damage done to him by the drug Nightthief, the one that made it possible for another dimension's Theo to possess him and spy on us for months. Paul had endangered himself to find a cure and save our friend's life. "About time you got here," Theo said with a wry smile.

"Good, you made it. How do you feel?"

"I've been better." His faux-vintage Beatles T-shirt hung on his too-skinny frame. Dark circles shadowed his eyes. So his first question seemed natural. "But, hey, you got the juice, right? The data for the juice, I mean." He meant the treatment for exposure to Nightthief.

"Right. You'll be feeling better in no time." I looked around for my parents, who needed to hear about Triad's plans ASAP. We had believed only one other dimension was spying on us, trying to manipulate events, but I'd found out that the real threat was a third dimension, the powerful Home Office, which had plans so much darker than mere spying. "Where are Mom and Dad?"

"They were out when I got here. Probably at the university labs, trying to figure some other way out of this, or building another Firebird."

I nodded absently. No point in calling them—my mom and dad, the illustrious scientists who created the most miraculous device in existence, rarely remembered to turn their cell phones on because *that's* too much technology. But they weren't the only ones I worried about. "Have you checked to see if Paul has come back yet?"

"You found him, huh?"

As I sat up, dizziness overtook me—nausea and vertigo both.

That was the sign. The warning. The moment I should've protected myself.

Instead, I only thought I'd moved too quickly. "Whoa. What was that?"

"You've been through a lot," Theo said. In the moment I didn't recognize the gleam of triumph in his eyes. "No wonder you're tired."

Still I felt strange. Uneasy. But I didn't suspect what was coming.

"So, Paul was going to come back at the exact same time as you?" Theo asked.

"That's what he said. Where did I leave my phone? I want to call him."

"Don't worry," Theo began going through the constant mess of papers on the rainbow table; I thought he was looking for my tPhone. "Take it easy. You'll find him, Meg."

Meg.

Only one person ever called me that. Theo—but not my Theo.

Only the spy from the Triadverse.

I turned to him in horror, realizing he would attack, but it was already too late. Theo and I scrabbled and fought until he pinned me on the wooden floor and injected me with a syringe filled with emerald-green liquid—Nightthief.

At first I thought he was a fool. Nightthief helps

interdimensional travelers take over their hosts and retain full consciousness and control. But I was home in my own body. Was he trying to poison me? Nightthief took months to kill—

—I shuddered, and then I couldn't move. Not my head, not my hand. Yet my lungs breathed without me, and my voice spoke someone else's words: "About time."

Theo smiled as he rose to let me up. "Always a pleasure to meet anyone from the Home Office."

I would've screamed if I could. The three dimensions in which Triad existed were my own; the Triadverse, a world very close to my own but only a few years ahead in technology; and the Home Office, a futuristic hellscape where ruthlessness ruled and profit was God.

During my adventures in different dimensions, I've lived within many of my other selves and learned who I would be if history had unfolded just a bit differently. I could dwell in a Russian palace or under the sea. Sometimes other versions of me made choices I didn't understand; sometimes they dealt with depression and solitude. But none of them had horrified me more than my Home Office version.

She did Triad's bidding. She wouldn't hesitate to kill. She loved to cause pain, which she called her art.

And she had hijacked my body, leaving me powerless.

She seemed to be in charge, too, because Theo asked her, "So, what's our first assignment?"

"Figure out what they're up to." She smiled. Feeling her smile, knowing that she enjoyed turning my body into a prison of flesh and bone—it revolted me more than anything else ever had. "My parents aren't the kind of people to surrender even if it's the smart thing to do, in any universe. But once the versions here have been outsmarted a few times, sabotaged a few times more . . . well, we might be able to bring them in line yet."

Theo nodded and helped her to her feet. "And if we don't get them to work for our cause?"

She laughed. "Then it's time for this dimension to die."

The Firebird only allows you to visit universes in which you exist, because your consciousness can only leap into another version of yourself. I prided myself on taking good care of the other Marguerites, on getting them out of any danger I got them into. But then I caused some problems I couldn't solve. One version of Theo may never walk again because of me. Another Marguerite has been caught up in a multidimensional conspiracy she should never have had to be part of.

And a second me—one I inhabited for nearly a month, one in which I realized I was in love with Paul Markov and went to bed with him—is now expecting the baby I conceived for her.

So I'd come back to my own dimension humbled. Ashamed. Determined. There had to be more ethical ways of traveling through the worlds, ways that wouldn't endanger or violate our other selves.

But I had no idea how profound the violation was until another Marguerite leaped into me.

"Look at this mess," sneered the other Marguerite in my body, the one I'd already begun to think of as the Wicked Marguerite. She shoved a stack of papers covered with scribbled formulae, and they fluttered to the Turkish rug on the floor. As she glanced around the room through my eyes, at the books and the potted plants, the blackboard-paint wall with its chalk equations, and the rainbow table Josie and I hand-painted as children, she didn't see home. Instead, my lips curled in contempt. "Primitive. Disorganized. They might as well live in a cave."

"Yeah, well, you have to stick around in this cave for a while, so get used to it." Theo kicked back in one of the chairs, resting his Chucks on the edge of the table. "What's the game plan?"

"We pretend to belong here." The Wicked Marguerite looked down at the bracelet on my wrist with distaste, then slid it off. "You're good at that, I know. We don't sabotage them right away—we wait, let them think the crisis is over, catch them off guard. But there's one problem we have to take care of right away, and that's Paul Markov."

My terror deepened. Paul knew about most of this; I'd been able to tell him the most important parts back in the Cambridgeverse. But that knowledge had put his life in danger.

My parents had never imagined any of this when they invented the Firebird—a device that allows consciousness to travel through quantum realities, which are what non-science-geniuses call "parallel dimensions." They only wanted to study the countless ways history could unfold. Because

11

everything that can happen *does* happen. Each time we make a choice, or luck comes into play, reality splits in two. This has been going on for infinity and always will.

My mother, Dr. Sophia Kovalenka, became fascinated with the multiverse at the beginning of her career in physics. She didn't only want to prove the existence of alternate realities; she wanted to see them for herself. Since traveling to parallel dimensions had previously been less scientific endeavor, more *Star Trek* episode, she very nearly got laughed out of her academic career. But a few people believed in her, including the English researcher Dr. Henry Caine, who became her collaborator in every way possible. (In other words, he's my dad.) They've worked with other scientists and many grad students as well, including their two current doctoral candidates, Paul Markov and Theodore Beck, and after years of painstaking effort, finally created the device. The Firebirds may look like crazy-complicated steampunk lockets, but they're the most powerful and miraculous scientific creations since the atomic bomb.

Unfortunately, like the bomb, the Firebirds turn out to have significant downsides.

As I said, you can only travel to worlds in which you exist. If there's a world where you died as a child or your parents never met? You'll never see it. Whatever situation your other self is in, you're stuck with it. And you're lucky the Firebird can remind you of your true identity, because otherwise you'll sink into the corners of your host's mind as that person takes over their body and life again.

Unless you're a "perfect traveler"—someone with the ability to maintain memory and control no matter what universe you're in. You can make only one in a dimension. Wyatt Conley made sure this dimension's traveler would be me.

"Let me take the lead, Theo," the Wicked Marguerite said as she checked herself out in a mirror, scowling at my messy hair. "You've been detected before, so they'll suspect you first. But me? Nobody would imagine a 'perfect traveler' could be conquered so easily. Shows how much they know."

"Feel free to take charge. But I should warn you . . ." Theo paused. "It's harder than you think. Separating them from your own versions. Emotions get, uh, confused."

"Maybe yours do. That's not one of my problems." Wicked began braiding back my hair. She pulled tighter than I would, enough that my scalp hurt. But the hairstyle wasn't so dramatically different that it would tip anyone off. "I admit, I wasn't sure about the Nightthief. Whether it would work this well. Nobody's tried to leap into a perfect traveler before."

"You'll probably need a hell of a lot more than I do." Theo sounded maddeningly calm about the damage they were doing to Theo's body and mine. "Keep it close by. Use it the instant you feel the first flicker of—you know."

Wicked wasn't her dimension's perfect traveler. That had been my older sister, Josie. In my visit to the Home Office, I'd seen how much Josie adored journeying between alternate universes; the work was an ideal fit for my sister, who was both a science geek and an adrenaline junkie.

But visiting parallel dimensions is dangerous even for a perfect traveler. The rest of us had all been at serious risk during our trips, and Josie had died.

Not only died. *Splintered.*

Splintering is what happens when a traveler's consciousness rips into two or four or a thousand pieces. Fortunately it's very, very difficult to do accidentally. But in the past few days I had learned two ways a person's soul could be torn into fragments. One was what had happened to Josie: her host had been seriously injured, and she'd tried to leap out in the last seconds before death—because if your host dies while you're inside them, you die too. The Home Office's Josie had nearly made it, but not quite. Instead, as she leaped, she splintered into countless parts, through dozens of dimensions, each so tiny and ephemeral that there was no putting her back together again.

This drove the Home Office versions of my parents to madness. And God only knows what it did to Wicked, because she'd been twisted into something I could never imagine being.

Yet this evil, too, had to be an essential part of me . . .

"You know where you need to go after we settle the situation here, right?" Theo said as I helplessly watched Wicked finish with my hair. "You've got the calculations?"

She rolled my eyes. "I don't need calculations if they're in my Firebird, and they are."

"I want to double-check," Theo insisted. The Triadverse version of him had learned to be more cautious. As he began taking notes, working through whatever unfathomable physics governed this, he said, "If you want to talk to Conley, seize the moment, before Sophia and Henry get back. Nothing will tip them off faster than evidence you've spoken with him."

Wicked frowned. "Which Conley?"

"This world's. But he's on board with everything."

Wyatt Conley: tech genius, business mogul, and America's most powerful geek. I've seen him on newsfeeds wearing jeans and a blazer over an Iron Man T-shirt, his rumpled, boyish look as manufactured as his tPhones that took over the cellular market a few years back. Not yet thirty, people say, and he's accomplished so much. If they knew what Conley's really done, they wouldn't smile when they said it.

"So, where's her phone?" Wicked asked. Theo took it from his back pocket, where he'd apparently hidden it from me just in case, punched in the number, and tossed it to her. I felt its screen hard against my hand and wanted to cry. To need to speak so badly but to be unable to say a word . . .

"You're here," Conley said in my ear, as I hoped my hatred of this man would at least make Wicked Marguerite nauseated. I'd gladly puke if it meant she had to do it too. "Glad you made it. Obviously we need to get rolling. My thought is, start with Josie."

"Always Josie," Wicked said sourly.

Conley went on as if he hadn't heard her. "Tell Dr. Kovalenka and Dr. Caine that much about your home universe, nothing more. They'll respond to hearing that their older daughter died in a world not so far away. That news will make them . . . sentimental. Once we have their sympathy, we can manage the rest."

"I doubt it's going to be that simple." Wicked walked through the house, familiarizing herself with the layout. "Trust me, once Mom and Dad go after something? They make it happen. And right now, the Mom and Dad of this dimension are going after us."

"But they don't have access to our tech, and they don't know the game plan. We're a few steps ahead, Marguerite, and we're going to keep it that way."

It shouldn't have jarred me so badly, hearing Conley call her by the name we shared. Yet it did. I didn't belong to myself anymore.

She said, "Why doesn't the other you just get started already? He's a perfect traveler, so he can destroy dimensions and still get out alive."

Only by destroying the dimensions containing each and every shard of Josie's soul can the other versions of my parents get her back. They will kill her a thousand times over, unmake trillions of lives so that people were never even born, just to have Josie alive in their own world again. This is the cruelest, most selfish thing I've ever imagined—and yet, Wicked is right. Mom and Dad know how to accomplish the impossible.

"It's risky, okay?" Conley snapped. Obviously he didn't like the idea of any other version of himself being in danger. Too bad I wasn't able to tell him that the Home Office had targeted our universe for destruction too, if my parents didn't take their bait. "Besides, you know as well as I do that I'm not located anywhere near Doctors Kovalenka and Caine in some of the critical universes. So you're more effective than I am even in the best-case scenario. And obviously we'd need you to slam the doors, if it comes to that."

Slamming doors? That made no sense to me. But I mentally filed it away, willing myself to recall every detail. Possibly Wicked didn't realize I remained aware within her, unlike most people dosed with Nightthief, who were basically unconscious within their own minds. Otherwise, she wouldn't have been speaking so freely.

Unless . . . slamming doors . . .

My train of thought derailed when I heard the sound of my parents' car pulling into the driveway. Wicked said, "Mumsy and Daddums are about to walk in. Let's wrap this up. What we need you to do is stop Markov. He's back, and he's probably headed this way."

"I'll take care of it," Conley replied, so easily it gave me chills. He wouldn't hesitate to have Paul killed, and he had the money to pay off guys who would do it in an instant. "Besides, the guy's been splintered. He's never going to be the same. We can use that."

Never be the same? Paul? I had just raced through the dimensions to collect all four splinters of Paul's soul—to put him back together again. When I'd finally managed to do it, however, Paul had been depressed, angry, even fatalistic. I'd already sensed that some of the darkness from the other

17

Pauls had seeped into him, but I'd told myself it was terrible but temporary, like the pain from a broken bone.

Had Paul instead been changed forever?

"Gotta go." Wicked hung up the phone just in time to run to the front door, where Mom and Dad stood. They looked like themselves again—in their shabby sweaters, Mom with her messy bun and Dad with his rectangle-framed glasses. When their faces lit up with smiles, I wanted to scream. *Please, no. It's not me. You have to know it's not me!*

"Sweetheart, you're home." Mom enveloped Wicked in a hug. Unfortunately the thick cardigan I had on kept her from feeling the second Firebird locket dangling beneath the fabric. "Thank God."

"And Paul?" Dad said, blue eyes wide with concern. "Paul's all right, isn't he?"

That took Wicked aback. Her head jerked slightly, like people do when they're startled. In the Home Office, Paul Markov was my family's enemy—a courageous rebel trying to stand up to the Triad Corporation's evil. She had to know that wasn't always the case, but still, she hadn't been ready to see proof of how much my parents love him, nearly as if he were the son they never had.

Unfortunately, she covered well. "He's back, and in one piece—his soul, I mean—but he's not himself."

Mom and Dad exchanged a look. "What do you mean?" my father asked. "Did the splintering affect him badly?"

See, that's the second way a soul can be splintered: someone can do it on purpose, if that someone were a total bastard like Wyatt Conley. What happened to Paul wasn't a terrible accident—it was an attack. Conley tore Paul's soul into four pieces and held each part hostage, forcing me to do his dirty work if I wanted any chance to put Paul together again.

"The fragments of Paul's soul went to some dark places," Wicked said, voice tremulous. "Worlds where we both saw another side of him. A dangerous side. And I hate to say this, but I think the splintering has changed him. Maybe forever. Like the terrible things all those other Pauls did stained his soul."

"Oh, no." Mom's hand went to her lips. "We'd realized splintering was dangerous, but—surely the damage isn't permanent."

Wicked shook my head in dismay. "I don't know. Mom, Paul . . . he scared me a little."

How could she say that? She was the scary one. Paul was only injured, and lost. Overcome by despair. Fate brought me and Paul together time and time again—but we had learned that we didn't always wind up with each other, that sometimes we hurt each other terribly. Our destiny had abandoned us, and Paul took it even harder than I did. Maybe he would have anyway, even without the damage from the splintering—but with it, Paul seemed to have lost all hope.

Wicked was turning Paul's anguish into her weapon. My parents, even loving him as they did, would be suspicious of him immediately.

"Heya," Theo called from the great room. "How did you make out on Firebird construction?"

"Better than you'd think," my father began, but then his voice trailed off as a taxi pulled up in front of our house. At first I couldn't imagine who would drive up in a cab, but then the door swung open and Paul stepped out.

He's here, I thought. *He made it!* Paul got here before Conley could even start to look for him.

That gave us a chance, unless Wicked had already screwed him over for good.

She opened the door and ran into the yard, eager to greet him. It's what I would've done—but I would've leaped into his arms, told Paul I loved him, and began trying to talk him back from the terrible despair that had taken him over. Wicked, on the other hand, went right up to him and then stopped short, as if taken aback.

"Hey." Wicked smiled sweetly, or tried to. It didn't feel quite right. "Are you okay?"

"I feel fine," Paul said, stoic as ever. "How I am isn't important right now." Then he walked straight past her, shoulders squared. This coolness would've wounded me at any other moment. Now it gave me hope. Already Paul had raised his voice to speak to my parents in the doorway. "Sophia, Henry, how much has Marguerite told you?"

My muscles tensed with Wicked's fear. She hadn't realized that I'd been able to explain everything to Paul before the end. Probably she thought I'd pieced his soul back together and come straight home. Her impatience was my one opportunity.

But if she could stall long enough to get Theo in on

it, they had a chance to discredit Paul. To hurt him, even kill him, and make it seem like self-defense. By that point I knew there was nothing they wouldn't do. She followed Paul inside, my heart thumping fast with her determination to take him down.

"She got us started, Paul." Mom's tone was tactful. "Come in. Sit down. We'll take this step by step. All right? And how are you feeling?"

"Strange." Paul shook his head. "Like . . . I have to choose who to be. Every moment." My parents gave each other worried looks as Paul stepped inside—and then he stopped. Slowly he turned his head and looked back at me.

Has he guessed? How could he have guessed? But if anyone knew me, truly knew me inside and out, it had to be Paul.

He stared into my eyes, searching for something I couldn't name. Wicked smiled back at him as she folded her hands around his arm. "Welcome home," she whispered.

Please, I thought. *Don't be fooled. Look inside my eyes and see the difference. It's our only chance.*

Please, Paul. Know me.

And he did. He did.

"Marguerite . . ." Paul's voice trailed off. "Are you—"

"I'm fine," she whispered. "You didn't hurt me."

My parents tensed at the idea that Paul had caused me pain, which was just what she wanted. But it was also the moment Wicked tipped her hand, because Paul knew there was no reason for me to say anything like that.

21

Paul slipped his arm out of her grip, then grabbed my wrists so tightly they hurt. Wicked gasped in shock. My dad took a step forward, hand outstretched, ready to act. "Paul, what are you doing?"

"I don't know how this is possible." Paul looked down into my eyes and saw through her straight to me. "But this is not our Marguerite."

3

"WHAT ARE YOU TALKING ABOUT?" MY FATHER LOOKED back and forth between Paul and me, still more suspicious of his grad student than his daughter.

"I don't know which world she's from," Paul said. "But Marguerite isn't our Marguerite."

Oh, thank God, I thought. I should've felt relieved, but my body was taking its cues from the Wicked Marguerite. The emotion surging through me could've been fear or fury. My skin flushed warm, and I pulled free from Paul. "I told you," she said, and the tremble in the words was real. She kept backing away—deeper into the house, toward Theo—as she continued, "Paul's been twisted, poisoned by his splintering. The other versions of him, where they hid his soul? They were some of the worst, most evil Pauls that could ever exist."

"Evil?" Mom pronounced the word like she didn't

23

understand what that even meant. Never had she ever imagined thinking of Paul as evil. But if Wicked got her way, everyone would turn against Paul at any moment.

"One of them shot Theo. Injured him so badly he might have died." Wicked's voice shook. She even dared to imitate my grief. "Another one got in a fight with me in a car, and hurt my arm so badly I might never paint again. There was even a priest who violated his vows—"

Oh, come on! I thought. The gentle Father Paul from the Romeverse wasn't evil, only conflicted. But Mom and Dad didn't know that. They only heard that Paul was capable of hurting their baby girl.

Paul tried to explain himself. "This isn't about me. This Marguerite . . ." His voice trailed off. Not only was Wicked making my parents doubt him, she was also making him doubt himself. He finished, more quietly, "Something's not right."

Wicked slipped my hands behind me as if I were just going to lean on the rainbow table. But one palm covered my father's old letter opener, an antiquated thing with a carved wooden handle and a metal blade. My fingers were close to the sharp edge. "Paul?" she said in my voice. "Come on. You're still messed up after being splintered. I don't blame you. Okay? I know it was hard. But I still believe in you."

And dammit, that got to him. Paul hesitated, just long enough for my mind to scream, *Come on, Paul, you know me! Don't doubt yourself now!*

24

I might have put Paul's soul back together again, but there were still . . . cracks. Vulnerabilities. Although I'd recognized the emotional damage, I'd thought of it as something that would pass.

Only at that moment did I understand Paul might be changed forever.

Wicked knew. She'd always known. And her knowledge told her just where to strike. "Paul, just because things are, well, weird between us right now? That doesn't mean I'm not me." She pronounced the words as if confessing some terrible tragedy. Paul's depression and doubt had become her weapons. If she could turn him against himself—make him pause before acting against me, even for one more minute—she would win.

My dad took a step toward him, hand outstretched as if he were about to check Paul's forehead for fever. "The splintering—what happened to your soul—we hadn't fully considered the aftereffects. Are you feeling disoriented?"

"Yes," Paul admitted. But his eyes remained locked on my face. His body betrayed his inner tension. He didn't trust his own judgment, but he didn't trust Wicked, either.

This was when Theo stepped in, the Triadverse version within using his pale, weakened body as a marionette. "Hey, man, it's okay. Marguerite's okay, and so are you, and so am I. Just took my first trip through the dimensions, and wow, does that mess with your head. I get how you could be confused. Take a deep breath."

25

"You drove us half mad with worry, you know," Dad said to Theo. "As soon as you're well, you're in deep trouble, Mr. Beck."

"I can live with that." That roguish grin was Theo's—in every dimension I'd found, everywhere—so the deception seemed complete.

My mother remained silent, her hands clasped in front of her. Then she said, "Were you experimenting with the Nightthief treatment?"

I didn't get why Mom was thinking about that at this very moment. Neither did Wicked. "We just got back, Mom."

"But the Nightthief is on the table," she said.

The vial of emerald-green liquid—the drug that had been used to hijack my body and Theo's—sat on the rainbow table, bearing silent testimony to the crime.

My mother's eyes went wide. Dad stood up straighter. Paul's gaze sharpened from doubt into terrible certainty.

Theo lunged forward. Even though he was a good four inches shorter than Paul, he barreled into him at full force, driving his shoulder into Paul's gut. As Paul doubled over, my parents ran toward me—and my hand closed around the letter opener. It was as sharp as any dagger. Horror flooded through me as I realized I might have to watch my parents die at my own hand.

But Wicked didn't stab the blade at them. Instead, she held it to my—our—throat.

Mom and Dad froze. The point pressed against my skin so

hard I could feel the pain increase with every beat of my heart.

"This is the carotid artery," Wicked said. All pretense was gone. I could feel the contemptuous sneer on my face. From the kitchen, I heard dishes clatter to the floor and break, and a heavy thud against the cabinets. Paul and Theo's fight had turned brutal, a blur of fists at the corner of my eye— but I couldn't focus on it, because Wicked didn't look. She was too busy drinking in the terror on my parents' faces. "In other words, this is the blood vessel that leads directly from the heart to the brain. If I sever it, your perfect traveler bleeds out in about thirty seconds. Maybe a minute. Long enough for me to save myself with my Firebird, but short enough that nothing will save her. You'll get to stand here and watch her die."

"Please, no." I'd never seen my mother look so afraid. So small. She held her hands out toward Wicked, as if to plead. "Tell us what you want, and why you're here."

"Oh, now you're worried about her." Wicked spat the words at them. "When did you decide to start caring about Marguerite? And call off your dog Paul Markov before he—"

A heavy thump on the floor was followed by gagging and a groan. Wicked finally looked, and I saw Paul leaning over Theo, whom he'd beaten down to the floor, but Triadverse Theo grabbed the Firebird at his neck. A shudder was the only sign that he was gone. Then our Theo weakly whispered, "What the hell—?"

Tension tightened my chest. Wicked hadn't realized Theo

would bail out on her so fast. "I said, call Markov off."

Dad wheeled around. "Paul, please, do what she—"

Paul didn't listen. He rushed toward us, and even as Wicked tightened her grip around the letter opener, he grabbed at her.

She expected him to go for the blade. Instead, Paul yanked at the front of my cardigan, savagely ripping it open. In that instant his broad fist clutched both Firebirds in his hand, towing me closer, off-balance. The cold, terrible anger in him now reminded me too much of his Mafiaverse self—that, and the potential for violence just beneath the skin.

"Put the blade down," he commanded Wicked, "and I'll give you back your Firebird long enough for you to get out."

She lifted her chin. "Let go of me or your Marguerite dies in your arms."

The point of the letter opener pressed harder against my skin.

"You won't do it," Paul said. "Because if you hurt her, I've got the Firebirds, and that means you'll bleed to death along with her. You might be willing to do anything else for Wyatt Conley and Triad, but I don't think you're willing to die for them."

Silence. My parents hung on to each other as if they were holding each other up. Behind them, out of focus, I could just glimpse Theo pushing himself onto his elbows, head sagging. Paul's gray eyes remained focused on mine.

"You think you know me?" Wicked's smirk twisted my lips. "You didn't even know yourself, until yesterday.

Because you're not a single, whole human being any longer. You're Frankenstein's monster, all sewed together out of pieces of other people you'll never be again. And the stitches could rip at any minute . . ."

But Paul didn't back down. "I don't know whether you're an opportunist or a sadist. I don't know whether you're a coward or a conqueror. But I know you're smart enough to recognize a no-win situation—and I don't think you're the type to commit suicide out of spite."

My voice dropped to a whisper as she said, "Oh, I do lots of things out of spite, Mr. Markov."

"I don't doubt it," Paul whispered back. "But you do those things to other people. Not to yourself. Now get out."

"Now I know how we're going to play this," she said. "Time to slam some doors."

Wicked let the hand at my throat drop, but before I could even register relief, she slashed at Paul. Blood sprayed warm against my skin and clothes as he jerked back his injured arm, pure reflex. It gave Wicked the moment she needed to seize her Firebird. My hand worked the controls—

—dizziness swept over me again. The world went dark and swirly, but even as I swayed on my feet, I knew my body was my own again.

Wicked was gone.

"Paul, are you okay?" I reached toward his arm, and Paul jerked back from my touch. For a moment we could only stare at each other. Then I realized I was still holding the blade, now stained with his blood.

Paul had reacted instinctively. Intelligently, given that I was still holding the weapon that had injured him. But seeing him pull away from me sent a chill through my veins.

Already he'd been questioning himself, refusing to believe in our love.

Now he couldn't believe in me, either.

4

"IF ONLY GETTING RID OF THE . . . IMPOSTORS SOLVED OUR problems," Mom said a few minutes later. I was kneeling in front of Paul, who sat on the sofa as I bandaged the gash on his forearm. Dad, meanwhile, was trying to get Theo to drink a cup of tea. (My father is English, so he thinks tea solves everything.) "But based on what you're telling us— the other two dimensions of Triad are now switching to a new strategy, one far more dangerous than before."

"They're willing to destroy entire dimensions, every one that contains a sliver of Josie's soul," I said. "Even this one. All to get Josie back. I still can't believe you guys would ever do that."

"I can," my father said quietly. Mom gave him a look, but she folded her arms across her chest, the way she did when she got defensive, as Dad continued. "That bout of meningitis you had when you were two, Marguerite . . . the disease works fast. You were in a pediatric ICU, and the doctors told us we could lose you. The state of mind I was in then . . ." He trailed off, and when he spoke again, his voice was hoarse. "I would've made a deal with the devil. Any deal, any devil."

I remembered my mother's rage at Paul in a universe where he had only injured me. That alone had been enough to turn all her love for him into hate. My parents pride themselves on being rational, logical people, like the scientists they are, but maybe that's made them more vulnerable to strong emotion. The same grief that wounds the rest of us deeply is something they can't even begin to bear. No wonder Josie's death had driven them mad.

"We have to act immediately." Paul hadn't looked me in the eyes since I'd become myself again. His head remained slightly bowed, as though he were too ashamed to lift it. "To do something to protect the dimensions in danger of being destroyed. Triad needs a perfect traveler's cooperation to accomplish their plan quickly—but even without Marguerite, they have the Triadverse version of Wyatt Conley."

"It didn't sound to me like Conley was going to do any of this personally," I said. Being a perfect traveler could be dangerous, as I'd learned. Conley talked a big game, but he preferred to protect himself and risk others. "And what does 'slamming doors' mean? Conley mentioned it, and so did she, but I don't get what they're referring to."

My dad sighed. "Unfortunately, neither do we."

"Wait a second." Theo frowned as he stared down at the rainbow table. He lifted his cup of tea from the papers laid across its multicolored surface. "We have some very, very interesting equations here."

Mom walked to his side. "What do you mean?"

"Not exactly a road map—but maybe a hint to the kinds of places they're trying to go. The universes they'll try to kill first." Theo grabbed the pencil his doppelganger had left and picked up the work mid-equation.

"We know what they'll all have in common—they'll be the dimensions that version of Josie had visited before," I said. "Those are the ones where the splinters of her soul are . . . buried, I guess."

The splinters were too small to be collected with a Firebird, they'd told me. Nothing of Josie's consciousness remained intact. She was dead, truly dead, and yet the Home Office had traced a bloody path to resurrection. By destroying the worlds in which Josie's soul had existed, they hoped the splinters would slingshot back to their own universe—until finally enough splinters would come together to restore Josie body and soul.

Though if Paul was still so damaged from being splintered into four parts, what would Josie be after shattering into a thousand pieces?

"I've been thinking about the theoretical implications." Paul sounded grateful to be dealing with math again rather than messy human emotions. "Triad will want to destroy source vectors as well—to take out multiple dimensions at once."

All these years surrounded by scientists, you'd think I

would've already learned every bit of technojargon I would ever need. Apparently not. I said, "What are source vectors?"

"Universes that generated many other universes valid for Triad's purposes," Mom said. No doubt my expression gave away my confusion, because she stopped and backed up. "For instance—in our world, and the Triadverse, and several others we've seen, Abraham Lincoln was assassinated by John Wilkes Booth. If you could find the one core universe where that event originated, and destroy that universe, you would in effect destroy all universes in which that event took place. That core universe would be a source vector. Do you see?"

"And you must understand, the timing of the significant event is completely irrelevant," Dad cut in. "Dimensions wouldn't just collapse. They would be . . . unmade. Even if the event took place centuries or millennia ago, destroy that source vector here and now, and it would unravel all the way back to the beginning of time."

"Shortly after the Big Bang," Mom interjected. We were literally talking about the apocalypse, but she still needed to be precise about when time began.

Every choice, however trivial, made a new quantum reality—another dimension unique in the multiverse. Each of the many worlds I'd visited so far, every other Marguerite I'd been: All of them would be demolished in an instant if someone found the choice back in time that led to my being born. Without that choice, that universe, none of the other Marguerites would exist. They would be unmade along with their dimensions, completely.

"Yes," I said. "I get it. So the Home Office wants to destroy all the worlds Josie got lost in and some, uh, source vector worlds. How do we stop them? Wait. Hang on. How do they even do that? How do you destroy an entire dimension?"

The four scientists in the room exchanged glances. Their expressions looked almost . . . guilty.

I said, "Are you guys about to tell me Firebirds are way more dangerous than you ever said?"

"No!" Mom drew herself up, offended. "Honestly, Marguerite. We wouldn't take those kinds of risks, ever."

"Indeed not." Dad paused, then added, "However, that doesn't mean there's not potential for danger with the Firebirds."

"It's sort of like when they fired up the Large Hadron Collider," Theo offered. I knew all about this, even though it happened when I was hardly more than a baby. For physicists, the activation of the LHC was like the Super Bowl, the Oscars, and New Year's Eve wrapped into one, and my parents still talked about it once in a while. "Everybody was freaking out, like, 'ahhh, the scientists are going to create a black hole.' Which totally didn't happen. Because, while it's technically possible, it's so incredibly improbable that the LHC could run for a billion years without a black hole opening in the center of the Earth."

Theo's explanation helped, but still, it gave me a turn—realizing I'd been carrying even a one-billionth chance of an apocalypse around my neck.

I looked down at my Firebird, which still dangled from

its chain—blood-spattered from Paul's wound, like the torn remnants of my green cardigan and the white dress exposed beneath. For me the Firebird had always meant hope, genius, adventure. But in that moment I knew I would never forget the bloodstains.

"So, how could the Firebird destroy a dimension?" Although I figured the answer probably involved an equation longer than a Harry Potter book, I felt like I had to say something.

But Paul had learned how to translate the hidden poetry of science for me better than anyone else ever had. "Remember what I told you when we went to see the redwoods? About the fundamental asymmetry of the universe?"

I could never forget that day. Muir Woods' beauty made me feel like Paul and I had stepped into our own precious sliver of eternity. But I remembered the physics-lesson part of it too. "Most forces in physics are symmetrical. But somewhere in the nanoseconds after the Big Bang, matter and antimatter got thrown out of whack somehow, and nobody has any idea how. That asymmetry between matter and antimatter is what makes the universe possible. Is that right?"

". . . close enough."

My artist brain doesn't wrap itself around the science stuff as easily as Paul's does. He'd never make me feel bad about it on purpose—but tact is not exactly Paul's wheelhouse.

Hastily he added, "It's important because the Firebirds could restore the symmetry between matter and antimatter."

"What? How?" My mind was reeling. "Why would you

ever make a device that could do that?"

Theo had overheard us. "Marguerite, that's close to how Firebirds work in the first place. The dimensional resonances we're always talking about, the ones that make your eyes glaze over? Those are the imbalances specific to each universe. The Firebird basically . . . surfs that imbalance, finds where it's supposed to be, and brings you along. Tune the Firebird to attack that imbalance instead of detecting it, and . . ." Theo's voice trailed off, and he just spread his hands outward, as if miming an explosion.

Paul, of course, couldn't let a gesture end a scientific explanation. "The rest would take care of itself. Dimensional collapse would fold outward wthin—no. There's no point in saying how long it would take, because the collapse would even destroy time."

"But the Firebirds could also increase the asymmetry!" Dad said, lighting up. "It would be trickier, by a measure, but still, we could do it. The Firebird's power might require a booster, of course . . ."

"It would." Mom's quicksilver mind was already a few steps ahead. "But if we could enhance the Firebirds' power, through a fairly simple device—some sort of stabilizer we could construct in each universe, then we could increase the asymmetry in each universe. That would make it much more difficult for Triad to collapse those universes. We could slow down Triad's work. Maybe even stop them altogether."

It made more sense to me then—the potential within the

Firebirds. Their power could unmake a world or preserve it forever. Infinite good and infinite evil, all enclosed within one locket that hung right above my heart.

By that point, Mom, Dad, and Theo were deeply embroiled in the equations. I wanted so badly to steal a few moments of privacy to talk with Paul. He needed to remember who he was, to shake off the melancholy and fatalism that still haunted him.

If he couldn't overcome it, I hadn't actually saved Paul. I'd only put together the pieces of a man broken beyond repair. Even thinking that made me want to hug him tightly, as if I could sink into him so deeply that my love could seal all the cracks, heal him, make him whole.

But like I said—I had more urgent problems than my love life. So did the rest of the multiverse.

"I have to go after her," I announced. "Don't I?"

Everyone else exchanged worried glances. I realized they'd all independently come to the conclusion that I'd have to go back into danger, but nobody had wanted to be the first to say it. Dad replied, "Sweetheart—as much as I hate this—we need to know which worlds they're targeting. For certain. Theo's equations will help, but the only way to be certain which dimensions are most in danger is for you to check them out."

"I could go." Paul's voice was rough. "Theo too. Or the two of you. It doesn't have to be Marguerite."

"Yes, it does," I insisted. His protectiveness moved me, but I couldn't let him get away with it. I was the perfect

38

traveler, which made me the one who slipped into each universe most easily. The one who could retain focus and control throughout. For any other trip, that might be no more than a matter of convenience. But for this? We had to respond as powerfully and quickly as we could. That meant me. I turned to my parents. "My Firebird should be able to track hers, right?"

It was Theo who finally managed to answer. "Yeah. Your two Firebirds were together for a while—we could pick up on her traces fast."

"Do it." I held the Firebird out to Paul. Although he hesitated, he got to work.

My mother said, "Your counterpart can't collapse the universes without killing herself. But she could be . . . laying groundwork. Preparing each world for your eventual cooperation, or for suicide missions by others."

If the Home Office versions of my parents and Wyatt Conley were willing to destroy entire dimensions to get Josie back, they'd think nothing of asking one person from their own world to die too. For a moment it hit me with dizzying force: Literally trillions of lives were at stake, and I was the only person with the power to save them. But I held on. "Wait. Wouldn't the universe's destruction slingshot her home? That's what your Home Office selves think will happen to the splinters of Josie's soul."

Dad nodded. He looked as if he'd aged five years in an hour. "That's probably what would happen to a perfect traveler—you or the Home Office's Josie—but not to your other self or to anyone else trying to destroy a universe with a Firebird. That destruction has consequences. It forges chains. It's as if . . . as if you were freeing a ship from anchor, but the only way to do it was by taking hold of that anchor yourself. While the ship sails free, the anchor drags you down to the bottom of the ocean. A perfect traveler would be able to overcome that, with the Firebird's help. But anyone else would be done for."

As unnerved as my parents were at the prospect, I felt slightly reassured. Maybe that should've embarrassed me—the fact that I could kind of handle the idea of an entire universe's death if I knew I could escape. But traveling between dimensions involved enough danger already; any protection at all made me feel safer. So I let my parents show me how to use the Firebird to stabilize a universe. I refused to learn how to destroy one, because that was not a thing I was ever, ever going to do. Paul remained nearby, grave and quiet, still not looking me in the face.

It was Theo who raised a question I hadn't considered. "Are you even going to be able to follow her?"

"What do you mean?" I said.

"If she's not in her own dimension, then she's already occupying a version of her in another world. Can two people leap into the same host?" He shrugged. "Seriously, no clue."

Mom made a face. "I knew we ought to have run simulations on that."

It didn't seem like a big deal. Either I'd be able to do it or I wouldn't, and if I could, I'd be in charge, because I was the perfect traveler, not Wicked. Then a ghastly possibility occurred to me. "We wouldn't, like, fuse together or something, would we?"

At once, all four of them said, "No." Dad helpfully added, "Different resonances, no matter what. Like oil and water, sweetheart."

Good. I could imagine Wicked's malevolence covering me like an oil slick, viscous and black. Better that than carrying it inside me. "You guys—remember what I told you about the Cambridgeverse?"

It took them a minute. I didn't blame them. The story of my last chase through the dimensions was one I'd told in a rush while blood was still gushing from Paul's arm. Paul winced at the mention of the place, because that was the world where he'd damaged my arm in a car crash that tore us all apart. But the most important aspect of the Cambridgeverse was something else entirely.

"Our counterparts are working on communicating through the dimensions," Mom said. "You told them to reach out to us. Which means we're poised to reach back."

"We considered this, early on," Dad mused, rubbing his chin in the way that meant he was either deep in thought or listening to *Rubber Soul*.

"If you could let them know what's about to happen, to look out for Triad, it would give them a chance." I looked at my torn, bloody clothing and, absurdly, felt like I ought to change before I went. When I returned home after all this and my body became observable once more, would the

41

blood have dried? Or would it still be wet against my skin, proof of how my hands had hurt Paul?

She could've gone for his throat. What would I have done if I'd had to watch myself murder him?

Paul broke into my reverie, saying, "Are you ready?"

"No. But it doesn't matter." I reached up—he's so tall, so heavily muscled, a Michelangelo in a world of Modiglianis. Still, I could cradle his face with my hands. "Follow me. I need all the help I can get."

He hesitated from fear—not for himself. "Theo could go, or Sophia and Henry could finally use the Firebird for themselves—"

I whispered, "I need you."

Paul didn't believe me. He couldn't, yet. But he nodded, and that had to be enough.

So I backed up, sat down in a far chair in the corner, hit the Firebird's controls to leap after Wicked—

—and that's why I'm now hanging from a cable about four hundred feet over the river Thames.

"Marguerite!" Paul shouts. I glance back to see him sliding out the observation window despite the cries of dismay from people nearby. My Aunt Susannah leans forward, her tears tracing streaks of mascara down her cheeks. Paul yells, "I'm going to come get you."

"Don't!" It costs me to shout that, because oh, God, I want him to come get me. I want him to save me. And from the glint of metal around his neck, I know this is my

Paul—that he followed me, that as damaged as he is, at least something inside him still believes we can make it.

But I'm pretty sure he can't save me. He'll only get himself killed.

My sweaty palms slip against the cable; my fingers cramp so hard it's like every nerve and bone is on fire. If I let go, the Londonverse Marguerite will die.

She was the first alternate self I ever entered, the first time I had to interpret the life I would've led in an alternate world. I think of her white, empty room. Her party-girl existence that she doesn't enjoy a moment of. When I last stood inside her, I willed her to remember our parents—the ones robbed from her in childhood, the ones whose love I was able to share with her, at least a little. Now I know she kept those memories. She came out with Aunt Susannah to do something fun, and Paul Markov seems to have found her. Are they only friends, or something more? Regardless, he must be one of the only honest, real people in her life.

In other words—during the past few months, her life has been worth living. Now Wicked has taken it away.

That's what they mean by "slamming doors," I realize. They know now I'll never do what they want. So they want to keep me from protecting these universes. The only way they can do that is by locking me out, forever.

And the only way to lock me out is to kill every Marguerite, everywhere.

My hands slip. I grab again as people scream—one hand

43

snags the cable, but the other doesn't. Now I'm swinging, and my shoulder hurts, and every muscle trembles. This is it.

I have to jump—but what if Wicked's blocking my way? What if I can't jump where she is? There's no time to set a new course back home—if I could even touch my Firebird, which I can't, because that would mean letting go, and if I let go—

Paul can't see this. He can't.

"Paul!" I cry out. "Get back inside!"

"Marguerite—no!"

I try to turn and look at him again. That's one movement too many. My slick hand slides off the cable, and I fall.

For the first instant it's like I'm not moving downward at all. It's more like floating, while intense wind blows around me. But then the force of it presses in, and my stomach's in my throat and the river's rushing up to meet me and I'm going to die.

Firebird! As I tumble, I clutch at the Firebird beneath my shirt. It's hard to grab it because now I'm rolling, my clothes are blowing all around me, the water's so close, so close—I hit the controls—

My body jerks to a halt. For one terrifying instant I think this is it, I hit the river, this is the moment of death.

But no. I'm sitting in a dark, cool chamber—no, a passage-way, only about four feet high. Light flickers in the distance; stone walls surround me; sand almost completely covers the floor: That's all I know, besides the fact that I'm in another dimension, one that saved me.

The other Marguerite is dead.

She was murdered. By Wicked and—because I had a chance to save her and totally failed—by me, too.

5

HOW DO YOU GRIEVE FOR ANOTHER YOU?

The strangest sorrow fills my heart. The injustice of her death is unbearable. Especially when it seemed like she might finally have discovered some things in her life that made her happy. The Londonverse Marguerite could've found her path. Even her Paul was there with her. . . .

You don't know that. He could've just been on the same hover-ship. He lived nearby, so it wouldn't be such a coincidence. You didn't have any chance to figure out how things had really changed for her, if they had at all.

But that makes it worse, thinking that she led this lonely, unhappy life until the moment that life was taken away.

The only things I know for sure are that she died through no fault of her own, and that she died so horribly, horribly afraid.

A sob escapes my throat. Misery and guilt press down,

squeezing the breath from my lungs and the knot from my throat. I bring my knees up against my chest and lower my head to let go and cry.

That other Marguerite—her body and her life helped me when I really needed help. How did I return the favor? I couldn't hang on to the cable. I let her go. The Firebirds crashed into that Marguerite's dimension and through her life; her death is the scar we left behind.

Finally, wiping tears from my face, I lift my head and start trying to figure out who I am this time.

Okay. Focus. I don't feel physically different in any major way. My hair is pulled back in a complicated bun or braid, and held in place with several pins. Its formality reminds me of the Russiaverse, but that's obviously not where I am. My surroundings are too grubby, my clothing too plain . . . and I'm not pregnant. Those physical sensations linger in my mind still, strongly enough for me to feel their absence.

The dark passageway around me provides few clues so far. Although the lighting is odd—I can't see the source, so it must be from around a bend in the passage—I can tell from the flicker of the distant glow that it comes from candles or a torch. The Middle Ages again? This doesn't look like any part of the Romeverse I remember, but there could be other dimensions at medieval levels of technology. But no, my clothes are all wrong for that. The khaki cotton skirt reaches past my knees, heavy but apparently sewn by machine; the lace-up boots fit my feet too well. (Take it from me: medieval shoes suck.) Slender bands of lace trim the long sleeves and high neck of my thin, white cotton blouse. No pockets, no purse—which means no smartphone, map, money, or any kind of identification.

I only know one thing for certain about this world and this Marguerite: she's in danger. Wicked wouldn't have it any other way.

The terror of the Londonverse floods through me again—that dark water rushing up at me, ready to crush my bones and steal my breath forever—

At least it was quick, I tell myself, taking a deep breath. After that long a drop, the impact with the water would've killed her instantly.

That doesn't help.

My mind starts up the refrain of why, why did this have to happen—and then the question becomes real. Wait, why *did* Wicked go to the Londonverse? Why would that world be marked for destruction? No version of Josie could ever have traveled there, because in that dimension, she died about a decade ago.

Then I remember what my parents said about source vectors. One universe could lay the foundation for many others. Destroy it, and the rest crumble. Because the entire timeline gets destroyed, it doesn't matter if the critical choice took place long ago—past, present, and future will all collapse at once.

How many worlds are now doomed because I let go?

Although my brain keeps replaying the moment my hand slipped from the cable, rationally I know it couldn't have gone any other way. I tried to hang on, so hard, like it was both our lives and not just hers. For all I knew, it could've been.

No doubt Wicked hoped to kill me too.

But what did she mean by stranding me in a weird passageway? I can't see how to get out, but obviously there must be a way, since Wicked was able to get here in the first place. This is hardly mortal peril; it's more annoying than anything else.

Why would Wicked have chosen such a slow way for me to die? She could've done so many other things: hanging herself, leaping from another great height, weighing herself down with rocks before jumping in water—okay, the possibilities are starting to creep me out.

But then I realize she's not going to do any of those things, not from now on. Anything that dramatic and absolute wouldn't give her time to leap away from this dimension and save herself. She killed Londonverse Marguerite so quickly and violently because she meant to take me out with her. I hope she thinks she did. Better if she doesn't know I'm still on her trail.

Even if she does know, though, her future traps will probably take longer to spring. Not only does she need time to leap out, but she also needs time for me to leap in, if she's going to have any chance of killing me, too.

From now on, the situations she puts me in will be less immediately terrifying. I have to remember: the danger is the same.

So, first order of duty—get out of here.

I start crawling forward, moving toward the uncertain light. Sand grits beneath my hands and knees. It's so dim in here that I can't see any doorway. No windows either. The air is cool, almost cold, and it smells musty. This has to be what it's like to be buried alive . . .

A chill runs along my spine. *Pull it together,* I tell myself as I keep going. *You can see firelight, right? Fire requires oxygen to keep burning. As long as it burns, you have air.*

I reach a sharp angle in the passageway, and finally I see a door. The wood is old, worn, and dry, and there doesn't seem to be a handle, but this has to be Wicked's way in and my way out. I slide my fingers around the door's ragged edge, where there's just enough space for me to get a grip on it and pull forward. With one big tug, I feel the door give way—

—and the wall caves in, tumbling over and around me, a tsunami of sand.

I scream until sand falls into my throat. Coughing and spitting, I try to wriggle out of the crush, but dirt and sand just keep coming, burying my legs and immobilizing me. Even if I'm not completely smothered, I won't be able to escape without digging myself out—and if the stuff pins my arms, too, I really will be buried alive.

Then I hear a voice echoing in the distance. "Marguerite?"

Paul. My heart floods with relief. "Yes! Help me! It's all falling in!"

Another voice, this one my father's. "Hold on! And whatever you do, stay still!"

I freeze. As hard as it is to let the sand keep tumbling over me, the pace slows the longer I don't move. I can hear scraping and motion not far away. My heart still pounds with terror, but at least now I know help is coming. Wicked failed. I'm going to get out of this . . .

A shape emerges within the sand—something solid jerking forward through the avalanche of grit, more defined as it gets closer. It falls toward me and *oh my God it's a dead body.*

I can't help it. I scream and try to scramble backward, unleashing new waves of heavy sand over me. Now I'm buried to the waist, but that is not nearly as horrifying as the dead person leaning toward me. His—her—its corpse is dark and desiccated, hardly more than a skeleton. Pelvis, sternum, and half an arm are all falling apart right on top of me. Worst of all is its open-mouthed death's grin and its empty eyes.

"Marguerite!" I turn my head to see my father crawling toward me. In the distance I can just glimpse a wooden ladder, and I realize that the light was coming from above. What underground death trap did Wicked bring me to? It doesn't matter as much now that Dad is here. In the distance I see a pair of legs descending the ladder and know that Paul will soon be with me too.

When my dad reaches my side, I grab his hand. I'd hug him if it weren't for the fact that I'm scared of collapsing yet more sand and burying us both. "Please, get me out of here."

"In a moment, sweetheart. We've got to shore up this

part of the wall first." Dad seems totally at ease, which I should maybe find more soothing than I do. The firelight flickering behind us catches his wire-rimmed spectacles, hiding his gaze.

With one hand I gesture toward the grotesque skeleton dangling in the sand, held together by some kind of garment or bandages. "But—this—"

Dad grins. "Amazing, isn't it? Just think, you found it all on your own!"

Over my father's shoulder I can see Paul's silhouette as he crawls toward us both. Paul seems to be carrying along some boards or metal bars, stuff they can use to build a barrier to replace the door I tore away.

The door Wicked meant for me to tear away so I'd bury myself alive. Knowing that I fell into her trap feels even worse than being face-to-face with this skeleton.

That doesn't make the skeleton any easier to deal with. I imagine I can smell its rotting flesh, even though it must have decayed years ago. Decades, even—or centuries—

"We told you specifically not to chance this area until we'd worked on it some more," my dad says. He's not angry. His fascination with my grisly find has cheered him beyond any need to scold me. "Whatever were you thinking?"

"I—got confused. I thought you meant one of the others." That explanation ought to work—it usually does. In every universe, everywhere, people just plain screw up.

Dad seems satisfied, anyway. He pets my shoulder. "You must be more careful, Marguerite. But I have to admit, there's a bright side—we'll put you down as the discoverer! You may wind up the most illustrious family member in the trade."

Since when is my family in the "trade" of digging up rotting corpses?

Paul finally crawls into view. The narrow passageway doesn't allow him to come around Dad and reach my side, but right now it's enough to see him; the firelight paints his face in rich, warm gold. Paul wears a white linen shirt, olive-colored pants, and high boots—just like Dad, it seems. The line of his neatly trimmed beard accents the sharp angles of his jaw. Paul's trim beard reminds me of Lieutenant Markov in Russia—and as always, thinking of Lieutenant Markov tightens my throat, makes me close my eyes.

When I open them again after only a moment, I can tell that Paul looks concerned and a bit confused—not relieved. If this were my Paul, and he had already followed me to this universe, he would be grateful to see me alive and well. He'd understand how I'd wound up in a place so dangerous my parents specifically warned me against it. So it's this world's Paul who has come to rescue me.

Mine must have remained in the Londonverse, waiting for a dead body to be dredged from the Thames.

That grisly image lingers in my mind for the few minutes it takes Paul and Dad to reinforce the wall. They dig the mummy out first, then me. Priorities, people. But I'm too relieved to see them, and my anger is reserved for the person who deserves it. For Wicked.

I bet she deliberately questioned my parents about the most dangerous places to go and went straight there, I think, while Paul's broad hands scoop away the sand from my legs. If Dad and Paul hadn't been close to the edge of the tunnel when I screamed for help, her plan could've worked. I could easily have been suffocated by sand. This world's Marguerite and I would have died together.

As soon as I'm free, I slide between my father and Paul. "I need to get out of here," I gasp. Sand is heavy in my boots, and right now I just want to breathe fresh air again.

"Go right along, sweetheart." Dad only has eyes for his new skeleton friend. "We'll be here for hours."

Paul's body brushes mine as I scoot past him. His eyes glance toward me, electric with both uncertainty and hope. He says—his voice thickly accented, like he left Russia yesterday—"You're certain you are well, Mar—Miss Caine?"

"Yes. I'm sure." I smile for him as best I can. Even in the reddish firelight, I can make out his blush of pleasure. So we're not together in this world. Not yet, anyway. But we're thinking about it. As beautiful as that is, his bashful hope only reminds me of the despair within my own Paul. . . .

Time to deal with that later. I crawl toward the ladder and start up it, grateful to see a sliver of night sky above. The stars shine brightly. Must not be much electric light around here.

I emerge from the tunnel and gasp. The moonlight illuminates a vast desert, several tents—and the Great Pyramids, towering majestically against the night. In the distance I can make out the profile of the Sphinx as it stares into the distance. Although the city of Giza is very close to the Pyramids in my dimension, it doesn't seem to have been built yet. There's nothing but rolling sand for as long as the eye can see—well, besides the tents, the ancient monuments, and various shovels, pans, and tools I recognize as ones for an archaeological dig.

They're Egyptologists. Mom and Dad went into archaeology. That wasn't just a dead body—that was a mummy.

I remain frozen at the top of the ladder, caught up in astonishment and awe, until I hear a rifle being cocked. Turning, I see Josie and Theo standing behind me. Armed. And ready to fire.

6

AT FIRST I DON'T EVEN KNOW WHAT TO DO. PLEAD WITH MY
sister not to shoot me? I find myself raising my hands in surrender, like I've seen on TV.

Josie and Theo simultaneously groan as they lower their
weapons. "It was you down there?" Josie's rifle remains in
one hand, pointed at the ground but obviously still ready for
action. She's wearing khaki jodhpurs and a white linen shirt
not quite as frilly as my own. Her hair hangs in a long braid
that nearly reaches her elbows. "We thought we had a tomb
raider on our hands."

Can't quite see myself as Lara Croft. I'd have a lot of trouble filling out her tank top. "Sorry, guys. Didn't mean to
raise a false alarm."

"You could've gotten hurt." Theo sets his rifle down. He
seems less comfortable with his weapon than Josie is. "What
were you doing?"

"I got mixed up. Confused. That's all." I brush more sand from my skirt. By now the grit has burrowed into my boots, my blouse, even my huge, old-timey underwear. The physical irritation only aggravates my inner misery. "Can I apologize tomorrow? Right now I need to lie down." Which is code for *I need to be alone so I can try to leap into the next universe.*

Josie, obviously, does not know this code. "You can do your drawings in the daytime, Marguerite. When it's safe, and you have someone with you."

She looks more annoyed than concerned, although that's pretty much how Josie is. Don't get me wrong. My sister can be sympathetic and caring when people need her. But she expects you to watch your own butt. Carrying that rifle—well, for her, it looks natural.

"I'm sorry," I say. "It won't happen again."

Will it? Will Wicked ever backtrack and make a second attempt on a Marguerite's life?

Yes. Of course she will.

It finally hits me then: It's not enough to chase after Wicked, fixing everything she's broken. I have to protect the other Marguerites, every single one that could be in danger from Wicked's schemes. Not only to mess with Triad's plan for destroying the universes—though that would be reason enough—but also because this is my responsibility, the most sacred one I can imagine.

My travels have endangered many Marguerites. Affected some of their lives forever. But Wicked is attempting a mass murder of countless Marguerites, and it's my job to save them.

I have to follow Wicked into her traps. Face danger after danger. Complete rescue after rescue. Failure means the deaths of billions.

"Come on." Theo steps closer. He's dressed more rakishly than any of the others I've seen in this dimension so far, with a brightly colored cloth tied at his neck and a wristwatch glittering so much in the moonlight that it betrays the diamonds set in the hands. He helps me up the final rungs of the ladder. "Go gently, Josephine. Can't you see Marguerite's shaken up? She's pale as a ghost."

Josie sighs. "I know. I'm sorry, Marguerite. Are you certain you're all right?"

"I just need to lie down. I promise."

"You want to walk her to her tent, Theo?" Even in the darkness, I can see the glint in Josie's eyes as she points toward the tent that must be mine. Maybe she thinks something's going on. Oh, please, not this world too—

Yet Theo doesn't leap at the suggestion, only looks awkward. That means we're not an item here either. Thank God. "I'm all right." I start walking, not waiting for any escort. "See you tomorrow."

"Only if you promise not to go crazy again," Josie calls after me. Her tone is different now, though. She's only teasing me.

Never have I felt less like joking around—but I have a role to play. So I glance over my shoulder and stick out my tongue. "Crazy, huh? Then how come I just discovered a mummy?"

Both Josie and Theo are instantly galvanized, dropping to their knees to call down into the passageway where Dad and Paul are hard at work. Me, I'm grateful for the chance to be alone.

The splendor of the Egyptian night is almost overpowering. A shudder ripples through me as I look once again at the Pyramids on the horizon. Their majesty blinds me to everything else at first, in the most comforting way. Sometimes, a truly beautiful painting or sculpture calms my spirit when nothing else can. Artwork can lift us up like that if we let it. The stark nightscape around me has the purity of art.

But as I walk on, slowly I begin to take in more details of our encampment. We have at least nine tents set up around here, plus a central fire over which a cooking grate has been set. The tents aren't the small nylon pop-up types I remember from the few times Josie convinced me to go camping with her; these are enormous, each of them the size of a large room, and they're sewn of thick white fabric that sways slightly in the night breezes. In the darker distance beyond the tents lie several woolly shapes that I suddenly realize are sleeping camels.

Camels? I can't help it. I laugh. The thought of my mom riding a camel—or Paul, who's usually so grave and calm, attempting to balance atop the hump—

But then I imagine him falling, and once again I remember my own terrible plunge in the Londonverse, the one that killed another me. My smile fades. It's going to be a long time before I feel like laughing again.

My tent turns out to be even more luxurious inside than out. There's a sort of makeshift floor, atop which we've laid what looks like a Turkish carpet. Small wooden folding tables hold my sketchbooks and a flickering lantern. Brightly patterned swaths of fabric hang at the corners and seams of the tent for maximum privacy. A handmade quilt in various shades of dark blue covers my little camp bed. Nearby, an upturned, leather-covered steamer trunk seems to serve as a chest of drawers, and lying atop it are a lace scarf and a pith helmet.

Too bad I didn't find this universe earlier, when I could've enjoyed it, when traveling through the dimensions almost seemed like a game. Now all I can do is try to move on as fast as possible, to save the next Marguerite.

I sit on the camp bed and unbutton the high neck of my blouse. Sand has even found its way into the Firebird, though after I give the locket a good shake, the mechanism seems to be none the worse for wear. Thank God. I don't think I could handle this thing getting broken in another dimension, because the last time that happened I got stranded for nearly a month.

Not to mention pregnant.

My Firebird remains tethered to Wicked's, capable of following in her footsteps as soon as she has moved on. So I take a deep breath, hit the controls, and—

—nothing.

Damn it. When I double-check that the Firebird is working properly—and it is—I know what the deal is. Apparently I can't leap ahead into a universe if Wicked is already in it. Each Marguerite has a maximum capacity of two: one host, one guest. I have to follow in Wicked's footsteps, so I can't move forward until she moves on.

And she won't move on until she's dreamed up a grisly way for another Marguerite to die.

What nightmare is she concocting this time? My predicament down in the mummy's tomb could've gotten me killed, but by now I feel sure this is far from the worst Wicked can do.

Just wait until I get out of this universe, Wicked. You're going to pay for this.

But how? It's not like I can ever catch up to her. One visitor in a body at a time means one Marguerite to a dimension. This chase could go on forever.

"Marguerite? Are you decent?" My mother's voice is just outside the fabric-draped flap that counts as my tent's door. She has a stronger French accent than usual.

"If 'decent' means 'not naked,' then sure, I'm decent." I tuck the Firebird back into my shirt with a sigh and start buttoning up.

My fingers pause, though, when my mother finally steps through, lantern in hand. Unlike everyone else I've seen here, she isn't dressed in classic aristocrat-adventurer-of-the-Gilded-Age style. Instead, she's wearing a long, flowing, richly patterned robe and a silk scarf knotted into what looks

61

like a pretty decent turban. Leave it to Mom to finally find her fashion sense in the desert.

"Are you all right, dear?" Mom sits on the edge of my bed. "It's not like you to go wandering into an active dig."

"I know, Mom. I'm sorry."

"You were acting so strangely this evening—"

When Wicked was here, something about her behavior concerned my mom. Not enough to make her realize how seriously things had gone wrong, but enough to draw her attention. Which means now she'll be watching me more closely. That's not necessarily a problem, but it's one more factor for me to juggle in this universe.

"I need to sleep. That's all."

"A good night's rest never made any situation worse," she agrees. Her arm slides around me, a caress that invites me to rest my head on her shoulder. Maybe I should be too old to take so much comfort from being hugged by my mom, but after plunging to my near-death, I'm not ashamed to need a snuggle. Her fingers comb through my few loose curls; she used to do that when I was little, after nightmares, when she was coaxing me back to sleep. "I must say, Mr. Markov hurried down to help you very quickly. I doubt anyone could've held him back."

Mom's Team Paul in this universe too. "I can't believe he let Dad go first."

Mom laughs softly. "It's not like you to play the coquette, Marguerite. You'll make up your mind about him soon, won't you?"

Probably, I think. When I leap out of this world—the Egyptverse, let's call it—this world's Marguerite will remember my feelings about Paul. She'll remember that he's come through for her in world after world, that we've loved each other time and again. But will she also remember the darkness within Paul? The nightmare visions from other worlds that neither of us can forget?

Out loud I say only, "You want me to be sure, don't you, Mom?"

"Of course. But you know these Russians. They feel things so deeply."

I laugh again. "As if you're not Russian."

"Of course, but a few generations back. The Saint Petersburg snows have hardly melted on Mr. Markov's boots."

So, he's a native of Russia in this dimension, like his accent suggested. My accent is odd here—not quite English or American, somewhere in between, just like Josie's was. Probably that's the result of a life spent traveling back and forth to Egypt and to museums all over the world.

Mom continues. "If the tsar's own Egyptologist isn't enough to impress you, what will be?"

She's only teasing me. But that reminds me of the Russiaverse where my mother was married to the tsar—and where I was the result of a clandestine affair between her and my father, the tsarevich's tutor. Mom always wanted tons of kids, but pregnancy was dangerous for her, which is why in my universe, she and Dad stopped with me and Josie. In the Russiaverse, she died giving birth to her fourth child. The

63

monstrous Tsar Alexander basically bred her to death.

I hug her tightly. She smells like roses. "I love you, Mom."

My mother obviously has no idea what inspired this out-burst of emotion, but she's too wise to ask. "I love you too."

After she leaves, I try once more to leap away, but no such luck. I undress, which takes a while; frilly collars and stock-ings and lace-up boots aren't easy to deal with. Again I try to leap; again, nothing. As I slip into the loose, thin nightdress I find in one of the steamer trunk's drawers, I decide to stay awake as long as I can, attempting to leap away every ten minutes or so. This Marguerite has been saved from being buried alive. Who knows what the next one has to face?

But I'm tired. So tired. Body and soul. No sooner do I pull the quilt over me and rest my head on the pillow than I pass out.

Nightmares chase me all night long. Yet I never dream of the terrible fall in the Londonverse, that last fatal plunge. Instead I'm back down in the tomb with mummified corpses tumbling out of doors and passages, dozens and dozens of them.

And in the dream I somehow know—every one of those dead bodies is mine.

When I wake up in the morning, I try the Firebird again. Still no escape. Apparently Wicked's having trouble coming up with something deadly this time. I hope, for the next Marguerite's sake, that she lives in a place so safe, so guarded, that Wicked can't find anything to do to her.

Although that would mean I'm staying in the Egyptverse for quite a while.

Well, I've dealt with worse dimensions.

Starting back in the Renaissance, many painters used a pigment called mummy brown. It had an umber tint to it—a natural, earthy shade that was never dull—and it could be slightly transparent, which made it good for glazes. The color remained popular right up until the middle of the twentieth century, when the Pre-Raphaelites first used it with abandon . . . and then realized the shade got its name because the pigment was made from actual, real, ground-up Egyptian mummies. Apparently a couple of painters actually buried the tubes of paint when they found out the truth. Even that didn't bother some people, though, and the production of old-fashioned mummy brown only ended when there were no longer cheap mummies.

I think about this story a lot as I look at the various vials and tubes of paint in my art box. Please, let me not make my own paints in this world. Please don't let me be somebody who would grind up a dead body for a painting. That's something Wicked would do, not me.

If only I could manage to be useful in this dimension—but I don't have the scientific know-how to build a stabilizer device. That's probably going to be even trickier here than at home, since the level of technology is more primitive. I've saved this world's Marguerite, but now I have nothing to do except wait for my next opportunity to move on.

Finally, accepting that I have to deal with my life here,

I put on clothing nearly identical to what I wore yesterday, just less sandy. Although I couldn't recreate the complicated hairstyle this world's Marguerite wore, I use the lace scarf to tie my hair back in a ponytail. Hopefully that will look appropriate. Beneath my blouse hangs the Firebird, which I'll keep trying throughout the day. Once I put on the pith helmet, I feel ready for adventure. So I walk outside, prepared to see an archaeological expedition in all its glory.

Instead, I see my parents, Josie, Theo, and Paul all sitting around the still-burning central fire. A metal coffeepot sits atop the grate, and Mom slices bread from a loaf wrapped in what looks like waxed paper. She's still wearing her robe, and Dad is reading a newspaper in German. Paul's eyes meet mine only for a moment before he shyly looks away and accepts the bread from Mom.

"Not like you to be late for breakfast," Theo says, grinning. He's got another jaunty scarf around his neck now, and his sunglasses are tinted dark green. "Did the mummy keep you awake all night?"

"No." Somehow I think he'd take some weird satisfaction from my nightmares, so I don't add anything else. "Sorry if I slept late. I don't want to miss anything."

Which is true. As long as I'm stuck here, I might as well take a good look around—and exploring ancient Egyptian tombs will be fascinating as long as no more mummies leap from the walls.

My parents exchange glances before my father says, "You do remember that it's the Sabbath, don't you, Marguerite?"

I guess Mom and Dad had to be religious in at least one universe. "Oh. Of course. I forgot."

"Good thing you're wearing that pith helmet," Josie says. She lights a cigarette, which startles me until I remember that probably nobody in this world knows yet that smoking causes cancer. "Because otherwise I'd be worried you're suffering from sunstroke."

"Marguerite is only eager to get back to work." Paul's thick Russian accent—so like that of Lieutenant Markov—melts my heart. I look over at him just as he hands over a piece of bread on a blue tin plate and a mug of coffee. He fixed my meal before he served himself. I smile at him as warmly as I can manage, and he ducks his head. The moment should be adorable, but instead I find myself thinking of Paul as I left him back home: head bowed, as if the shame and despair he felt—the residual effects of his splintering—were literally weighing him down, making it hard for him to move.

"Are you certain you're all right?" Dad peers at me over the rims of his spectacles. "You look pale, Marguerite."

"I'm fine." I try to brighten up—that way I won't draw extra attention.

Time to concentrate on what matters most about Paul at this moment: He's still this world's Paul, at least eight hours after I jumped into this universe. My Paul remains in the Londonverse. Apparently he feels the need to find the body before he follows me here, but that can take a while. Dredging a river for a corpse is lengthy, tedious work with no guarantee of success.

This is a subject I know way too much about. After they told us my father had died crashing his car into the river, I spent a lot of time researching that, mostly after I knew he was actually alive and okay. Having him back with us didn't erase the trauma of thinking he was dead. I don't know why, but it didn't. For weeks I had nightmares in which I found out I'd gone to the wrong universe, that the father I'd brought back wasn't mine, whatever my brain could invent to convince me Dad had died after all. Learning more about what might have happened to him if he had gone into the river . . . well, it helped somehow. But now it means my knowledge about what a water-bloated corpse looks like is way, way too vivid.

Please don't let Paul have to see that, I think. *Please.*

"If Marguerite doesn't feel the need to rest, then I don't see any reason why she shouldn't get something done today," my mother says. "We need the work crews for excavation, but not for her sketching. In fact, she really should have more time down in the tombs when she can draw uninterrupted."

"And the sooner you get down there, the better." Dad lifts his coffee to me, as if in a toast. "We don't want last night's little incident to spook you."

I raise my mug to him and take a drink—and then stifle the shudder that passes through me. Oh, my God, that coffee is strong. Crazy strong. Like, if I drink this whole mug, I might be able to see through time. Apparently, if you wanted to drink coffee before the invention of the filter, you had to *mean* it.

"She shouldn't go into the tombs alone again," Paul suggests. "I'm happy to go with her."

Theo's face falls as he sees the opportunity one second too late. Maybe I ought to feel sorry for this world's Theo, but I figure he can take care of himself. "I'd like that," I say, and Paul smiles. It feels good to see him smile again.

Twenty minutes later, he leads me into another tomb—down another ladder, this time into a far larger passageway, one where it's easy to stand up and walk. The lantern in Paul's hand illuminates a long corridor that seems to stretch into infinity. As he holds it up, its light reveals the hieroglyphics and paintings on the wall. The entire Egyptian pantheon stands before me painted in ochre, cobalt, and gold: Horus with his curved beak, Isis with her arms outstretched like wings, Anubis with his dark jackal head waiting to take the dead to the underworld.

"This is amazing," I whisper. My fingers reach toward the symbols, but I know better than to touch them.

"Almost intact." Paul sounds proud. "With the help of your sketches, we'll be able to translate them. People who died three thousand years ago will speak again."

I flip open my sketchbook, which I hadn't yet taken the time to look through. Here, I draw as much as I paint, if not more—sometimes with colored pencils, sometimes with plain—and my work reveals much more meticulous detail than I've ever used in my artwork back home.

"You're the only one who hasn't studied Egyptology," Paul adds. "Not formally, at least. But you're the one who might make the greatest discoveries of all."

That's when it hits me: My dad wasn't joking about me being in the "family trade." Here, I'm an Egyptologist too. This time, I'm not just along for the ride. I work alongside Mom and Dad. I'm part of the team. That's never happened before.

Wait, no. It's true for Wicked—she's as much a part of the Home Office's plans as anyone. But she shouldn't get to be the only one, because this feels incredible.

See, my parents have never made me feel bad for not inheriting their science-genius genes the way Josie did. They've always encouraged my artwork and never even suggested that my kind of creativity was less important than theirs. Still, they're the ones who have redefined the laws of physics. I'm the one who has had exactly one gallery show in my life. It's hard not to feel insignificant when your parents are basically Marie and Pierre Curie. What would I have to create to match the Firebird? The Sistine Chapel, maybe.

But here, my parents need my artwork. I'm part of their discoveries and their triumphs. The knowledge fills a hole in my heart I hadn't even known was there until this second.

Maybe you'd think being a perfect traveler, a journeyer through the dimensions, would have been as fulfilling. The difference is, that's something that was done to me. As great a gift as it is, the burden of it is real. And the danger. And the wrong I've done. This, though—these sketches of Ancient Egyptian hieroglyphics—this is pure. Totally my own, born out of the art I love.

Compared to the terrible stuff that's happening through-out the multiverse right now, this consolation isn't much. But maybe I need it more. I'm grateful for even this brief wonder, this moment that could almost be called happiness.

I hug my sketchbook to my chest, and Paul laughs softly. "You seem . . . excited to get to work."

"I am." For as long as I'm stuck in this universe, I intend to do my best.

Paul hesitates before saying, in his thick Russian accent, "I always wished I could draw and paint as you do."

"Really?"

He nods, his eyes not quite meeting mine. Sometimes it's adorable how such a large, strong man can be so shy. "We find so many artifacts of a lost civilization. A broken statue. A buried jar. We see shards and scraps. Mere pieces of what was a glorious whole. When I think about this, I wish I could put it back together again. Not as it was before—that is of course impossible. But enough to see it, truly see it, as it once was. The art you create—that's as close as we ever come."

Not as it was before. I remember racing through the dimensions, trying desperately to put the pieces of Paul's soul back together again. Can he ever be the same? Or will I only see him the way this Paul sees Ancient Egypt—in paintings, in memories, and in dreams?

I refuse to believe that my Paul's soul is lost. He's not broken. Not one of the ruins that surrounds us. He can make it.

Then Paul's eyes widen, and he steps back, grimacing as if

in pain. He slumps heavily against the wall as if the paintings weren't even there.

"Paul!" I go to him, alarmed. "Are you—"

My hand touches his chest, and beneath his shirt I feel the unmistakable outline of his Firebird. It's my Paul, here at last.

I want to hug him, but he holds out his hands as though for balance. He's still disoriented. "Where are we?"

"Egypt. This is an ancient tomb, and we're all exploring it together. As dimensions go, this one is pretty freakin' awesome, right?" I'm trying to make him smile, because if I can, that means he didn't have to see the dead body of London-verse's Marguerite. But Paul's face is pale, and his gray eyes tormented, and I know the last thing he saw in that world. "I'm sorry."

"You could've died." Then his body tenses. His eyes widen. His voice drops to a growl as he says, "Maybe you did."

"Paul?"

He doesn't answer—instead he pushes me back so roughly that I nearly hit the opposite wall. Something in his gaze reminds me of the cold-blooded Mafiaverse Paul, who unloaded bullets into Theo without even flinching. "Prove who you are."

"What?"

"You could be her," Paul says. His hands grip my shoulders so tightly that I could never wrench myself free. "You could have killed her, and waited here to kill me too. So prove it. Prove that you're my Marguerite or I promise you—"

Paul doesn't finish that sentence. He doesn't have to. He just saw one Marguerite lying dead in front of him. Now he's willing to kill another with his bare hands.

My Paul would never do that—ever—or he wouldn't have.

But the splintering has damaged him, left rough edges and paranoia where love used to be. To my horror I realize that I may not even know Paul anymore

And if he doesn't know me . . . would he hurt me?

Oh, God. He would.

7

"PAUL—" I CAN'T TALK. FOR A MOMENT I CAN HARDLY breathe. His gaze burns into me with the cold blaze of ice, and he steps closer, as if preparing to do his worst.

I remember Lieutenant Markov shooting the traitorous guard who would've murdered the grand duchess, and, from another world, the Russian mafia lord's son who blew away Theo's knees in cold blood. The potential for violence, whether for good or for evil, lies within every Paul—including the one I love.

My own Paul had overcome that, long before his splintering. Before I even met him. He'd struggled through the darkness in his past to become a good person, and a strong man. But the cracks in his soul remain, and at any moment the good man I love could fall apart. Become someone else, someone dangerous.

So I'd better defend myself.

"Okay," I begin shakily. "I just got hijacked for the first time in my own body, because Wicked—"

"Wicked?" Paul squints, as if assessing a suspicious stranger.

"Oh, right! That's what I'm calling her, the one from the Home Office, because—well, it's easier, for one, and I don't even think she deserves to be called Marguerite. But she knows about Nightthief, doesn't she? Then—then I bet she doesn't know about that terrible spring break you and Theo had in Vegas—"

"Stop." Paul takes a deep breath, and then he looks like himself again. My nauseating dread fades. Of course I didn't have to be afraid of Paul. Splintered or not, he's still himself. He has to be. "I knew it was you as soon as you told me you nicknamed the other one Wicked."

I don't want to ask this next, but I have to. "What happened in the Londonverse?"

"What do you think happened? Do you need me to say it out loud?"

I nod like the hypocrite I am, demanding that Paul speak when I lack the courage to even ask the question.

"She's dead," Paul says heavily. "I watched her die."

The knowledge crashes into me, nearly as hard and cold as the water of the Thames must have been for her. I would give so much to have stayed in one second longer, to have spared her the awareness of her fall until the very last instant, when she might not even have had time to understand what was happening.

You can't cut it that close, I remind myself. *It wouldn't save*

75

her, and it would only endanger you. True. Doesn't make me feel any better.

Paul and I remain silent for a few moments. The ancient gods surrounding us stare with their identical, arched eyes, and now this passageway feels like the tomb it used to be. *Did you think death was a game you could cheat?* The painted figures seem to say. *The people buried here thought that too. Now you're digging up their bones.*

"I waited for them to find the body." Paul stares at the wall behind me, looking past my face as if I were just another hieroglyph—no. That's not it. He sees the dead Marguerite in his memory more clearly than he can focus on the real me, here and now. "I realized seeing her wouldn't tell me anything—even if it had been you, and the Firebird had been around your neck when you hit the water, surely the impact would've broken it. Or the current could've snatched it away. But I still thought I needed to see her for myself." He closes his eyes. "I wish I hadn't."

They say that hitting water from that high up is just like hitting concrete. My Londonverse self might have been in pieces. Nausea ripples through me, and I have to swallow hard. "Did—did Aunt Susannah have to—"

"I identified the body for her."

"Thank you." Aunt Susannah wouldn't have been able to bear that, I don't think. Then I realize the full meaning of what Paul has just told me. "Wait. Aunt Susannah knew you? Well enough for you to—well, to do that?"

Paul nods. "After you left the Londonverse the first time, your other self remembered who you were. Everything she'd done. So apparently she looked for Paul Markov at Cambridge, hoping he had some explanation. Then they began . . . spending time together."

It breaks my heart all over again. Another world where Paul and I might have been together, maybe forever—and Londonverse Marguerite finally had some kind of shot at happiness—ended in one fatal plunge.

"Aunt Susannah explained some of it to me, while we were waiting for—while we were waiting," Paul continues. "The rest I put together for myself."

"See? We really do have a destiny. Because if there was any world where you'd think we didn't have a chance, that had to be the one." I feel shallow, talking about my love life at a time like this. But I'm not doing it for me—I'm doing this for Paul. He needs something to hold on to. Otherwise, the grief and guilt he feels from all these universes will continue to drag him down. The cracks left within him from when his soul was splintered could deepen and weaken until he truly falls apart.

My distraction works, at least a little. Paul takes another deep breath and straightens. "Did you say Egypt?"

I hold out my hands to gesture at the hieroglyphics. "No, actually, this is Wisconsin."

He almost smiles. "Egypt. My accent is stronger here—"

"You're the tsar's own Egyptologist, working with Mom

and Dad on the expedition. We have these huge tents, and this crazy strong coffee, and real live camels. Mom's even wearing a turban."

Paul's dismay brings me closer to laughing than I've been in a long time. "Do we have to ride the camels?"

"I don't know. Hasn't come up yet."

"I hope not." Just when I feel like we might be getting past the worst of it, he tenses again. "Wait. The other one—Wicked—she came here to kill you? Just like the last Marguerite?"

"She's slamming doors—shutting me out of more and more universes." The twisted plan has become clearer to me after a night to mull things over. "Triad is trying to make sure that I can't save the universes in question. I can't save a universe I can't reach. I can't reach a universe where I'm already dead. So they're going to kill all these Marguerites— one after another—unless I follow Wicked and put things right. I have to keep after her, Paul. I have to save the other Marguerites. Not only because it lets me reach those dimensions and protect them, but because . . . I can't just let the other versions of me be slaughtered. Not if I have the power to stop it."

Paul wants to object, I can tell. No doubt he thinks my plan for rescuing the other Marguerites is too dangerous. Honestly, I agree. It *is* too dangerous. But that's what I have to do. Maybe he senses my determination, because instead of arguing, he simply asks, "What happened in this dimension? How did she attempt to murder you?"

"She tried to bury me in a cave-in. One of the passage-ways wasn't as stable. I got through it fine, except for the part where an actual ancient mummy fell on me. Way less fun than it looks in *Raiders of the Lost Ark*."

Paul frowns. "That sounds survivable. Obviously. But—"

Quickly I explain why Wicked's methods are going to be less immediately dangerous in the future, and at first Paul nods, agreeing with me. But his gaze slowly becomes more distant, even confused. Then he strokes his short beard—a gesture that seems familiar, even studied—and says, his consonants thick and blurred with his Russian accent, "Wait. Remind me, I know this. Who is Wicked, Miss Caine?"

Crap. This world's Paul is bleeding through again. I step closer, which ignites hope in his eyes until the moment I reach into his shirt, take hold of his Firebird and set a reminder.

Paul staggers back, swearing under his breath in Russian—even though he's my Paul again. "Let me reset this for more frequent reminders."

"You could make some Nightthief." No sooner have I spoken the words than I realize how unlikely that is. "We probably don't have the supplies out here in the desert."

"Probably not. I'll look later. Right now I want to set the reminders just in case."

He starts manipulating the controls, his large hands sur-prisingly deft with the tiny mechanics. Instead of stepping back, I remain close in an attempt to preserve the fragile bond restored between us.

So of course that's when I hear Theo shout, "Hello in there!"

"Hey, Theo," I call back. Paul steps back and drops his Firebird back within his shirt just in time for Theo to appear.

Somehow Theo's grin looks even more devilish when set off with that mustache. He could pass for a lothario from some old silent movie. "How goes the sketching, Marguerite?"

"Oh, it's—" Great, I want to say, but the sketchpad is closed and Theo isn't a fool. "Still getting started. I'm a little nervous in these passageways after what happened last night."

"Who could blame you?" Theo steps closer and puts one hand on my shoulder, an unmistakably flirtatious touch. "Next time we're in Cairo, I'm making it my sworn duty to distract you from your troubles. What about a trip to the moving pictures?"

Oh, my God, even movies are new here. This would be amusing if it weren't for Paul's gaze on us, heavy and disapproving. I step out of Theo's reach, clutching my sketchpad to my chest. "Drawing is the only distraction I usually need. Which is why I should get started."

The rebuff doesn't affect Theo much. He simply shrugs. "Let me know what you think, next time we're in Cairo."

"Sure. Definitely." I mean it as a brush-off, but Theo grins again.

As soon as he's gone, Paul says, "You're with him, here."

"No, I'm not!" I would have picked up on some sign of that last night or this morning. "He's only flirting, or maybe just being Theo."

"Maybe you have a destiny after all." Paul turns away to follow Theo out. "It's just not with me."

"Why are you acting like this?" I could shake him. "Why are you being so—so jealous, so angry—when you know that I—"

Paul whirls around. The anger is back, but subsumed in grief that's even more terrifying to see. "I'm not angry. I'm not jealous. I'm relieved. You shouldn't be tied to me anymore, Marguerite. Theo would be better for you."

"Excuse me, but who I love isn't something you get to prescribe for me, like a doctor with some pills."

"Don't you understand?" His voice rises nearly to a shout, echoing from the stone walls. "I see Theo near you and I remember shooting him. I see you near him and I want to shake you until you fall. This brutal . . . thing my father tried to turn me into—I thought I'd buried it. Maybe I had. But the splintering set it free. I'm no good for you any longer, Marguerite. I never will be again."

"It's only been a few days. How can you know?" I'm sympathetic to what Paul's going through, but this defeatist attitude has to stop. "Paul, you didn't hurt me. You would never hurt me."

"You don't know that. And neither do I." When I start to protest, Paul holds up one hand. The wind blows at the collar of his white linen shirt, ruffles his reddish hair. "You don't know what it feels like, being splintered. You don't know how it is to know that . . . that you've been stolen from yourself."

That catches me short. I hadn't thought of it that way before. The profoundness of the violation—the intimacy and brutality of it—makes me shudder. "You're back together now. I know it was terrible, but you'll get better."

"This isn't a cut you can fix with a Band-Aid. It goes deeper." Clearly struggling for the right words, Paul remains silent for a few long seconds before he speaks again. "My thoughts don't unfold the way they should. My feelings control me too much. From as far back as I can remember, I fought to be a different kind of man from my father. But sometimes I find myself wanting to react the way he would. Other times, the anger or sorrow seems to come out of nowhere; it doesn't have anything to do with me but it takes me over."

"You're not going to turn into your father." This much I believe absolutely.

"Maybe not. But I have no idea what I *am* going to turn into. Only one thing is certain. I'm not the same person you fell in love with. I've changed more than you could ever realize. And I will never be the same again." His gray eyes finally meet mine. "You should get out while you can."

He walks away, so now we are both in despair, both alone.

After a moment, I decide to stay in the tomb.

I wasn't lying when I told Theo my work would be the ideal distraction. That day, I remain in the passageway for hours, sketching as delicately and accurately as I can. The beauty of the paintings on the walls touches me even through my misery, and I imagine my long-ago counterpart, no doubt wearing the thin white cotton robe and elaborate beaded collar they always show in movies about ancient Egypt. Copying that person's work with every detail, every highlight, is the highest tribute I can pay to the original artist. And getting it right lets me feel like I've succeeded at something amid all this failure. I need that feeling more than I should.

The only time my work becomes difficult is when tears blur my vision. But I dab them away and keep going.

Although I want to go after Paul, I don't. As badly as he's hurting, maybe right now that's what he needs. When we're in pain, people are too quick to say, *Get over it, move on, it's not that bad.* But we don't get over grief by denying it. We have to feel it. We have to give it its due. Sometimes that means doing the exact opposite of "moving on." We have to dive down to the very depths of our sorrow, relive every terrible moment, and endure the torture of asking what could have been—and what will now be. We have to bleed out before our hearts can start beating again.

That's what Paul is doing now. Bleeding out.

After a few hours, I finally hear footsteps in the stone passageway. Hope lifts me away from my work, and I look in that direction, eager to see him. Instead, Theo walks in. It takes all my self-control not to let my disappointment show.

"How's the work going?" Theo steps closer, hands behind his back. "Our Russian friend seems to be in a terrible temper. Has been ever since he left you behind."

"I wouldn't know anything about it." This Theo probably believes Paul and I had a spat, and this is his big opportunity. I have exactly zero patience to deal with that.

He wipes his brow, which has a fine sheen of sweat. "The only escape from the damned heat is in the homes of the dead. Strange, isn't it?"

"Never thought of it that way." The air is cool and musty in here, which wouldn't seem like such sweet relief if the alternative were anything but the scorching sun of the desert. "I should probably go back to the campsite, huh?"

"No rush. Take your time, Meg."

Meg.

No wonder he sounded so familiar. The Triadverse Theo has followed me here.

I turn to look at this Theo—the one who kidnapped my father, framed Paul for murder, and helped Wicked hijack my body. When he sees the recognition in my eyes, he sighs. "I knew it. Am I really the only one in the multiverse who nicknamed you Meg?"

"Yes. Are you here to inject me with Nightthief again?" I demand.

"No," Theo says as he steps closer. Now I can see that he's pale, and his movements have become slow, reluctant. Whatever he's here to do is bad.

My only potential weapons are a box of colored pencils and a sketchpad. But I bet a pencil to the eye would stop almost anyone.

"Listen to me." He holds up his hands, and I pause, unsure

what he's going to pull next. "I know you're angry with Conley and Triad, and I don't blame you. But don't let your temper blind you to what's really going on here. You can turn this whole thing around in a second, just by agreeing to cooperate."

"Stop trying to negotiate with me!" I back away from him, although this only leads me farther into the tomb, away from the exit. "When will you guys at Triad get it through your thick skulls that I'm never, ever working for you? How do you not see that this is crazy?"

"Actually, yes, I do see it," Theo says, and this may be the first time he's ever told me the entire truth. "If I'd known at the start this was what I was getting into, no way in hell would I have signed up. But now I'm here. Now I know. And if any universes are going to be destroyed, I intend to be in one of the ones left standing."

I can't argue with his goals, but I have a big problem with his methods. "This isn't just about saving your skin. It's about saving trillions of lives. Literally! How can you not fight this with everything you've got?"

"Because everything I've got isn't enough to stop them! Meg, will you calm down and think? It's too late. Triad is too far ahead. You want to start running a race with them while they're about an inch short of the finish line. How pointless is that? Conley and Triad still want you on their side, despite everything—"

The sound I make can only be called a snort. "Oh, yeah, they've got so much to forgive me for."

Theo grimaces in exasperation. "Dammit, why are you doing this to yourself? There's still time for you to save your whole dimension! Billions of people there, every animal, every plant on the entire Earth—you're risking them all in this crazy chase. Don't you owe them your loyalty first?"

I never thought about it in terms of loyalty. If I could only protect one dimension, wouldn't it have to be the one I call home?

But I refuse to let Theo turn this around on me. "I'm not the one putting my universe in danger. That's Triad's responsibility."

"All I'm saying is, your actions have consequences." Theo's face is heavily shadowed in the dim passageway. He has yet to take up the heavy flashlight dangling from his belt. "Those other universes could be no more than—choices nobody ever made."

For the length of one breath, I am no longer in Egypt. Instead, I lie beneath warm furs in a dacha in Russia while a snowstorm rages outside and Paul holds me close. At the same time, I sit in an opulent Parisian hotel room, hand splayed across my belly, dizzy with the new knowledge that in that dimension I carried Paul's child.

I have regretted making that choice for the grand duchess ever since—and yet it would be infinitely worse to erase that choice, all those lives, that dimension forever.

"Those people deserve a chance to live," I tell Theo. "They have the right to create their own destiny."

"You haven't always respected your other selves' choices so carefully, have you?" Even in the darkness I can see the spark of anger in Theo's eyes.

"I've messed up," I admit. "More than once. But what you're talking about is different."

Theo shoots back, "So where do you draw the line, Meg? Anywhere you like, as long as I'm on the wrong side of it?"

I could scream. "Cut out the stupid word games! I made a mistake, but you're deliberately committing genocide! That is way, way off the scale of anything I would ever do. And you know what else? My Theo wouldn't ever do that either. So how did you get so screwed up?"

He lunges toward me. His tackle catches me under the ribs, knocking the breath out of me and sending my pencils flying. I claw at his face as Theo grabs my lace scarf, which comes loose from my hat. His knee presses down my left arm as he straddles me and fumbles around my throat.

The Firebird! He's going to steal the Firebird! I struggle to get him off me, but I can't, not even when I realize he isn't going for the Firebird at all. Not even as the lace scarf tightens around my throat.

I can't breathe.

Theo is strangling me.

My larynx feels like it's being smashed into my spine. My pulse is fast and hard and with every beat the scarf seems to be cutting into my skin.

"Jump," Theo says. He's crying; tears trickle down the

cheek he's turned toward me so that he won't have to see my face while he does this. "I left you one hand free. Grab the Firebird and jump."

I could do it, but then this Marguerite—and maybe this entire dimension—dies.

Desperately I thrash beneath him, or try to thrash. I paw feebly at his tense arms. It's no use. Theo has me pinned with all his weight and strength, and I can't breathe. Dizziness floods me. My tongue feels too thick for my mouth. I can hardly hear over the roar of my own blood in my ears.

"Meg, please!" Theo sobs once. "Please, don't make me kill both of you."

I'm about to black out. With my last strength, as Theo begins to blur and darken above my eyes, I hit the controls on the Firebird and—

I am surrounded by the void.

Complete darkness. Complete silence. I have no weight, no body.

Oh, God.

I'm dead.

8

I CAN'T BE DEAD.

I mean it—I can't. My heart beats in my chest, harder and faster as it responds to the mortal fear of another dimension, another Marguerite. So I must have leaped through dimensions. But I can't feel where my arms and legs are. There's no up, no down.

Before I jumped, I had no chance to ask myself whether or not I could. If Wicked hadn't moved along, I would've been stuck there with Theo strangling me to death . . .

I shudder. I must be alive, if I can shudder. And yet now I remember how it feels to die.

Did I leap into the same body as Wicked after all? I know that's impossible, but I can't come up with any other explanation for why I'm here in a total void. Am I just stuck in the corner of this Marguerite's mind until Wicked moves along? Maybe this is how it feels to exist only in someone's imagination.

Something brushes against my cheek, and I startle. The hands I couldn't sense a couple of seconds ago automatically come to my face to check. Turns out my curls are floating around me as if I were underwater. Okay, body parts intact equals good, but what the hell is going on?

Metal begins to clank and whirr, the unmistakable sounds of machinery at work. Light filters in from behind me, dim at first, then brightening. Turning around is difficult; I have to writhe with my whole body to do it, and by now nausea has begun to wring my stomach. Finally I manage to get a look at what's going on. Enormous plates are shuttering upward as if being folded, and as they fold they reveal—

—Earth. As in, the whole planet. Which I am not currently on.

Outer space. You're in outer space. Deep breaths. I can't talk myself down. Oh, my freaking God I'm in outer space! There's no oxygen in space!

Of course there's oxygen here—wherever this is—because I'm breathing. But for how long?

Never, ever have I liked heights. I'm not phobic or anything, but I'm one of the ones you have to tell not to look down no matter what. Now there's nowhere to look but down.

Red lights begin to flash, and I hear a female computer voice say, "Warning. Plasma venting in four minutes." A male computer voice says something else afterward in another language, one I can't identify, because I'm facing my second life-or-death crisis in five minutes and this is the closest I've ever come to passing out from terror.

Pull it together! Nobody's going to save me but me. Now that there's enough light in this chamber, I can see tons of openings—most of them square and small, as well as a single, large, round one that looks like it might be some kind of door. Please, let that be a door. It's the only chance I've got.

I try to move toward that opening, basically attempting to swim through whatever air is in here, but that doesn't work. It leaves me simply flailing in space, barely moving forward at all. Quickly I scan the area being revealed around me, this section of whatever enormous machine contains me now. If I could touch one of the walls, I could pull myself along the surface until I reached what I really, truly, sincerely hope is a way out.

The closest one is beneath me, if "beneath" has any meaning up here. So I wriggle in that general direction, moving so slowly I want to scream.

"Three minutes to plasma venting," intones the computer voice, with her male echo just after. Three minutes isn't long enough—at least fifty feet separate me and that opening, and I don't even think I'll be able to touch the nearest surface before then.

Another voice echoes through the chamber. "Marguerite? What are you doing?"

"Mom!" Where is she? I can't see her, but it doesn't matter. She can see me. "Get me out of here!"

The metal plates stop moving. My vista on planet Earth gets no wider. The computer voice intones, "Plasma venting aborted."

I should be happy. I should be cheering and laughing, especially now that a mechanical tow arm is unfolding from the wall to bring me in.

Instead, I want to cry.

I lost the Egyptverse Marguerite too. I had chances to save them and failed. And this time Theo was the one who did it—*Theo*—

Will I be able to save anybody? How many Marguerites have to die?

"What were you thinking?" My dad is questioning my sanity for the second time in two days, and I don't blame him. Wicked leaves a trail of crazy wherever she goes.

Dad and Mom sit on either side of me in the space station *Astraeus*—at least, that's the symbol and name stamped on the sleeves of the pale blue coveralls we wear. Mercifully, this place has gravity, or at least a good approximation of it, in its rotating central sphere. This appears to be the safe area where scientists and their families work and live. The four huge fans that spread out around it collect solar energy; the pods beneath the fans collect unnecessary plasma (whatever that is), the better to vent it into space.

I was less than three minutes from being shot into outer space along with the plasma when Mom picked up on some odd readings in the atmospheric chamber.

"The sensors in there don't warn us about human intrusion, because no one's supposed to bloody go in!" Dad only gets this angry when he's scared. "What possessed you?"

Possessed. That's closer to the truth than he can ever know. And it tells me how to play this. "Dad, something's wrong with me. I mean, mentally. I've been doing this stuff I can't understand, and sometimes I don't even remember doing it. This time I could've gotten killed. What happens next time?"

Mom's and Dad's eyes both widen, and Mom puts her arms around me. "She may need medication, Henry. Certainly she needs to see a doctor."

"On Earth?" I say hopefully. Maybe I should think it's supercool being in outer space, but I want to be back on the ground. I want all the air I can breathe. I want real gravity. I want a sky. I want to stop thinking about Theo strangling me to death.

"It won't come to that. You can stay on the station." Mom seems to think that will make me feel better. "We'll take you off-duty for a few days and let you rest. Get some sleep."

What kind of duties could I possibly have on a space station? Probably it's a little like the deep-sea station from the Oceanverse, where everyone has to help out—but there I only had to check some weather readings and tie down some cables. The potential for screwing up seems way, way higher in outer space.

"You *have* been behaving strangely of late," Dad admits. His hand brushes through my hair. "Yesterday you were in such a mood—and you didn't seem to remember who the Beatles were, which makes no sense whatsoever."

I laugh despite myself. The Beatles appear to be another universal constant: If they can exist, they will. And if the Beatles exist, my father will be their number-one fan. "I remember them now. But I don't remember not remembering them, if that makes sense."

My parents exchange worried glances. They're probably afraid I'm on the verge of some kind of psychotic break. Good. Because they need to keep an eye on this Marguerite until I stop Wicked, who could come back at any time and try to finish what she started.

But other dangers chase us, too. I put one hand to my throat, haunted by the memory of pain.

Mom gets to her feet, towing me with her, and Dad follows suit. I can feel the difference from Earth gravity. I'm slightly lighter here, which adds a surreal edge to every moment, every move. "Come on," she says. "Let's get you checked out."

The *Astraeus* turns out to be neither as cramped as the real space stations I've seen on TV in my dimension nor as roomy and comfortable as they are in the movies. The walls and floors are made of brushed metal, slightly dinged from long wear. The ceilings are black and lined with small, faint lights. Handles jut out from odd places—up high, down near the floor, etc.—but the handles don't seem to lead to anything. Huh. The few windows are small, revealing only the smallest circles of blackness; I make it a point not to look through any of them. Corridors are short and lead to broader spaces, which aren't divided like they would be in an office but clearly have defined roles—various scientific stations. My parents both wear small Canadian flag emblems at their collars, and I bet I do too, but I also glimpse the flags of Mexico, Russia, the United States, Great Britain, Japan, and what I think is the flag of India. Some flags I can't identify, but this definitely seems to be an international setup.

If anyone knows about what nearly happened with the plasma venting, nobody gives any sign.

The *Astraeus* has a large enough staff for there to be a resident shrink, Dr. Singh, who has me lying down for an exam within seconds. Her black hair is cropped short and a bit spiky, and she looks like she's no older than Josie. Yet I find myself trusting her instantly. "Are you experiencing depression?" she asks.

"No." I mean, I guess not. There's no telling what might be going on in this Marguerite's mind, since she's now been inhabited by two trans-dimensional visitors in a row. "I've been really stressed out, though."

Dr. Singh nods. "Have you had suicidal impulses?" Mom and Dad look at each other, stricken. The doctor notes their reaction and leans closer to me. "If you'd rather speak to me without your parents in the room . . ."

"No, no, it's okay. They should hear this." I take a deep breath. How can I keep this Marguerite safest? "I'm not suicidal. But some of the stuff I've been doing during these, uh, blackouts—it's dangerous. I don't know why, and it doesn't make any sense, but it's happening and I'm scared."

"Okay," Dr. Singh says, laying one hand on my shoulder. "I agree with your parents—you should be taken off duty immediately. You need sleep, rest, and relaxation. Exercise, too. The logs say you haven't been keeping up with the requirements. You're not at the reprimand stage yet, but you will be soon. And if your body is out of whack, sometimes the mind follows suit. Maybe this would be a good time for you to concentrate on your art."

They really need to understand the key point here, so I say it out loud: "I should be watched."

Again, the three adults in the room exchange glances. Dr. Singh says, "You reported no hallucinations, no violent impulses—"

"But what if that changes?" Which it will, if Wicked ever returns to the Spaceverse. "What then?"

"There's no reason for us to assume that's going to happen," Dr. Singh insists. "The psychological strain of space duty affects many people adversely for a while, but the vast majority of them get over it. If I put everyone who'd ever acted strangely on the *Astraeus* into lockdown . . . well, we wouldn't have much of a crew left."

"Can you do a brain scan?" Mom straightens and folds her hands in her lap. Her posture looks almost laughably prim, but I've learned that's how Mom gets when she's scared. "If Marguerite has developed a brain tumor—"

"Sophie, no." Dad puts his hand on her shoulder and gives her a little comforting squeeze. "Don't let your worries run away with you. You'll upset Marguerite."

But my mother won't budge. "I'm not upsetting Margue-rite. I'm trusting her judgment. Our daughter has told us something is seriously wrong with her. She's hurting, and she's frightened. We need to obtain as much information as we can through every possible diagnostic test. Only then can we form any meaningful hypothesis about Marguerite's condition."

I wanted a guard at my door, not a battery of medical tests. Still, I can't help smiling weakly at Mom. It feels good to know she'd go to bat for me, even when I'm behaving weirdly, even when the doctors are telling her to let it go. Not all parents support you that much; Paul's never have, never would. I got lucky with Henry Caine and Sophia Kovalenka.

Dr. Singh capitulates with a small smile. "I suppose it can't do any harm, and I don't have any physicals to run until tomorrow. Lie down, Marguerite. This won't take a second."

Obediently I take my place on the medical table. Instead of the paper covering I'm used to, here the table is sleeved in clear plastic, which must be sterilized after each use. What kind of tests are they about to run? I've never been a baby about shots or blood draws, but that doesn't mean I enjoy getting poked with needles. Or maybe they'll do something more dramatic. Would a space station have an MRI machine?

But Dr. Singh simply takes out what looks like a metal headband, thick and elaborate, and slides it over my head so that the two points press in on my temples. The band itself doesn't quite touch my skin. I feel a warm, electric sort of prickle—not pleasant, but not painful either—and readouts begin to stream along nearby screens. Dr. Singh watches them, nodding and at ease, until she gasps.

"What do you see?" Dad says sharply. "Dear God. When Sophie talked about a tumor, I thought—"

"It's not that." Dr. Singh steps closer to the screen, looks back at me, then stares at the screen again. "There's no tumor. Body chemistry is largely within normal parameters. But Marguerite's brain activity, particularly in the precuneus— that's a section of the parietal cortex, the core seat of our consciousness—well, I've never seen anything like it."

Mom rises to stand by Dr. Singh as my father's hand closes reassuringly over mine. My mother says, "Can you draw any conclusions? Even speculate?"

Dr. Singh shakes her head, not in negation but in wonder. "The levels of activity in the precuneus are higher than I've ever seen. Higher than should even be possible."

"Is that good or bad?" Dad squeezes my hand tighter.

"I don't know," Dr. Singh says. "It looks like—almost like—no. That can't be."

"Things are only impossible until they're not." Mom's tone goes firm. "Say the first thing on your mind, doctor. The first conclusion you came to."

After a moment, Dr. Singh sighs. "If I didn't know better, I'd say there was more than one mind at work inside Marguerite's brain."

Holy crap. They found me.

9

FOR A SPLIT SECOND I CONSIDER TELLING THEM THE TRUTH. *Hi. I'm a visitor from a parallel dimension, an alternate version of your daughter hitching a ride in her body for a while. I'm here to protect you from yet another version of your daughter, who just tried to kill her. See? It's a very simple explanation, really.*

Yeah, no. For now, I'm playing it safe.

"What could that mean?" I ask Dr. Singh, trying to sound natural.

She gapes at the readouts. "I have no idea. This is completely unlike any results I've ever seen. Nobody's even *theorized* something like this before."

"Is it dangerous?" Dad has wrapped both of his hands around one of mine, probably meaning to comfort me, but I think he's the one who needs reassurance.

"If you'd shown me these readings on their own, I might have said yes." Dr. Singh looks back at me and shrugs. "But

Marguerite is awake, alert, apparently healthy, and displaying no stranger symptoms than some short-term memory loss. So while this clearly has some deleterious effects, and we need to keep an eye on her . . . her mental function is more or less intact."

"I take it monitoring is the next step." My mother is trying very hard to act impartial about this, but her hand trembles slightly as she tucks a loose curl behind one of her ears. "We wait to see whether this activity—spikes, or diminishes, and so forth."

"Exactly," the doctor says. "We keep her under observation, twenty-four/seven." Then she frowns. "I keep using that phrase even though it doesn't apply up here. . . ."

That makes Dad chuckle, and even Mom smiles a little. Good—I don't want them to be too frightened. The weird activity in their daughter's brain will resolve itself as soon as I take off with the Firebird. If Wicked ever returns for a second murder attempt, they'll cue into her weird behavior right away.

Mission accomplished.

Except—how do I get back down to Earth?

The answer is obvious, in one sense. I return to the sweet, sweet ground I will never take for granted again the next time I use the Firebird. Chances are that whatever dimension lies ahead, I'll find myself back on terra firma. But I'm trapped here until I get a moment to myself to try to leap away.

Part of me wants to obsess about what Wicked might be doing in the next world over. She nearly launched me into the absolute zero of space this time, so how could I even guess what might be waiting ahead? But I'm too freaked out by memories of the world I left behind.

Theo *killed me.*

He strangled me with my own scarf, his body on top of mine, so he had to have felt every convulsion, heard every choking sound, and eventually felt the other Marguerite go limp beneath him as she finally died. As awful as I feel about what happened to my Londonverse counterpart, the death my other self faced in the Egyptverse was even more terrible. Every time I let my mind wander for even an instant, memory jerks me back to that moment, to the visceral sensation of Theo's fingers tightening around my throat. It's like an adrenaline shot to the heart or an electric shock, every single time.

Sometimes the memory of horror is worse than the horror itself. You only live through the trauma once, but a memory can last forever. Memory never has to let you go.

I think this one's going to keep its hold on me for a very long time.

How am I supposed to beat Wicked? I can never catch up to her. Do I have to just chase her endlessly, fixing the disasters she created?

Yes. I do. Until we have another plan, the best I can do is help to save these other Marguerites. I couldn't rescue Londonverse or Egyptverse . . . but Spaceverse is fine.

Well, if "under psychiatric observation" counts as fine.

Dr. Singh decides I should rest in my own room, so Mom and Dad take me there. My quarters turn out to be private, which is nice. They're also small, which I guess I should've expected. In here the walls are covered with some white resin, and decorated with my own charcoal drawings, which are kept in place by magnetic metal corners. The bunk is hard-molded into the wall and comes complete with a safety harness, just in case we lose gravity in the night, I guess. No window, thank God. I open a few drawers, looking for something more comfortable to put on, but apparently in space it's all jumpsuits, all the time.

"Do you need anything else?" Mom gently pats my shoulder. "Anything at all?"

"Maybe something to eat?" I'm not hungry. But my parents need something to do, to feel like they're helping. They nod and hurry into the corridor, which gives me my first moment of privacy in this universe.

I slump onto the bunk and rub my head with one hand in an attempt to massage away a headache before it begins. If I think any more about what happened to the last Marguerites—the two Triad killed, the two I lost—I'll lose it completely. The flashbacks shake me up too much to think straight. Concentrate on something else, I tell myself. Anything else.

The charcoal drawings interest me the most, so I focus on them. Sometimes analyzing the artwork of another Marguerite tells me how she's different from me, or a little more about what her life is like. Here, Marguerite either isn't as motivated by color as I am or she doesn't have as wide an array of art supplies to choose from. The more I study her work, the more I think it's the latter, because I see energy in her work. Vitality. Every stroke is bold. Josie's eyes are as vivid in black, white and gray as I've ever painted them in color.

This Marguerite lives under tight constraints, I think. The rules for living in space must be strict on every score, from the exercise regulations to the infinitesimal amount of private space. So she finds ways to be creative within those boundaries. It helps me to connect with her, get some sense of the life she lives, because she's the only one I've been able to save so far.

That's as long as it takes for my parents to return with my meal (a fairly ordinary sandwich and juice, though everything is bagged and sealed). Then they make me lie down under the covers as if I were a little girl again, running a fever. "You should rest," Dad says. "Rest helps everything."

I smile up at him. "I thought that was tea."

"Tea *solves* everything. So I'll bring you a cuppa later on." Dad leans down and kisses my forehead, something he hasn't done in years.

"We'll restrict access to your room," my mom promises, "and there's an electronic sentry on your door. You can leave whenever you want, but you'll be tracked when you do. I realize that's a high level of surveillance, so if you'd rather we didn't—"

"No. Keep on tracking me. This isn't something you can leave up to my mood on any given day, all right?" My parents have to understand. "I'm going to be fine, as long as you keep watch."

"Then watch we shall." My father smiles at me, though worry has dulled the usual twinkle in his blue eyes. "Call us if you need us."

Then they're gone, and for one moment I simply lie there, indulging in the luxury of stillness. But then I put my hand to my Firebird. Lucky thing medical exams in space don't require you to strip down; while people native to each dimension find it difficult to see a physical object from another—i.e., the Firebird—they can spot it if they look hard. A doctor performing a physical would be looking hard. The automated instruments ignored the Firebird completely.

Obviously I should attempt to leap out of the Spaceverse immediately—but after two terrible deaths, it's hard to brace myself to dash into yet more mortal peril. The first time I tried in this universe, I was almost relieved not to move on. Not only will I have to face danger, but I'll also take on the responsibility for saving another life . . .

You saved this one, I remind myself. *Now try to save another.*

One deep breath, I hit the controls—and nothing. Wicked still hasn't moved on. I slump back down on the bed, suddenly so tired I think I could sleep for days. Maybe that's the best thing I could do, for now. Let this Marguerite rest, take what comfort I can in my dreams.

Then the door chime sounds as the door swooshes open automatically. My parents had promised to seal my quarters, so whoever this is has permission to enter. Probably it's Doctor Singh . . .

Instead, I look up to see Paul, clad in his own *Astraeus* jumpsuit. He's with us in space, too. Before I can say anything, he reaches his thumb under the neck of his jumpsuit and reveals his Firebird.

"Paul." I want to jump up, to hug him, to bury myself within his strong arms and imagine he can protect me from everything. That's a lie—but the illusion would be so comforting right now, like the warmest, softest blanket in the world.

Yet I remain on the bed. He's pushed me away so many times that I don't think I could bear another rejection. Besides, right now Paul looks even more shell-shocked than he did when he first appeared in the Egyptverse.

For a long moment, neither of us speaks. Finally Paul says—very quietly—"Was it me?"

"Was what you?"

"Was it me who hurt you?" Paul's voice shakes. The only other time I've ever seen him so close to the brink was when I told him my father had died. "No. Am I the one who killed you?"

"No. No!" I scramble up from the bed to stand in front of him, close enough to touch—even though we don't. "It was Theo. The Triadverse's Theo. He followed me there."

Paul slumps against the plastic wall, like he couldn't

have held himself up one moment longer. "I was between reminders—I didn't know. When I came back to myself, I saw you dead again." He breathes out heavily, like someone struggling not to cry. "Again."

"Hey." I step toward him and put my hands on his shoulders. "I'm here, okay? I'm your Marguerite, and I'm all right."

His gray eyes search mine, and I wonder whether I'm still *his* Marguerite.

"Your parents found the body," he says quietly. "Theo had left on some kind of errand—nobody knew who had done it—but when Theo doesn't return, I guess they'll realize who the murderer was."

I wonder about the Egyptverse's Theo, who might have been a dandy and a flirt but wasn't a murderer. He'll come to in Cairo or some other Egyptian city, completely unaware of what he's doing there. If he's caught, he'll go to prison or be executed for a crime he didn't commit. Wicked's destroying more lives than just mine.

"Why did you think you could've killed me?" Is that a question I really want the answer to? I'm not sure.

Paul crosses his arms in front of his broad chest. "Why did you think I couldn't have?"

"Even the worst version of you I met"—the Mafiaverse Paul (we both know this; no need to say it out loud)—"even he wouldn't have done that."

"You don't know what it's like in here." Paul's gesture indicates his head, his mind. "I can't describe it. It's like . . .

like the pathways between my thoughts and my actions have all been ripped apart, or rerouted. Emotions I could set aside before—anger, jealousy, or even hate—now it's as if they take over my brain. I could have made a mistake, Marguerite. I could have done it."

A chill traces its icy fingers up my back, but I refuse to give in to paranoia. Somehow I have to help him to believe.

"You didn't. Okay? You weren't the person who hurt me. So let's stop freaking out about what could've happened and concentrate on what did." But now I can only think about the Egyptverse—one of the most beautiful worlds I've ever visited—and how it's just been ruined for so many people I love.

"When the reminder brought me back, I heard Sophia screaming, and the sound of it . . ." Paul winces, shuts his eyes. "I knew you were dead just from that. Just from the sound of her scream."

"I'm one for three." My voice sounds hollow in my own ears. "Wicked tried to throw this one into outer space—but I made it back in. At least this one is going to be okay."

Paul looks at me, gaze hard, as if he might spot some injury I'd missed. "If I can create the device that would help the Firebirds to increase the asymmetry and strengthen this universe, then we can keep her safe. The technology should be at hand here. This could be the first world we have a real opportunity to save."

Which is absolutely true. Yet to my bruised spirit it sounds a little as if he's saying, *You obviously can't protect anyone, but I can.*

I force myself to stay positive, to think constructively. "So. We're in outer space. Wow."

"I used to think I'd like to go into the space program," Paul says. "When I was small."

"I'm glad you didn't," I say softly. "Otherwise we'd never have met."

Paul doesn't reply. He has withdrawn even deeper into himself.

I try again. "Want to hear something interesting?"

Paul gives me a look. "As bad as the past few weeks have been, they weren't dull."

"I guess not. But listen. When the doctor looked me over here on the station, she ran some kind of futuristic brain scan, and they could tell there were two Marguerites in here."

His eyes widen. "They realized you were visiting from another dimension?"

"No. But they did figure out that this Marguerite's brain is, like, twice as busy as it should be."

"Intriguing." Paul sounds almost like his beloved Mr. Spock. His science-genius brain seizes on this new information, and he's distracted from his troubles, at least for now. "I want to see those test results for myself. The data might help us come up with a device to detect unwanted visitors."

"That would definitely come in handy." If only we could've ID'd Triadverse Theo when he first came into our world. We all would have been spared so much trouble.

Paul adds, "And maybe we can see how badly the splintering has damaged me."

"Hey. Come on." I can't stand to hear Paul like this. "It's an injury. You'll heal."

"You don't know that. We have no template for this. No idea how badly splintering affects the psyche—or whether 'healing' is even a possibility." He stares down at his boots. "Maybe a soul can be broken, just like a destiny."

"Our destiny isn't broken," I snap, before catching myself. We're both exhausted, we've been through experiences we haven't had any chance to recover from, but we shouldn't take it out on each other. So I calm myself as best I can before adding, "You walked right through my door, even though it was supposed to be locked to everyone except a few people my parents approved. So we must be together here too, right? If destiny brought us together in outer space, then it has to be pretty powerful."

"Destiny has led me to hurt you. It's led you to hurt me. It brings Theo back to us over and over, sometimes so you can love him instead." Paul looks uncomfortable. His height and his powerful musculature mean that the world often seems slightly too small for him. In this tiny room, he might as well be in a cage. "If our destiny is nothing more than a prediction of a collision, an intersection between two paths, then we don't have a destiny at all."

Can that be true? As often as we find each other—as often

as we love each other—is it only a matter of chance if we end up together? I don't want to believe that.

But whatever Paul and I have, it's not a story with a single happy ending.

"I guess this wrecks your thesis," I say dully, "about fate and mathematics." He winces as if in pain. Never joke with a PhD candidate about their thesis, especially not when it's a stupid time to make a joke. But I don't know what to do. I wish for magic words, for a spell, for a script. I'd pay all the money I have or ever will have for the right words to say at this moment. Instead, I am powerless and silent.

"There are parallels in the equations." Paul's voice sounds as flat as it did back in the days when I was first getting to know him, and his awkwardness was so extreme that I called him the caveman. "But they didn't mean what I thought they meant. Maybe I believed in destiny because I wanted to believe."

"We're more than a set of equations, you know." I reach for all our best memories, even though they seem so far away. "The night we made lasagna, or the time we went to Muir Woods, or Valentine's Day—that's all real."

"You fell in love with me in another dimension," he says without looking me in the face. "Maybe it was only ever Lieutenant Markov after all. Maybe, instead of being your destiny, I'm only a . . . stop on the way."

Okay, I know we've both been through a lot, and Russians are fatalistic, et cetera, but this has to end. "Don't say that! This is just the splintering talking, don't you see? You're ignoring everything we've done together. Everything we've been. Or was I never anything more to you than a math equation?"

That was supposed to be a rhetorical question. Apparently it isn't.

"Math doesn't lie," Paul says. "Our emotions do."

I'm too flummoxed to argue. Without some grand cosmological destiny tying us together, Paul . . . doesn't believe in us.

He continues talking, staring at his own shoes. "We deceive ourselves into believing we can have what we want most in the world. But it doesn't always work out that way. We know that now."

"Stop talking about us like a physics experiment!"

"You're not being logical about this," Paul replies.

When a scientist tells you you're not being logical, you have to get out of the argument immediately, because they're recalibrating the scales to make sure you lose. I hug my knees to my chest as I curl in the far corner of my bunk. "Don't you have some experiments to run with the Firebird?"

Paul looks like he wants to say something else, but instead he heads out, unhappy even as he has a chance to save the world. As soon as the door slides shut behind him, I grab my own Firebird and try to leap out of this miserable dimension.

No such luck. I'm stuck here, adrift in space, hopelessly far from home.

★ ★ ★

Valentine's Day was only a few months ago. Lots of people, including my parents, say it's a stupid fake holiday to sell greeting cards, and if you're only reinforcing your relationship one day a year, you're in trouble. I thought I agreed right up until the moment Paul brought me red roses and chocolate.

"I thought those were the right things," he said as we snuggled together on the back deck, near the small fire in the cast-iron fire pit. We'd draped a single quilt around both our shoulders, bundling us together. That night, even the blue-and-orange glow of Josie's tropical-fish lights on the deck railing seemed vaguely romantic. "That's what they always show in movies. But on the way over here, Theo told me it was cliché."

Paul had never had much of a love life before me, which is why he put so much stock in Theo's advice. "Theo would probably give somebody craft beer and a trucker hat." With relish, I plucked another candy from its crinkly wrapper. "And there is never, ever a bad time to give me chocolate. Remember this."

He nodded solemnly. "Forever."

"Do you like your books?" I was more worried about my own presents. Growing up surrounded by scientists, I had more or less absorbed the entire geek canon before I turned twelve. Mom and I had watched our way through *Star Trek: The Next Generation* together on Netflix, and Dad and I do a mean version of Monty Python's dead parrot skit.

But Paul—always grades ahead, without any kind of social life and surrounded by people older than him—had missed a lot of the fun stuff.

"I've heard of *Dune*," he said, his gray eyes glancing toward the novels stacked at the edge of the firelight. "And I always meant to read Ursula K. LeGuin. But the compendium—what is it, the hitchhiking guide?"

"*The Hitchhiker's Guide to the Galaxy*. Essential reading. And hilarious." I leaned my face even closer to his, so that our noses almost touched. "You need to laugh more."

"Never had as much reason to laugh before." His broad hand weaved through my curls. "Nobody else ever made me this happy."

"Same here," I whispered. But loving Paul—it was as if he had lit a candle inside me, and that inner glow seemed to illuminate the entire world.

Paul drew me closer, kissed my temple, and whispered, "The firelight reminds me of the dacha."

Our one night of passion. Back then I didn't know the price it had cost. Back then, I reveled in the memory as pure hours of bliss. "Me, too. Let's pretend we're back there."

His eyes brightened. I wasn't suggesting we have sex on the deck—ugh, splinters—but he knew how much I wanted him to kiss me, and once we began kissing, it seemed like we'd never stop.

Valentine's Day wasn't even three months ago. Not long after, here I am, broken-hearted, unsure whether Paul and I will ever get back together, miserable. And in geosynchronous orbit. Yay.

My parents suggest that I have breakfast in the "mess," under the theory that socialization is a good thing. I go early, just because I don't think I can stand another second of moping around in the plain white box of my room. When I arrive, a breakfast shift seems to be just ending. Half a dozen jumpsuited people file out, talking to each other about solar flares and the breakup between people called Min-Ji and Cedric. One of them waves at me, and I wave back. Are we friends? Acquaintances? I guess everyone here must know everyone else.

One flash of blond hair makes me freeze. My brain whispers *Romola*—Wyatt Conley's henchwoman in half a dozen worlds so far, including the Home Office. But no, this is someone else. The Spaceverse is one dimension where I don't have to worry about her.

Looks like that's the only lucky break I'm going to catch for a while.

As I sit alone at the cafeteria table, pushing reconstituted scrambled eggs around my tin plate, Paul comes in. His night must have been as sorrowful and lonely as mine, but his expression is so closed-off. Anyone who didn't know him better might call him cold. Paul no longer expects to find any comfort with me, but I can't help wanting it from him. My torn-in-two heart only knows that its other half is near, and yearns for him so desperately my chest aches.

Are we . . . broken up? The term sounds so childish for

the terrible rift that has opened between us. When I think of it literally, though, it sounds closer to the truth. We have been broken. We are in pieces. We can't be put together again.

He slides onto the nearest plastic bench. "How are you?" The way he says it makes it clear this is bare minimum politeness, period.

If he wants to talk about irrelevant stuff, then fine. "Well, this morning I found out that the exercise requirements on the space station demand three freakin' hours of workout per day. Apparently it has something to do with bone density, not that I cared after an hour on the treadmill."

Paul opens his mouth, probably to explain the bone-density thing. I give him the *no science now* look. Thanks to my parents, I'm pretty good at that one. At any rate, he stays quiet.

"So." I keep poking at my food. "Any progress?"

"I think so," he says, surprising me. This is the first good surprise I've had in a while. Paul continues, "Your theory about the slammed doors—that they're convinced you won't help and trying to shut you out of universes marked for destruction—I think that's correct."

"That means the Egyptverse and Londonverse are toast, doesn't it?"

"Maybe not. I can return to either of them. So could Theo, or even your parents could travel to the Egyptverse if they could create a new Firebird in time, and use the materials on hand to build a stabilizer."

"Are you going to be able to show me how to build a stabilizer on my own?"

"The term is inadequate, really—since *stabilizing* is only part of . . ." He gets this look on his face whenever he realizes he's gone off on a scientific tangent and left me behind. "I'm afraid the device is fairly complicated. We protect a universe by increasing the asymmetry of its matter-antimatter ratios. The Firebird can do that if we enhance its power enough. What we're calling a stabilizer would really enhance the Firebird's power so *it* can operate as a stabilizer. A more accurate scientific term can be developed at a later time."

Mom and Dad will love coming up with some funny acronym, or maybe choosing something else from Russian mythology for the proper name. But at least I know we're on the right track. "Okay. We're on the verge of being able to undo Triad's work."

Paul nods, but then he adds, "We have to assume that at some point, Triad may consider creating another perfect traveler."

"But they don't want to bring anyone else in on the conspiracy. Conley sent me around to sabotage other dimensions that might create the Firebird technology, remember? Triad doesn't intend to share its power."

"You're assuming they would act in good faith, which is an unreasonable assumption." When Paul's uncertain about how to act, he gets like this: hyperprecise, scientific, almost icy. It used to irritate me, before I realized that he does this to cover up his sense of isolation. Behind that rigid facade, he feels as lonely as I do. "The most likely scenario is that Conley would recruit a potential traveler, use that person to do some of the dirty work he had for you, then betray that traveler and destroy their home dimension."

Now that Paul has said it out loud, I don't know why I didn't see it before. "Damn," I mutter as I let my fork drop onto my plate. "We'll never be able to stop them."

"Maybe not. If they were creating other travelers already, I doubt they would still be so focused on limiting your influence. But we have to act fast."

"Okay." I can do this. It helps to focus on the big picture, on the countless lives who are relying on Paul and me to get this right. "How is the work on the stabilizer going?"

"I think I'll be able to start construction today. This dimension—the Spaceverse—it's our trial run. In another several hours, I should have the data I need to set up the trial device." He makes a gesture with his hands suggesting that the device is roughly circular, something the Firebird will fit into. "Then I'll give it a try, and if it works . . ."

"Then you and I run around through the multiverse, saving lives and shutting Triad down." If I have nothing else, at least I might get the satisfaction of permanently wiping the smirk from Wyatt Conley's face. "You'd head back to the Egyptverse and the Londonverse right away, wouldn't you? I want you to."

Paul frowns. "The order is probably irrelevant. Why do you want me to prioritize those two?"

"Because I failed those Marguerites. I had chances to save them, and I didn't."

"It's not your fault." His voice gentles, and for a moment it sounds like he still believes in me. Somehow that hurts more than his coldness did—the momentary illusion that he's back, we're back, and our schism is no more than a nightmare. "You were put in situations you couldn't escape from."

Maybe he's right, but that doesn't keep guilt from pressing down on me every second, every breath. "I just feel like it would be a way of . . . paying tribute to them, at least. If we save their dimensions, we keep them from being completely erased, you know? They'll still have people who remember them. They'll still be real. And they'll matter, because they played some part in protecting their entire universes."

Paul weighs that, then nods. "Those two first."

"Thanks." I take a deep breath and focus on the task ahead. "And the Spaceverse is going to be taken care of, because you'll fix things here, and I already saved this Marguerite. This is one we can cross off the list right away."

As the word *away* leaves my mouth, red lights start to flash. An alarm begins blaring and the computer voice says, "Overload imminent in plasma venting mechanism. Overload imminent. All hands to escape vessels. Repeat. Overload imminent."

Plasma venting? As in, the place where Wicked left and I leaped in?

Fear floods into me—pure, horrifying mortal terror, as

if Theo's hands had closed around my throat again. Wicked had a backup plan. She created a second trap, sabotage that could take out this entire space station at any moment.

We're about to be thrown into outer space, and there's nothing I can do to stop it.

10

"OVERLOAD IMMINENT," THE COMPUTER VOICE CHANTS, like everyone wasn't panicking already. "Prepare to abandon station."

Paul and I run from the mess hall to see astronauts hurrying every which way. Everybody else knows what to do, where to go. We have no idea. "Escape vessel," I say. "If we follow the others, we'll find one."

"Come on." He grabs my hand, and we start to dash in what looks like the main direction of the crowd. But then the speakers whine and the computer voice snaps off.

Instead, I hear my mother. "This is Commander Kovalenka. Only nonessential personnel are to abandon ship. We have a chance to localize the decompression, but only if the rest of you return to your posts, now!"

Mom must be a really good boss, because almost everyone immediately heads back to their posts.

"I'm nonessential," I say. "Probably."

"I'm essential here," Paul answers. Which is no doubt true, but he still sounds arrogant as hell. But then he turns to me and puts his hands on my shoulders. "Get out of here while you can. Save this Marguerite. Save yourself."

As much as I'd like to be on an escape vessel right now—which is a whole lot—I don't know if I can leave with my parents and Paul still aboard. Would this world's Marguerite evacuate and leave them behind? Somehow I doubt it.

To Paul I only say, "Go. See if you can figure out what they need you to do."

He runs. While he has no memory of what to do in this situation, maybe his genius brain has a chance to figure it out. Or maybe his reminder will lose power soon and let this universe's Paul back in, just in time to do his job.

For me, the path is even more uncertain. I'm not sure whether to escape or remain and be useful, but the fact is, I don't even know what to do to make either one of those things happen. Finally I keep running in the direction Paul and I had chosen, hoping I'll see a new flow of traffic, figure out where it's going, and be able to decide.

I turn the corner and there's Mom, frantically working on a computer panel. They must have rerouted primary controls to her nearest interface. Even as she types at supersonic speed, she spies me from the corner of her eye. "What are you still doing here?"

"I don't want to leave you," I say, which is the truth. Whatever she orders me to do next, though, I'll do. As much as I hate the idea of leaving the others, I came here to save this Marguerite, not to put her in even greater danger.

But Mom nods toward a nearby console. "Handle Earth communications. You should be able to manage it."

Oh, crap. I go to the console and poke experimentally at the interface. To my surprise, this actually looks fairly simple. Like figuring out how a tPhone works—you go from clueless to proficient within a few minutes. It only takes a few strokes of my fingers to send the right calls to engineering, to ops, to commander_astraeus (a. k. a. Mom). Having a task to perform makes me feel stronger.

As Mom continues to work, she says, "I have to ask you something."

Is this really a great time for a mother-daughter chat? "Uh, sure."

"Yesterday, when you were in the venting apparatus—did you do this?"

My gut sinks. "I don't remember doing it," I say honestly. "But I think I must have."

"Marguerite." I've never heard her say my name like that, so pained and so lost.

"I'm sorry. I'm so sorry. I should never have been here." *I should have figured out how to stop Triad by now. If I had, your world wouldn't be in danger. This space station would be safe. But I messed everything up. Oh, God, Mom, I'm so sorry.*

Sirens continue blaring. My mother continues typing. After a couple of seconds, she answers, "You told us you needed to be watched. You tried to warn us that you

122

weren't well. You're not to blame."

Hearing Mom take the responsibility for Wicked's plotting and my mistakes is too much. I want to argue with her, but this is when the gravity goes out.

In the movies it always looks like this magical moment straight out of Disney's *Peter Pan*—you can fly, you can fly! Astronauts grin and do somersaults like being in zero-G is the most fun humanly possible. To me, it feels like I've just been thrown from a spinning swing—queasy, disoriented, too dizzy to function. Only the dark ceiling with its red flashing lights remains as any hint of what "up" might be. My stomach rebels, sending fresh waves of nausea through my gut.

Mom's feet are now floating above her head, but she just grabs a cable from her belt, hooks it onto one of those brackets on the wall, and keeps typing. Does my jumpsuit belt have one of those? Yes, and now I'm reminded that the small brackets are everywhere. I clip on and continue working with my screen, routing the communications from Earth as fast as I can.

Then my screen blinks with a new message, one I haven't seen before: Mission Control General Admin to Astraeus Comms. If *comms* means *communications*, this call must actually be for me. I double-tap the screen, which seems to be the way to answer—

—and my busy computer screen is replaced with the image of Wyatt Conley's face.

This is who we're relying on to save us? We're all dead.

Conley says, "Comms, this is Mission Control. We haven't been able to raise Kovalenka. Was she injured in the original malfunction? Over."

"She's kind of busy right now! We have a crisis going on, in case you hadn't noticed. Uh, over."

Conley's sigh of frustration is audible in outer space. "We need an official report."

"No, you need a working space station and astronauts who are alive!"

My answer is half bluff, but it actually gets through to him. "Can you patch any system controls back down to Houston? We could lift some of the load from you guys."

I have no idea whether or not that would work. But apparently my mother can hear him. Over her shoulder she calls, "I'll reroute atmospheric controls. If they can keep those stabilized while I seal off the vents, we have a chance."

"Did you hear that?" I say to the Conley on my screen, and he nods.

This Wyatt Conley isn't the enemy. He's using his genius in a better way here. At least, I have to hope so.

The scene within the *Astraeus*'s corridors has turned into a Salvador Dali canvas. Drops of dark fluid, probably coffee, float in perfect spheres. A sneaker drifts along close to the floor, laces trailing behind. My hair coils and bobs around me like I'm wearing my own personal storm cloud. Voices shouting in alarm rise in pitch, and I instinctively tense even before I hear my mother swear in Russian.

What happens next feels and looks like the station gets

shoved out from under us. I hit the far wall; Mom's face mashes against her screen. A low vibration ripples through the very framework of the *Astraeus*, and if we're going to die, it will happen any second.

But I keep breathing. After a few endless seconds, the vibration stops. My mother stares at her interface, then sighs heavily in both relief and remorse. "We lost the primary solar generator. But we preserved atmospheric systems and backup power. That gives us a chance to fully evacuate and potentially salvage." She turns to me, her eyes red with unshed tears. "Patch Houston through. I must personally report the loss of the *Astraeus*."

We're not lost! I want to protest. *Okay, it's broken, but you can probably fix it eventually, and everybody lived. That ought to be a victory.*

Then I realize—Mom has to report that her own deeply unstable daughter sabotaged the station.

Numbly I work the screen as best I can. After only a blink, Conley appears on her screen. I push myself down the hallway, far enough that I don't have to listen.

This world's Marguerite is going to pay a terrible price for what has happened here. Will she be institutionalized? Medicated? Whatever treatment she'll be given will be wrong, because there's nothing the matter with her. She just had the bad luck to be hijacked by Wicked, and then by me. Of course, she'll remember the truth, but after everything that's happened, will anyone believe her if she starts talking about having been possessed by a traveler from another universe?

Maybe Paul will save her dimension. Maybe I saved her life in the literal sense. But in every other sense—everything else that makes up a good life, a reason to live—I may have destroyed her.

Within a few hours, gravity has been restored and more orderly evacuations have begun. People trudge past carrying duffel bags of their stuff as they prepare to return to Earth months or years before they ever wanted to. Some of them whisper to each other as they go: The commander's daughter had some kind of breakdown. Makes no sense. She had her whole family in orbit with her. If that's not enough to help you, what is?

Meanwhile I sit in a small room within the medical area that apparently doubles as a holding cell for the criminal and dangerous. I'm grateful for the return of gravity, not least because I'm so upset I might throw up, and the last thing I need is vomit floating around.

This room does have a window, which I force myself to look through. The view reveals the damage to the station; the area Wicked sabotaged is crumpled and asymmetrical, an ugly blight amid the silvery arcs of the rest of the *Astraeus*. It might as well have been crushed in the fist of an angry giant. Whatever incredibly critical thing it does for the space station—well, it's not doing that anymore.

The door makes sounds that must mean it's being unlocked. I stand up, ready for the space police or whoever it is who's going to take me into custody. When I see Paul instead, hope bubbles up inside me.

Yet his expression remains as rigid as stone.

"I have to be quick." He steps in with me, not quite closing the door behind him. The red-violet beginnings of a black eye have begun to draw semicircles around his eye. "Nobody told me I couldn't be in here, but I would guess this is against the rules."

"You're okay." I want to touch his arm and reassure myself that he's still here—but do I even have the right to do that anymore? Are we together or not? I don't know. It shouldn't matter, maybe, what with everything else that's happening. But it does. I close my eyes. "Was anyone killed?"

"No. But several were injured by a plasma leak in the solar power core. Some of them seriously."

"You say that like that's no big deal." I bear some responsibility for those injuries. No, I wasn't the saboteur, but I should've realized Wicked would have a backup plan. Traps within traps: That's her game. Angry with myself for not seeing it, angry with Paul for being so cold and callous, I hug myself and refuse to meet his eyes.

Paul's only reaction is to look away. His rejection stings until I realize he isn't ignoring me, he's working with Dr. Singh's computer.

"She didn't have time to sign out," he mutters as he searches through the files. One sharp keypunch brings up a screen that looks like a seismograph reading—jagged lines up and down, packed densely together. The name at the bottom reads CAINE, MARGUERITE K. "This is your brainwave function?"

"Yeah, that's it."

"What did she use to take these readings? Is there an MRI, or—"

"They keep it simpler here." I realize, now, what Paul wants—and why, to him, this would be his top priority. Which drawer did Dr. Singh pull that headband-sensor from? When I find it, I hand the silvery semicircle over.

Connecting the sensor to the computer turns out to be as simple as connecting a Bluetooth headset and a phone. Paul settles back onto the medical bed, I hit the control, and—

Oh, my God.

My brain scan looked like up-and-down lines packed closely together, twice as dense as they should've been, apparently, but otherwise normal. Paul's scan is chaos. Lines radiate in every direction at once, as though someone had smashed his fist into the center of the screen and shattered the glass. The borders of the screen turn red; a small box in one corner says CHECK INSTRUMENT FOR MAL-FUNCTION.

It's not malfunctioning. This chaos is what's happening inside Paul's head. This is what his splintering has done to him.

Paul and I stare at the computer screen in silence for what feels like a very long time. Finally I venture, "Maybe it's not forever."

"Maybe it is." He sits up, takes off the sensor, and places it carefully in the drawer where it belongs.

Paul gets to his feet and, for the first time in days, looks me steadily in the eyes. The desolation I see there is terrible. "Do you understand why I can't be with you?"

No. No no no.

"I'm not fully in control of myself right now. I don't know if I ever will be again. At any second, I could—break. Don't you remember how I acted when I got to the Egyptverse? I was so close to hurting you, even without knowing for sure whether you were Wicked or yourself." Paul's voice wavers, but only for a moment. "Please, Marguerite. I have to live with the memories of my other selves hurting you. Don't endanger yourself again. Let me go."

I want to argue. But the cobweb pattern on the still-glowing medical screen tells me this isn't only Paul's fatalism at work. What happened to him, the consequences of it: This is very, very real.

One time, Josie told me something important: "When someone tells you who they are, believe them." If a guy tells you, I have trouble trusting women, you don't assume he's just had bad experiences and you can fix things by being the nicest, best woman of all time. You go, *Thanks for the warning. Good luck with that. Nice knowing you.* Then you walk away without ever looking back. And if someone says they're going to hurt you? Don't stick around and wait for them to prove it.

Paul is telling me he's dangerous. It's not his fault, and maybe it won't be forever, but I have to believe him. I have to trust him, precisely because he can't trust himself.

Even though it's the last thing in the world I want, I have to let Paul go.

"Okay," I whisper, stepping away from him. He blinks, surprised. He must have expected more of a fight. Those first seconds of silence echo with all the memories we've shared, all the moments we should've gone on to experience together. The multiverse just divided again, creating a future where Paul and I aren't together . . . and this is the one I have to live in.

Paul takes a deep breath and shifts back into science mode. Maybe that's easier for him to handle. "We should concentrate on the quantum realities that need our protection. Leap out of here the first second possible. I'm going to remain here long enough to test the stabilization function of the Firebird. If that works, I'll track back to the Londonverse and Egyptverse, and then I'll catch up to you."

"Thank you for saving them first. For keeping your word."

"Marguerite . . . I would never break a promise to you." Our eyes meet, and I see all the pain he's trying to hold back. "Never. Not even if it means my life."

For a few fragile instants, we are connected again. I feel it as surely as I feel my own heart beating inside my chest. He brings his hand to my face, and I close my eyes as his fingers brush my cheek. When he steps closer, I hold my breath, hoping for an embrace, a kiss, whatever goodbye I can have.

Paul brushes his lips against my forehead, a touch so tender it breaks my heart. I lift my face to his, hoping for a farewell kiss, but already he's moving backward, away from me.

Whether Paul believes it yet or not, we have something left to save. If he can overcome the splintering, the two of us still have a chance.

He turns away from me as he takes out his Firebird, no doubt beginning the process of figuring out how to build a stabilizer to pair with it. Hoping to restore that temporary connection, I confide, "When Mom asked me if I'd done this, I confessed because I knew this Marguerite had to be watched in case Wicked came back. But . . . did I just ruin her whole life?"

"You did what you had to do." Paul's gaze is again remote; the gray of his eyes turns to ice. "You can make hard choices, Marguerite. You can even be ruthless. You just don't want to admit it."

"I'm not ruthless—"

"The potential's inside you. It has to be. Otherwise, Wicked would never exist."

He's right. It's Paul and Theo's turn to judge me by my worst self. To judge my darkness. Because whatever else Wicked is, she is me.

Paul's too good to rub it in, make it worse. Instead, he drops his Firebird back under the collar of his jumpsuit. "I have to go. Get out if you can, and don't stop trying. Because when you're taken into official custody, you'll be searched, and they could find the Firebird."

"Okay," I say in a small voice.

Paul nods before he steps out of the room and locks the

door behind him without a single word of goodbye. He thinks that makes him seem strong and resolute. It only reveals that this parting hurts him as much as it hurts me, maybe even more.

I'm sorry, I tell this world's Marguerite. She'll remember everything that happened while I was within her—yet another of the things that's different for a perfect traveler. We leave a trail of memories for our hosts to follow. But will Dr. Singh's readouts be enough to prove she's telling the truth about what really happened?

At least the Spaceverse Marguerite will know it was for a good reason. She'll know her freedom has been sacrificed for the safety of her entire dimension. I have to believe she'll think that was worth it.

I put my hand on my Firebird for the next of my many futile attempts to move into the next universe, thinking to my host, *I'm sorry, I'm so sorry*—believing that this is only the first of many times I'll repeat those words inside her head. But this time the Firebird snatches me away in an instant.

Should've finished my apology first.

11

ABOUT TWO FEET IN FRONT OF MY EYES LIES ADAM, COM-
pletely naked.

The Biblical Adam, I mean. The serpent coiled around
the nearby tree tells me that much. This picture has been
painted skillfully—incredibly so, with color both vivid
and expertly shaded, vital composition that draws my eye
to Adam's outstretched hand reaching up toward God, and
enough subtlety that the expression in Adam's eyes carries
as much emotion as any human's could. He's thinking: I'm
scared, but I want this.

If I were looking at this in a gallery, I'd assume it had
been painted in one of the workshops of the Old Masters at
the height of the Renaissance. Just two problems with that
scenario—first, this work is so new I can still smell the fresh
paint.

Second, not only am I not in a gallery, but I seem to be lying on wooden scaffolding. While I'm flat on my back, the painting looms above me, so broad I can't see the edges.

What's the mortal danger here? I can't see anything. Is the scaffolding rickety, about to collapse? Feels steady enough to me. The air doesn't smell of smoke. My body feels absolutely fine, not injured or punctured in any way.

Carefully I roll over, taking note of the clothing I wear—rough-woven cloth dyed the color of rust, bad shoes, some kind of scarf tied over my hair—

—and look down to see that I'm roughly forty feet above the marble floor.

Once I was nervous about heights, but after dangling from a helicopter and being in Earth orbit, a mere forty feet feels like a relief. Was Wicked hoping I'd roll over too quickly and plunge to my death? She can do better than that . . .

"Do you not see the heresy?" calls a proud, authoritative voice. Her words echo in this space, which must be large, even if I can only get glimpses of it around the scaffolding. "How can you excuse your mistress now?"

I shift farther along the platform until I can see who is speaking to me from below. A small group gathers down there beside enormous columns holding up a vast arch. Most of the people wear long dresses or robes obviously more luxurious than my own. Their garments are bright with the shine of silk or the sheen of velvet. A few wear the deep red cassock and cap I know belong to cardinals of the Roman Catholic Church. There's no doubt who the speaker is, though—that has to be the woman wearing a tall, peaked hat and white robes richly embroidered with golden thread that glints in the light.

Although we've never met before, I know who this is: Her Holiness Pope Martha III.

I tell myself, *Welcome back to the Romeverse.*

"Do you refuse to answer?" she shouts. Even at this height, I can see her frown lines deepening. "Do you endorse your mistress's heretical work?"

I know enough world history to be sure I do not want a pope to be angry with me. Is that Wicked's plan? To feed me to the Inquisition? "No, ma'am—Your Holiness!"

"Then why did you not stop her from painting this abomination? To depict Adam alone at the Creation, without Eve, mother of humanity?" Pope Martha waves some kind of golden staff around the enormous space enclosing us.

Finally it hits me that this is the Sistine Chapel—only now coming into existence, only now turning into a masterpiece. Instead of Michelangelo, another painter has the honor of creating this work, and apparently I am one of that painter's apprentices. Awestruck, I roll onto my back again and stare at this painting, which I now recognize as a wholly original interpretation of the creation of man, the moment Adam receives the spark of consciousness from God. I get to help paint the Sistine Chapel! That makes this absolutely, utterly, the most magnificent universe I've ever been to. My misery about my split with Paul evaporates for one beautiful moment, leaving me to feel nothing but pure wonder.

"Still you refuse to answer!" bellows the pope, which reminds me to move.

"Forgive me, Your Holiness," I call. "May I come down and address you directly? With, uh, the respect you deserve?" That sounds like the kind of thing you might say to a pope.

After a moment's silence, Pope Martha III replies, "It shall be permitted."

Turns out this scaffolding was built by people with hugely exaggerated ideas of how acrobatic most artists are. It takes me a while to work my way down, and I'm panting by the time I do. But I use that time to think about how I can possibly answer her question, since I have no idea who my "mistress" is, why the pope isn't bitching at her directly, or the reason behind any of the artistic choices she made.

Pope Martha can't be taller than five foot two. She's older, nearly elderly, and her shoulders have begun to stoop. But a sense of power radiates from her as surely as any light. This woman knows her anger can make emperors tremble—and right now, she's angry with me.

"Your Holiness," I begin. Should I curtsy? Can't hurt. So I do it, then start talking fast. "As I understand it, my, um, mistress plans to paint the creation of Eve as an entirely separate panel. She wants to individually portray the Father and Mother of humanity before she brings them together to tell the rest of the story of the Creation."

Pope Martha says nothing, and I find her silence ominous. If Wicked somehow figured out how to frame me for heresy in medieval times—well, I'd have to give her points for creativity. But I don't think that's it. Honestly, I don't seem to be in any danger at all.

Instead of fear, I feel only the quiet anguish of knowing that Paul and I have been divided from each other . . . maybe forever.

The pope finally proclaims, "If true, that explanation is satisfactory. But I shall expect a full accounting of her plans for the ceiling when Mistress Annunziata returns from the Dolomites."

I nod. "Absolutely. Your Holiness." Gotta remember to add that every time.

"She keeps her plans secret, and still has the audacity to complain about what she is paid!" Pope Martha begins to pace, and her elegant flock of courtiers moves back, with rustles of silk, to give her room. "Does she dare to dicker with her pontiff? I have seen her wearing golden chains, fine dresses, even jewels." The pope's hand goes to her throat, like she's pantomiming some necklace she saw on Mistress Annunziata. Then her eyes focus sharply on me, and she cries, "Look at this! She is so generously compensated that even her apprentices can wear chains!"

With that, she grabs the chain of the Firebird and yanks it off my neck.

Damn! Most people from this dimension would never see the Firebird unless their attention had been drawn to it, but Pope Martha was thinking about the exact right thing at the precise moment her eyes focused on me. Since she was thinking about what someone wears around her neck, she saw what was around mine.

My first instinct is to tackle her and get it back, immediately, but my guess is that physically attacking the pope would not end well. I try to think of an explanation that might work. "That isn't something I bought," I manage to say. "It's a—a family heirloom, Your Holiness. My mother handed it down to me." Which is more or less the truth, actually. "Please, I—"

"Her Holiness would never wish to deprive a lowly apprentice of her one valuable possession," murmurs one of the courtiers as she steps forward. "Her mercy and generosity are praised throughout Christendom."

I've seen this courtier before, in this world and several others: It's Romola Harrington. My entire body tenses, because in the Home Office, she's one of Wyatt Conley's many underlings. She's slipped into various dimensions to interfere with me before. And yet I've also run across her in worlds where she was only herself, and even where we were friends. She's someone on the very farthest reaches of the orbit that contains my family, Paul, Theo and Conley— someone who might be tied to us, or might not.

Has the Home Office's Romola come here to entrap me? Or is this merely the Romeverse version behaving the way she normally would?

"You should ask forgiveness for doubting your pontiff's charity," Romola says. She's supposedly scolding me, but

I can tell she's actually playing to Pope Martha's vanity to make sure I get the Firebird back.

"I do. Please forgive me, Your Holiness." I drop another curtsy, just in case.

Pope Martha airily holds out the Firebird and gives it to Romola. "Return this trinket to the girl, Lady Romola."

Oh, no. Romola's got the Firebird. If this one is working for Conley, there's no way she'll ever give it back. But I could tackle her, at least once we're no longer in the pope's presence . . .

No need. Romola only runs her hands over the Firebird in a show of admiration—over and over, almost creepily—but then smiles and hands it back to me. "What an interesting necklace. How good of your mother to give it to you."

I manage a smile as the locket settles into my palm. "Yes, milady."

Maybe "milady" is laying it on a bit thick, but I don't care. I'm swimming in the relief of knowing this Romola is the one who belongs in this dimension, and having the Firebird once again around my neck. It's one small victory to set against the devastation of losing Paul.

Pope Martha dismisses me, saying, "Back to Trastevere with you, girl. And tell those lunatic parents of yours that I expect to review their planetary charts shortly."

"Thank you, Your Holiness." This time I bow deeply, and with sincerity, because I really don't want to spend any more time around a touchy pope. Yet I take my time walking out, traversing the nave at a leisurely pace. I'd be a fool to waste a single moment I can spend looking at the wonder of the Sistine Chapel, midcreation.

When I step outside, into the late-afternoon light and the bustle of Rome's streets, I'm able to clear my head and think.

That wasn't an attempt to kill me. Yeah, the pope was unhappy, but it was Mistress Annunziata she was really angry with. Besides, I don't think she'd have had either of us executed. Michelangelo acted like a total brat with Pope Julius II for years, and I think the worst punishment he ever faced was a delay in payment.

So why did Wicked bring me here?

Maybe her trip to the Romeverse was accidental. Theo once told me some universes are "mathematically similar" to others, meaning that if your calculations were the smallest bit off, you might wind up in a completely different dimension. Wicked could've come here, realized she was in the wrong place, and hung around just to keep me trapped on the space station she'd scheduled for destruction. When she couldn't think of an effective way to kill off this Marguerite, she decided to use this universe as a holding cell rather than a potential murder weapon.

That makes perfect sense, I say to the Paul in my mind, as if he were here to work through this with me. In fact, that's got to be the most likely explanation. The next universe is the one I should probably be worried about.

Still, as long as I'm in the Romeverse, I have to stay on guard.

My breakup with Paul should hurt more than it does.

Right now it's as if I'm in shock—numb to the pain. They say people who have an arm or leg amputated often feel it for months or even years afterward, the nerve endings still sending signals about itches and sensations that are no longer real. A phantom limb, that's what they call it. Maybe that's what I'm feeling now, this sense that Paul can't really have broken up with me, that he's still by my side.

He is, in the most important ways, I remind myself, squaring my shoulders. *He's working with you to save the other Marguerites and protect the multiverse. So concentrate on what matters.*

Although I've never visited the Vatican back home, I know from movies and TV that it's this gloriously old-fashioned palace and cathedral, usually surrounded by flocks of tourists. St. Peter's is, if anything, even more imposing here, where no other buildings seem to be even three stories high. Its enormous dome soars above the various earthen-colored brick buildings clustered nearby. The city keeps no respectful distance. Instead the dirt roads around the Vatican are crowded with groups of rosary-clutching pilgrims, vendors selling fruit or bread from mule carts, or intently chatting monks in their cassocks. My last journey to the Romeverse was brief and frantic, taking place entirely at night. Looking at the scene in the late-afternoon light gives me the chance to truly experience something very like our own Middle Ages.

It doesn't take away the fear and urgency I feel. Doesn't mend my broken heart. But I can't let Conley and Triad turn the Firebird into nothing more than a weapon. The chance to see other worlds is a gift—priceless and irreplaceable. Even now, I have to hold on to my sense of wonder at the knowledge that I'm standing in a whole new world.

I walk into the crowd for a bit, mostly just to take in the sights and smells. The smells dominate. This is ye olden days, in which they had no deodorant. Also, nobody has the job of cleaning up after the mules. Even the stink is kind of interesting, though. It makes me appreciate home.

I need to find my home here in the Romeverse. That's not someplace I reached on my first trip, and it's not like I know my way around the city. Nor were medieval people big on road signs. When a nun walks near me on the road, her wimple almost comically broad-winged, I stop her. "Excuse me, Sister, but I'm lost."

Like every other word I've uttered in the Romeverse, I say this in either early Italian or late-stage Latin. The language skills we learn as babies are more deeply ingrained in the memory than almost anything else, meaning dimensional travelers automatically speak whatever languages their hosts do.

The nun smiles beatifically at me. "Can I help you, my child? Where do you need to go?"

I want to say, *To the Castel Sant'Angelo.* That's where Paul is—Father Paul, in this dimension, a priest who should not love me but so desperately does. I want to feel Paul's love for me again.

But if it doesn't come from my Paul—the one I love most of all—it's not enough for me. Not anymore.

"To Trastevere," I say instead, hoping I remember how Pope Martha pronounced that. "Do you know where the inventors live?"

Finding Trastevere turns out to be easy enough. The neighborhood isn't very far from the Vatican, nestled below the hills and right by the bank of the Tiber. Most of the city lies on the other side, including the majority of the crumbling monuments of the Roman Empire. The houses here are humble, made of whitewashed brick or stucco in various shades of earthy orange, pink, and gold.

As for finding the inventors—the nun had no idea, but it turns out I didn't need any extra help. Atop one of the taller buildings, I see a copper dome approximately the size of a MINI Cooper, with a wide slit in the middle. From that opening projects what has to be this dimension's very first telescope.

Yeah, I'm home.

"Hello?" I call as I come through the door. "Is anyone here?"

"We're up here, darling!" My mother's voice comes from above, no doubt from the observatory/attic. In one corner of the room is the wooden ladder that leads up and down. The room itself looks like one Vermeer might have painted, with its simple wooden furniture, its wide fireplace, and only a couple of images on the wall for decoration—sketches of mine, showing my family in robes and caps.

"Just polishing the lenses." That's Dad, who must be

beside Mom upstairs. "Tonight promises to be clear, which means we'll finally get a good look at Jupiter!"

My parents: always different, always the same. I want to see them wearing their medieval clothes—this could provide prime fodder for teasing later on, once we've gotten through all of this. I need to feel like eventually I will laugh again.

But first we have to get through it, which means continuing the chase the very first moment I can.

Probably Wicked won't have moved on yet. That last scenario of hers was crafty, so I think she's taking her time. Planning things out more carefully. Setting traps within traps. That's not the kind of thing you accomplish in only an hour or so. (This world's technological level allows for more sundials than clocks, so I can only estimate how long I've been here.) Still, I have to try. So I sit down on one of the benches by the table, take the Firebird from my robes, and hit the controls to jump.

I don't shift universes. Not surprising.

But at that moment—the exact same instant—the ground lurches, sending crockery tumbling to the floor and making my parents cry out. I hear yells from outside, too. We're experiencing an earthquake.

As a native of the Bay Area, and therefore someone who has spent most of her life perched directly atop the San Andreas Fault, I'm familiar with tremors. The one that just shook Rome wasn't even that strong.

Still, it happened the very moment I activated the Firebird. In my head I can hear both my parents saying, as they

144

have a hundred times before, *Correlation is not causation.* Just because two things happen in proximity to each other doesn't necessarily mean one of them caused the other.

When one of those things is a device capable of destroying entire dimensions, though . . .

That's incredibly unlikely. They all said so, and I know them well enough to understand that they'd never even have considered building a Firebird if it weren't absolutely true.

Unlikely. But not impossible.

The ground shudders again, longer this time. Longer earthquakes are more powerful.

What if—what if this was Wicked's plan? What if she came up with a way to destroy this dimension without my help, set it in motion, and fled?

This time she might not be murdering me. She might be murdering this entire world.

12

COME ON, I SAY TO MYSELF AS I SWEEP THE PLANK FLOOR after the shaking dies down. If this dimension were collapsing, it probably would be a whole lot more dramatic than an earthquake that's barely a five on the Richter scale. And I didn't do anything unusual or weird with the Firebird, just hit the exact same function I've hit dozens of times before.

Besides, the tremors have stopped. It's been at least twenty minutes since the earthquake. That's long enough for my family and the rest of the neighborhood to start cleaning up.

"If we could only understand the principles that cause these tremors," Mom says. She's wearing what looks like a workday dress of brown cloth, and her hair is tied up in a kerchief much like mine. Given how haphazardly she dresses at home, honestly, this getup doesn't even look that much different. "But I have never hit upon an explanation that could satisfy all the possibilities. People are so willing to declare them the work of God, without ever asking how God accomplishes his will on Earth."

Dad has on breeches, a loose white shirt, and a cap that looks so much like an elf's that, despite everything, I nearly laughed out loud when I first saw it. As he examines the plates on the floor for chips or cracks, he says, "I feel certain it is connected to mountains, somehow. Does not the terrain rise or fall after some earthquakes? Are not new crevasses cut into the ground?"

"It's definitely connected to mountains," I babble as I brush the dust over our threshold, into the street where neighbors are mending shutters or soothing startled horses. *Right, yes, think about the textbook explanation of an earthquake. That's the reason. It doesn't have anything to do with your Firebird. Not a thing.* "I'm guessing that, uh, the surface of the earth is made up of enormous tectonic plates that cover large sections of the globe. When the plates move together or apart, they create earthquakes. Over time the friction between plates builds mountain ranges. Volcanoes, too."

There is nothing more priceless than the looks on my parents' faces as they stare at me. For once, I actually know more science than they do. If only I could enjoy this more, instead of struggling to swallow my panic.

"Remarkable," my mother finally says. "When did you begin to draw such conclusions?"

Oh, man. How did people figure out plate tectonics again? "Um, logic, I guess. And it's not like you can't see on a map how Africa and South America used to fit together."

My parents exchange confused glances, and Dad asks, "What is 'South America'?"

Whoops. "Oh! That's just—it's irrelevant. But you should look into the whole plate tectonics thing. I bet my theory checks out."

Mom's and Dad's big genius brains go into simultaneous overdrive, a state of mind that can leave them in conversation for hours, their words and thoughts overlapping so fast that nobody else could ever understand.

My mood darkens again as I recall the first tremor, and the way it exactly followed my attempt to use the Firebird. No matter how convincing the plate tectonics explanation is, this coincidence is too neat for me to dismiss. Nor have I tried to leap out of this dimension again. It's going to be a while before I feel safe doing that.

Not causation, I think. But correlation can be meaningful in other ways. Maybe my Firebird didn't cause this. Maybe my device and the earthquake were just . . . linked, somehow.

Oh, no. My eyes widen as I recall what Paul told me back in the Spaceverse. He said that once Triad had really, truly given up on my ever working for them, they would begin to create new perfect travelers. People they could convince, or deceive, into doing Triad's dirty work—namely, destroying universes.

What if that's what happened here? What if something about my attempt with the Firebird signaled this other perfect traveler that it was time to begin the final countdown?

My gut churns, and I have to lean against the plaster wall.

I try to talk myself down. This dimension is still here. The shaking ended. Sometimes an earthquake is only an earthquake.

Then the earth trembles again. Nothing falls. The lanterns hanging from the ceiling sway in only the shortest arcs.

"Aftershocks," I say out loud. My parents nod, not overly concerned. Earthquakes have aftershocks. That's normal.

But my hair is standing on end, and I know—I *know*—that I must find out what's really going on.

"Mom, Dad, I have to go." I put the broom down and grab my cloak.

"Where can you possibly be headed at a time like this?" Dad says.

I slip the cloak over my shoulders. "The Castel Sant'Angelo."

My parents know what that means. Mom folds her hands in her lap. "Oh, sweetheart—I know how badly you must want to see him, especially after a scare. But is it safe for either of you? Is it kind to Father Paul?"

"The two of you chose to end this madness." My father sounds grave. "Don't let your resolve falter now. If you do, you're endangering Father Paul's standing within the church. Her Holiness may have agreed to protect our research, but if she ever learns you've tempted a priest from his calling . . ."

Me, a temptress. "I have to talk to Paul," I say as I head out. "Even if it's for the last time." When I shut the door behind me, my parents don't follow.

I ask for directions from some of the many people in the streets cleaning up earthquake-related messes in the last of the orange sunset light. Luckily, I soon come across a cart leaving the masons' guildhall, whatever that is. Some of their members have been called to help with repairs at the Castel Sant'Angelo, and they offer me a ride and an earthenware cup of weak beer.

I drink it. Beer's not my favorite, but I need some courage, even of the liquid variety.

When I see Paul again, he might be this universe's Father Paul—tender with love for me, so greatly at risk because of the clandestine relationship we must have recently ended. But of course I'm hoping for my Paul. If he ran the final tests right away, and those tests worked, then he could have saved the Spaceverse already. Of course he'll go back to the Londonverse and Egyptverse first, at my well-meaning-but-in-retrospect-unnecessary request. How long will it take him to construct the necessary stabilizers? It could be a while, especially in the Egyptverse, where Paul will have nothing more to work with than the few, low-tech materials my parents took along on their archaeological dig.

However, I have to think positive. Paul said the machine wasn't actually that complicated on its own, so it's possible he could put one together pretty quickly, right? Then he could show up here in the Romeverse at any moment.

Or hours from now. Or days.

I close my eyes tightly and hope against hope that I'm wrong about the tremors.

★ ★ ★

By the time we reach the Castel Sant'Angelo, dusk is falling. The castle guards are the exact same two guys I saw last time. Same mustaches, same brilliantly colored, striped costumes, and the same sarcastic looks on their faces: Seems like old times. One of them says, "The usual chamber?"

"Yes, please. And if you could let Father Paul know I'm here, I'd appreciate it."

The other guard ambles off to find Paul, muttering under his breath, "Some people never learn."

I'm shown to the same small chapel I visited last time. One of the stained glass windows has broken, littering the stone floor with green and scarlet shards, but the earthquake seems to have caused no other damage. If the iron frames holding the hundreds of small candles near the altar fell over, they've been righted, and all the little flames burn brightly enough to provide some light.

Each candle represents a prayer, I think. My nonreligious parents mostly taught me about various doctrines in a historical context, not about details like this. But I'm pretty sure you light a candle for someone when you're afraid for them, praying for them, wishing that someone up there would take care of them. I take one small candle, devote it to the two lost Marguerites, and light it with the flame of another.

I can't truly pray for people who are already lost, but at least I can remember them.

Then I hear my name spoken softly. "Marguerite?"

I turn to see Paul in the doorway of the chapel wearing

151

his long, black priestly robes. The glint of gold around his neck pierces me with sudden hope. The Firebird. *It's my Paul! He's saved all the other worlds and come here to save this dimension too!*

No. The item hanging around his neck is a cross. It promises salvation, but not the kind the multiverse currently needs.

"You've come." Father Paul steps closer to me, his hands clasped together as if to keep himself from reaching for me. "I didn't think you would."

He's so different from my own Paul, and yet so familiar, too. When I look through the priest's garb and longish hair, searching for traces of the man I love, I feel as if I'm seeing Paul again for the first time. . . .

A new grad student, a head taller than anyone else in the room, more muscular than a construction worker. His cheap, faded clothes, bought from Goodwill with the few dollars he had left over from his scholarship, because his parents had shut him out. He never even looked up from the floor except to talk physics with my parents, as though he spoke only in numbers rather than words. I looked at his strong jaw and hulking form and mentally dubbed him "the caveman."

Songs and movies tell us that when you meet the one you love, the planet stops spinning, the clouds open up, and your heart begins to sing. Reality is messier than that. The truth is, we meet new people all the time, but we can never tell exactly what they might mean to us. You never know who you'll forget, or who you'll need forever.

Father Paul says, "You had told me we shouldn't meet

again." The sorrow in his voice sounds too familiar. For the length of one breath, I'm back on the *Astraeus*, standing in front of the computer readouts that reveal just how shattered my Paul's soul has become, and the pain is as fresh as it was the moment he told me to let him go.

We share this, Father Paul and I—the terrible knowledge of what it means to love someone more than life, and still to have to give them up.

"I'm sorry," I say, meaning it. "But when the earth shook like that—it felt like the end of the world."

Paul crosses the space between us in two steps and folds me against his chest. I hug him tightly, grateful for his comfort, and for his love.

Despite the holy vows keeping us forever apart in this dimension, Father Paul's love for me is so pure. So uncomplicated. He doesn't question why we care for each other. He doesn't demand that the entire mathematical foundation of reality work out in favor of our relationship. No one has tortured him by splintering his soul. He remains whole, and gives his entire heart to me.

I imagine running endlessly through the multiverse, through world after world, finding the one where we know how to love each other, where no one is chasing us down or keeping us apart. Everything that can happen must happen, so there has to be a world like that out there. One perfect world where Paul and I get it right.

"Are you still afraid?" Paul murmurs against my forehead.

"Yes," I admit. By now I've figured out that even in the

worst-case scenario, this plan won't kill me. If there's any warning about the collapse of the dimension (and there would have to be, right?)—well, I've still got my Firebird. I can't leap into the same dimension where Wicked currently resides, but I could always head back home, or into another dimension altogether.

But I'm afraid for Father Paul. For the versions of my parents who are gazing at the planets through a telescope for the first time. For the Sistine Chapel that deserves to be finished. And for this Marguerite, too.

I already failed two other versions of myself. I don't want to fail an entire universe, too.

"The shaking seems to have ended." Paul's voice can sound so soothing, so strong. "You know you cannot stay here."

But if my Paul shows up, we might need to find each other in a hurry—and how are we supposed to do that in a medieval world where nighttime is impassably dark? "You have to come to me when you can," I say. "All right? Come to my house. My parents won't tell. They won't mind."

Father Paul hesitates, but finally he nods. "You're finally ready," he whispers. "You believe at last that I'm willing to leave the church for you." The yearning in his eyes is as beautiful as it is painful.

Even in this world, with the entire Roman Catholic Church in the way, Paul and I have found a way to be together. I clasp his hands in mine. "You're sure?"

"Surer than I have ever been about anything. God led me

to the church, but he did not give me the charism of chastity. So I cannot be meant to be a priest. My prayers have led me to believe that God brought me to Rome because that would bring me to you."

His shining faith in our destiny takes my breath away. If only my Paul could find this. . . .

I don't want to steal a moment that should belong to this Marguerite, but I'm afraid the world might be ending. Even if she never gets to kiss him, he should get to kiss her at least once.

And maybe I need the chance to kiss my Paul goodbye.

"Come here," I whisper as I slide my hands on either side of his face. Paul doesn't make a move to respond, but he doesn't pull away as I bring my lips to his. Our kiss is tentative at first—gentle—until the moment something catches fire inside him.

His mouth opens, just slightly, enough for me to capture one of his lips between both of mine. With a groan, Paul pulls me closer, and finally I'm back in the comfort of his embrace. I clutch the folds of his black robe in my hands as he kisses me harder, until the fever between us is as passionate as any moment I've known with any Paul, anywhere.

When our kiss breaks, Paul gasps for breath. I expect him to apologize or repent. Instead he squares his shoulders, newly determined. "I will come to you," he says quietly. "Nothing will keep me from you again, Marguerite."

"I hope not. I hope everything's going to be beautiful from now on." Oh, please don't let me have messed things up for these two. Please let the timing of the earthquake have been a coincidence. Please don't let me have failed these people's worlds.

Father Paul doesn't understand the true nature of the fear haunting me. He simply runs one hand through my hair as he says, "I've prayed about this for months. In the past days when we chose to part, I thought I would find peace. Instead, peace was farther away than ever." Paul doesn't look like a guy making excuses so he can finally get some. He smiles as if he's experienced divine revelation. "Only with you does my soul find comfort, Marguerite. Whatever I must do to be with you—even leaving the church—that is the path I must follow. Nothing will keep us apart now, nothing in this world."

Tears well in my eyes. Although I try to blink them back, one trickles down my cheek. "Good," I whisper. If this universe survives, one more Marguerite and Paul will have a chance to be happy.

For now, I simply have to figure out how to stay with him until my Paul can reach this universe and explain what's going on. . . .

A dog outside begins to bark loudly, every yip carrying clearly through the broken windows. At first I'm annoyed, but then I remember that dogs always know when earthquakes are coming. Scientists still don't understand exactly when quakes will happen, not even with all their degrees and instruments and Nobel Prizes, but dogs always know.

This time the tremor jolts the entire castle, sends me and

Paul toppling to the floor. The remaining windows shatter, and I cover my head as glass sprays in every direction. Paul shoves me roughly to one side, which I don't understand until I see that the racks of candles have fallen over, only inches from where the edge of my robe would have been. We hang on to each other as the ripples continue for at least two or three minutes—in earthquake terms, a very long time.

Finally the tremors stop, but I continue shaking. "This is wrong," I whisper as Paul and I huddle on the stone floor together. "This isn't only an earthquake."

"You're right. This is something more," Paul says, surprising me. Is he going to attribute this to our sinful kiss? No. Instead he points at one of the windows, and my gaze follows the line of his finger through the broken glass at the edges to see the moon—which is even now being blotted out by darkness.

"It's just an eclipse." After everything else, this is blessedly anticlimactic. "Eclipses aren't supernatural, you know. Not God being angry or anything. You can ask my parents."

Paul gives me a look. "I know this, of course," he says, politely enough, but I realize that this dimension must at least be advanced enough to know a demon's not eating the moon. "But no eclipse was predicted for tonight, was it? Surely your parents would have informed Her Holiness."

"Maybe they did." And yet—Mom and Dad were excited about getting a good look at Jupiter tonight. As far as they were concerned, that was the evening's number-one attraction. Is an eclipse too mundane for them to get excited about anymore?

Or is the increasing darkness in the sky evidence that my worst fears are coming to pass?

Shouting down the corridor means others are beginning to panic. Paul presses his lips to my forehead, one quick kiss. "I must speak with the others, learn whether this is a mere calendar error or—"

I kiss him back, on the lips this time. "Go. But come to my parents' as soon as you can, okay? The very first moment."

Paul takes my hand and presses it to his chest. I feel no Firebird, only the rapid beating of his heart. "Always," he promises. "Always, Marguerite."

He dashes from the chapel as I get to my feet and dust off my robe. Despite my fears, I try to remain calm. To think of rational alternatives. The darkness overhead could be only clouds rolling in before a storm. Or my parents could've gotten so caught up in their personal enthusiasms that they forgot to warn Pope Martha III about the coming eclipse— which is one hundred percent something they'd do.

All possible. And yet my inner voice repeats the mantra, *I can leap out whenever I need to.* The Firebird's weight against my chest has never reassured me more.

As I go to the doorway of the chapel, I find myself remembering the last time I was here. All the candles flickered in their orderly rows. The stained-glass windows remained intact, carving light into spectacular imagery with frames of slender iron. Now it's almost in ruins. I can't help imagining

my love for Paul lying here with all the other broken, abandoned things.

I hurry out of the Castel Sant'Angelo to find that the
guards have abandoned their post at the door. Instead, they've
joined the throng of people huddling on this hill, staring up
at the sky in dismay. I lift my head to see that the moon has
completely vanished—and now, in a widening circle around
it, the stars are winking out one by one.

There goes my last hope that this was an eclipse.

Oh, God, I think. This is it. This is really it. If Paul doesn't
get here soon with a solution, the Romeverse is going to die.

At that exact moment, someone runs into me, knocking
me down hard.

The stony ground bruises my flesh. Hot blood runs from
a scrape on my cheekbone, but I have never cared less. I push
myself onto my hands and knees, not even bothering to look
at whatever poor panicking person ran into me. Who could
blame them for freaking out?

Then a hand grabs at the front of my robes, pawing at me.
In the first flush of shock I assume some jerkwad is trying
to sexually assault me, which I would find terrifying if the
frickin' apocalypse weren't about to descend. I pull back my
fist to punch him in the face—and see Romola getting to
her feet.

And she is now clutching my Firebird, the match of the
one she's wearing around her neck.

"Give that back!" I launch myself at her, but Romola
knocks me to the side with the heavy staff in her other hand.

I tumble down again but scrabble back out of her reach. "What are you doing?"

"Completing an experiment." She smiles in total contentment. "One we weren't sure would work. But it looks like it has."

The earth rumbles beneath us again, enough to knock me off my feet. Romola stays up with the help of her staff.

If she thinks that stick can protect her forever, she's wrong. I don't care how hard she hits, how viciously she hurts me. The only thing that matters is getting my hands on that Firebird again.

"How could you do this?" I say as I struggle back to my feet. "How could you destroy an entire universe?"

"I didn't," Romola says. "You did."

What are you talking about? I want to protest. *That's impossible. I didn't do anything to destroy this universe. I never would!*

But already my mind is taking me back to earlier today. To my first glimpse of Romola, which put me on my guard— but not enough. To that moment in the Vatican when Pope Martha claimed the Firebird from me.

"You took it from the pope," I say to Romola as we stand there beneath the ominously darkening skies. The torches still burning around us are the only remaining light. "You touched it. And when you did that, you did something to the controls—something that—"

"Ensured you would instigate the destruction of this entire dimension the very first time you tried to leap out of it. Lucky moment, that. I thought I'd have to drug you and

160

slip it off your neck while you slept. But between the papal meddling and your overeager first attempt—well. We've accomplished this even faster than we'd hoped." Romola's smile belongs on the cover of a bridal magazine, not at the end of a world. "Granted, we knew this could only work on one single occasion. Once you knew what to look for, the ploy wouldn't fool you twice. But it doesn't look like we have to worry about that, do we?"

This isn't only about destroying the Romeverse. It is also Triad's very specific, very personal plot to murder me.

Luckily, it's a stupid plan. The Home Office's sick plan to save Josie has told me what happens when someone's in a universe when it ends. "If this universe is destroyed, my consciousness will just return home. Which means I can come after you the minute I get my hands on another Firebird." However long that might be.

Romola laughs out loud, even as the crowd's murmurs of dismay grow louder. "That's what would happen to almost any other traveler. Even to a perfect traveler—after her soul had been shattered. If not, we wouldn't be able to save Josie. But an intact perfect traveler with her full power, ah, that's another story."

Excuse me? "What are you talking about?"

"You've become used to being privileged, haven't you? Comfortable in your talents. Everything's so easy for a perfect traveler." Romola makes a show of studying the Firebird, the prize she's lording over me. "That's because perfect travelers mesh more closely with other dimensions. But, you see, there's a price to be paid for that. You're so in sync with this universe that you can retain control—and so in sync that, without your Firebird when this universes blows up . . ."

Her voice trails off, making me wait for the rest. A rush of cold panic sweeps through me as I realize what she's telling me. I say it first: "When this universe dies, I die with it."

13

ROMOLA SWINGS THE FIREBIRD BACK AND FORTH LIKE A hypnotist's pocket watch, taunting me. "I'm in so few useful dimensions, and Mr. Conley so rarely lets me undertake anything important. I think that's about to change, don't you?"

Billions of people are about to die, and this idiot is psyched about her promotion. Even my own survival hardly matters compared to that, but I'm ready to fight for all our lives. I ball my fists together and steel myself to take a blow to the head, a stab from a knife, anything. "Last chance, Romola. Give me back my Firebird."

"Last chance," she echoes. "And you just lost it."

Romola drops the staff. I see her hand reaching for her own Firebird to leap away, and I launch myself at her—

—and land on bare ground as she swiftly dodges me.

I scramble up from the ground and look around

desperately, sure I could see Romola even amid the gathering chaos—there! Her yellow velvet gown, bright in the darkness, reveals her in the crowd gathered just below. I dash downhill, ignoring the cuts bleeding on my face and arms, desperate to reach her. Amid the throng, I lose sight of her, glimpse her again, lose sight once more. But finally I catch sight of yellow velvet, focus on it, and start to gain. Once I'm within arm's reach, I grab her by her shoulders, wheel Romola around, and snarl, "Give. It. Back."

"What do you want of me?" Her smirk is gone, replaced by pure, honest terror. My stomach clenches as I see that she's not carrying a Firebird in her hand or wearing one around her neck. This is the version of Romola who belongs here, in this universe. The one whose counterpart just betrayed her. "What is it you think I have done? I promise you—the strange portents in the sky, they are not my doing—"

"I know." I back away, half in a trance. "I know."

Romola just ditched this dimension, carrying both her Firebird and mine.

Meaning I'm stranded here at the end of the world, without any chance for escape.

I flop onto my knees, too stunned even to scream.

They needed a perfect traveler to destroy a universe, I think in a daze. They got one.

And now I'm going to die as far away from home as anyone has ever been.

There is truly, literally, nothing I can do. Without my Firebird, I'm powerless. I am trapped in a dying world.

Paul—my Paul—could still save me. He's the only one who can. But in order to do that, he would have to have already tested his plan to protect a dimension against destruction, made it happen in three different universes, and managed to have traveled here in the nick of time. How many hours does the Romeverse have left?

Wait. No. My heart sinks as I realize Paul couldn't save me. He would arrive in this dimension with only one Firebird—his own. I know him well enough to be certain he would try to put that around my neck, let me be the one to survive while he died. I also know that I would never let that happen.

For me there is absolutely no way out.

Someone cries out in horror. A few other people faint. I follow their panic-stricken gazes, looking up toward the Castel Sant'Angelo.

It's . . . melting.

Literally, melting. The stone bricks glow with heat, then soften, then begin to sag and drip down over the others. A castle is turning into a volcano before our eyes. And as far as I know, Father Paul is still inside.

"Paul!" I shriek. "You have to get out of there! Paul!"

Crowds of priests and guards are escaping; my eyes can just make out the silhouettes of a few people dashing from a faraway exit. But for the rest, it's already too late. As the lava begins seeping downhill toward us, radiating blistering heat in a wave ahead, the entire Castel Sant'Angelo collapses in on itself.

My scream feels as if it's torn from me. As if nothing could be left inside my skin now that I can't reach him again.

Now the lava is a wave, flowing faster, downhill toward us. Everyone around me picks up and runs. After one more moment, I do too. Tears blur my vision, but it doesn't matter what I see. It doesn't matter where I run. Even if Father Paul wasn't killed in the collapse, we could never get to each other now. The thought of him, so tender, so kind, dying in that molten hell because of me—I would have died in his place rather than let that happen. It doesn't matter if Romola and Triad tricked me—I should've known better. Been smarter, been braver.

He might have escaped the castle, I think. Yet that's even worse. If Father Paul is still alive, then he has to die along with this world. Already I know that death will be horrible.

I ought to drop to the ground and let the lava burn me to death. I deserve to know how the people in that castle felt as they died, being charred to the bone. My death is inevitable now anyway. Only my Paul could've saved me, and whatever slim chance I had of that was lost with the Castel Sant'Angelo. At least if I let the lava claim me, the terror would be over.

Yet I keep running. Even though my brain knows it's hopeless, some unstoppable part of my heart keeps demanding *live, live, live*.

The fleeing people in front of me suddenly stop short, sending me thudding into someone's back. He shoves me back harshly, which I don't understand until another person does the same thing a few feet away, and this time the person hit from behind falls—into the enormous crevasse that I now see just in front of us. It's still opening wider as it swallows the woman whole. Her scream echoes a long, long way down.

"Satan's furnace is revealed to us!" one man cries. "The final judgment is at hand!"

Most everyone scatters, running right or left, the only two directions that remain for us. Stupefied by terror and guilt, I stagger to the very rim of the crevasse and stare down into it. It's depthless, an almost infinite black abyss gaping wide like the jaws of a monster. The distant fiery glow beneath must be the planet's core.

Mom and Dad should be here, I think numbly. *Then I could really explain plate tectonics. They'd understand if I could show them the planetary core. And then Mom and Dad would be here with me. They must be so scared and I want them here, I want my parents so bad—*

"Take heart!" someone shouts. "I have found her, and we can yet be saved!"

I know that voice. It belongs to Wyatt Fucking Conley.

When I wheel around I see him standing there in red robes, a blazing torch in his hand. He's Cardinal Conley in this world, and I don't doubt for a minute that it's only the Romeverse version. No way would any Conley from Triad be stupid enough to come to a collapsing universe.

"This is the girl." Cardinal Conley points at me with a shaky finger. Soot stains his face and his scarlet robes.

Behind him are massed a couple dozen people, a few of them priests but mostly townsfolk, all of them as disheveled and wild-eyed with fear as I must be. Conley's wavering voice gains strength as he condemns me. "Only two weeks ago she claimed she had been overtaken by an evil spirit! Her sorcerer parents used their spells to convince Her Holiness that she was only ill, but I knew this one had been possessed by a demon!"

I can't even argue with him. The Romeverse Marguerite must have believed it herself—how else could a medieval person understand my visit from another universe? Certainly no evil demon could've visited a worse fate on this world than I have.

"I argued that the demon inside her should be exorcised," Cardinal Conley says. Sweat has beaded on his skin. There's nothing of the cocky, power-hungry schemer left in him now. He feels nothing but terror, wants nothing but revenge. "No one listened, and now the demon has brought us hell on earth."

People shout in agreement. I just stand there at the lip of the crevasse, wondering if he'll shove me in. If he does, how long will it take me to fall?

Conley steps closer to me, his crazed eyes gleaming. "We still have a chance. If we destroy the demon now—destroy it in its earthly vessel—God may yet spare us!"

Something inside finally snaps me out of my stupor and despair, and I'm pretty sure it's hate.

I come back to life. Yeah, I'm going to die here. I know

this. There's no way out. But I'll be damned if the last person I ever see is Wyatt Conley.

"Yes, destroy the demon." I ball my hands into fists at my side. When I step forward, Cardinal Conley skitters back like a cockroach. "But do you know where the demon really is? Do you think the devil would even bother going after a mere girl to do his evil here on Earth? I'm a painter. Only an apprentice! I don't have the power Satan wants. You know who does? A cardinal."

"She lies," Conley says quickly. "The devil speaks with forked tongue—"

"I was possessed by an evil spirit, but he hasn't told you the whole story! The cardinal has kept the truth from you!" It feels good to yell at him. "The spirit was cast out, and immediately afterward I revealed absolutely everything. Her Holiness the Pope knew my soul was clean. But someone else was possessed that day. Someone who still can't remember anything that happened to him for hours. Someone who never presented himself to the pope to be judged!"

Even by torchlight, I can tell Conley's face has gone stark white. I wasn't sure how he'd handled the complete amnesia that must have followed the visit of Triadverse Conley—but without his pride and wealth and rank, he's nothing but a coward. So it wasn't hard to guess he'd kept his inexplicable lapse a secret. Every line of his expression testifies that my words are true.

The crowd sees it too. They've begun to murmur and shuffle in discontent, and their angry glares have shifted from me to Cardinal Conley.

"Am I lying?" I say to him. "If so, prove it. Tell me what we spoke of the last time we met in the Castel Sant'Angelo. Or can't you remember?"

Conley's mouth opens, then closes again. He looks like a fish gasping in air.

"He is the demon." I point to the now-trembling cardinal. "He's the reason we're all going to die. He is the murderer of this world!"

The crowd rushes forward, ready to tear him to pieces. Conley dashes from them in blind terror—and tumbles into the pit. Briefly I see a red blur in the blackness, before the febrile glow of the core beneath erases even that slight glimpse of him. Now Conley's scream is echoing all the way down to hell.

While the torch-wielding mob celebrates, believing they might have saved all of creation, I wander away along the narrow patch of ground that remains passable. By now the earth is trembling underfoot constantly, but nobody pays it any mind. I ignore the gravel skittering around my feet, the sticky blood on my cheek and legs from cuts that will never be tended. They don't matter. Pretty much nothing matters anymore

If there's nothing left for me to do but witness how a dimension dies, I want to at least face it bravely.

When I find a large stone in the hillside in an area where no one is lingering, I slump down onto it and turn my face up toward the night sky. The moon has reappeared, but is now four times too large, as if it wanted to devour the

170

horizon. Around it the stars whirl and blaze as they flare in fitful shades of orange and gold. It's a nightscape Van Gogh might have painted in his final, suicidal frenzy.

The faces of those who defeated me loom in my mind, as if they were gloating—Conley, Romola, the Triadverse version of Theo—but I refuse to let those people dominate my last moments. They have no more place in my mind. No time remains for anyone but those I have loved the most.

So I think of Mom humming to her countless houseplants as she waters them from her pressed-tin pitcher. Dad sitting at the rainbow table and drinking Earl Grey tea from his Beatles mug. Josie speeding ahead of me on the waterslide when we were kids, holding up her arms and shrieking with glee as we headed toward the big final splash. Even Theo—my Theo, the real Theo—the day he took me for a ride in his muscle car all along the coast, and we played the Kills at top volume and left the windows down to feel the wind in our hair.

And always Paul, in so many ways, so many worlds. I think of the Egyptverse version with his adventurer clothes and shy courtesy, and the Mafiaverse one, so savage and cold and yet vulnerable too, willing to show a complete stranger his tattoos and his weaknesses just for the chance to be seen. Warverse Paul, who wanted me so much he couldn't stop caring even after I betrayed him. The guy from the Cambridgeverse who made one stupid mistake he'll punish himself for his entire life long. And my beloved Lieutenant Markov, waltzing in the Winter Palace, standing in the Easter Room, making love to me in the heart of a snowstorm—

I don't try to check the tears flowing down my cheeks. I only turn my thoughts to the Paul who was so briefly mine. This big, muscled, wordless guy who hulked around in doorways that hardly seemed to fit him, in his thrift-store clothes and his cheap, ragged haircut. Who made lasagna with me last Thanksgiving eve and laughed as we tried to keep the noodles from curling up. Who knows every concerto by Rachmaninoff but probably wouldn't recognize Beyoncé if she were standing right in front of his face. Who gave up everything he'd ever earned and risked his life for the chance to protect me. Who watched me paint and told me I knew how to see people as they truly were.

But you were the one I never really saw, I realize. *Not until it was too late.*

"Marguerite!"

I turn and stare into the darkness. Am I dreaming? No. It's him. It's Father Paul, running toward me.

A sob escapes from my throat. He escaped the destruction of the Castel Sant'Angelo, only to die along with the rest of us. Maybe I should have wished for him to have that faster death, the one where he would've suffered less fear and despair.

But I'm selfish, and I'm small, and I need Paul more now than I ever have before.

I leap up to run toward him, but the quakes are strengthening. It's all I can do to cover more than five or six feet at a time before falling down again. From what I can see, Paul's having trouble too. But we don't stop. We keep running, crawling, struggling toward each other for nothing more than the chance to die in each other's arms.

Distant screams rise in the distance as the light overhead glows brighter. I glance upward to see the sky ripping apart as if it were made of cloth, and that cloth were being shredded by claws of fire. It makes no sense, but maybe the laws of physics are beginning to collapse along with everything else. Gravity may let go of us at any moment and send us spiraling into the dying sky.

Just let me get to Paul, I think, or pray. There doesn't seem to be much difference between those things anymore. If I can only have that, I can face the rest. I have to reach Paul.

As I stagger to my feet again, the quake stills—maybe only for a few moments, but those moments are all I need. I run as fast as I can toward Paul, who's racing even faster toward me. We collide, embrace, and I'm crying and laughing at the same time, "We made it, we made it, we—"

And then I realize what I'm feeling against my chest: the hard edges of a Firebird. I pull back and gasp as I see Paul isn't wearing one Firebird—he's wearing two.

"How did you know?" I whisper, hardly daring to trust my own eyes. "You couldn't have known—"

"We have to get out of here," Paul says with his usual gift for understatement. He slings one of the Firebirds from his neck, ready to drape it over mine.

I still can't believe it. In a daze I say, "You made it here to rescue me. . . ."

My voice trails off as I finally focus on the locket on its chain. I don't know what that is, but it's not one of our Firebirds. Now beyond shock, I gape at him in bewilderment.

This isn't my Paul. Who the hell is it?

"Marguerite, please," he says.

When he tries to put the Firebird around my neck, I lift my hands to block him. Where is this person trying to take me? What is this about? "If you're not my Paul—then who are you?"

Paul looks down at me, his gray eyes searching. "Another one who loves you."

I don't understand any of this. Can I possibly believe him? Do I have any choice?

But I do. The last time someone else from the multiverse deceived me, it was Romola, and the result of her trickery was the destruction of an entire reality. I can't let that happen again, ever, not even if the cost is my life.

The ground trembles beneath us again. Buildings in the far distance begin to disappear and crumble, maybe collapsing into yet another crevasse that leads to the center of the Earth. A low, terrible, vibrating groan emanates from deep below—the death cry of a planet.

"Please," Paul shouts over the ever-louder roar. "Trust me, Marguerite. Believe me."

And I do. I believe him.

I duck my head for the Firebird. He drops it around my neck and wraps one arm around me to steady me against the tremors. "Take hold of the Firebird and hit the controls on my mark. Ready?"

"Yes." Lines of fire have begun to race along the ground in intricate spirals, rising ever higher into an apocalyptic blaze. Smoke and sulfur bellow from the tears in the earth. William Blake couldn't have imagined this hell.

"Now!" Paul shouts, and I leap away, leaving the end of the world behind.

14

I SLAM INTO MYSELF AND STUMBLE INTO THE WALL. SHAK-
ing, I brace myself with both hands long enough to take a
few deep breaths. I'm alive. I made it.

Paul—whichever Paul that was—rescued me from a
world on the verge of collapsing into eternal nothingness
and brought me here. But where is "here"?

Wherever it is, gravity works, the sky isn't spiraling into
fire, and the earth isn't caving in with lava-filled crevasses,
so I'll take it.

I'm inside, out of any rain or wind or unholy flame. Lights
are on, and I'm not in pain, and never before have I been so
keenly aware that this is all anyone really needs. Everything
else about human existence is merely . . . extra.

But I still need to understand exactly where I've been
brought, and why.

My attention turns first to the Firebird hanging around

my neck. The metalwork on this one has been more crudely fashioned—it has rough edges compared to the ornate curls of my parents' handiwork at home. The locket hangs shorter, too, thanks to a more compact chain with thicker links. Even the weight is different—heavier, both the Firebird and the chain. What universe's creation is this?

I step away from the wall and look around the room I'm in. First I see a bed, a simple metal frame with a plain black blanket, but nearby there's a desk of battered wood, atop which sits an old-timey electric typewriter, connected to the wall with an absurdly thick black power cord. In one corner stands a metal filing cabinet. To judge from that and the uninspiring fluorescent light tubes overhead, I'd guess this is an office repurposed to serve as a bedroom. But why?

One door. I go to it and try the knob. It's locked. At first I think I must have locked someone out, but that's not how door locks work. Someone else has shut me in. Why?

The final step is studying myself, though there's not much here to go by. I'm wearing slightly clunky black shoes, a plain, dark blue skirt that hangs just past my knees, a button-up shirt of cheap cloth, and—I lift my hands to my curly hair—a shorter style this time, maybe a bob.

This feels familiar. . . .

Two sharp raps on the door make me jump, but I pull myself together quickly. Whoever is on the other side of the door must be my captor. "Come in."

Paul steps through, wearing a military uniform I recognize. As he looks at me, his expression shifts from the deepest relief to what he must hope looks like calm. "You made it."

"We're in the Warverse," I say. "Where Theo and I came a couple of weeks ago."

"You remember me." Paul can't meet my eyes any longer. "I wasn't sure you would."

"It hasn't even been a month. . . ." My voice trails off. He didn't literally believe I would have forgotten him so soon. He just thought I wouldn't care enough to think back on him often, if at all.

When Wyatt Conley splintered Paul's soul, sending each part to another dimension as blackmail for me to do his dirty work, he sent one sliver here. While the Warverse possesses technology as advanced as our own, all that tech has been turned to military use. This nation—whichever it is, because I never learned the name—it's embroiled in a desperate global war and has been for decades. The overall impression I got of the Warverse was that it felt like World War II would have, if it had lasted for fifty years.

Conley sent me here to sabotage this universe's Firebird project, which was on the verge of success. In this world my parents are top military scientists, Paul is one of the researchers working with them, Josie has become a bad-ass fighter pilot . . . and Theo is the guy Warverse me apparently fell in love with. But Warverse Paul cares for me, and I realized I might be able to use that to my advantage. Believing I had no other choice, I let Paul take me out for a romantic night on the town, flirted and talked with him, and even wound up kissing him passionately on the streets of San Francisco.

Our kiss lasted until the moment Paul recognized my Firebird, and I was busted.

In the end, I negotiated a truce: We manufactured fake evidence of sabotage while actually giving the Warverse the data they needed, and in return I got my Firebird back. But Paul was angry and bitter about my deception to the very end. I thought he hated me and would forever.

Instead he just risked his life to save mine.

"Thank you," I say very quietly. "What you just did—what that meant—"

"This isn't only about you." Paul averts his gaze from my face. "It's about Triad, too. Come on."

I start toward the door. "Where are we going?"

"A Firebird project staff meeting." Paul steps aside from the doorway as I walk through it, making sure our bodies don't brush against each other. "Time to come clean."

From the way Paul says that, I expect my parents to feel as betrayed as he does. When he shows me into a small conference room down the hall, however, my parents in their stiff military uniforms look up from their work spread on the table and smile.

"You're the other one?" Dad says, in the same tone of voice I would expect him to use if he someday recognized Paul McCartney on the street. "The Marguerite who visited our world recently?"

"I—uh—yeah." This is not a situation I prepared for.

My mother shakes her head, smiling in her you-silly-thing

way. "Why didn't you just tell us who you really were? We'd have been so delighted to speak with you!"

"I thought I had to sabotage you," I admit. "It didn't seem like the beginning of a great relationship."

"Fair enough." My dad drums his fingers on the edge of the table. "But you and Lieutenant Markov here found a way around that, didn't you? Now we've got our own Firebird technology and have been able to put it to good use."

"But I was here only a week or two ago!" Honestly, I've lost track of the days, especially while I was in outer space, but I'm positive it hasn't been that long in "real time" since I left the Warverse. "How do you have Firebirds already?"

"Two reasons," Paul says. Although I've gratefully sunk into a chair at the conference table, he remains standing at the door, more as if he's guarding this meeting than taking part in it. "One, we were almost there to start with. We had the materials on hand. We had most of the know-how. All we needed was a boost, which the information from your Theo Beck provided."

If they hadn't been close to success, Conley wouldn't have wanted to sabotage them in the first place. "Okay," I say, "but what's the second reason?"

My parents give each other a conspiratorial smile as Mom says, "Well, for the past few days, we've been having some very interesting conversations with others who have built Firebirds of their own."

"Others?" What, are there tons of people in the Warverse

on the verge of dimensional travel? That sounds completely unbelievable. "How many scientists are working on this here?"

"No, no, sweetheart, not here." Dad sighs. "We've been speaking to our own other selves from various universes, including yours."

Conversations between dimensions? Of course—the Cambridgeverse! They were working toward this ability, and the very last thing I did before leaving that world was internally ask my other self to please, please try to reach out to the other parallel dimensions.

She actually listened. They did it. And now . . . "We're joining forces." I feel a smile dawn on my face. "We're all going to work together against Conley and Triad."

"Exactly." Mom leans across the table, so pleased with herself I'd call her "smug," if it weren't for the fact she has every reason to be this proud. "The counter-conspiracy to defy Triad has already been born."

If someone set off all the fireworks from the Fourth of July right now, the spectacle still wouldn't be fabulous enough to express how completely freakin' ecstatic this makes me. We've done it! We're finally, finally ahead of Triad, ahead of Wyatt Conley. We can stop reacting and start acting.

And as one of the very few perfect travelers in the multiverse, I just went from being a pawn to being a weapon.

Being a weapon is going to be lots better.

"We can defend the universes now," my mother says.

"Experiments conducted by the Berkeleyverse Paul—"

I hold my hands up in the time-out signal. "Wait. Berkeleyverse?"

"Well, the different universes have to have different names." My dad says this so smoothly you'd think he was the one who'd been traveling between worlds for months instead of me. "It helps keep things straight, especially since we're mostly communicating with other versions of ourselves. Can't really address a message to 'Henry' when I am one of the Henrys, can I?"

"Mostly we adopted the names you chose," Mom adds.

Okay, but there's one name I'm sure I never chose. "Which dimension is the Berkeleyverse?"

Paul folds his arms in front of his chest as he leans against the wall. "Yours."

"But—" My first impulse is to say something like, *but my world is the real one*, which makes no sense. Everyone's dimension is as true and valid as any other. No one universe is the center. Now that we're all talking, my home dimension needs a name too. Still, though—Berkeleyverse? "My parents teach at Berkeley in lots of universes."

Dad raises an eyebrow. "I feel bound to mention that lots of universes also have wars, and yet we are the Warverse. Sophie and I also teach at Cambridge in many quantum realities, but there is only one Cambridgeverse. And while absolutely every dimension discovered so far has an ocean, we have nonetheless designated an Oceanverse. In other words, my darling girl, the names are all sort of arbitrary and rubbish and it's not worth making a fuss over, is it?"

"I guess not." Berkeleyverse is going to take some getting used to, but I'll deal with that in my own time.

"As I was saying," Mom continues, "experiments conducted by the Berkeleyverse Paul Markov indicate that we can, in fact, use the Firebird to stabilize dimensions past Triad's ability to destroy them. So far, two such universes have been protected: someplace called the Spaceverse, where we first contacted him, and also the Londonverse." She frowns and looks over at my father. "Those are the right names, aren't they, Henry?"

"They are," I reply. Paul kept his word—he protected those worlds first. The two Marguerites slaughtered by Wicked and Triad—we've repaid their losses in the only way we ever could. "And the Egyptverse?"

"He's there now," Dad says. "Harder to build a stabilizer device there, it seems. Markov's working on it."

It helps me to know where he is, to be sure he's safe. However, I can only feel so much relief with the acrid smell of smoke from a dimension's death still fresh in my mind. "But—the Romeverse—you didn't save that one."

"By the time we tracked you there it was too late." Dad's smile fades. "We barely had time for Lieutenant Markov here to leap in and rescue you. Another ninety seconds and it would've been too late."

Ninety seconds. That's going to give me nightmares— but what part of the death of the Romeverse won't? I force myself to focus on the thing Dad said that I didn't already

183

know. "You tracked me?"

Mom explains, "Our dimension was ahead of yours in only one respect: We had already projected how to track travelers through the multiverse, both their Firebirds and their unique resonance patterns. Once we had learned the correct resonance for you, we were able to determine precisely where you were. Then we saw your Firebird leave the Romeverse without you, which seemed to be, at minimum, an extremely serious problem."

My dad chimes in: "When Markov here realized the irregularity in the signal meant your dimension was collapsing— well, you lived through the rest, didn't you?"

My memories aren't even fifteen minutes old, and yet already I can hardly believe them. "I saw . . . claws ripping apart the sky. And stone melting to lava. Crevasses opened up in the ground, and when I looked down, there was the planet's core. . . ." Shuddering, I wrap my arms around myself. "That can't be real."

"It wasn't." Warverse Paul's tone becomes more stern and forbidding each time he speaks. "The disintegration of that dimension involved a complete collapse of the laws of physics. Your brain couldn't possibly have processed the reality of what was happening."

"Humans simply don't have the capacity for that sort of thing," Dad says, more gently. "It sounds like your artistic mind supplied a few colorful metaphors, shall we say, to make sense of what was going on around you."

Mom folds her arms. "Henry, have you considered that

a purely logical mind, or one with a more scientific orientation, might quickly have become overwhelmed in such a situation? Lieutenant Markov here only endured two minutes of exposure to the chaos, but if he'd been there longer—or if you or I had become trapped there—we would have attempted to process the information rationally, and so become overwhelmed. We might well have been rendered incapable of thought or function in short order."

"Whereas Marguerite's aptitude for symbols and images protected her?" Dad nods. "Fascinating theory."

"I never want to test it, okay?" My voice shakes. I can't stop imagining the fiery, surreal end of the Romeverse. "Because I never want to see another dimension die. And I didn't just see it—I made it happen, it was me—"

My parents both go very still. Paul straightens, pulling away from the wall. "What?"

I explain what happened, wondering if they'll hate me for it. Instead, they all look at each other darkly. "A bloody sneak attack, that's what I call it," Dad mutters. "Underhanded, even by Triad's standards."

"It will be all right, Marguerite." Mom leans across the table to touch my arm. "Now you know what to look out for. They won't be able to do that to you again."

Please, let Mom be telling the truth. "What happens next?" I ask. "Do you—take me home, take your Firebird back?"

My parents and Paul exchange glances. It's Mom who answers. "We intend to give you this Firebird. It's a sacrifice because we still only have the two, but it's worth it. You alone stand a chance of saving the other Marguerites and stabilizing the universes in time. We've tracked the Home Office Marguerite—"

"Wicked," I say. "Call her Wicked."

My father's eyebrows couldn't be raised any higher. But my mom smoothly continues, "We've tracked Wicked to her next destination. As soon as she moves on, you can pick up her trail."

At that moment, Klaxon alarms begin to wail. I cover my ears with my hands as my parents and Paul all look upward, dawning horror on their faces. In an instant, Mom has grabbed my arm to drag me behind her as the three of them rush out of the room, leaving all their work behind. "What's happening?" I shout over the shrieking alarms.

"We're evacuating!" Paul runs faster, getting ahead of us to open the door. "Southern Alliance troops are moving in on the Bay Area."

Whatever the Southern Alliance is, the last time I was here, their fighter planes nearly bombed me. "They're invading today? Now?"

"Soon." My mother remains calm, even as she quickens her steps and tows me along. "We have orders to transfer the entire Firebird project to the aircraft carrier *J. A. Quinteros* within two hours. And as of this moment, Marguerite—the project includes you."

15

THE MILITARY BASE SEEMS QUIET AND ORDERLY, AT LEAST our section of it. As soon as we run from that room to begin our escape to the *Quinteros*, however, we are plunged into chaos.

Military vehicles crowd every roadway. Soldiers and sailors carry huge boxes of equipment if they're assigned to help with evacuation of war materials; if they aren't, they mostly run for their designated escape vehicles. I sit on the back of a jeep between my parents, Firebird around my neck swaying with every pothole and bump in the road. Paul's behind the wheel, driving with what I first see as a cold-blooded indifference to the safety of anyone around us. Then I realize everyone else is driving or running the same way.

Low-hanging gray clouds mask the sunlight—hardly unusual in San Francisco. But not all of the sky's darkness is due to the clouds. Smoke hovers at the horizon in several directions, sometimes many miles away, sometimes closer. The smoke doesn't look like the product of a currently raging fire; instead, it reminds me of the smoldering aftermath of a wildfire. As bad as it is to see the fires consuming hundreds of acres of countryside, it's worse to see that smoke coming from downtown, and maybe even Berkeley, too. How many hundreds or thousands of people must have died?

After the destruction of the Romeverse, though, I can't work up enough energy to panic. Instead, I feel numb to everything but my astonishment that I am still alive—and that this world's Paul came to save me.

The gargantuan scale of aircraft carriers is familiar to me because of the USS *Midway*, which is permanently docked in my version of San Francisco Bay. That doesn't make the *J.A. Quinteros* any less intimidating. It towers overhead, stretches into the distance. Boarding it is going to feel a little like climbing a mountain. My parents begin commandeering some sailors to help tote equipment and files across the boarding ramp as Paul leads me onward.

"Shouldn't you be helping haul top-secret stuff?" I nod at the guys laboring under heavy boxes.

Paul gives me a sidelong look. His grip tightens on my elbow. "I am."

He didn't say it to be funny, but any break in the tension is too precious to waste. When I start laughing, his stern expression cracks—just a little—enough for the light to get in.

Another one who loves you, he said to me in Rome. . . .

From the crowd of soldiers just beneath me, someone shouts, "Marguerite!" I turn, and in the middle of the frenzy, I see Theo—this dimension's Private Theodore Beck—waving his cloth uniform hat back and forth overhead, desperately signaling me.

And I can no longer breathe.

In a flash, it feels as if I'm back in Egypt, pinned on the floor of a tomb, eyes filling with tears and neck crushing in the viselike grip of my own scarf, Theo crying as he strangles me to death.

"Marguerite?" Paul steps closer, and his hand on my arm becomes less possessive, more protective. "You look terrible."

Blunt in every universe: That's Paul. I whisper, "Theo. I saw Theo."

Frowning, Paul looks from me to Theo—still waving, apparently unaware I've seen—and then back at me again. "Then why aren't you happy?"

"They must have told you I died in the Egyptverse. But I guess they didn't tell you how."

"No, but what—"

"Theo killed me." The words haven't gotten any easier to say. The reality remains almost too horrible to believe. I know it's true—I could never forget that terror and pain, not as long as I live—and yet nothing will ever make that feel entirely real. "Not my Theo. Not your Theo. The one from the Triadverse. He wrapped my lace scarf around my neck and choked me until I was strangled to death." I catch myself. As terrible as that was for me, I wasn't Theo's main victim. "I mean, I leaped out just before losing consciousness. But that world's Marguerite would've died only seconds later."

Paul staggers back a step, as though he were the one who had been attacked. When he looks down at Theo again, raw anger darkens his gray eyes. "How could he ever . . ." Then he swears in Russian and turns his head so he doesn't even have to see Theo.

Meanwhile, poor Theo waves with both hands, broad arcs, desperate to get my attention. Although the sight of him fills me with terror, I know that fear should be directed at the Triadverse's Theo Beck. Not this world's, and not mine.

My Theo deserved better, just like this Theo deserves a chance to tell his girl goodbye, if I can bear it.

Determined, I turn to Paul. "I should go to him. Do we have five minutes?"

Paul stares at me in disbelief. "You can't want to be with your murderer."

"I don't, but he's not my murderer. This isn't about me, okay? It's about this world's Marguerite, and it's about him." I point to Theo, who, encouraged, begins struggling through the crowd toward us. "If we're evacuating the entire city of San Francisco, I'm guessing the situation is beyond scary. This might be the last time he ever gets to see the girl he loves, and he should get a chance to say goodbye. So that's what I'm going to give him. Could you get over yourself long enough to show some grace?" The anger I've felt toward my own Paul's fatalism has begun to bubble over, but that's not fair—this is another man, with another fate. "I love you in so many worlds, Paul. Maybe now you can actually see how many there are, and you'll finally believe me. But this world belongs to Theo."

With that, I start down the boarding ramp, and Paul lets me go.

"Marguerite!" Theo disappears from my view for a moment, because now I'm too low down to see him through the crowd. He's lost amid uniforms and shoving and the smells of sweat and salt water. So I push myself toward the sound of his voice until finally I see his face. He pulls me into his arms so tightly—

—and again I remember the lace scarf, the agony of one of my infinite deaths—

—but I don't forget the lesson I learned on my last journey through the worlds. Each universe's version is an individual. Triadverse Theo is a deceitful, homicidal son of a bitch. My Theo is one of the kindest, most selfless friends I'll ever have. As for the Theo holding me close at this moment, all I know is my other self loves him tremendously. That's what I'm honoring now.

"Where have you been?" Theo kisses my throat, my cheek. "Ever since that weird episode we had at the base— they haven't let me see you, you haven't been home, not even once, because God knows I went there every chance I could."

"It's classified." My parents didn't have to tell me that; it's obvious. "I'm sorry, Theo. You know I'd explain everything if they'd let me."

He frames my face with his hands. Theo's soulful brown eyes drink me in. "Just tell me it's not dangerous. If you're safe, the rest doesn't matter."

"I'm safe." For me, actually, that's far from the truth. But I'm speaking for the Warverse Marguerite, who is now being protected as a key asset in the Firebird project. That's probably as secure as anyone in this dimension gets. "What about you? Where are they sending you?"

"We're being sent east, into the Rockies. That's all I know so far. I'll write as soon as I can, care of your parents, and tell you everything except the name of the camp. I swear."

"You better."

When Theo pulls me in for a kiss, I kiss him back with all the love in my heart. If this Marguerite feels for him what I feel for Paul, this is how she would kiss him goodbye. I embrace him tightly, open my mouth, as the sea breeze ruffles my hair and his warm hands stroke my back. After I leave this dimension, Warverse Marguerite will remember this moment. For her sake, and for his, I want it to be beautiful.

A whistle pierces the air, making Theo break our kiss. Already several of the soldiers around us have begun to surge in another direction, a wave that will carry Theo away. He gives me his lopsided smile, charming as ever. "If you think this was good—just wait till I tell you hello again."

"I hope it's soon." Though the way this war is going, I can't imagine how long it will be before they see each other. Months? Even years?

Or longer. During a desperate war, every time you say goodbye, you know it could be forever.

Theo kisses me once more and whispers, against my lips, "I love you."

"I love you, too."

I'm using her voice to say it, using her body and mind and heart. That makes it true.

He gives me one last heartbreaking look, then turns to follow his orders and march into a war that may kill him. I watch Theo go for as long as I can make out his shape among the hordes of soldiers around me, then as long as I can convince myself that maybe I'd glimpse him again. Only when I know he's truly, finally gone do I turn around and board the *Quinteros*.

I have said goodbye to this Theo forever. What will I do when I'm reunited with my own?

But I don't doubt for one second what I'm going to do when I see Triadverse's Theo again.

I can't feel the ocean bobbing and swelling beneath me. The enormous scale of an aircraft carrier allows it to remain steady against the waves. But as vast as this ship is—big enough to house dozens of fighter planes and a basketball court on its broad deck—once I go down inside it, claustrophobia closes in. Hallways are narrow, stairs are skinny and steep. Paul takes me to my parents and walks off without a word. I can't worry too much about his reaction because I'm too busy trying to acclimate to my new surroundings.

The quarters my parents lead me to are about the size of my closet at home, barely big enough for the fold-down bed and the small table and chair bolted to the floor. "I think this room is even tinier than the one on the space station," I say as I set down the small cardboard suitcase they brought for me.

"Space station?" Mom says, frowning.

"You know. From the Spaceverse. You guys heard of that one, I know you did."

Dad pushes his glasses up his nose, the way he does when his curiosity is going into overdrive. "Yes, but we weren't certain how that world got its moniker. Is it, well, more spacious in some way?"

"Or perhaps livable areas are rare in that universe," Mom hypothesizes. "And a 'space station' could then be a place where people are able to dwell in great comfort."

After the strange whirlwind of emotions that came from kissing Theo goodbye, it's a relief to smile. "No, it's nothing like that. Space as in outer space. You know, outside Earth's atmosphere." I point skyward.

Mom and Dad light up, and Dad is breathless as he says, "As in traveling to another planet?"

"Orbiting this one, actually." As creeped out as I felt being up above the Earth, I can see how the idea fills them with wonder. "Mom was the commander."

Their bedazzled expressions last only for a moment, fading so quickly that I wonder whether I've said something

194

wrong. Then my mother says, "If we weren't fighting this stupid, futile war—think of the things we could be doing, Henry. The discoveries we could have made. Instead we're only allowed to look at other dimensions so they can teach us new weapons to build."

"I know, Sophie." Dad hugs her from behind, a gesture startlingly familiar despite their military uniforms and these stark, blank, gray metal surroundings. "I know."

They're so sad, so lost. My parents find a way to be discoverers and innovators in every world, but I never thought I'd see one where their love of invention had been even slightly soured by the uses for their creations.

"So," I say as I hang on to my suitcase, trying to move us along. "Do I get a ship's map or floor plan—or whatever you call it on a ship? I'd like to find the cafeteria eventually."

That was supposed to be a joke, but my mom and dad give each other a look that clearly means, *You tell her.* Dad's the one who finally says, "Well, sweetheart, you've got your bed and your table, a few books in your suitcase, plus a door to a private head right here—quite a luxury, by the way—and we'll bring you your meals personally. So no worries about getting lost, no need to go wandering about."

I remember the room I appeared in, the half-bedroom, half-office with locks on the door. At the time I was too shaken to analyze it, but now its purpose is clear. "You're keeping me under guard, in case Wicked decides to drop by."

"Once the Berkeleyverse warned us of the danger," Mom

says, "you volunteered. I mean, our you, not you you."

"Got it. Good. That was the right thing to do." What damage could Wicked possibly do to an aircraft carrier? I don't want to find out. "It's okay. I won't leave this area, no matter what."

"Of course you understand." Dad looks at me the same way he did when he realized I'd grown an inch taller than Mom—proud but wistful. "To tell you the truth, Marguerite, when we first learned what was going on, I didn't understand why Josie hadn't been the perfect traveler. She's the one who can't wait to plunge into the fray." Josie has dragged me onto countless roller coasters and zip lines; the first time I learned she was the Home Office's choice as perfect traveler, I knew that made perfect sense. Before I can agree with my dad, however, he continues, "But this role doesn't need an adventurer as much as it needs someone who can . . . look at each world with fresh eyes. Who can perceive things deeply. Not an adventurer—an artist. You were the one we needed all along."

It's like the moment in Egypt when I realized that, in their dimension, I got to be a meaningful part of my parents' work, but even better. Times a thousand. "Thanks," I manage to say, despite the catch in my throat.

Mom sighs, both in satisfaction and as a signal that they have to go. "We'll bring your dinner in a couple of hours, sweetheart. If you need more books, let us know—or I could bring a pack of cards."

"Actually, could you send Paul down with dinner?"

Maybe he's not ready to talk with me again yet, but who knows how much time we'll have? I can't afford to waste a single chance. "We need to talk."

Within five minutes, I have explored every inch of my Spartan new surroundings. The bathroom, or "head" as they call it here, is clean but tiny, and weird, too—instead of a real shower, there's just this handheld nozzle and a drain in the floor; basically the whole bathroom is your shower. Instead of glass, the mirror is polished metal, providing a blurry view of myself in the vaguely old-fashioned style I remember: my curly hair cropped to chin-length and pulled to one side with bobby pins, very little makeup besides the dark red lipstick that even Theo's kiss couldn't smear.

For once, I don't have to try leaping out of this universe in every quiet moment. Instead, I get to curl up on the bed. While I'm too on edge to truly relax, it's a luxury just to lie there. Just to be, for a while. Thanks to the new interdimensional tracking, my parents will be able to tell me when Wicked's finally moved along.

Through the drowsy haze of my not-quite-a-nap, I think that she seems to be taking her time. Is that because the Home Office thinks I died with the Romeverse? Or is that because Wicked's figuring out an even deadlier trap? Though I have no idea how anything could ever top that.

A knock jolts me back to the here and now. From the other side of the door Paul says, "Dinner."

I roll off the bed, take one deep breath, and then I open

the door with a smile. Paul remains so stiff he might as well be at attention before the captain, a tray of food in his hands. "Hey," I say. "Thanks. Please come in."

He does, setting the tray down on my table as quickly as possible. When I close the door behind him, though, he tenses. Obviously he was hoping for a very brief visit.

"Didn't my parents tell you I was hoping to talk?" I ask.

"Yes. But I couldn't imagine what we would have to talk about. Aside from the Firebird project, of course, but you can have those conversations with your parents. That would no doubt be more productive." Each word is clipped, and his posture is formal. I've got my work cut out for me.

"I don't want to talk about the Firebird. I want to talk about Paul. My Paul." How can I get through to him? "I love him, but he's in trouble—so much trouble—and I don't know how to help. I thought, if anyone could help me understand, it would have to be you, right? You're so closed off sometimes. So hard to read. Only another you could ever really understand."

"We're not the same," Paul replies.

"No. But you're not totally different, either." *Not everything from that night in Chinatown was fake,* I want to say, but I know better. "Please. He needs us."

Paul's stoic face betrays nothing, but he sits on the edge of my bed. His posture remains so stiff that he might as well be seated in a church pew.

I'm nearly as ravenous as I am curious, so I sit at the table to eat the sandwich he brought me. Hungry as I am, though,

I can only manage a couple of bites. Warverse bread tastes like cardboard. Given the severity of the rations here, it may actually be cardboard. "Okay," I say, setting the sandwich down. "You remember how Paul was splintered before. How part of his soul was hidden inside you."

"I assume you were able to find and reunite all four splinters of his soul. Otherwise we wouldn't be having this conversation."

"Yes, but that wasn't enough." I ought to have taken an image of that terrible brain scan from the Spaceverse. If I could point to that now, the damage would be undeniable. "Paul's messed up. All these darker impulses—violent impulses, even—it's like he can only barely control them. He doesn't trust himself around me or around anyone, and he doesn't believe he'll get any better."

"He won't heal from the injury." Paul's tone is so cool, he could be discussing a stranger instead of another version of himself. "If the splinters didn't synthesize correctly while being spliced back together, they never will."

I sag back in the chair. "You can't know that."

"Injuries to the soul aren't like injuries to the body. Splintering isn't the same as cutting through skin. It's more like—shattering porcelain." Paul's hands trace an indistinct shape in the air, some broken thing he has imagined. "You can put it back together again, even glue it so well the cracks barely show. But the cracks will always be there. They won't heal."

Then Paul and I will never be together again. I lean my

elbows on the table and rest my face in my hands. Every other emotion I could feel is drowned in terrible, final loss.

After a moment, however, Paul says, "But just because something's been damaged doesn't mean it's ruined." When I look up at him, he continues, "I, uh, manage violent impulses of my own. I've never lost control. That's a choice I've made. Discipline I've learned. Your Paul could learn that too."

Could he? I don't know. But we'll never find out if my Paul won't even try. In order for him to try, he has to believe.

"The violent impulses," I begin. "Those come from your parents, don't they?"

He always goes so rigid when anyone even mentions them. "That's obvious. But I don't have to be the man my father is."

"No, you don't. But the cracks still linger, don't they?"

Paul breathes out heavily. "If this conversation isn't going to be constructive, then—"

"Wait. No. It's just that I think something about how you grew up convinced you—made you doubt—" At last I find the right words. "It made you think nobody could ever love you for yourself alone."

As badly as I needed to say it, I almost wish I hadn't, because Paul's flinch tells me that hit him like a bullet.

He doesn't reply right away, but I let the silence linger. There's no time for anything but the truth between us from now on.

Finally Paul says, "My parents . . . you know that they're corrupt people."

"In my world and a few others, they're mobsters. Gangsters? Whatever word you'd use here."

"Mobsters." He slumps back against the wall, weariness replacing his formal rigidity. "That doesn't surprise me. Here, they profit from the black market. They resell food, equipment, even medicines at exorbitant prices, all because they bribed the right people to make sure they received those shipments, while ration storehouses remain empty."

"Did they want you to be a part of it?"

"It sickens me, and they always knew that. Always mocked me for it. Said I thought I was 'too good' to fight for my own place in the world. Mama and Papa don't see this as a war against the Southern Alliance. To them, it's every man for himself, always, forever."

Maybe that's their constant—the one thing that's true for the Markovs in every world. I feel sure it's true in mine. "In my world, Paul's parents don't even speak to him anymore. They don't give him any money. All because he became a scientist." I'd always known something was seriously messed up about a mother and father who were angry their kid got into college at age twelve.

"Mine are more understanding," Paul says. "Because military service is mandatory, and because they hope that someday, I'll achieve a high rank and be able to funnel stolen goods in their direction. They're sure I'll do it eventually. That I'll 'see sense.' People like them understand the concepts of right and wrong. They just convince themselves that they're in the right. It sounds like your Paul's choices force his parents to know just how selfish and small they are." His smile is as thin as the line of a scar. "People can forgive anything except being proved wrong."

I think about my Paul's bare dorm room, where he can't afford anything but a single set of scratchy sheets he bought from Goodwill. He owns two pairs of equally battered blue jeans and a series of not-new T-shirts; even his one big indulgence, a pair of good boots for his rock-climbing adventures, he got secondhand. My parents bought him a new winter coat, and when they baked him a birthday cake he was so surprised. So grateful. I don't think he'd had a birthday cake in years.

Maybe his father, Leonid, wasn't merely being mean. Maybe he was trying to awaken something angry and cruel within Paul. If Paul had chafed at his poverty—if he'd thought at any point, *This is ridiculous. I don't have to live like this. It would be so easy to separate the idiots around me from their money*—everything would have changed. If he'd turned his genius to identity theft or hacking into banks, he could have made himself a millionaire within weeks. Days, even. The Firebird project might've collapsed without him, while Paul would have turned into exactly the man his father wanted him to be.

But he never flinched. Not even once.

"It was hard for me to accept that Paul and I don't wind up together in every world," I say. "Still is. But I know I love him, and that something between us—in so many worlds—it goes beyond random chance. For Paul, it's different. It's like now that he's been splintered, he assumes we'll never wind up together."

Paul considers that, his gaze turned deeply inward. Learning about another version of yourself—about the array of people you could be that would all still truly be you—it's intoxicating. Despite my desperation, I'm fascinated to watch someone else go through it too. "You always seemed so out of reach," he finally says. "Not only because of Theo. Because it's so hard to believe anyone would love me back without wanting something in return."

Although I already knew how badly my betrayal here must have hurt him, I realize now how much deeper the wound struck. "I'm sorry," I whisper.

But Paul isn't listening. He doesn't need an apology anymore. He wants to understand. "If it's hard for me, it must be almost impossible for your Paul Markov. The idea of fate gave him hope. Then when that fate was torn away, he couldn't believe any longer."

"He knows my parents love him," I say. "And my Theo, too. But he probably thinks it's all about the science. About what he can help them do."

"I don't know. I'm not him. But . . . I could believe that was true."

Paul and I sit in silence for a few moments. I take another couple of bites of the sandwich, but on autopilot, hardly tasting the bland food. How am I ever supposed to undo damage like that? How can I make Paul believe in us when his whole life, and all these other universes, tell him we're impossible?

Once I thought of running from world to world, trying to find the one where Paul and I loved each other perfectly. Now I don't know whether a world like that could ever exist.

"Why Theo?" Paul says, breaking the silence between us. "Why do you think you chose him and not me?"

"Probably he poured on the charm. At home he works with you guys, my parents are his thesis advisers, and so maybe he held back because he didn't want to step on their toes. Then I fell for Paul, and Triadverse Theo came and screwed everything up for him, and that was that. In a world where he didn't have any reason not to go for it . . . well, I guess that's this one."

"So there's no real difference between us in terms of how you could feel." Paul tries to make it sound reasonable, but I can hear the hurt he still hasn't managed to bury.

"I know this world's Marguerite loves this Theo. But when Paul and I have been together—in Russia, in Rome—" My voice breaks. "I didn't even know you could love someone like that, until I loved you. I mean . . . him."

"I know what you meant." This time Paul's voice is gentle. He believes me now.

"Maybe, if I've finally been to enough worlds to put all the pieces together, then maybe I can make it right. Maybe I'll finally really understand him."

"It wouldn't matter if you visited a million worlds. You never know everything about another person—not even someone you love. You can't, and you wouldn't want to." To my surprise, Paul smiles, his expression as warm and adoring as it was that night in Chinatown. "You have to love the mystery. You have to take a chance."

A speaker's squeal startles us both. Only now do I see the small, perforated screen in one corner with a toggle that must be my communication with the rest of the ship. Dad's tinny voice says, "Marguerite, we have confirmation on, um, Wicked's movements. She's shifted universes again."

I rise from the table and hit the toggle that lets me reply. "I have to go, right away. The Marguerite she just left is in danger."

"Understood," Dad says. "Safe journeys, and know that we're watching you. We'll help if we can."

"Thank you. Love you, love to Mom." Which is sort of stupid, when their own Marguerite is about to reclaim control of her own existence. But it feels right, especially when the reply comes back: "Love you too."

Paul stands, and we're face to face. Only a short week or so ago, I hoped I'd never have to confront him again. And now it's so hard to say goodbye.

"I'd like to kiss you," I said. "Bad idea?"

"Probably. This Marguerite wasn't thrilled with what happened," he says, referring to our makeout session on a Chinatown sidewalk. "She didn't blame me. After we learned the full truth, she didn't even blame you. But I'm not going to take advantage of the situation."

"I knew she'd remember that. But I hope she also remembers how much you helped me. How good you can be."

His eyes drink me in. This may be the last time he sees

me gazing back at him with love. "I hope so too. And good luck."

"Thanks." I'll need it. What will Wicked have planned for me this time? All I know is, it's going to be bad. I look up at Paul again, take courage from his face, hit the Firebird's controls—

—and slam back into my airplane seat, hard enough that it rocks. Behind me I hear someone grumble. I think I knocked their drink off their tray table.

The stewardess is standing in the aisle next to me, a quizzical expression denting her prefab smile. "Miss? Are you all right?"

"Good. Yeah. Definitely."

"Can I get you anything else to drink? This is our final service of the flight." Her voice has a faint accent—she's Latina, I think. "Coffee, tea, water?"

"I'm okay. Thank you."

As the stewardess moves on, I think, *Wicked put me on a plane.* My mind fills with nightmare images of jetliners being blown up, fiery crashes into the runway, or some terrible oceanic disappearance that doesn't get solved until a year later. I clutch the armrests, because if that's what Wicked has done, then I have no chance to save myself, none at all.

But could Wicked get this theoretical bomb past security? And where would she buy explosives? I don't have any idea, and she's from a world so different from my own that I doubt she'd have a clue here. This world is pretty obviously close to mine; everything about the plane and the passengers looks totally normal, plus I'm wearing leggings and a lacy top from Anthropologie that I'd been coveting but—back at home, at least—never managed to save up enough allowance money for. Also, if this is the final service of the flight, Wicked rode this plane for at least an hour or two, possibly much longer. She wouldn't wait so long if a bomb were going to go off midflight anyway. I'd have been trapped here just the same.

Maybe the danger isn't on board this plane. Maybe the danger waits at my destination.

My inner ears tighten. I swallow hard and feel them pop just as the pilot's voice says, "We are now beginning our final descent into Quito, Ecuador—"

Ecuador? I know now what universe I'm in, and who will be waiting for me on the other side. This was where Triadverse Paul escaped to, after he turned against Triad in an effort to protect me. This is where he must still be living in hiding from Wyatt Conley's goons.

Why would Wicked travel to Ecuador? She hates Paul, or at any rate doesn't mind causing him pain. But then I realize the one reason she could possibly have. If she made arrangements to meet Paul at the airport, then she could have told other people to meet him there too. Say, people who work for Wyatt Conley.

My heart sinks as I realize that Wicked set a trap for Paul . . . and I'm the bait.

16

THE ONLY PLAN I CAN COME UP WITH DURING OUR LAND-
ing is to try to get out of the airport without Paul seeing me.
Wicked must have called or emailed him, told him to meet
my flight, but if Triad's people are looking for our reunion
as their cue to move in, then that reunion can't happen. Of
course they might be watching for him outside the airport,
in which case nothing I can do will help. But if avoiding
Paul now has any chance of helping him, then that's what
I'm going to do.

I'll pass up baggage claim, see if I can get into another terminal or something before I exit, and hope the credit cards
I've found in my wallet will work in Ecuador. If my tPhone
works too, I'll call Mom and Dad back home and see how
much they can tell me.

After that—well, I'll figure it out as it comes. Maybe I'll
just walk back to the ticket counters and buy a seat on the

next flight back to the United States. Hope I can afford it.

Airports all pretty much look alike. As I stroll along with the other deplaning passengers, my bottle-green messenger bag slung over one arm, I keep my head down. I don't want Paul to see me . . . but I want to see Paul, so I can't help glancing up to scan the crowds waiting just outside the security zone.

Within moments, I see a familiar face—then another—and I freeze.

Paul hasn't come to meet me.

Instead, Theo and Wyatt Conley stand just behind the barricade. Theo's wearing sunglasses that hide the expression in his eyes, but Conley's smiling, grinning even, lifting one hand to wave to me.

In the other hand, Conley holds a sign that reads WEL-COME BACK.

I stop short. Another passenger bumps into me from behind, then mutters something in Spanish that probably means *idiot* while other people swerve around me. My hands tighten around the strap of my messenger bag. One thought in my mind swells until it presses out all the others: Triad found Paul.

"Hello there, Marguerite," Conley says, like he's an old friend I've come to visit. "Glad you finally got here. We have places to go and so much to talk about. But first of all, I'm afraid I need to ask you for some ID."

My breaths feel like they aren't drawing in enough air. Dizziness makes me sway. But I stand my ground and stare at Conley as I ask, "Are you high?"

"Just answer this," Conley says. "What color was the Beatles' submarine?"

It feels like a trick, a trap. My first impulse is to begin screaming that Conley and Theo are terrorists, that they should be shot down immediately. But I know by now that it's rarely that easy to get out of Wyatt Conley's games. For now I have to play along. So I remember the moment I convinced a mob to throw him, shrieking, into hell. Then I smile with all the warmth of that memory and give the correct answer: "Purple."

"And that's our perfect traveler, come back at last." Conley gestures me to join them on the other side of the barricades. Theo has turned his head, because apparently his sunglasses aren't enough of a shield.

Merely being close to this Theo horrifies me on every level. I can bear it only because being close to Conley is somehow even worse. My hatred for Wyatt Conley can eclipse everything else, even my murderer.

I keep playing it cool. "I'm pretty sure I'm not the only person who knows the answer to that question," I say as I come around, though I keep several paces' distance between us. "The Beatles aren't exactly obscure."

"No, they aren't," Conley answers. "However, creativity can bend in different ways. Only in your dimension did the Beatles sing about a purple submarine. There are a couple of 'Big Green Submarines' out there in the multiverse, but usually it's yellow."

210

"Yellow Submarine"? Weird. Not nearly as fun. I remember my dad holding my hands and dancing with me in front of the cartoon when I was very tiny, barely a toddler. We'd sing about the purple submarine together. Suddenly I wish I were back there—just a little kid, laughing with my parents, loved and safe and sure nothing in the world would ever be any scarier than the Green Meanies.

Oblivious to my reaction, Conley continues, "It's interesting, isn't it, how many things we think of as universal are actually unique to one very specific point in space and time?"

"Yeah, it's fascinating." I don't have any patience left for Conley's grandiose speculations. "Why did you bring me here?"

To my surprise, Theo answers. "We needed to find out if you were still alive."

"No thanks to you guys." I put my hand on my Firebird and raise one eyebrow. "I guess I'll be going."

I won't be. I wouldn't ditch Triadverse's Marguerite in this situation. I've let down too many of my other selves already. But I also intend to put up with exactly no more crap from Wyatt Conley.

"Stick around," Conley says warmly. He flips the sign over for Theo to take, then tucks his hands in the pockets of his designer jeans. Between his deliberately casual demeanor and his long, freckle-dusted face, he'd blend in at college with Theo and Paul—a grad student, seemingly as lazy-casual as the others, but subtly more sophisticated, with the faint sheen of confidence and wealth. No doubt Conley thinks he comes across as nonthreatening, and his act might work on people who don't know him. "We need to talk, don't you think, Marguerite? You know more now. You've seen more. And I think you might almost be ready to hear me out."

Not even. "You're putting some other Marguerite in danger right now. This very second! You can't tell me what great friends we ought to be while you're killing another me one universe away."

He holds up his hands as if in surrender. "As a show of good faith, I sent your Home Office counterpart to a 'neutral' universe—one that isn't slated for destruction, one without Firebird technology, totally off the grid. These are peace talks, all right? And that makes this a cease-fire. Maybe we can even turn it into an armistice."

"I have only your word for that," I say. Would Wicked really follow his orders?

"That's right," Conley agrees. "You can't test what I've just told you. So you have two choices. You can trust me, or you can leave here as ignorant as you came and try to pick up your counterpart's trail. I don't think you'll find it very easy. Do you?"

I have her trail already, thanks to the tracking information I got from the Warverse. But Conley can't know that. If he finds out the Warverse wasn't sabotaged but is instead leading a counter-conspiracy of several alternate dimensions, we'll lose whatever advantage we'd managed to gain. So, for now, I just have to deal.

"Okay," I tell him. "I'll stay and hear you out on one condition. Tell me what you've done to Paul."

Conley's smile broadens. "Absolutely nothing."

"Bull. You've hunted him to Ecuador—"

"We'd done that within the first two days," Theo cuts in. He's staring at his red Chucks, one of which he keeps sliding back and forth across the tile floor. "But nobody's hurt him, Meg. I promise you that."

"Meg," I say. "The last time you called me that, you were strangling me to death. Forgive me if I don't take your word for it." Theo flinches and says nothing more.

But Conley adds, "Maybe I should've been more precise. We haven't done anything to Paul . . . yet."

I thought I was the bait on Paul's hook. Turns out he's the bait on mine.

One step brings me right into Conley's face. He's not much taller than I am. "Show me that he's all right. Let me see Paul. After that—okay, we'll talk."

"See? I knew you could be reasonable." Conley claps his hands together. "So, did you bring any bags?"

"How would I know?" I snap. But as I start heading toward baggage claim, my head whirls, and once again I have trouble catching my breath. It felt a little like this when Wicked leaped into me—but when I put my hand to my chest, only one Firebird hangs there.

"Altitude sickness," Theo mutters. "Quito's more than nine thousand feet above sea level. It takes some people a while to adjust."

"And you don't look like you slept a wink on the plane."
Conley puts one hand on my shoulder to guide me, which
sends clammy chills through my body. "You know what?
Let's run by, see Paul, and give you a chance to rest. After
you've had some sleep, we can really talk. Then we'll have
all the time in the world."

Turns out I brought a flowered duffel bag of mine, which
Theo has to lug out to the limousine waiting out front. I
hope it's heavy. I hope I packed hardcover books, a dozen of
them. In the limo, Conley sits facing forward, which means
I'm stuck riding backward. My queasiness worsens as we
duck into hilly, chaotic Quito traffic.

And when I say chaotic, I mean it. People here seem to
regard lanes of traffic as vague suggestions at best. Cars and
trucks swerve and skid, ignore signs, zoom through lights,
you name it. Even though my stomach churns, I'm kind of
glad I can't see what's ahead of us or I'd probably have a heart
attack.

I make a point of not seeing what's in front of me, i.e.,
Conley and Theo. My blackmailer and my murderer, both
so close I can hear them breathe. My nausea peaks at the
thought of it, and it's all I can do to hang on.

The queasiness reminds me, for a moment, of the morning
sickness I experienced on my last journey to the Russiaverse.
Almost without thinking, I slide my hand across my belly
and try to remember the weird, watery heaviness of early
pregnancy. I only felt the baby move once—I think—and

even that was more of a goldfish wiggle, because it hadn't been quite four months since that night in the dacha.

Paul's baby, and mine, still in the Russiaverse waiting to be born. I am fighting for all the people Triad has put at risk, but deep down, I think I'm fighting for that baby most of all.

"Are you about to throw up?" These are the first words Theo's spoken since the airport. He sounds sulky, even petulant, and yet every syllable cuts me like a knife. "If so, would you please roll down a window first?"

"If I throw up, it's going to be in your lap." I fold my arms across my chest and stare out the window. Better to look at that maniacal traffic than this Theo's face.

When we finally turn off from the clogged highways and wind into one of the neighborhoods, I'm struck by how, well, ordinary everything looks. The signs may all be in Spanish, and the stores and vehicles may mostly be slightly smaller than they would be at home, but otherwise this is a strip mall like any other, complete with open-air cafés. The limousine slows to a crawl as we pass a Juan Valdez coffeehouse, and Wyatt raps softly on the window. "And there you go."

My heart rises as I recognize Paul—Triadverse Paul, so like mine that only a few issues of timing divide them. He sits at a round stone table, typing at his old laptop, which has a panel held on with duct tape. I wonder why he's frowning. Is this when we usually chat, and I haven't signed on as usual? Since he turned out to be the "bait" in this particular trap, Wicked wouldn't have given him any clue she was boarding a flight to Ecuador.

It would be so easy to just open the door and jump out. The limo isn't even going five miles an hour. I want to launch myself at Paul, show him this Firebird and explain about the counter-conspiracy, all of it. In this moment, there is nothing I want more.

I don't move. I have to find out how much Conley knows. So I keep pretending that I'm willing to play ball.

Paul's broad hands continue working on his keyboard as he searches for something, or someone, in vain. How ironic, that we can only get perspective on the people we want to be close to when we pull away—or when they do.

Did I have to lose Paul before I could fully understand him?

"What has he been doing down here?" I murmur. "I know you know."

"Not everything," Conley admits, surprising me. "Markov's skilled enough to cover his tracks. He seems to have picked up some programming work and even a little translation on the side. Lives in a youth hostel not far from the historical colonial section of town. Makes the occasional friend from other students passing through, but don't worry, Marguerite. No visiting girls have tempted him to wander . . . at least, as far as we know."

He's trying to make me jealous. What a waste of time. I know Paul well enough to know that he's hardly even kissed any girls besides me, and he's way too bashful to turn into a womanizer.

Even if he weren't shy, Paul would never cheat. Even the

thought of me with another Paul was almost too much for him to bear. His fidelity is something I never have to doubt.

"All right," I say. "Paul is okay. Thank you."

"My pleasure." Wyatt Conley smiles, like he's done me some huge favor.

"He'd better stay okay." I allow myself to look at Conley with some fraction of the hate I really feel.

His smile hardens. We both know the reality of this game. "That's up to you."

Afterward, the limo drives straight to a luxurious hotel and drops me off—with Theo right behind. "Get her settled in," Conley says to him. "Make sure she's safe and tight."

The way he pronounces tight is unmistakably a reference to the lace scarf this Theo used to strangle me. Maybe such cheap, obvious tricks shouldn't be so effective, but I can't help feeling a wave of fresh fear, and an uncomfortable knot within my throat.

There is, of course, a room waiting for me in this hotel, posh enough to have marble tiled floors and a waterfall in the lobby. A penthouse suite, even, because Wyatt Conley doesn't do anything by halves. Theo and I ride up in the elevator together in stony silence. Once he offers a hand to take my duffel bag, but I only grip the handle more tightly. I don't want this scum touching me or my stuff. I've had enough of his "help."

Which, of course, is exactly why Conley made Theo accompany me. Given that I'm in a strange country, without much money, dizzy and nauseated, the chances of me running off are minimal. But he wants Theo there as a reminder of just how bad things can get. For all his promises of safety and cooperation, Conley still wants me to fear for my life.

The thing is, though—now that I'm forced to really look at Theo, I can see that guilt lies so heavily on him that his shoulders sag. His usual bantam swagger has been reduced to a shuffle, and still, more than an hour after landing, he has yet to meet my eyes.

Theo murdered me, and Theo hated it. I remember how much he cried, how he pleaded for me to jump out so he would at least only have to kill one of us. If Theo or Conley thought killing would be easier after that, they were wrong.

The mere idea of confronting him terrifies me. But it turns out I affect Theo even more profoundly than he affects me.

Theo taps the key card against the lock before stepping back to let me through. I shoulder the door open to walk into pure elegance. The living room has a panoramic view looking over the city and is set up with chic, modern leather chairs and sofas, even a glass dining table ringed by gilded cane chairs. A mirrored wet bar sits in one corner, in case I suddenly start preferring Scotch to seltzer. Lush rugs cover the marble floor, and the artwork hanging on the walls actually looks like art. I step in far enough to see into the bedroom, where a king-size canopy bed is draped with soft veils of netting. It's not the Ritz, but still—this looks like the kind of hotel room J. Lo would get.

I drop my duffel bag on a carved teak bench and motion toward the wet bar. It's hard, acting casual in front of my killer, but somehow I manage to keep my voice even. "I only drink on major holidays and at the apocalypse. But do you want something?"

"Better not." Theo doesn't know what to make of this. Good.

I make a show of checking the wet bar, which is basically a minibar without the mini. My back is to Theo, so he can't see how my fingers shake in front of the rows of bottles and cans. Choosing a can of club soda, I sit down in one of the gilded chairs and try to pretend it's a throne. "Tell me, Theo. What was it like, killing her?"

He stares at me, his face waxen.

I crack the tab of the club soda, acting casual, like my stomach isn't heaving inside. "The other Marguerite couldn't have had any idea why you were doing it. She thought you were this cute, dashing European, with your greasy porn-stache and your bright little scarves. And she didn't even remember being led into that tomb. She came to in the last couple seconds of her life." *I'm sorry,* I think to her. *I'm so sorry.* But I bet she wouldn't mind my using this memory to bludgeon her killer. "Did she try to speak to you? Did she have time to cry?"

"Please, Meg." Theo's voice breaks. "You know I hate this."

"Yeah, well, obviously you love something more. Is it money or power? Wait, don't tell me. I don't actually care."

Theo steps closer to me, and finally he takes off his glasses. Those puppy-dog eyes of his are filled with tears. "She died fast. Almost the moment after you left. And that didn't make it one bit easier. I sat there beside her for—nearly an hour, I think, I don't know—and when I crawled back out into the open air, I saw my rifle, and I thought, I should shoot myself. Just grab the rifle and sit down in the nearest camp chair and blow my damned head off."

"Instead you escaped on a camel." My lip trembles, but I manage to cover it by taking a sip of club soda. "Dignified. And proof that you didn't actually feel that bad about it, no matter what you say now."

"Don't say that!" Theo insists. "You don't know what it did to me, Meg. You don't."

Something inside me snaps. "What it did to *you*? You strangled me nearly to death, murdered another me in cold blood, and I'm supposed to be worried about how it affected *you*?"

"No—that's not what I meant—"

"Yeah, Theo, I think it is. Whether you know it or not, that's exactly what you meant. Because no matter how much you claim to care about me, you're only looking out for yourself." I want to throw the can at his head, but I don't. The beatdown I need to give him is going to hurt worse than any bruise. "I bet it's not just greed driving you, either. I bet it's jealousy, too. All those worlds where Paul and I fall for each other while you lose out. So do you hate Paul for loving me, or me for loving him?"

Theo neither denies it nor agrees. He just shakes his head. "Seems like I'm always finishing second."

I laugh out loud, in surprise I genuinely feel and contempt he deserves. "There are worlds where we're together, Theo! Worlds where I love you so much. I've jumped into a universe to find us lying beside each other in bed. I've kissed you. I've felt you touch me. Paul was the only one I ever loved, but the other Marguerites? Some of them chose you. Some of those worlds are yours and hers to share. But Wyatt Conley is trying to destroy those worlds—and you're helping him."

I push back from the table. Theo edges back from me. But the disbelief and anger on his face is all too clear. Exhilarated by the rush of my own fury, I keep going.

"You're killing a thousand mes and a thousand yous who could be happy. Every chance you and I ever had? It's just one more log for you to throw on the fire. So that's how I know you can't possibly love me, Theo. If you did, you couldn't destroy us over and over again."

"It's not over and over—not a thousand—Christ, Meg, it's going to end, soon. It would end today if you'd just hear Conley out."

"Oh, yeah?" As I walk him closer and closer to the door, I continue, "Did Conley tell you that, when you heard him out? That it would end soon? I wonder if he'll still be telling you that after the tenth version of me you murder. Or the hundredth Paul. Or thousands of both of us. You're the scientist, so why do I have to be the one to tell you the multiverse is infinite? Conley wants total control, and total control is impossible. The killing is never going to end. Which means you don't ever get to stop." I point to the door. "Now get out."

Theo bolts through the door like he's fleeing a fire. Most of the Theos are braver than this one, I decide. He seems like a total coward.

But if he's as selfish as I think he is, he's going to want to find one of those worlds we share. He's going to want to keep it safe from Wyatt Conley. And if I can shove even one wedge between Conley and his number-one henchman—

—but I can't. If anything could have stopped the Triadverse's Theo from blindly following Wyatt Conley, it would've been the command to murder me. Instead he obeyed that order. So there's no stopping Theo now. In fact, I bet he'll justify himself more and more in an attempt to hide from what he's done.

Will I be able to do anything in this universe but stall? Learn anything that will do us any good? Get any closer to the Paul who even now waits halfway across Quito, vulnerable and alone?

We'll see, I tell myself as I sink, exhausted, back down into the chair. *We'll see.*

17

I WAKE UP IN THE CANOPIED BED, BLINKING AND UNSURE. The sky beyond the windows is dark, though the horizon is beginning to brighten.

Dawn is a time of day I usually feel no need to experience. But instead of burrowing back under the feather duvet and trying to go back to sleep, I push myself upright and take stock. The nausea I felt yesterday has died down, and while I'm still slightly short of breath, it no longer seems like a crisis. So I've adjusted to the altitude well enough.

My belly rumbles, reminding me that I have no idea how much Wicked ate in this body yesterday, if anything. Although I don't read much Spanish, I can make out the hotel info book well enough to know it's still an hour before room service will start serving *desayuno*. Time for a nutritious breakfast from the minibar.

Jet lag really doesn't sum up how unreal everything feels

after you've jumped all around the globe in different dimensions, I decide as I choose a bag of trail mix and a Coke. We need another word for it. Universe lag? Firebird lag?

I hate waiting. Suspense wears me down worse than stress ever could. Even jumping into worlds where I know Wicked's latest deathtrap is waiting doesn't grind me down as much as this: sitting on a leather sofa, watching the sunrise against my will, eating junk for breakfast while I wait for Wyatt Conley to show up and be creepy.

I know our next conversation serves a purpose. I know how important it is to find out just how much Conley has learned about the alliance between the other dimensions. And yet when I am traveling, I am brave. I do what has to be done. When I am waiting, I only feel small and hollow and scared.

If Paul were with me— I think, but I stop myself before even finishing. Reaching out to him here in Quito would endanger him, maybe even lead Conley to kill him. At this point, honestly, I would settle for absolutely anybody I love. My own world's Theo, even. Or Josie. Or Mom and Dad . . .

The caffeine must be hitting my bloodstream, because my eyes finally focus on what's been sitting right in front of me this whole time: a landline phone.

I sit up straight. I'd tried my tPhone almost as soon as Theo left, but it had been remotely shut down, no doubt by Triad. In my exhaustion it hadn't even occurred to me to think about a landline. And for Wyatt Conley, genius of the cellular age—I bet he doesn't even remember landlines exist, even though every hotel room has them.

Swallowing the last of the Coke, I pick up the phone and examine it. I don't see anything that looks like a listening device, at least not according to the few spy movies I've seen where they check for this stuff. If Conley tapped the line, well, there's nothing I can do about that. Still, I'd bet everything he didn't think about the landline. The only other people who continue to rely on them are eccentric, slightly absentminded people . . . such as my parents.

Our landline number is one of the few I know by heart.

It takes a little negotiation with the hotel operator to place the call. Then I hear the odd, purring double ring of an international call until, finally, a sleepy voice says, "Hello?"

"Mom! It's me, Marguerite. I'm sorry, I know it's six in the morning—"

"It's five here, but never mind." Already Mom's wide awake again. "I take it this is the Marguerite from the Berkeleyverse?"

"Uh, yeah, it is." They've been brought in on this too? Wow, the Cambridgeverse works fast.

I hear my mother shouting, "Henry, get out of bed! It's the other Marguerite!"

In the farther distance, Dad says, "The good one or the bad one?"

"The good one," my mom replies, and I have to grin.

When I hear her pick up the receiver again, I hastily say, "Listen, Mom, I'm so sorry about not telling you guys the truth the last time I was here."

"Perfectly all right, sweetheart. I won't deny it was strange when our Marguerite informed us of the situation—but uncovering the full truth behind Conley's plans made your subterfuge worthwhile for everyone involved."

While she speaks, another receiver picks up, and Dad interjects, "Honestly, we should've suspected it."

"And you know it was Wicked who came here last, right? I mean, the Home Office me. You didn't . . . listen to her, do anything she asked you to do?"

"Wicked," Dad says. "An appropriate name. But no, we knew how to work around her. We'd been on the lookout for her more than twelve hours before she arrived, and we knew our own Marguerite almost certainly wasn't at risk."

"How could you be so sure?" Wicked hasn't hesitated before killing any of the others.

"Because the last universe Wyatt Conley's ever going to destroy is his own." Dad's voice has that tone that means, *sweetheart, you haven't been thinking.* It irritates me, usually, but this time my father has a point. "He murders tactically. Not out of pure cruelty. Otherwise we'd all have been goners long before now."

Mom adds, "Also Conley clings to the hope of working with a perfect traveler, particularly you. Your dimension has the technology and represents a threat. You're the only possible way he has to ameliorate that threat, save destroying the dimension altogether."

"He'd do that," I say quietly. "He's already destroyed at least one."

My parents are both silent for a moment, as if paying their respects to the dead. Mom finally continues, "He still wants your cooperation. Wicked, as you call her, is so fanatically devoted to the cause that she makes him believe he can persuade you. And we must keep him focused on that goal—because it won't be long before he realizes we're tracking Wicked's movements. He has to suspect already."

"He does." I fiddle with the chain around my neck. "He didn't ask me where I got this Firebird, even though that should've been his first question."

"Bloody hell." Dad exhales sharply. "Well, when you speak to him next, try to figure out how much he knows. Of course you're going to do that already, aren't you? But keep on him. Give away nothing. Let him hint and guess."

"Okay. I can do that." I flop down on the sofa, feeling as if I could fall asleep again just from the comforting sound of my parents' voices. "Thanks, Dad. It's good to have something to do besides just . . . chasing around after Wicked, even though I can never catch her."

Mom says, "Don't say that. You're not wasting time, Marguerite."

"But the Romeverse is gone—and two other Marguerites died anyway—"

"And you saved another from a fatal accident in outer space," Mom insists. "You're distracting Conley from what the rest of us are doing, and buying us time."

"We need that time," my father adds. "It takes a while for the asymmetries to spread throughout a dimension and protect it fully. So don't doubt yourself for a moment, sweetheart. You're doing good work."

If they're talking to the other dimensions, maybe I'm not the only one they're keeping track of. "Can you tell me where my Paul Markov is?"

"Still in the Egyptverse," Mom says. "Building the stabilizer must take a while there, and by now we assume he has to find a way to recharge his Firebird, which must be at low levels. But the technology of that world, if it's like our own at a similar stage of development, should allow him to do so if he can get to a city, Cairo perhaps—"

Assume? Of course. Just because they can track us through the dimensions doesn't mean they can communicate with us. Communication is only possible between worlds at a high enough state of technology. While Paul is in the Egyptverse, he has no idea what else is happening.

"Does he know I'm alive?" I ask.

The next pause lasts long enough that I know the answer before my dad says, "He hasn't learned what happened to the Romeverse at all. So he has no reason to fear for you. Well, besides the homicidal maniac version of you on the loose, which I suppose is reason enough."

"He doesn't know how to follow me. He could only track my Firebird, and that's going to lead"—my gut sinks—"to the Home Office."

"We'll try to send a warning." My mother obviously doesn't want to drag me down. "Hang on, Marguerite. Stay strong."

I want to. I will. But it seems like my dangers are multiplying every moment. Like I tried to smash through a glass barrier and am now surrounded by a thousand tiny shards, each one sharp enough to draw blood.

My invitation to lunch comes as a note hand-delivered by the concierge. My ride is provided by a hulking limo driver who either speaks no English or is fully committed to pretending he doesn't. I wear jeans and a dark red T-shirt from the depths of my duffel bag, both wrinkled in the extreme. Wyatt Conley isn't worth the effort of dressing up, much less ironing.

I'm taken to a restaurant in a sort of closed-circle area with a central green space large enough for a few tropical trees to loom high overhead, and plenty of other greenery frames the other shops and salons. Many of the buildings here have an open-air structure, even the kind of businesses where I'd never expect it, like banks. The road loops around the circle before stretching straight again not far past this restaurant where I've been shown to a table just under shady palm fronds.

No sooner do I pick up the menu than I hear the roar of a V8 engine. The reason I can identify that sound is behind the wheel of the red sports car speeding into the circle, namely Theo. He parks on the far side of the green area, and I'm not surprised to see Wyatt Conley getting out of the passenger side.

"Limos are elegant, of course," Conley says as he walks up

to me, Theo lagging behind. "But I tend to prefer a sexier ride."

"Seems about right." I fold my arms across my chest. "Men have been using sports cars to compensate for small penises for a long time. Why shouldn't you?"

Conley's eyes narrow, but he collects himself after only a moment. "Enough childishness, Marguerite. It's time to deal."

As he takes his seat, I steal a look at Theo. He looks neither smug nor ashamed. He's not avoiding my gaze like he did yesterday, but he's not engaging with me, either. It's like he's deep in thought, although I have no idea what could be more important than this. Maybe he really doesn't care what becomes of me at all.

A waitress brings us coffees and presents the heavy-bound menus. Conley doesn't even look at his before laying it across his plate. "I want to be clear about a couple of things from the beginning. One, the offer of a true partnership that I came to you with months ago? That's no longer on the table. Matters have progressed too far for that. But I think we can still come to terms you'll find reasonable—and certainly more inviting than the alternative."

Pollo *means chicken,* I think, as I refuse to look away from the menu. Just get something *pollo* and you're safe. "I don't think the offer of a true partnership was ever on the table. But go ahead. Hit me with these exciting terms."

"I guarantee your safety, and your family's, and that of your world's Paul Markov. We will make no attempt to destroy your home universe, and nobody of your acquaintance will ever be splintered—at least, not because of anybody at Triad. That's all you get." Conley sighs with satisfaction. He thinks he's finally worn me down. "In return, you travel when I want you to, where I want you to, and do what I want you to. If that includes the destruction of a universe, you do it. And if that prospect troubles you, well, just think of it as their world dying to save yours."

I don't say anything, just cover my face with one hand. Is that enough for him to think I'm wavering? If he thinks I'm at least unsure, at least considering what he wants, then maybe he'll tell Wicked to leave whatever "neutral" universe she's in so I can get on the move again.

And if he sees that I'm tired—that I'm afraid of never getting Paul back, that I can't bear the thought of endangering even one more world—that's nothing but the truth.

"You're going to lose," Conley continues, his voice quieter now. Deadly. I am finally hearing the snake beneath his skin. "You know your world doesn't have a chance, not against this dimension and the Home Office united. Of course you won't admit it. It hurts your pride just having to sit here and take this from me. You think I don't understand how much you hate me? Do you really think you're hiding it so well behind your little menu? Give up, Marguerite. You can't win. All you can do is save yourself and yours. Is swallowing your pride really too much to do for the people you love?"

I think of the sacrifices I've made—the sacrifices Mom, Dad, Paul, and even my Theo have made—and I know that

Wyatt Conley has no idea how much someone would do for the people they love. Like this silent, morose Theo at his side, he loves no one but himself.

"Let me think," I say. "I have to think."

"What is there to think about?" Conley's voice rises enough for diners at other tables to glance at us, the rude Americans having a fight over lunch. He controls himself better as he adds, "You don't get a better offer."

I shrug. "The Home Office might give me one."

Impatiently Wyatt Conley says, "I speak for both of the other two universes of Triad—"

"You think you do. But I've visited the Home Office for myself." That gaudy, twisted megalopolis had choked off both earth and sky. "And if you think they're huge fans of yours, wow, are you wrong."

Theo lifts his head now. I've actually piqued his interest. Conley remains quiet for a few seconds before smirking. "Amateur-level theatrics? I thought you were smarter than that."

"It's not theatrics. It's the absolute truth." The one truly pleasant memory I have of the Home Office is of the moment when I learned this. "They think you go too far, and they intend to 'rein you in' pretty soon. And what was it your Home Office self called you? Hmmm . . . oh, yeah. He called you a 'total asshole.' That's verbatim."

The waitress approaches to take our orders, gets a good look at the facial expressions around the table, and then walks off. She's smart.

"You're making this up," Conley says flatly.

"If you believed that, you'd be laughing at me now." It's safe to put down the menu and spear him with my gaze. "But you know I'm being completely honest. The three founders of Triad in the Home Office loathe you, and they're counting down the days until they can put you in your place."

Conley shoots back, "We have an alliance."

"Three founders. One of them is another you who can't stand you. The other two are my parents. Who love me—any version of me!—a whole lot more than they'll ever care about you. Face it, Conley. If you want a deal, you'd better improve your offer. Because I know exactly where to go to find a better one."

All of his studied casualness drops away. "They gave you that Firebird, didn't they? I knew it! I knew they wouldn't leave well enough alone!"

I hadn't even thought about that as a cover story, and it's better than anything I could've come up with. "Do you want to go back and reconsider your options?"

Conley pushes his chair back from the table. He's always looked like an overgrown middle schooler, and now he's acting like one. "I'm going to go back and have a few words with the Home Office. In the end, we need only one perfect traveler, and it doesn't have to be you. If you have a preference for which dimension you'd like to die in, this is the time to speak up. All I can promise you at this point is that your home is going to go up in ash and smoke, and I'm going to enjoy watching it burn."

No. Oh, no. I pushed him too far, and I've made him desperate. "Wait—I didn't say you couldn't make me a better offer—better than the Home Office—"

"Too late," he says. "Beck, come with me."

"I'm with you, boss." Theo's voice sounds oddly distant. "Got the keys in my hand already."

"Please." Tears are coming to my eyes. "Don't, please!"

"So you finally learned to beg. I like the sound of that. But not enough to care." With that, Conley stalks off.

I slump back in my chair as he and Theo go to the car, my vision blurring as I start to cry. Why did I do that? I was only supposed to be figuring out how much he knew, not pissing him off. It felt so good to tell him off for once—to use the truth against him—and now my big mouth may have condemned my entire dimension to death.

Would I die with it? If my spirit is in another dimension when my body is destroyed, do I perish or become some kind of . . . ghost?

At least my world knows how to defend itself. By now surely they've created the asymmetry that will protect them. Still, it takes time for that to work; Dad said so this morning. Have they had enough time? If Wyatt Conley moves against them now, can they possibly survive?

I wipe my face with the napkin, determined to find another landline phone and warn the other worlds of the multiverse what's about to happen. The sports car's engine roars to life—that would be Theo behind the wheel, revving it up. I guess even now, with the death of an entire dimension at hand, Theo loves his horsepower. With a squeal of brakes, the sports car pulls out of its parking space and starts coming around the circle.

But as the car takes the curve, it accelerates, moving so fast I gasp. It passes by me in a red blur, the loud engine not quite drowning out the worried murmurs of the other diners. When the road straightens at the end of the loop, Theo floors it, pushing the car to at least seventy miles per hour and probably more—

—and he doesn't take the final curve.

He doesn't even try.

I stare, open-mouthed, as Theo drives the car over the curb, sending it airborne for the split second before it crashes.

18

SCREAMS ERUPT FROM EVERYONE AROUND ME AS THE RED sports car smashes into the thick concrete column of the streetlights. The deafening slam of metal shifts into the hiss of a demolished engine, and through the thick smoke I can see the car almost torn in two.

How could Theo have crashed the car? I think, stunned, before the truth descends:

Theo crashed on purpose.

My body and brain can't agree on what to do. I stand there swaying, wanting to faint, then take a few lurching steps forward before bracing myself against a lamppost to keep myself from falling down. Within a few seconds, though, I'm able to push myself on and run to the wreckage. Someone shouts at me in Spanish, probably warning me to pull back to safety, but Theo explained once that crashed cars only explode in the movies. Nothing short of an explosion could keep me away.

I come up on the passenger side, where the door has been knocked off, and Conley—

It's all I can do not to throw up. I hate this man . . . I mean, I hated him, when he was alive. But looking at him now nauseates me. Never did I need to see Conley's head split open. I never wanted to learn how brain fluid smells. Now I can never forget it.

The coldest, most calculating part of my mind—the part Wicked would understand—knows that this dramatically changes the odds. In this dimension, Triad had only one leader, who was also their only perfect traveler. This world will never be a risk to mine again.

Yet none of that seems important compared to the fact that Theo is somewhere in this wreckage. He did this on purpose, and instinctively I know that he did it for me.

"Theo?" My voice cracks as I edge around the back of the vehicle. *Please let him not be torn up like this, please don't let him be split open, please, please, please.* "Theo, can you hear me?"

"Meg?"

Finally I reach the driver's-side door. Theo slumps in his seat, which hangs unnaturally far back—the impact must have dislodged it. His face is already swollen and purple. Blood trickles from his nose and ears. One of his arms, obviously broken in multiple places, lies limply across the gearshift. With the other, he reaches for me.

I take his hand, pretending not to notice the blood pooling between our palms. This is the same person who murdered the other me, the same fingers that gripped the scarf he knotted around my throat. Yet I can't look into his bruised, despairing face—without accepting his grip. His hand is weak and shaky in mine. "Theo, what did you do?"

"I knew . . . knew I could take him out." Theo tries to smirk, but then he coughs and winces from the pain. "The son of a bitch never . . . wore his seat belt. Always . . . always wear your—"

His seat belt cuts into his torso so unnaturally. Several of his ribs must be broken. Maybe his sternum, too. "Hang on. They must've called an ambulance, so the doctors will be here any second. Okay? Hang on."

"That's not . . . how this goes." His head lolls toward me. His eyes seem to meet mine, but I'm not sure he can even see me. "I took a life. You can . . . you can only pay for a life with a life."

"Oh, God, Theo—" I hate this Theo so much. I've hit him, cursed him, even attempted to kill him. But I'm not made of the kind of stuff that could enjoy watching him die.

My mind shows me an image from my second night in an alternate dimension: the Londonverse, where I wore the body of a girl who's already dead. I believed my father had been murdered, and I staggered around drunk in a nightclub in the vain hopes that the alcohol would numb the endless pain inside. Theo came to me then, picked me up in his arms and held me right there in the club, cradling me against his chest while I sobbed, even as the drumbeat throbbed and the dancers swayed around us. He was pretending to be my Theo—manipulating me, even using me—but that night, I know, he genuinely hurt for me too. That moment might have been the realest I ever shared with this Theo, until this one, right now.

"Conley . . . he . . . he told the other one to move on." He swallows, winces, gasps. "You have to follow her."

"I will," I promise. "Right away."

"You asked me . . . how she felt. The other you. While I killed her." Theo tries to smile, but his cut lip makes it grotesque. "Now I know."

He shudders—no, spasms. He coughs again, and the trickle of blood from his nose turns into a heavy flow. His eyes roll up in his head, and his breath rattles in his chest.

"No," I squeeze his hand more tightly. As much as I've hated him, it turns out I can't bear to watch him die. "No, Theo, hang on. You can still help us. You can be the one who brings the Triadverse around! You could undo some of the damage—help bring things back. . . ." My voice trails off as I realize he can't hear me anymore

The rattle in his chest stops, and for a moment I think that's it, until Theo whispers, "Meg . . ."

His hand goes slack in mine. Blood flowing from his nose and ears slows, then stops. Theo's head falls back, free of the broken car seat. Nobody is here any longer.

Trembling, I take my hand from his and touch his face. Closing his eyes feels impossibly strange, his eyelids thin and fragile against my fingertips. When I pull back, I see the bloodstains I left behind.

I stagger away from the wreck, oblivious to the gore

dripping from my hand. Far away I hear sirens. Whatever limo driver or security guard or goon Conley had watching me obviously thinks I'm no longer a priority, or figures he's no longer on anybody's payroll. At any rate, nobody is trying to capture me or hurt me. I'm on my own in Ecuador, completely alone.

Think. I reach the coffeehouse on the corner, where all the patrons have gathered to gawp, and sink into one of their woven-cane chairs. *You can reach a landline and call your parents again. They'll come and get you.* I mean they'll come get the Triadverse Marguerite. As soon as I'm sure she's okay, I intend to follow Theo's advice and return to pursuing Wicked.

No, I need *Paul.* He's here in this very city. But how do I find Paul in the middle of an enormous city I don't know and where I don't speak more than three dozen words of the language?

I focus again on the shattered wreck smoldering in front of me and realize—one of the world's richest men just died violently in public. This will be on YouTube within minutes, if it isn't already. News crews will get here before the ambulances do. Paul will find out as fast as everyone else on the globe, and if I'm in any of the pictures or video being taken by the zillion smartphones I see being held up by the murmuring crowd, he'll see I'm here.

Paul will know to come for me.

I have Theo's blood all over my hands. The thought seems simultaneously incredibly important and a thousand miles away. Some paper napkins have been left on a nearby table. I grab a couple and start scrubbing away the red. There's so much red. Paul can't see this, he can't know what happened to the guy who used to call him little brother.

Blood stains my shirt, my jeans, my skin, but the Firebird remains spotless. The cause of all this turmoil glints in the noonday light, bright as ever.

Theo said Conley had already signaled to Wicked. How? They can't communicate the way we do, or else they'd already know . . . wait. Of course. Romola. He called her, she swapped universes long enough to make a phone call, and it's done. Maybe he has other henchmen, other imperfect travelers willing to leap between worlds and screw stuff up for the rest of us, but I bet Romola's the only one in on the whole scheme.

The point is, Wicked's gone. I have a chance now to leap to this so-called "neutral universe," since this Firebird picked up her trail as soon as I got here. Then the race begins again.

At the moment, a neutral universe sounds like an almost unbelievable luxury.

I take a pen and my dog-eared boarding pass for the San Francisco–Quito flight and jot down a few notes. While I know my other selves remember my time in their bodies, this might be too much of a shock for my Triadverse self to handle in the first several minutes. I put down the hotel name and room number and underline the words *Paul will be here soon*. Part of me wants to linger until he arrives, to take momentary comfort in his arms . . . but he should be with his own Marguerite when he sees this. They need each other.

No need to mention that Conley's dead, that Theo gave his life to protect us, or that she shouldn't walk back to the car and look inside. What I saw there—what Theo did—neither she nor I will ever be able to forget that as long as we live.

I tuck the boarding pass in the front pocket of my T-shirt, take a deep breath, and leap away.

After seeing two people die in a violent car accident, it's jarring to jump into myself behind the wheel of a car.

But this car isn't on the road.

It's in the water.

Oh, my God. Oh, my God! Frantically I paw at the door, look out at the river or bay or whatever is now lapping over the hood, and feel the first trickles dampening my feet. Panic rushes in along with the water. I look up for the sunroof—our new car at home has one—but not here. Water closes over the hood completely, and the car tilts as it begins to sink.

My fingers clasp the handle before I remember, *Don't open it.*

Back in late November, when we believed my father had been murdered, we thought he'd drowned when his sabotaged car crashed into the water. Dad turned out to have been kidnapped into a parallel dimension instead, but none of the rest of us discovered that for nearly a month.

And the thing is, when you mourn someone's death for that long, you don't get over it instantly, even if you get them back.

I had nightmares about Dad's crash for more than six weeks after he was back home safe and sound. Paul insisted that knowledge was the answer, that if I understood what to do in that situation, eventually I'd save myself in the dream and the nightmares would end. It didn't exactly work that way—the bad dreams trailed off on their own. But those dozens of videos of safety experts or TV reporters I watched, all of them explaining how to escape from a sinking car, told me the water pressure makes the door hard to open. You're supposed to try to get out through the window instead.

My finger finds the window controls, and the glass slides halfway down, then stops. At the exact same instant, the entire dashboard goes dark. Water has shorted out the car's electrical system.

The opening at the top of the window might be wide enough for me to squeeze through.

Might.

I slip my head through, angle my shoulders, and start pulling myself out. But the glass snags on my belt, and even as I wriggle desperately, the car keeps sinking. With one hand I fumble at the belt, manage to undo it, and then brace both my palms against the car door and push myself out as hard as I can. The force pulls my jeans down to my thighs, but now I can get my hips through the window. Almost free.

The car tilts and I splash into the water, my lower legs still trapped between the window and the door. I struggle, but my feet catch in the opening. For one sickening moment I think the car's going to tow me down like an anchor, all the way to the bottom. In the last instant before I go under, I suck in a deep breath.

I go under. Everything turns so cold. My hair swirls around me in a dark cloud. Sunlight turns the muddy water amber. The car still drags at my legs, its weight sure to drag me to my death if I can't shake it. Desperately I kick and kick and—yes!—my feet slide free. My jeans and shoes went with the car, and now I'm able to swim upward.

When my head breaks the surface, I gasp for air. A small crowd has gathered on the road, near the smashed rail that must show where my car plunged in. No strong current drags me down, and thank God, because I'm not sure I could fight it. The lack of oxygen, combined with extreme physical exertion, dizzies me—but adrenaline has begun to kick in. I have the strength to keep going. Struggling, I head for shore.

Thank you, Dad, I think as I feel the first riverbank slime beneath my bare feet. *Thank you, Paul.* All those nightmares and videos just saved my life.

For a while, I just lie on the riverbank, too exhausted to even cover myself. If the world wants to look at my butt through my wet underwear, it can go right ahead. At the moment I couldn't care less.

I can handle a lot. I know this about myself by now. But those two moments, back to back, have left me so ragged and tired that I am beyond action. Beyond caring. Some kind woman who keeps a first-aid kit in her car covers me with one of those silvery safety blankets. So I allow myself a few moments to simply exist. To say nothing to myself beyond the thought, *I'm warm.*

By the time the police arrive, though, I'm able to talk again.

"Witnesses said it looked like you drove off the side on purpose," says the cop, who squats in front of me with a notepad in his hands. "But then you fought like hell to get out of there."

"I didn't mean to drive into the water." A droplet makes its way down one of my curls before falling on my cheek. "I—I think I fell asleep at the wheel."

"Fell asleep? If I run a field sobriety test on you, what's it going to show me?"

I wouldn't put it past Wicked to do a couple of shots before driving into a river, but I feel totally, almost brutally sober. "I'm clean. I swear. But I've been putting in a lot of all-nighters, and—"

"You're lucky you didn't hurt somebody else." The cop seems to believe me, but he heads off to get the Breathalyzer anyway. "Hang tight. Who can we call for you?"

My phone, if it was on me at the time of the crash, is now at the bottom of the river, completely ruined. So I give the cops my home landline number, but when nobody answers, and I can't remember any of the other numbers off the top of my head, they agree to give me a ride home. If everyone's out, well, I know where the spare key is kept.

In my universe, anyway. But this one looks close. The license plates are all from California, and although I'm not positive, I'm pretty sure I've seen this area before. It can't be too far from our house in Berkeley. Even this sweater is one I own at home.

A neutral universe, Conley said. One not marked for destruction—one where this world's Marguerite didn't have to die. Wicked tried to kill her anyway.

Was Conley lying to me? He never hesitated to when it served his purposes. This time, though, I think he was telling the truth.

I think Wicked tried to kill this Marguerite . . . just for the fun of it.

She calls it an art form, Paul told me in the Home Office. What brushes and paints are to me, manipulation and murder are to her.

And I know—from my own heart, and from the experiences of so many other Marguerites—I'll never give up my art.

When we get to the house, Mom's car is out front, but the mail is jammed in the box like she hasn't checked it in days. The cop who brought me here frowns. "Your parents on a trip?"

"They go to lots of academic conferences." Which is true, though they always remember to put through a stop-mail order. Well, I guess one time they forgot. I tilt one of the flowerpots over to see the spare key just where it always is, outlined by a dusting of soil. "See? I'm good."

The cop shows me in, gives me a citation report, and tells me to come down to the station tomorrow to talk with them about this. Although I don't think I'm going to be in serious trouble, I suspect a suspended license is in this Marguerite's future. But she won't mind. Not when I leave here and she remembers what happened, and what nearly happened. Calling Uber for six months is a small price to pay compared to drowning.

Once the police car finally pulls away, I lock the door behind me and walk toward my room. My steps slow as I take a good look around. This is my house, but something's not right.

In fact, something is very, very wrong.

Mom's houseplants, her pride and joy . . . they're all dying. Some are already dead. Their leaves have turned brown and curled at the edges for lack of water. The sight shocks me so much that I turn to get the watering can before I think, *Shower and put on some clothes first.* I'm still wearing the silvery blanket wrapped around me and not much else.

Then I hear my mom's voice from her bedroom. "Who is it?"

"Mom? Were you asleep?" None of this makes any sense to me. "I was in a car accident—I'm okay, but the car sank—"

My words trail off as Mom shambles into view. She's never been a fashion plate, wears sweaters nearly as old as I am, and so far as I know is allergic to makeup. But the shapeless sweatpants and T-shirt she's wearing now are filthy and food-stained; her hair seems not to have been washed in at least a week. "Marguerite? What happened?"

"I think I fell asleep while I was driving."

That should shock her out of her doze. She'll come to me, ask questions about trajectories and velocities while she strokes my hair and tells me to take a warm bath.

Instead, Mom gets furious. "You can't even bother to take care of yourself! You yell at me for not caring, and then you go and do something like this?"

"I didn't mean to!" My mother is so even-tempered that I've hardly ever had to deal with her when she's this angry. Maybe not ever. Her eyes burn with a feverish light, and suddenly I'm afraid. Not *of* her. *For* her. Because whoever this unstable person is, she's not the Sophia Kovalenka I know. "I'm sorry, Mom. I'm sorry. I'll—I'll sell some paintings, maybe, start to pay you back for the car—"

"Right. It's all going to be fine once you're painting again, and I go back to the university. The new car will be just as good as the old one." Her smirk is bitter. "Any day now."

What can I say? "I'll make it up to you. I can. Somehow."

She puts her arms around me then, and I'm shocked by how thin she is. We're both bony, well beyond "fashionably thin," into the area where doctors quiz you about anorexia even though you came in for a flu shot. That's just how we are. But my mother has lost even more weight, to the point that it can't possibly be healthy, even for her. "I'm sorry, sweetheart." Mom murmurs into my damp hair. "I'm sorry. You know I love you."

"I love you too." As much as I mean those words, I say them mostly because I think she needs to hear it.

"If anything happened to you—"

"It won't. I promise. Look, see? I'm fine." I try to smile for her.

But Mom's expression darkens. "You can't promise me nothing will happen. No one can."

We stand facing each other for a few long terrible seconds, until I finally say. "I need to shower."

"And put on some dry things." For one brief moment, she kind of sounds like herself. "Then we can get some sleep."

"Pizza," I find myself saying. "Pizza, then sleep."

"Okay." Mom wanders back into her bedroom. Although she could be going for her phone to call the delivery guys, I suspect I'll have to be the one to do that.

Why does Mom look so terrible, and why did she act so weird about my car accident? How could she ever have let her plants die? I don't see any equations on the chalkboard wall; long-ago ones linger as mere shadows of white dust. Do Paul and Theo not come by here, or any other graduate students either?

And where's my dad?

As soon as I'm rinsed off and clothed again, I have to start exploring each of these questions. But I already suspect I won't like the answers.

All I know is that this version of my mother is the

weakest—the most broken—that I've ever found. If Wicked had murdered this version of me, already I know Mom wouldn't have been able to go on.

But Wicked tried anyway. Even in a neutral world, with no reason for violence, no orders from Wyatt Conley, Wicked still went in for the kill.

19

THE VERY FIRST GOOGLE SEARCH REVEALS THE DARKNESS hanging over this house.

LOCAL PROFESSOR, DAUGHTER MURDERED IN CARJACKING GONE WRONG

Although Dad and Josie were in his car, Josie was behind the wheel. This detail is only a random one in the story, because the reporter couldn't have understood the significance. If Josie had been driving her own car, nobody would have tried to carjack it, because carjackers aren't interested in bright yellow Volkswagen Beetles that the cops will spot within seconds. And if Dad had been the driver, he would've done exactly what the carjackers wanted: gotten out, made sure Josie did too, and handed over the keys.

But Josie's quick temper—the way she responds to any risk by rushing straight at it—that made her reckless. She "resisted leaving the vehicle," the story says, without specifying exactly how. Whatever she did, it spurred the would-be carjacker to fire his gun.

Ms. Caine, 21, died on the scene. Dr. Caine was able to speak with first responders but lost consciousness during transport to Alta Bates Medical Center, where he was declared dead on arrival.

You'd think I'd be used to finding worlds where one or more members of my family have been lost. It's happened often enough that I handle it better now. But it never gets easy.

If Josie was twenty-one when she died, that means this happened three years ago. Since then Mom's been . . . broken, I guess. Devastated. Is she even still teaching? On leave? We're still in the house, but to judge by the mail piling up outside, she's not coping well, if at all.

Which is why this makes me so completely furious.

I sit in my room, knees balled up to my chest, staring down at the glowing laptop screen. Josie's senior portrait smiles out at me from the screen, as does Dad's last faculty picture. How could Wicked try to take away the one person my mother had left? A chill goes through me as I realize my mom might even have committed suicide. That's what Wicked set her up for—she went after both of our lives this time.

The venomous cruelty of it goes beyond anything else I've seen of Wicked, especially because, according to Conley, there was no tactical reason for this Marguerite to die.

Wicked might enjoy her other murders, but I always thought that at least part of her motivation was getting Josie back. I've underestimated her sadism. I never guessed how low she would go.

And yet somehow, I have to acknowledge, Wicked and I must be the same.

I learned about the potential for darkness within Theo early on. Then I learned about the darkness Paul hides inside. But I turned out to be the darkest one of all.

Once in my life I planned to kill another human being. When I believed Paul had murdered my father, in that first rush of hate and loss and pain, I honestly thought I could kill. But even then, when the moment came, I hesitated—and thank God, because Paul was innocent and Dad was alive. And it wasn't even the strength of my hate that fueled me—it was the strength of my love for my dad. That brought me to the point of murder when nothing else could.

So what twisted another version of me into Wicked?

I look up at my walls, where my paintings decorate the room as usual. However, this is one of the few worlds I've visited where I don't focus on portraits. Instead, I've turned to landscapes, cityscapes, even some still lifes of fruit and vases, that kind of thing. This Marguerite's color work shows real depth, as does her treatment of light—I could learn from this. But I can sense the pain that has led her to avoid painting human faces.

With a deep breath, I sag back in my easy chair. I've

probably done everything I can do for this version of me. I definitely don't want to hang around this depressing universe any longer. I hate leaving Mom like this, but I can't bring back Dad and Josie for her. And another Marguerite will be put in danger any time now.

I take hold of the Firebird, try to jump. Nothing.

Exhaustion claims me, body and soul. Physically, my muscles still ache from my desperate car escape, and the bruises around my hipbones and knees have begun to throb. Emotionally, I'm so drained that I'm not sure I'd care if the house caught on fire.

Bed, I tell myself. Now. I'll set the alarm to go off every three hours or so; that way I can keep trying to jump out as soon as possible. But then I remember my phone sank in the river along with my car. Great.

In my own dimension, Josie gave me a Hello Kitty alarm clock for my sixth birthday. It doesn't get cooler than that when you're six. Josie took pride in having picked out such a great gift, and the alarm clock remained one of my prize possessions until well after the age when Hello Kitty felt like "my style." Even when I replaced it with my tPhone, I didn't throw out the alarm clock. It's still sitting in the back of my closet, serving as a makeshift dummy head for my knit winter caps.

If Josie gave me the clock in this dimension, too, then Hello Kitty is about to get called back into action. So I shuffle to the closet and flip on the light to start rummaging around, then stop.

My portfolio case has been jammed in the back corner, crumpled like paper, and all over the floor lie old canvases of mine. Frowning, I kneel to examine them. My first glimpse chills my heart.

It's a portrait of Josie—with the eyes scraped away.

I keep going through them, and over and over, the destruction is the same. Josie, Dad, and Mom, their eyes or mouths or both missing from their original portraits. The mutilation makes their faces look hollow and ghoulish—the stuff you'd expect to see in horror-movie posters. At first I wonder whether this Marguerite made an artistic choice to deface her old pictures as a symbol of the destruction of her family. But then I see the tiny flakes of paint on the floor of the closet. No, this was done within the past day or two.

In other words, Wicked did this.

Last of all I find a self-portrait, very like one of my earliest ones back home. The me in the picture is even wearing a blue flowered T-shirt I still own. But her entire face is missing, scraped away so violently that Wicked's knife tore the canvas in several places.

She hates herself more than any of the others. Sitting cross-legged on the closet floor between my rows of shoes, I study each of the faces in turn. But why does she hate them? Does she just hate everyone? Maybe something went wrong in utero, and my brain didn't develop into a normal person's. Wicked might be a psychopath, only the shell of a human being. . . .

But that answer is too easy. It lets me off the hook. If I'm going to beat Wicked at her own game, I have to understand her. That means I have to stop shielding myself behind all the ways I'm different from her.

I have to face the same darkness Theo had to acknowledge. The same darkness Paul is doing battle with even now. I have to take a hard look at Wicked and learn what we share. I have to learn how the two of us are the same.

So I try to imagine being the girl from the Home Office. Being me, there, in that dangerous, status-obsessed megalopolis, the daughter of two of that world's greatest inventors. Why would that mess me up? I don't understand how that would make me a murderer, but I can see how it would make me vain or snobbish. I can even see how it might distract me from my painting, or make me think less of it. In my own world, Mom and Dad have always encouraged me: buying brushes and canvases, convincing professors in the art department at the university to let me audit technical classes, and never once asking questions like *But how will you make a living?*

In the Home Office, though, money is more than power— it's also virtue. You are what you make. You bring cash value or you are worthless.

So Wicked would always have been overlooked. Underappreciated. And when Triad chose Josie to be that universe's perfect traveler, and Wyatt Conley even fell in love with her . . . she must have felt totally invisible.

It's not an excuse. It's not even an explanation. But on a fundamental, inexpressible level, I know that I have finally seen something in her soul that might be like mine.

The vandalized canvases lie across my legs, staring up blankly. When Josie died, both my parents and Conley became obsessed with getting back the splinters of her soul, because they believed that might bring her back. They plunged into this multi-universe conspiracy and became willing to collapse other universes. Josie eclipsed the other me even more completely after her death than when she was alive.

The Home Office's Paul told me my counterpart there was Triad's most enthusiastic volunteer. Home Office Theo, less politely but maybe more accurately, called her a bitch. Now I see her doing everything she can to prove herself— braver, more ruthless, more unstoppable than even Josie had ever been, all for the sake of people she must have resented deeply.

If she wins, what's her reward? Josie returns to life to overshadow her once more.

Wait. This happened three years ago? My eyes widen. This universe wasn't a neutral one chosen at random—this was the one where their Josie died. When Wicked came here, she would've found my mom broken and depressed. She would've seen this house falling apart even though I was still here. Instead of having empathy, Wicked must have thought, *See, I'm still not enough. I'll never be enough for her. When she realizes she lost me too, then she'll finally be sorry.*

It's almost as if I can feel myself in the driver's seat of that car, looking at the water. *I'll show her,* Wicked would've thought in the moment before she stomped down on the gas.

There's more to it than this, I'm sure. Wicked's glee in what she's doing is still unfathomable and unforgivable.

But I've gotten at the root. I know what drives her. Behind her endless malevolence is pain she can't heal, no matter how many universes she tears down.

Maybe the time will come when I can use this knowledge against her.

Already I know that I have to start fighting back wherever and whenever I can every single time.

"Mom?" I call as I walk toward her bedroom. I've spent hours mulling this over. The sky outside has started to lighten, hinting at dawn. "Mom, get up."

From behind her door I hear her mumble, "Marguerite?" I take that as permission to come in, and I do. When I see what her room looks like, I wish I hadn't. It smells like unwashed laundry in here, and the other side of the bed—where Dad would've slept—is piled high with junk mail, crumpled socks, and a couple of used paper plates. Mom sits up from the rubble, scratching her head. "Sweetheart, what's wrong?"

"Mom, you do research on parallel dimensions, right? On different quantum realities?"

She frowns in consternation. "I—you know I'm on academic leave—"

"But that's your field of research. Yes?"

"Of course it was. Your father and I worked on that together." Now she's irritated. "Why did you wake me up to—"

She cuts herself off the moment I reach for the chain around my neck and pull out the Firebird. "I'm not your Marguerite, Mom. I'm here from another dimension."

"What is that supposed to be?"

"Look at it, Mom." I sit beside her on the bed. "Look at the Firebird and tell me you didn't make this."

"What the—" Her hands curve around the locket, and her jaw drops open.

"You've invented the Firebird in several dimensions now." For the time being I stick to the simplest part of the explanation. I'm not sure how much Mom can take all at once. "I've been traveling through several of them, and the Firebird finally brought me here. It brought me to you."

My mother says nothing. She just sits there examining it, not saying a word—until she starts making a sound I think must be crying. But when Mom looks back up at me, she's laughing. "We did it," she says, tears in her eyes and a huge smile spreading across her face. Thin and filthy as she is, suddenly she's Mom again. "Henry and I. We did it."

I hug her tightly. "You better believe you did."

By the time we eat breakfast, I've filled Mom in on the essentials. Although we're both exhausted from lack of sleep, I can tell Mom is awake again in a way she hasn't been since Dad and Josie died.

"You were acting strangely the past couple of days." She sips from her cup of Darjeeling. "But never in a thousand years would I have suspected this."

"Did you ever work with a grad student named Paul Markov in this dimension?" I ask. "Or Theo Beck?"

Mom shakes her head no. "I haven't served as an advisor for any students since . . . well, since."

Both Paul and Theo probably enrolled in different graduate programs, in search of different mentors. "Do you have any former students you can reach out to who might work with you on this?"

"Xiaoting, perhaps. She's an assistant professor at Yale now. I've been meaning to call her—she emailed me, and I never got around to—"

"Reach out to her." Mom needs her support system back. Xiaoting and the other grad students who practically moved in with us over the years—they'd be a good place to start. "Get in touch with as many of your former students as you can. Soon you could make one of these yourself. Once all of this is over, I'll see whether Paul or Theo can come to this dimension and talk you through it for a few days."

"And if I can figure out how to communicate through the dimensions, I might be able to move even faster than that." Her expression is wistful. "It won't be the same as being with my Henry and Josephine again. I understand that. But even knowing how they are . . . how they would be, if they were here . . . it feels like I can breathe again. Like I stopped breathing the moment they died but didn't realize it until today."

I hug her tightly from behind, and once again look at the wilted, withered houseplants. "I guess I haven't been doing so well either." It's not like I couldn't have picked up a watering can once or twice.

"No. We've buried ourselves in here together. I suppose we ought to find a new place. One without—one where we can make new memories."

Even the idea of moving away hurts her, I know. This house is more than a shelter and a place to put our stuff. In the deepest, best sense, it is home. But a person can have more than one home. "That might be a good idea."

Mom breathes in through her nose, out through her mouth—a sign she's forcing herself to move on. "I'll start working on cross-dimensional communications immediately. And I'll know to watch for visitors."

"Come up with a security question, maybe. The others won't be able to remember the answer, and if I need to come back here, I'll always tell you who I am."

"Why did you decide to tell me?"

"I'm telling all the worlds from now on." My mind is made up. "At least the ones where I wouldn't be burned as a witch for it. You guys have a right to understand what's happening. Besides, the more universes that team up against Triad, the better."

The Triadverse itself is effectively taken care of. Conley kept the power and knowledge to himself there, and he's dead. So far as I know, I'm the only perfect traveler left in the multiverse.

We can take the initiative, I think. We can turn the tide.

"Tell me again something else about how they are," Mom

says. "Just one more thing."

"Let's see. Josie is considering taking up competitive surfing—part-time, so you don't have to worry about her dropping out. And Dad was so psyched about getting one of those cars that parks itself. Was he as bad at parallel parking in this universe as he was in ours?"

"Worse, probably." Mom turns toward me and brushes one of my curls from my face. "When will you try to leave this dimension? I'm not trying to rush you, sweetheart, but I really can't wait to talk all of this over with my own Marguerite."

"Soon. I ought to try now." All my good intentions to keep checking through the night vanished when I had my breakthrough about Wicked. At least her more elaborate scenarios usually take a while to set up.

"One thing," Mom says as I take the Firebird in hand. "Don't underestimate your will, Marguerite. Or hers."

I nod and hit the controls, expecting nothing—

—and then it's all I can do to catch myself against the tiles before I slip and fall in the shower.

Hastily I take off the Firebird and put it on the nearby toilet tank. It's endured being dunked in water a few times now, and Mom and Dad tried to make sure it was waterproof, but I'd rather not tempt fate if I don't have to. Apparently I landed in this dimension mid-shampoo, so I pretty much have to rinse before I can do anything else.

In some ways I feel cheated that I didn't get to say more of a goodbye to my mother in the . . . the Josieverse. I have to stop relying on the opportunity for a longer farewell. My mom could've used another hug, more information . . . something. But what would ever have felt like enough? I couldn't give her Dad and Josie back, but I gave her the best thing I could: hope. Maybe that will be enough.

For now, I just have to figure out where I am, and why, and what Wicked's done this time. Although hair-washing isn't a supremely hazardous activity, Wicked wouldn't have left this dimension without putting me at risk.

This bathroom is really tiny, I think as I step out and wrap one towel around my hair before drying off with the other. Like it was in the Mafiaverse, when we lived in Manhattan. But there's something about the fixtures—the oddly streamlined faucet, the unfashionable royal blue of the tile, the ten-kinds-of-shower-head—that makes me think this isn't the United States. Sure enough, when I search through the vanity for some anti-frizz crème, the information on the back is given in both English and . . . is that Chinese? Japanese? Well, I'll find out.

Hanging on the bathroom hook is a simple white T-shirt, jeans, and a yellow silk kimono jacket embroidered with flowers and birds of paradise. It looks almost like one my counterpart had in the Londonverse; it was the only piece of clothing she owned that made me feel like we had something in common.

My hands aching—losing their grip—the Thames below me—
I have to save this one.

As I get dressed, I take stock of my physical condition. I

have no cuts. The house doesn't appear to be on fire. What did Wicked do? Then I see something else in the vanity drawer: a bottle of Tylenol. I shake it and realize only one or two pills remain.

If she were going to overdose, wouldn't she have taken them all? But I can't be sure. I wouldn't put it past Wicked to know exactly how much it would take to overdose.

So far I feel fine, but it might take a while for the medicine to kick in. Could medics pump my stomach if I warned them now, got started in time?

I put my Firebird back around my neck, knot my damp curls into a bun at the back of my neck, and walk through a house I've never seen before—surprisingly large, given the tiny bathroom. Teak wood covers the floors, and the walls are all stark white. Following the sound of running water takes me into an enormous dining room, with a table long enough to entertain royalty but as cluttered as the rainbow table back home, and slightly different species of potted plants in the corners. Bamboo appears to be a favorite, its jade-green stems stabbing upward from squat, square pots with mustard-colored glazes. "Hello?" I call as I head toward what looks like the kitchen.

"Have you decided to stop sulking and come down?" That's my mother's voice. I poke my head through the doorway to see her in teal-green yoga pants and a racerback tank, rinsing off plates before putting them in an industrial-size dishwasher that looks absurd in an otherwise normal kitchen. She smiles at me, with none of the pain and loss from that last universe, and it strikes me suddenly how beautiful Mom is when she's happy. "Oh, Marguerite, it's you."

I guess Josie must be in a bad mood upstairs. "Yeah. Hey, do you remember whether there was much Tylenol in this bottle?"

"Only a dose or two left, I think. Why?"

Wicked didn't OD, at least not on this. "No reason."

Mom returns to her washing. "I don't know what got into your sister this morning. Trying to sneak out of the house at dawn? What could she have been thinking?"

Knowing Josie, she probably thought the surf was up. But then, Josie's old enough to leave the house whenever she wants, and Mom and Dad would never try to stop her. Huh. Do I have a younger sister here? My memories of sturdy, obnoxious little Katya from the Russiaverse make me smile. "Not a clue."

"Well, I told her she could come down for dinner, so I suppose we'll see her soon. I do hope she's managed to calm herself." Mom sighs and smiles as she closes the dishwasher door. "Thank goodness only a couple of you ever lose your tempers at the same time."

"Um, okay." The way she put that was kind of weird, but not worth getting into. I need to figure out what's up with this Marguerite, not her bratty younger sister. Before I explain the whole story to this version of Mom, I'd like to know exactly what kind of help I should ask for first.

So I continue exploring the house. In the kitchen, the appliances are all slightly odd—either too small or industrial-large, with rounded corners, and again the sink has slightly different fixtures that say we're not in California anymore. We must be in Asia, I guess, but where? The dining room table is of course piled high with papers, on which are printed or scribbled equations that won't tell me much. But wait—is that—?

I pick up the Nobel Prize, a heavy disk of solid gold. Alfred Nobel's profile stares into the distance, hoping humanity will remember him for this instead of the invention of dynamite. Mom and Dad had already won the Nobel in the Triadverse, too, which means this is the second dimension where I've seen one of humanity's top accolades being used as a paperweight.

"Heard from any alternate dimensions lately?" I call to Mom. If they won for inventing the technology, or at least proving their theory, she'll know what I mean. That's going to make this easy to explain.

But when my mother appears in the doorway between the kitchen and dining room, she's frowning. "Sweetheart, are you all right?" She steps forward and puts her hand on my forehead. "You were asking about the Tylenol. Is that because you're running a fever?"

"No, I was just—I'll explain in a minute." Obviously Mom has no idea what I'm talking about.

If they didn't win the Nobel for learning about parallel dimensions, then what did they win it for?

They might have been oceanographers again, I think as I keep going into a large living room where the windows all have heavy white cloth curtains, and look out on what seems to be yet more bamboo plants growing outside. In the distance is an urban cityscape. Or maybe Mom and Dad went into pure math.

The living room is more casual than the dining room, and about a jillion of my paintings are on the wall. Looks like I even do some sculpture, to judge by the molded clay hand on one bookshelf. And on the sliver of wall beside the main windows, I see some framed magazine covers with Mom and Dad's faces. One of the covers only has an illustration, though—an enormous aqua double helix, framed on both sides by identical profiles. At the top, just beneath the magazine title, is the bold headline THE CLONE AGE.

Clones?

"It's seven o'clock," says a voice that sounds familiar and yet strange. "That makes it dinner time, right? Are you going to let me out of prison yet, or do I have to go hungry?"

I look back to see my mother in the dining room with her hands on her hips, facing a very angry . . . me.

"Prison." Mom sighs. She is completely unfazed that my doppelganger just walked in. "Honestly, aren't you a little old for—"

"You know what I'm a little old for? Being treated like a toddler who threw a tantrum," snaps the other me. She's wearing a skater skirt and a T-shirt in almost identical shades of blue.

"Apparently you're not too old to act like one," Mom retorts. I just stand there, staring.

There are two of us. Two of me. Do I have an identical twin, or—?

I look back at that headline, THE CLONE AGE. Now I notice the line at the bottom, which reads WHAT THE CAINE FAMILY MEANS FOR OUR FUTURE.

I'm a clone. We're clones. In other words, in this universe, there is more than one person that the Firebird would count as being *me*. Multiple versions of me exist here, which means more than one Marguerite could travel to this dimension at the same time. . . .

Hurrying back into the dining room, I stare at this other version of myself. Sure enough, just at the neckline of her T-shirt, I can see the chain of her Firebird.

When I walk in, at first she's surprised—as shocked to see me as I was to see her. But then the realization hits her, too.

Wicked and I are standing face-to-face at last.

20

I'm going to hurt her first.

I launch myself at her, sending her smashing into the wall as Mom screams. Wicked tries to claw my face and winds up snagging my damp hair and pulling hard. Wincing, I grab for her Firebird and feel the chain give.

She pushes me down, but I have time to tug off my own Firebird and throw them both toward the corner before she's on me. Wicked shoves my head onto the floor, hard, then does it again. This time I grab her hair and yank to the side, hard enough that she topples beside me.

"Marguerite! Victoire!" Mom goes on her knees beside us, trying to get in the way. "Have you lost your minds? Stop this—"

Wicked lets go of me long enough to savagely elbow Mom in the face, which is almost as shocking to see as it is for

269

Mom to experience. "This is between us!" Wicked shouts at my stunned mother.

That moment of distraction lets me roll atop Wicked and pin her arms to the floor. "You didn't think I'd ever catch up," I mutter as I try to still her wriggling. "You didn't count on this world, did—aaah!"

Wicked's teeth sink through my skin as she bites down savagely, but I don't let go. Mom grabs me in an effort to pull me away from Wicked. "Girls! Girls! What has gotten into you?"

I'm able to shake my mother off, but only for a moment. Nothing will stop her except the truth. "Mom! Listen to me. Did you ever think about studying the multiverse? Parallel realities?"

Wicked's eyes go wide. Wow, I look weird when I'm surprised.

Mom finally says, "Long ago—in undergraduate—why are you—"

"I'm not from your universe." I nod down toward the writhing Wicked. "She isn't either."

"You're insane!" Wicked shouts. "She's gone psycho, Mom. I noticed a long time ago. I just didn't want to say anything. But now she's lost it and you have to stop her, Mom, or she'll kill us both!"

"I'm not going to kill anyone," I promise. "Mom, go look at the Firebirds. The lockets I threw in the corner. You'll see what they are!"

Will she? Mom did before, but that was in a universe

where she and Dad had worked on that technology for more than a decade. Here, my mother isn't even a physicist. The Firebird won't serve as such easy proof.

"They're going to toss you in a padded cell and never let you out." Wicked practically spits the words at me. I knew I got flushed when I was angry, but I had no idea my cheeks reddened so much, or the depth of the wrinkle between my eyebrows that comes with my scowl. But the rage inside Wicked practically glows from her, like heat. That fury belongs to her alone. "You'll be shut in the loony bin without your stupid necklace and you'll never get out."

Hopefully I can avoid institutionalization—or, at least, get Wicked locked up with me. Though only at this moment do I realize that I have no idea what to do with Wicked now that I've caught her. It's not like we have a prison for Crimes Against the Multiverse.

"Both of you, get up from there." Mom has recovered from her astonishment, enough to go Cossack on us both. "Get up!"

I look up at my mother, hoping she'll see how afraid I am. How real this is. "I can't let her up, Mom. If I let her up, she might kill both of us, and I *am not* exaggerating, I mean kill."

"See?" Wicked whines. Tears glimmer in her eyes—probably only from the pain of having her hair pulled, but she's using them like a master actress. "She's psycho. Mom, I'm so scared—"

"Stop this," Mom repeats. She still hasn't made a move

271

toward the Firebird lockets, which lie in the corner. Instead she starts backing toward the table, where her cell phone is probably buried among the papers. "I mean it."

Then we all hear the door, and footsteps thumping toward us. That's Dad, probably, or Josie. Will one of them believe about the Firebirds? Or will Wicked finally get her chance to turn the others against me?

From where Mom's standing, she can see into the hallway, and she sighs in relief. "Oh, thank God. Help me with these two."

"No worries, Sophia," Theo says as he walks in.

Theo. My mind fills with the horrible image of the last time I saw his face: Triadverse Theo bloodied and dying in the wreckage of his sports car. This Theo, whichever he is, has the same Chucks on his feet, same faux-vintage Beatles T-shirt, same stubble on his chin. When he sees two Marguerites on the ground, his face goes white.

That's when I see the Firebird chain at his neck. It's not just any Theo—this one is mine.

He mutters, "What the—"

"We're clones," I say. "We're clones and so we can both be here at once."

"I followed her here and she's trying to kill me!" Wicked cries, instantly shifting strategy.

"Do you know what they're talking about?" Mom says, but nobody answers her.

Theo pauses, closes his eyes like he's thinking hard, then asks, "What's the single most embarrassing thing that happened to us in the Warverse?"

Wicked only stares. I say, "Finding ourselves in bed together."

"Excuse me?" Mom goes pale.

"It's not how it sounds!" Theo holds up his hands. "Well. Actually, it is how it sounds. But not between me and my Marguerite—or your Theo or your Marguerite, at least as far as I know—"

"They're both crazy," Wicked growls, but she knows she's about to get busted. She thrashes beneath me until I think she's going to throw me off. That's when Theo sinks down to sit on her legs, and she groans in defeat.

"Okay," Theo says, "first of all, Sophia, or Dr. Kovalenka, whatever I call you here, we need to talk about parallel dimensions."

"I already told her," I say. "But can you make her believe us? Like, with the math?"

Theo grins at me. "Extremely convincing math, coming up."

Half an hour later, Wicked is tied to a chair, the dining room table is covered with about fifty brand-new equations, and my mom's mind is seriously blown.

"This is unbelievable." She sits at the table staring into an unseen distance. I don't think I've ever gotten to shock my mother with science twice in the same day. "My God. Henry will be beside himself."

"I know how that feels," I say as I glance at Wicked

literally beside me. For her part, Wicked is now ignoring all of us. She points her chin high like a captured soldier willing to give no more information than her rank and serial number.

Not that any of us have gotten around to asking her anything. Instead, I'm watching Theo compare his Firebird with the one from the Warverse. "This is kinda crude, but to have built it under that kind of time pressure? I'm impressed."

"I'm just grateful," I say. "Without it, I would have died along with the Romeverse."

Theo's dark eyes meet mine for a moment, then he turns back to the Firebird lockets. "If it helps, we think that's the only dimension Triad has taken down so far."

"It helps some." But not much.

"Henry was going into physics," my mother says in her daze, "before we met at Oxford. Then he switched to genetics, mostly so we could be in the same courses."

"You guys met at college this time around?" Kind of mundane. I prefer my own universe, where my parents had bonded over shared crackpot theories long before they ever met in person. "In my dimension, you went to the Sorbonne instead."

"Oh, that explains it." Then she shakes her head and is Mom again. "It explains one point of divergence in the realities. But this conspiracy you've described, the threat this Triad represents—how do we defend against it?"

"Knowing is half the battle." Theo nods his head in Wicked's direction. "The other half is making your universe sufficiently asymmetric, in terms of your matter-to-antimatter ratios. I can do it with my Firebird and a stabilizer that we can whip up in a jiffy."

"How are they supposed to do that?" I gesture toward the wall of magazine headlines about clones. "This isn't their field."

"Or mine, in this universe. Apparently I decided genetics was my bag this go-round. Still, Paul and I should be able to talk them through it." Theo picks up his phone and inputs the unlock code; the screen shifts into an image of Paul next to his contact info. Surprised, I say, "How did you know the code?"

"Same one as at home. It's, um, my mom's birthday." Theo looks slightly sheepish at this evidence of his sentimental side, but he moves on. "Always a relief to find 'Markov' in a new universe's contacts list, isn't it? I'd be even more relieved if I'd actually been able to talk to him. No luck so far either calling or texting, but I assume he'll show any time now."

"Paul?" Mom brightens, no doubt thrilled to once again understand some part of what's happening. "He went on a scuba diving trip today. The sun's going down, though, so he should be back soon."

Scuba diving? Maybe that's what Paul does when he lives somewhere that has no mountains to climb. "Where are we, anyway? What country is this?"

My mom blinks. "Of course—you wouldn't even know. This is Singapore, sweetheart."

Singapore? Theo and I exchange glances, and he says,

"This is the place where you can get caned for chewing gum, right?"

"That's slightly more draconian than the truth." Mom pauses. "Slightly. Be on your best behavior. On the plus side, it's very safe here—at least, from any known threats."

Wicked, the previously unknown threat, continues to ignore us all.

According to Mom, she and Dad were awakened this morning by the sound of Victoire—a. k. a. the clone Wicked leaped into—attempting to sneak out of the house. They had no idea why she wanted to do that, but they grounded her until dinner and made her stay in her room the entire day. She had a bathroom, internet access, and food brought to her, so it's not like my parents put her in some kind of gulag, but Wicked's mouth twists in a sneer as my mother tells us that part of the story. No doubt she used the time to research quality methods of committing suicide in a way that might take me out with her.

But because she was awake so early, and got caught upstairs, Wicked never saw any of the others or the magazine covers. When she heard the other voices in the house, she would've assumed they were simply sisters unique to this universe. She had no idea she was a clone, and so she didn't suspect the danger until the very moment she saw me.

I turn my head to see Theo studying me instead of the Firebird. He's noticed my fascination and dread about Wicked. When I smile, he says, "Your face normally looks nothing like that, by the way. We've got some serious grumpy overload going on over there."

"I can be grumpy," I say, but we both know he's talking about something deeper and darker than that. "You must be doing better, huh? The Nightthief remedy is working." Then I reconsider my optimism. "Or is it—did you need to be in a healthier body for a while?"

"The Nightthief treatment helps." Theo takes a deep breath, as if letting that fear go. "Given enough time, yeah, I think I'll be back to myself again. But I can't deny, it feels good to be in a version of me who never had to deal with this stuff. I think I work out here, even. All the abs, none of the suffering." He runs his hand over his taut abdomen with satisfaction. I laugh despite myself, and am rewarded with his warmest smile. Then he turns to Mom. "Sophia, do you think you can keep an eye on—what did you call her again?"

Mom says "Victoire" at the same moment I say "Wicked." Then we look at each other, and Wicked huffs in exasperation.

Unfazed, Theo says, "Can you keep an eye on her?"

"Indeed I can. I couldn't manage a houseful of eight teenagers without knowing how to keep them in line." My mother tosses her hair, focused again.

But I can't get over—"Eight?"

"We tried four sets of twins, thinking we might get two or three live births." Mom shrugs. "The experiment exceeded our wildest hopes."

Theo looks as astonished as I feel. "And the others?"

"Most of the others wanted to go see some movie, the newest *Star Wars* thing, I think." Mom waves her hand around airily. Pop culture is not one of her top concerns. "Henry took them. I suppose they'll be back in half an hour or so."

"It won't take that long," Theo promises. He nods toward the front door, and I get to my feet to follow him.

Stepping outside feels like being slapped in the face with heat and humidity. Our house appears to be even grander than I thought—a bungalow of white stucco about twice the size of our home back in the Berkeley Hills. Yet the bungalow is dwarfed by the skyscrapers beyond, dozens of them, some so futuristic that I could imagine them in the London-verse or even the Home Office. Palm trees sway along the roadside, where compact cars zip along, and in the distance I can see an elevated train snaking along its track, a silhouette against the setting sun. I tuck my messy, half-dry hair back into the bun Wicked had wrecked so I won't look like some kind of escapee to any of the hyper-vigilant Singapore cops who might come by.

"What is it?" I ask Theo as he shuts the door. "Is there some problem at home, something Triad's doing, that you didn't want to say in front of Mom?"

"I was going to ask you the same thing." Theo leans against the door. "You look at me like I'm a puppy you'll have to put down. What happened?"

At first I want to make up a lie, but why? Theo's strong enough to hear the truth. I look into his eyes and say, "You

278

killed me. Then you died for me."

He listens, slack-jawed, as I explain what happened in the Egyptverse and then in the Triadverse. "Conley thought that if he ordered you to kill me, it would force you to see me as an enemy," I finish. "But he was wrong. Once the Triadverse's Theo had to face what he was really doing, once he actually had to see it for himself—he couldn't do it anymore. He finally turned against Wyatt Conley, and I think he removed that entire universe as a threat."

"Jesus." Theo runs one hand through his fashionably spiky hair. "I don't know what to say to you. I don't know how you can look at me."

"I can look at you because that wasn't you." I touch his shoulder. "Our choices matter more than anything else. And you've always chosen to help and protect me."

Theo's smile is crooked. "What about Paul? How's he doing?"

"I haven't seen him since the Spaceverse. We left things badly." I take a deep breath to get through it. "Paul's splintering messed up his brain—for real. The scan we ran looked like shattered glass. One of the other Pauls told me that you could recover from being splintered, or compensate for it at least, but you have to try. To try, you have to believe. And Paul doesn't."

"Little brother." Theo groans and thumps the back of his head softly against the front door. "Don't worry, Marguerite. You'll get through to him eventually."

"I hope so." How do you undo the programming of a

lifetime? Paul was literally raised to believe there was no such thing as unconditional love, and I don't know how to convince him otherwise.

"You will." Theo's dark brown eyes meet mine, wistful and resigned. "You'll be one of those college freshman girls convinced she's going to marry the guy she's already in love with. Except all those other girls will have broken up with their long-distance boyfriends by homecoming. You and Paul? You're going to make it."

"Theo—"

"You're looking at me like I'm too wounded to ever recover." He slaps one hand on his chest, exaggerating the wound, even though I can sense the very real pain he still feels. "Trust me, Marguerite, I'm gonna be just fine. I broke enough hearts along the way, so I had it coming."

"Nobody deserves a broken heart. Everybody deserves to be loved."

His smile falters, but only for a moment. "I am loved. Just not the way I was hoping for. Right?"

"Right."

"Here's what's going to happen. I'll go do my postdoc work somewhere else, at a university far away from California, far away from all of you. You and me and Paul, we'll still Skype and text, just a little less often than we used to. I'll spend some time feeling sorry for myself and listening to emo music, then I'll spend some time partying too hard and probably sleeping with a few of the wrong people, and finally someday I'm gonna meet a woman who actually makes me glad I didn't get you. Because she'll be to me what Paul is to you, right? She'll be the one."

"Yeah. She will." My words come out hoarse, strangled by the lump in my throat.

Theo continues, "Someday you'll come to my wedding, and I'll come to yours and Paul's—where I expect to be best man, remember—and eventually we'll argue about whose babies are cutest. Mine, probably, because look at this face." He points at his own widening smile. "And we'll drift further apart, but you and me and Paul—we will never, ever let go."

"Because we're friends, always." I sniffle as I try to smile back. "How can you be so . . . okay with this?"

"Because I want you to be happy. With or without me, whatever it takes." Theo sighs. "That's the difference between wanting someone and loving them."

"Thank you. For everything."

"You're most sincerely welcome. Now—one final request—all these other versions of me get to kiss you. I'd like to kiss you just once, as myself." He hesitates, the mask of cocky self-confidence slipping for a moment. "Only if you're okay with it. I'm going for poignant, not pathetic."

"Poignant works," I say, and he takes my face in his hands.

When Theo kisses me, it's gentle, even tender—demanding nothing. We embrace in this one still moment stolen from time, surrounded by the currents and choices that could have swept me away from Paul and onto Theo's shore. In infinite worlds, we are together, our other versions loving each other with their own sense of a perfect, unshakable destiny.

We don't live in any of those worlds. We live in one where Paul is my only love. But Theo has accepted that. He is content to be here with me, to hold me close just this one time.

At last our lips part. We smile at each other. "Paul's going to get this right," Theo murmurs as his thumb brushes along my cheekbone. "He's going to come back to you."

"I hope so."

Our wistful mood is instantly shattered as we walk through the door to hear Wicked's voice. "They won't pay you anything. We can pay you everything."

"Money is merely a necessary artifact of late-stage capitalism." Mom perks up as she sees us. "Oh, good. You're back. There have been some bribery attempts since you left."

"You don't know Mom and Dad at all," I say to Wicked. "I would've thought that by now you'd seen enough alternate versions to know how little they usually care about being rich."

"Believe me," Wicked shoots back, "I know how little they care."

I pause. I want to use this knowledge against her—but is it possible I might get through to her?

So I pull out a chair to sit opposite from Wicked. "You think Mom and Dad don't love you, because they've been so upset about losing Josie. I know that's not true."

Wicked laughs. "You have the luxury of being sentimental. Me? I see the world the way it really is."

"Every Marguerite you've killed—we usually have a pretty

good life, you know?" Could anything still touch this person? Or is her soul completely dead? "It can be like that for you, if Triad would just stand down. There are ways to go on, even after the worst has happened." Mom proved that to me back in the Josieverse. Dad endured the loss of my mother in the Russiaverse. And if I hadn't kept going after I thought my father was dead, we really might have lost him forever. "They have to let Josie go."

"Precious Josie is the only thing that matters," Wicked retorts. "Even here! She's the daughter Mom had for real. Apparently the rest of us were farmed out to surrogates. We're just spares. Don't you see?"

Mom, unmoved by any of this, folds her arms. "I could hardly be expected to carry octuplets. That wouldn't have been healthy for me or for any of you. The surrogates were all enthusiastic volunteers for the experiment."

I try to hush Mom. "That's not what's bothering her. Listen to me, okay, Wick—I mean, um, Marguerite? You can't undo any of the things you've done, but you can stop here. You can show my—your parents that you have the power."

Wicked looks at me in confusion. Some of the hostility has left her, though, and that gives me hope.

"See, if you stop now, if you refuse to do anything else for Triad, you'll force them to deal with you and your feelings." In a lot of ways, I don't believe Wicked deserves a happy ending. But if getting one means other dimensions get to live—then that's the price we have to pay. "You could go home. Today, even! Just return home and tell them what's really going on with you. They'll listen."

"But—" Wicked blinks. "But—I don't understand—"

"What?" My heart is in my throat.

She looks down at herself and says, "Why am I tied to this chair?"

No wonder the hostility is gone. This is no longer Wicked but Victoire.

"Without her Firebird, she didn't get a reminder." Theo has caught on too and explains to my mother. "Wicked's been, uh, submerged inside your daughter's consciousness. She's not coming out until the Firebird reminds her again."

I sigh and lean back in my chair. I nearly got through to her . . . or did I?

"Um, seriously," Victoire says, eyes wide. "What is up with the chair?"

The front door opens, and I hear half a dozen voices talking at once about Rey and Finn and Poe Dameron—and every single one of those voices is mine.

Dad steps into the dining room first, wearing a white linen shirt and khaki shorts that emphasize his scrawny chicken legs. He never wears shorts at home, but here I guess the heat won out. "Hello, what's this?"

And then there are my other selves—six more of me—all of them in outfits I could easily choose, all of them with their wildly curly hair tucked into styles I've worn a hundred times. It feels like staring into a funhouse mirror, except that all the reflections are exactly right.

My mother gets up. "Marguerite, Theo, you know Henry,

and these are Elodie, Colette, Oceane, Giselle, Estee, and Amelie."

Dad folds his arms. "Why are you introducing me to one of our own children, and why is another of them tied to a chair?"

"I'd like to know that too," Victoire interjects.

"This is going to be one hell of a long explanation," Theo says.

"So get started." The sharpness in my voice surprises me, but now that I see all my other selves in one place, I know what has to be done. "They need to understand completely, because I have to ask their permission for something important. Something they have to fully comprehend before they say yes."

Theo gives me a look. Mom says, "Marguerite, what do you mean?"

"It's time we had a meeting." I take a deep breath. "All the Marguerites. Every one of us. We're going to come together at last."

21

THREE HOURS LATER, I CAN'T HEAR MYSELF THINK OVER the sound of my own voices.

All six of them.

"Do you realize that Theo lost his left leg below the knee?" Mafiaverse is so angry she's near tears, her fists balled up in the lap of her green skirt. We're all seated at the table, being watched by my gaping parents and Theo as we have this extraordinary meeting—a gathering of all the people I could potentially be. "He's going to need a prosthetic, and now I'm getting all these creepy emails from some guy in the Russian mob—"

"Paul and I are flying back from Ecuador tomorrow." Triadverse sits near me in an orange sundress, calmer than any of the others. "So far as we can tell, nobody else at Triad had any idea about the cross-dimensional stuff—"

"I have an evil phantom inside of me," says Victoire, who's

still stuck with Wicked. "Get it out."

"Don't get me wrong." Cambridgeverse wears a corn-flower blue T-shirt and a lot of dangly chain necklaces, and she rubs her left arm as she speaks in her crisp English accent. "Mom and Dad are super psyched about communicating between universes, but did you really have to go snuggle up to the guy who maimed me for life?"

Warverse is wearing a straw fedora, a pink dress, and a scowl. "Markov? Seriously? How am I ever supposed to explain all this to Theo? I mean, my Theo." Her eyes glance back at the Theo in this room, who winks at the version who chose him. She beams back.

Angriest of all is Oceanverse in black, who yells, "You wrecked a submarine!"

Then another voice cuts through the din, hushing us at once. "Everyone, be silent."

We all close our mouths and look toward the person sitting at the head of the table—the Grand Duchess.

She wears a crimson camisole and her curls tumble free down her back, yet she looks more regal now than I ever did in her jewels and furs. The grand duchess's perfect posture turns the ordinary dining room chair into a throne, and the command in her voice is undeniable. From this moment on, there's no question about who's in charge.

"You must all listen to this Marguerite from the shadow world known as the Berkeleyverse, as she is the only one possessed of all the knowledge that can help us," the grand duchess commands, gesturing at me lightly with one hand.

"The question of her actions while in our own worlds—that will be dealt with later."

Oh, God. Dread weighs me down. How am I going to look the grand duchess in the face as I apologize for getting her pregnant?

"You will proceed," the grand duchess finishes, with a nod in my direction.

"Okay. Well. First of all, thanks for coming—"

"I was kidnapped!" Oceanverse cuts in, though she immediately looks abashed when the grand duchess fixes her in an imperious stare.

"Sweetheart, we're merely borrowing you for a time." Dad smiles at Oceanverse encouragingly; he was the one who made the trip to her dimension. Between him, Mom, and Theo, at least one of us was near the Marguerite in each world—even the Russiaverse, where the Parisian chemist Theodore Beck was already visiting his friend in her new Danish home. We only had the two Firebirds to work with at first, which meant we could only undertake one trip at a time. Since then, though, both the Triadverse and the Cambridgeverse have contributed one each. They've needed reminders, but we can pass one Firebird around for that.

I continue. "However you got here, I'm glad you came. Because if we're going to stop the Home Office—the dimension that's trying to destroy so many of the others—we all have to work together. I realize some of you were already making a head start on that," I interject, nodding toward the three for whom this is true: Triadverse, Cambridgeverse, and Warverse. "But we need to be united, completely."

Mafiaverse folds her arms across her chest. "You mean, we should just forgive you."

I feel sick. "You don't have to forgive me. Ever. Just understand that right now, this moment, I'm doing my absolute best to keep every one of us safe."

"It's not so bad, what you did," Cambridgeverse says, surprising me. When she takes in my expression, she shrugs. "I mean, I wish you hadn't gone over to Paul's place, but he wasn't exactly your Paul, and I remember how we used to be—you know, it's awkward, but I get it."

"Not so bad? Tell that to Theo," Mafiaverse retorts.

"I'm right here," Theo says, "and even though I'm not the one who has to live with the consequences, I am the one who took the bullets. So believe me when I say what happened to, well, to us that night wasn't Marguerite's fault. At the beginning she had no idea the Russian mob could be involved. She couldn't have predicted what was going to happen. Me, I'm the one who knew she'd been kidnapped and walked right into a bad situation anyway. If what happened to your Theo is anyone's fault besides the guy who fired the gun? It's mine."

Oceanverse still looks livid. "So who wrecked the submarine?"

"That would actually be yet another version of me, who's now dead," Theo says. "So if you were hoping to file a lawsuit, you're out of luck."

Triadverse leans backward, putting her hands to her temples. "My head hurts."

This would be a prime moment for the grand duchess to bring up what I did to her, but she doesn't. Maybe it's beneath royal dignity to speak of such things in public. She looks at me and says only, "If the interruptions have finally ceased, please continue."

"Right. So, first of all, we have to make sure we strengthen all of your universes so that they can't be destroyed, ever. That process requires one Firebird"—I hold up my locket, even though the others are all familiar with the device by now—"and one stabilizer, which isn't hard to build in a technologically advanced dimension. Those of you who are already in communication with other universes have started working on that. Mafiaverse, you guys have the know-how. You just have to execute the plan. For the rest of you with different technologies, we have to figure out alternative solutions."

"Where are we even supposed to start with that?" Ocean-verse says. "I don't have that kind of knowledge, and in my universe, my parents don't either."

"But my parents do." I think fast. "One of them needs to go to your universe. Preferably Dad—my version of Dad, I mean—he stayed there for a month after he was kidnapped, and he still remembers some of it. That would give him a head start with the technology."

"I can head back and tell him." Theo shakes his head with a wry smile. "High time Henry did some dimensional

290

traveling of his own, don't you think?"

"Definitely." Mom and Dad have left the journeying to us—to me, mostly, because of the talent Wyatt Conley gave me. But they ought to experience some of this, both the chaos of it and the wonder.

"And my own world?" At the sound of the grand duchess's voice, everyone focuses on her again. She sits with her hands in her lap, and somehow she looks both older and more beautiful than the rest of us. People always say, *oh, beauty comes from within,* and I always thought they were being glib. But now I see that energy radiating from the grand duchess, intangible but undeniable, as she continues. "It appears our mechanical advancement is significantly behind yours."

Theo shrugs, like, *no big deal.* "All we need are the right metals and the knowledge, Your, uh, Highness? Was that it?"

"Your Imperial Highness," I whisper.

"Right, that's it. Yes. Your Imperial Highness. Since it turns out you and I are friends there, and I'm in your neighborhood anyway, we can work together on it. You commandeer the materials, and I'll get the job done." Theo sort of salutes her, then pulls his hand back, obviously feeling ridiculous. Warverse giggles.

Oceanverse raises her hand, reminding me she's one of the only Marguerites who attended something resembling a real school. "So, some other version of Dad is going to just take over my dad without any warning?"

"Ask his permission," I say. "Tell your dad everything. If

he doesn't want my dad to stay, then he won't. I promise. It's your dimension, so it's your choice."

"Okay." Then she adds sheepishly, "I guess since the alternative is getting our dimension blown up, Dad's probably going to say yes."

"Probably," I agree. Though I predict that later on my father will bitch at length about the inhuman suffering of being forced to return to a dimension without the Beatles.

"What about here?" Victoire says. "Will your Theo stay, or will another version of Mom come to our universe, or what? And who's going to get the evil phantom out of me?"

Theo and I glance at each other. How exactly do we deal with Wicked? If we just left her in Victoire forever, would Wicked remain trapped as she is now? Or might she grow stronger over time, work her way out? Even if she didn't, it's hard to imagine a soul that damaged, that poisonous not corroding the person who contained it.

And if my parents in the Home Office are willing to destroy entire dimensions to get one of their daughters back, is there anything they wouldn't do to rescue the only child they have left?

The front door opens, startling us all. Cambridgeverse whispers, "Wait, there's another one?"

But the footsteps are too heavy to be mine. The familiar sound brings a smile to my face even before Paul walks in.

His hair is slightly longer here, and at the moment it's mussed—air-dried and textured with salt water. A faint stripe of sunburn covers his nose, and over his shoulder is a backpack no doubt full of equipment. He's still wearing a long-sleeved black swim shirt and matching trunks.

But it's not the differences that strike me the most. It's the Firebird hanging around his neck.

It's my Paul, finally with me again.

The reaction ripples around the table, each one of us wearing a different expression, from loving to terrified and everything in between.

But it's the grand duchess I can't bear to witness. She grips the arms of her chair, and her lips are parted in awe. Her love for Lieutenant Markov defined and changed her life, and then she lost him forever.

Or she had until this moment, when—for her—Paul has returned from the dead.

Paul, meanwhile, must have gotten texts from Theo and my parents telling him to get here as quickly as he could, and Theo sent a couple of messages explaining the clone thing. But knowing the facts doesn't appear to have prepared Paul for the reality. He stops in the doorway, staring at each of us in turn, his jaw slowly dropping open.

"I know, little brother," Theo says with a wry grin, leaning against the wall with his arms crossed. "I had this dream too."

"You're from the Oceanverse." Paul points to the correct Marguerite, which surprises me. "And you're from Cambridge—from the War—" His gray eyes light on me, and he draws in a deep breath. "—and you're mine."

I nod yes. *Always, Paul.*

293

But now his attention has turned to the grand duchess, who still gazes at him, transfixed. After a moment, Paul bows slightly. "My lady."

The grand duchess half-turns, covering her mouth with her hand.

Tears well in my eyes. Paul knew her by sight. Knew all of us. Knew me.

Could anyone else in the multiverse read my entire history in a glance? Paul sees through to the truth of me. He always has.

Paul finally says, "I assume this isn't merely a social occasion."

"Got it in one, pal." Theo thumps him on one shoulder. "Let me catch you up on the conclave of the Marguerites."

As Theo goes through the entire spiel, I sit back down and try to read Paul as intelligently as he read me. I'm good at this, usually—so how can I love Paul so much and yet find it so difficult to understand the conflict within his heart?

But then, Paul tries to hide what he feels. His parents' cruelty must have taught him long ago to be cautious. Closed-off. Even afraid. They tried to keep him from everything he loved, which is how you teach a person to bury love deep inside where nobody else can see. It's how you teach someone not to hope.

"Now that we're all up to speed," Theo finally says, drawing the rest of us back into the conversation, "who wants to go home first?"

Mafiaverse raises her hand. No wonder she never wants to

be near Paul—or the rest of us—ever again. Cambridgeverse says, "Everyone needs to know the Triadverse is no longer a threat. With Wyatt Conley dead, there's one fewer perfect traveler, too. The sooner I get back, the sooner we can reach out to the new universes, since my parents have communication technology."

"So do mine," says Warverse. Everyone's eager to get back to their own dimension right away, except for the grand duchess. Without saying a word, she sits in regal self-possession, so still I could almost believe I was looking at a photograph—until the moment her hand brushes across her abdomen, as if searching for the child who should be inside.

Paul's child. What must it be like for her to see him again?

As my parents begin working out who's going where with whom, Paul finally comes to my side. He stands near enough that I no longer feel he's avoiding me, and his broad hand closes over my shoulder. "You're all right," he says. "When we realized a universe had fallen . . ."

"I'm okay. You rescued me." I smile crookedly up at him. "One of you, anyway."

"We need to focus. I've calculated a likely future target for the Home Office." Paul is trying to switch fully into Science Mode, the better to conceal his confused emotions, and only half succeeding. "This next dimension serves as a source vector for many others, which puts it greatly at risk. I'm surprised the Home Office didn't attack it earlier."

"Okay, then that's where we'll go next," I say. I'm heartened by the fact that Paul said *we*, that he still takes it for granted that we can go together. That gives me something to build on. "But first . . ."

"Yes?" His gray eyes meet mine for only a moment before he has to look away.

I nod toward the grand duchess. "You need to say goodbye."

Paul hesitates, then takes a few steps toward her. When she looks up, her eyes are red. He says, "If you don't want to talk to me—if it would hurt too much—"

"No, please." The grand duchess gets to her feet. "It does hurt. But this chance will not come again."

Maybe I shouldn't be listening. And yet, I was literally a part of her during every moment she was ever with my Paul. There are no secrets among us.

Paul holds out his arms to her, and she embraces him desperately. He envelops her in his hug, cradling her close in the way that's always made me feel so safe. So loved. When she finally pulls back, he says, "You understand the truth about the Firebirds now. That I'm not your Paul—"

"But another person he would have had the chance to have been," she says, her voice trembling. "Lieutenant Markov so loved studying physics and optics. I feel sure it meant a great deal to him, learning that in another lifetime he had the chance to become a scientist. To follow his dreams."

Paul nods. "It did. I was a part of him during those last few weeks, and I remember—" His voice breaks off, nakedly emotional in a way he's never shown before. But those days in Saint Petersburg, and that night in the dacha, remain some of the most powerful in either of our lives.

Remember that, Paul. I bite the inside of my cheek to keep from crying. *That wasn't only her. That was us, too.*

Finally he manages to say to the grand duchess, "He loved you so much. I will always carry that inside me. As long as I'm alive, in some way, so is his love for you."

The grand duchess kisses his hands, and tears well in her eyes. Paul looks like he might break down too. I should stop watching them, grant them at least the illusion of privacy, but I can't look away.

"The baby," she begins, then holds one hand up to Paul's mouth before he can begin to apologize. "If it is a boy, I will of course name him for you. But what name would you choose for a girl?"

He glances over his shoulder at my mom, who is even now preparing to take Warverse back home. With her yoga clothes and sloppy bun, she must look nothing like the bejeweled tsarina the grand duchess remembers, but she's so like my mom at home—the one who loves Paul nearly as much as she loves me. He says, "Sophia. In most worlds she means more to me than my real mother ever has."

"Sophia, then." The grand duchess smiles up at him through her tears. "I have so much to say, and yet anything less than a lifetime would never be enough time to say it. Just know that I am and will be well. When the day comes, I look forward to telling our child all about you." She clutches Paul's hand tighter and holds it to her heart. "I will love you until the end of my days."

Paul pulls her close again and kisses her.

I have no business feeling jealous. The hot rush that sweeps through me, as if I'd been slapped, can't even compare to how the grand duchess must have felt when she understood that I took the one night she could ever have had with her Paul. And later on I know I'll even be glad she had a chance to say her own goodbye.

That doesn't make it easier to watch Paul kissing anyone else, even another me.

When they break apart, to my surprise, the grand duchess walks in my direction, stopping only a few paces away. "It was you who visited my world," she says, her hands clasped in front of her. Even though a tear from her farewell to Paul has traced an uneven track down her cheek, her composure is already complete. "You were my shadow self."

"I am so sorry." The apology I gave her in my letter doesn't even come close to being enough. "The things I did—I got caught up in the emotion of the moment, and I took all these risks without asking whether you would have done the same—"

"I would not have," the grand duchess says.

Once again, I feel slapped, and this time, I've earned it completely. I hang my head, no longer able to face her.

But then the grand duchess continues, "I would not have had the courage." When I look up, she is—somehow—smiling. "My path had been laid out for me since before I was born, and never had I dared to deviate from it, even by a single step. Not even for the love I felt for Lieutenant Markov. You took me off that path forever, and I am glad of it. Glad for the memories I would never have known but for you, glad for the chance to know my real father, gladdest for the child I will bear. You have given me the chance to make my own fate, and there is no more priceless gift in the world."

It takes me far too long to find the breath to answer her. "You're being nicer to me than I deserve."

"None of us can know the full consequences of our actions. Just know that I am more than content with the consequences of yours." The grand duchess holds out her hand, as she would to a courtier, then frowns—like that's not quite right, but she doesn't know what else to do. Admittedly this is not a situation covered in most etiquette books.

I just clasp her hand and smile. "Have a really great life," I whisper. "You deserve it."

"I plan to try." The grand duchess looks over at Theo then. Her expression is no more than friendly, maybe a touch amused by the differences between her own dapper Theodore Beck and this one in his jeans and T-shirt. Yet it makes me wonder what might happen eventually, after she has mourned for Lieutenant Markov, and her friendship with Theo has deepened over months and years.

Probably I'm reading too much into it. But when I think of her raising Paul's child with Theo by her side, it seems like a beautiful future, one worth having.

"Oh, and one more thing," I say to her, thinking of one other person I got to know in the Russiaverse. "If Vladimir understands about the shadow worlds, if he ever believes— would you tell him hello? I miss him sometimes. Katya and

Peter, too. But especially tell Vladimir that if I'd had a big brother in this dimension, I would have wanted one just like him."

Slowly the grand duchess nods. "I think Vladimir would be pleased to hear that."

"Okay." Theo claps his hands together at the center of the room, bringing our attention back to the situation at hand. I realize only then that my parents are gone, taking Ocean-verse and Cambridgeverse with them, because now those two clones are huddled apart from the rest of us, deep in conversation, clearly freaked out. "I figure the Russiaverse is my last stop, since it's going to take me longest to help out there. Maybe I take Mafiaverse, and Paul can take Warverse back home?"

"I should move on to that universe you were talking about," I say to Paul. "But as long as Wicked is stuck here, maybe there's less of a rush. I can keep the others company, explain more of the details."

Victoire, newly untied, crosses her arms in front of her chest. "Is anyone going to do anything about the evil phantom inside me?"

Theo, Paul, and I exchange glances. Theo ventures, "Um, we don't actually have anyplace to put her that isn't going to unleash her on the multiverse again."

Paul tries to reassure her. "The chances of her unduly affecting you are undefined but unlikely."

Victoire raises her eyebrows. "'Undefined'?"

Paul isn't always as comforting as he thinks he is. I hastily

300

add, "We'll get her out, I swear, as soon as we're sure the multiverse is safe. Mom and Dad know to look out for you, and I can spend a while here before I have to move on—"

"I'm fine here," Victoire huffs. "A friend of ours is coming over to stay with us while Mom and Dad are off on their weird adventures in other dimensions, though Romy will never believe this—"

Once again I feel a sensation wash over me, but this time it isn't heat. It's pure cold. "What name did you just say?"

"Don't pretend you didn't hear her," says Romola, who must've been able to walk right through the front door while the rest of us were so completely distracted. "You should know me by now."

Maybe I should be unnerved by the Firebird around Romola's neck—proof that she's from the Home Office.

But I'm a whole lot more freaked out by her gun.

22

Worst is seeing the awful betrayal on Victoire's face, and her sisters' faces. They look so wounded. Even shattered. Did I look like this when I thought Paul had hurt my father?

Victoire rises to her feet, wobbly and uncertain. "Romy— what are you—"

"You can explain all this to your version of me later," Romola snaps. "But I think you know who I've come for."

She's here to set Wicked free.

Paul, Theo, and I all exchange glances. Between the three of us and the seven other clones in this room, we could take Romola out easily—if it weren't for the black pistol she holds. As it is, any attempt to disarm her could be deadly, and if one of the bullets hit a clone, Romola might kill two Marguerites with a single pull of the trigger. Theo's shoulders sag in defeat. But Paul—

Paul's eyes blaze with that cold fire I've found so menacing in the past. Is this the same anger he would have felt anyway, or proof of his splintering? The potential for violence deep within him has been re-armed, and it could explode at any moment.

At the moment, though, I'm nearly as angry as he is, no splintering required. It's galling to have to point to Victoire and say, "Your Marguerite is . . . with her. Asleep, but safe and sound."

"Very well." Romola motions to the chair Victoire was sitting in only a few moments before. "Go on. Take your seat. I'll handle the rest."

"Is this about the phantom?" Victoire asks. I nod. She turns to Romola then, still bewildered and hurt. "Romy, why are you doing this?"

"I'm not your 'Romy.' I'm from a dimension with higher technology and more realistic priorities."

"You're destroying billions of lives to save one," Paul says. Though he keeps his voice low, his anger simmers just below the surface. "Those priorities are twisted. Corrupt. But hardly realistic."

Romy shrugs. "In all honesty, I see your point. But gaining supremacy over all the other worlds in the multiverse? That makes more sense." Her eyes are cold as she glances at Victoire. "When is that one going to sit down?"

"Do it," I say to Victoire, this other me who's wearing the scratches and bruises I gave her earlier tonight. "There's no other way."

Trembling, Victoire takes her seat. The other two clones lean forward, as if they'll rush Romola the moment Victoire shows any pain, gun or no gun. Unfortunately recklessness seems to be a characteristic too many of us share.

Don't go after her, I think as I try to catch the others' eyes. If only clones could be telepathic with each other, so I could make it clear just how dangerous this is. Then they wouldn't do anything stupid—

—but they don't even get the chance, because Paul rushes Romola first.

As he smashes into her, sending them both stumbling into the wall, we all scream. He's such a huge man that the tackle would seem brutal if Romola weren't wielding a gun. But even her tumble down to the ground doesn't make her drop her weapon. Romola kicks away from him, skidding across the floor, and has the presence of mind to aim not at Paul but at me. "I'll do it," she says rapidly, not even glancing at Paul a couple of paces behind her. Her eyes remain focused on her target, which appears to be the dead center of my chest. "Don't try me. I will kill her."

Paul says nothing. Instead he grabs a meat cleaver from the knife block. Its blade glints in the light. The others in the room gasp, but Romola still doesn't look up. And Paul's standing close enough, at the perfect angle, to swing it down and split her head wide open.

Don't. Terror rushes through me. Not for myself, despite Romola's unwavering aim. She doesn't realize what Paul could do. She wouldn't even have time to know Paul was taking action before he'd stunned or killed her.

But if Paul kills Romola like this, in cold blood, he will have surrendered to that darkness within him. The damage from his shattering will be complete, if only because he'll never again believe that he could be anything but a murderer.

I can say nothing. Do nothing. This battle is Paul's to fight.

He stares down at her, hatred warping his expression into something I can hardly recognize. His hand tightens around the cleaver's handle as his knuckles turn white. Within him I see all the menace I remember from the son of a Russian mafia leader. All the recklessness of the Cambridgeverse Paul, who let a moment's temper and inattention mangle my arm forever. And I see a hard, bitter edge that belongs to my Paul alone.

Oh, God, he's going to do it. He's going to kill her.

At that moment Romola glances upward and sees what he's doing. She doesn't even flinch. "Your Marguerite is in my sights." Her arm hasn't wavered one millimeter. "The second I see you start for me, I fire. She'll be dead before I will."

Anger ripples over Paul's face, an ugly grimace that makes me wonder if he'll strike Romola down anyway. Instead he steps back and sets the cleaver down again.

Would he have murdered her? We can never know.

Now that Paul is no longer an immediate threat, Romola sits up and goes back into action. With her free hand,

Romola fishes a second Firebird from around her neck. She prepared herself for anything, then. As she lifts the heavy chain over her head, Theo says, "Where did you get a gun in Singapore?"

"Policemen carry them," Romola explains as she tosses the Firebird to Victoire, who puts it on with shaking hands. The other Marguerites have clustered in a corner, silent and pale, knowing they can't help. Only watch. "Odd, given that the officer in question obviously had no expectation of being attacked."

"I think you can get the death penalty here if you smoke a joint." Theo runs his hands through his spiky hair in frustration. "Maybe it's not that bad for pot, but attacking a police officer—you realize this universe's Romola will probably be executed for this."

She shrugs. "Not my problem."

"You're still just the errand girl," I try. "You're here to pick up your world's Marguerite. Not to do the job yourself."

"I took care of you well enough in the Romeverse, didn't I?" Romola retorts.

Again the molten hell of that universe's final moments writhes in my mind. "In case you hadn't noticed, I'm still alive and well. You can't say that for Conley or Theo in the Triadverse, can you?"

"We lost a perfect traveler, but we can always make another. You're not as indispensible as they all seem to think. This room would seem to prove it. Infinite copies, and yet you're still never enough, Marguerite. Never enough for your parents, never enough for anyone."

Romola, onto my game, is trying to wound me back. The thing is, it doesn't work. With all my self-doubt and uncertainty, I've never felt like my parents didn't love me, or that I didn't deserve to be loved. Only in these past few days, as I've realized how that sense of inferiority has gnawed at Wicked—and at Paul—have I fully appreciated how the lack of love can twist someone inside.

If you know you're loved, deep down *know* it, something deep and precious inside you will always be safe. If you don't have that love—or don't know that you do—then you're vulnerable. Unshielded. Exposed to all the hardness and horror of the world.

"You don't understand half as much as you think you do," I tell Romola.

"And yet I still seem to understand more than you." With that, Romola leans forward and activates Victoire's Firebird for a reminder. The jolt isn't visible; however, the pain it causes Victoire is. She jumps in her seat, twists around—and goes deadly still.

Wicked's back.

"Good try." Her smile is as sharp as a shard of a broken mirror. "But, as usual, not good enough."

Instantly Wicked's hand goes to her Firebird, as does Romola's. The lockets seem to vanish, leaving both Victoire and Romola there looking stupefied. Romola takes a couple of steps backward in utter confusion, then gasps in shock at the gun in her own hand. "What's going on?"

"Romy?" Victoire says. "Are you yourself again?"

Paul steps forward and carefully takes the weapon from Romola's hand, showing no sign of the homicidal anger that nearly consumed him only seconds ago. "Sit down. We'll explain later."

"Who is that?" says Warverse, from the corner where she and the others have huddled. "I've never laid eyes on her in my life."

"Her name is Romola Harrington." Mafiaverse answers, and I realize she looks paler and sicker than anyone else in the room. "In my universe, she works for Wyatt Conley."

"Here, too," says one of the clones who's already rid of her visitor from another dimension—Elodie, I think. "Conley funds Mum and Dad's cloning research. Romy's one of his assistants, so she lives here and handles PR, transfers of funds, that kind of thing."

"And she's one of our friends." Victoire goes to the very confused Romola's side in a show of solidarity. "She'd never hurt us."

"Neither would mine," Mafiaverse says.

"That's great. You guys got way nicer Romolas than we did. Maybe when you get back to the Mafiaverse, you could ask yours to help out?" Frustration is making me snarky. "I'm sorry. It's just—as soon as we take care of one threat from the Home Office, another one takes its place. I don't know what to do."

"We stick to the plan." Paul tries to sound logical and

confident, like he's only talking good sense. Yet he won't meet anyone's eyes, and he keeps glancing over at the cleaver he very nearly used on Romola. "Protect our own dimensions, continue to work together, move on quickly. This next world is important—"

"I'll go there," I say. Up until now, I've been following in Wicked's footsteps. With this step, with Paul resetting my Firebird to strike out in new directions instead of only trailing behind her, maybe I can finally beat her to the punch. "Right away. As long as I keep her out, the dimension will remain safe until you can meet me there."

Paul opens his mouth to speak, then closes it. He was going to object.

I beat him to it. "I mean, you or whoever can reach me. Whoever is closest in that dimension."

Because I don't know anything about this next world. Where I once assumed Paul and I could always find each other, now I know the multiverse has a million different ways of tearing us apart.

"Okay," I murmured one night in late February as Paul and I snuggled in his dorm room, listening to his beloved Rachmaninoff. The piano notes rippled down around us like raindrops on a windowpane during a storm—cascading, endless. "So you can mathematically prove the existence of fate."

"I hope so. If not, my chances of successfully defending my thesis are poor."

"But you can." I lay on my side, Paul spooned around my back. His hand splayed across my stomach, two of his fingers touching the bare skin exposed between my top and my jeans. "You can actually look into this snarl of equations and read what our destiny is fated to be."

"No, that's going too far." Paul kissed the back of my neck, as if apologizing for having to correct me in any way. "Yes, there are parallels in the equations that suggest parallels in the outcomes. But it's not as though one number tells me we get married, or another number tells me we never meet. It would take a lifetime of exploration and evaluation to even begin understanding how to interpret those findings."

"Do your equations explain why there are all these parallels? Why you and Theo work with my parents in so many worlds, or why you and I seem to manage to find each other every time?"

"I could only posit a theory."

After growing up with my parents and their menagerie of grad students, I was used to their jargon. Smiling to myself, I said, "All right, posit away."

"Have you ever eaten Pringles?"

It was such a non sequitur that at first I thought I'd heard him wrong. "Pringles? Like the potato chips?"

"Yes," he said earnestly. "They're very good."

"I know. I've had Pringles. I mean, obviously. But this is the first time anyone's ever used them as part of a cosmological theory."

Paul hugged me more tightly. "They all have to be shaped

the same to fit into the can. If they were too irregular, they couldn't be packed together."

"You mean—dimensions are like potato chips in a can." It began to make sense to me, which was either a breakthrough or possibly proof I'd been hanging around physicists way too long. "They have to be shaped the same, at least a little, or they couldn't co-exist."

"Exactly. See, we might make a scientist of you yet."

"You wish."

"No, I don't. I would never want you to be anyone but yourself." Paul kissed the back of my neck again, slowly this time, so that I felt the warmth of his breath on my skin. I took his hand and slid it up my body, inviting him to explore. It seemed like we had become our own tiny universe of heat and light and love, needing nothing else. . . .

And now Paul and I stand here, terrible bleak tension between us because he no longer has faith that our fate brings us together.

But if he can no longer believe in us, I want him to at least believe in himself.

I step to his side and keep my voice low. "You stepped away from Romola, okay? You thought of me first. The splintering didn't get you."

"I only stopped because Romola threatened you." Paul stares at an empty corner, again avoiding my gaze. "I nearly committed murder."

"Nearly doesn't count! You hung on and controlled

yourself. You can win this fight."

"But it will always be a fight. Always." He shakes his head as though he were about to pronounce a death sentence.

"And you can always win." I put one hand on his arm.

"Maybe. Maybe not." He steps away from me. Maybe the breakthrough is just too new, or maybe his despair runs even deeper than I thought.

As badly as I want to make things right with Paul, we have a multiverse to save.

"You've input the coordinates for this important dimension?" I take my Firebird back, determined to carry on. "I'm cleared to go?"

"I'll follow as soon as I can. If I can," Paul promises. Still he doesn't meet my eyes.

The Grand Duchess Margarita of all the Russias watches us in dismay. Although I see her eagerness to speak, she has far too proper manners to ever intrude. How angry she must feel, seeing me blow my chance to be with my Paul after she tragically lost hers.

But now I'm thinking about Lieutenant Markov, whose memory always makes me cry, and I can't afford to break down. So I just look around the room at my other selves, whether visitors from other dimensions or this world's clones. "These might not be the best circumstances, but I'm glad I met all of you. Seeing all these lives we could lead, and all the different ways things turn out—"

"It proves anything is possible," says the grand duchess.

I nod at her, then look again at Paul, who finally returns

my gaze in the instant before I hit my controls and—

—I wobble, because I've slammed into a world where I'm currently on top of a very tall ladder. I manage to recover my balance in time, saving me from tumbling to the tiled floor below. But I'm even more afraid. Because the one thing I know about this dimension is that somewhere, very close, a bomb just went off.

The only other time I've been near a massive explosion was during an air raid in the Warverse. One of the fighter planes dropped a bomb nearly on top of our shelter, and for a couple of minutes after that, the only thing I could hear was a dull roar, almost exactly like the one ringing in my ears now.

Did Wicked get here before me after all? Did she set off an explosive device, trying to frame me as a terrorist? But she hasn't had time for anything that elaborate, and besides—I don't smell smoke. I don't see any damage. A few people walk along on the tiled floor beneath my ladder, all of them headed in one direction but in no particular hurry. Their clothes look roughly modern, if kind of drab. A drop cloth is spattered with red, but the drops look more like paint than blood.

How can nobody care about the bomb? I look to my other side and see Paul's face, larger than life on the wall by my shoulder, the paint still wet. Clipped to the ladder is a box of paints, and I realize I'm wearing a smock.

From the corner of my eye I catch some movement and look down again to see a middle-aged man holding up a

313

paintbrush. He looks irritated, and he has a blue-gray stripe across one cheek. I must have dropped my paintbrush on him. And he's way more interested in that than the freakin' bomb.

The man waves at me again, signaling for me to come down. But he doesn't want me to evacuate. I can tell he just wants me to get my brush back.

Usually I try to piece together the most important clues about a universe on my own, but this time, I'm going to need some help. So I say to the man below, "What's going on?"

But I don't say it with my voice.

Instead, automatically and unconsciously drawing on the language information rooted deeply in this Marguerite's brain, I respond in sign language.

Oh. I'm deaf.

23

I THOUGHT BEING DEAF WOULD BE . . . QUIETER.

The man beneath the ladder signs back, but badly. "Brush. You. Get."

Shaking off my bewilderment and the dull roar in my ears, I head back down the ladder. My shoes are kind of clunky—lace-up boots—but not so much that I have to worry about falling. When I get to the bottom, this man hands me the brush. But then he smiles and shrugs, like you do when you realize you're in a bad mood for no reason.

"Work stop. Night. Goodbye." After this primitive fare-well, he begins packing up brushes and such, even heading up the ladder to collect the paints, which must belong to him. I back away from the dropcloth, looking up at the mural above us. Yes, that's Paul's face, but I'm painting him as one of a group of hardy peasants, marching through a field of wheat, being led by Vladimir Lenin to a glorious tomorrow.

315

I always likened Paul's build to the idealized, masculine ones shown in Soviet propaganda. Now I'm apparently painting him into it. This might amuse me a little if I weren't trying to adjust to the staticlike sound in my ears that erases all other noise. It's just so strange—people walking by me without the thump of their footsteps, no echoes of any kind against the tile, mouths moving during conversation as silently and meaninglessly as koi fish in a pond—

A hand waving at the corner of my vision startles me. I turn to see Josie, wearing a long black coat and a knitted cap. She smiles and signs—fluidly and fluently—"We got off work at the same time! Good, we can head home together."

"Great," I reply. "Let's go."

I wait for Josie to start walking in the right direction, but she stands there for a minute before scrunching her nose in confusion. "You don't want your bag and your coat?"

When I turn around I see, in a small pile next to the dropcloth, a dark blue coat and embroidered scarf that seem more likely to belong to me than to my supervisor. I put them on, uncovering a knapsack smudged here and there with dried paint. In my pockets are two cloth gloves. To judge by Josie's warm hat, I'm going to want to wear these.

By the time I return to Josie, she's shaking her head in affectionate chagrin. "You're in a dream world today."

"I'm sorry," I reply, slightly amazed at how readily my gloved fingers form the shapes. "I'm a little lightheaded this evening."

Josie laughs. "Not again already!"

Oh, no. Maybe Wicked has been here. But if so, did she just . . . drop a paintbrush on my supervisor and leave? That makes no sense.

When Josie sees my bewildered expression, she pats my shoulder with her free hand. "I was just kidding, and I should know better than to joke about that. Come on, let's get you home."

She doesn't seem set on continuing our conversation, which is good, because I need a minute.

I always believed deafness would mean profound, permanent silence. Apparently I was wrong. For me at least, now that I've had time to begin getting used to this, it sounds less like an explosion's aftermath and more like having a large seashell clapped to each ear—a rushing-roaring-ringing that never gets any quieter or louder. I'm constantly surrounded by white noise, basically, which either drowns out everything else I could hear or is simply the best my eardrums can do in this dimension.

Was I born deaf here? Possibly. But I also remember my father talking a few days ago about the time I had meningitis when I was two years old. Both he and Mom have told that story several times, either to emphasize how much they love me—which is sweet, if melodramatic—or to laugh about how they knew I was feeling better when I started spitting my hospital Jell-O at the nurse. I'm almost positive meningitis can cause deafness. Maybe, in this dimension, my parents took me to the hospital a few hours later, or the antibiotics were slightly less effective. This dimension's Marguerite survived just like I did, but her hearing didn't.

Thankfully this Marguerite learned sign early enough in life to have deeply internalized the language, so I have it too. And I have a little more time to catch up on the situation here, since for once I don't have to thwart either a murder attempt or a crashing dimension. Nor do I have to search for Paul, who is obviously in my life in this world too. My job is protecting this universe, which simply means staying here and keeping Wicked out. All I have to do is get along well enough for the hours it takes Paul to join me here and start building the stabilizer. So I only need to study my surroundings, and my hearing isn't necessary for that.

To judge from the scale of the mural and the tiles on the floor, I had assumed I was painting in some kind of civic building—whatever would come closest to a city hall here. But this turns out to be a train station so opulent it makes the BART look like a garbage dump. As we get closer to our track, the crowds thicken. Apparently we got here at the very top of rush hour. The train itself is clean, but sort of old-fashioned. No ads. Josie and I are crunched in together so tightly that there's no chance to talk. I'm not even sure I could get my hands in front of my face.

We hop off after only two stops, and I take careful note of the station and the directions, in case I have to navigate this on my own later. Then I follow Josie up onto the street.

Josie and I turn the corner, and I see a statue of Lenin, several stories high, seemingly standing against a powerful wind and pointing forward. When I let my gaze follow the direction of his finger, I glimpse the distant, multicolored onion domes of St. Basil's Cathedral.

Russia, I think, a wave of nostalgia washing over me. I'd known it might be as soon as I recognized Lenin in the mural, and the style of it, but something similar might have been painted in any Soviet Bloc nation since the Revolution. I could've walked out anywhere from Estonia to the Ukraine—and, since this is a new dimension with new rules, potentially even San Francisco itself. But no. I'm back in this country that has come to mean so much to me.

However, this is a very different Russia. Instead of beautiful, elegant Saint Petersburg, I appear to live in Moscow—and I bet in the universe ruled by Tsar Alexander, Moscow looks better than it does here. All the buildings constructed in the previous century are plain concrete, the architecture so dull and uninspiring that the effect has to be deliberate. The elegant subway stations testify to an earlier age, one that wanted its public places to create awe. Apparently that sentiment died out a long time ago. The cars moving past us are so square and squat they could be shrunk down to fit in with a Lego set. Mom told me the Soviet Union didn't believe in capitalist decadence, and decadence apparently included manufacturing automobiles in any style besides "ugly."

It's twilight. Josie must be tired after a day at work, but her attention is all for me as she asks, "Do you want me to walk with you all the way to your place? I don't mind."

The sunset light catches a glint on her finger as she talks to me, and I realize she's wearing a slim band of gold. A wedding ring? Oh, please don't let her be married to Wyatt Conley in this universe. After the carnage of that final, fatal car wreck in the Triadverse, I will never again be able to see his face without remembering what it looked like after it had been split open. And even the worlds where he's an okay guy, where his love for Josie is true and good, remind me that his grief for her is fueling the Home Office's brutal slaughter of the dimensions.

"Hey." Josie frowns. "Did you catch what I said?"

"Yes, sorry. I'm really not feeling well. If you could walk me home, I'd appreciate it." My smile probably looks pretty weak, but Josie will assume that's because I'm tired, or coming down with something. Sure enough, she offers her arm to me so I can hold on. It's an oddly formal gesture, yet an affectionate one—something Josie wouldn't do at home, even while she fussed over you. Maybe it's something distinctly Russian, or maybe it belongs to this dimension, which I hereby dub the Moscowverse.

Apparently Josie and I don't live in the same home anymore. Well, if she's married, no wonder. She must live with her husband, Mr. Anyone Who Is Not Wyatt Conley. Now that I take a good look around, I can see a number of other people her age, and even my age, who definitely seem to be coming from work instead of school. The schoolkids all wear uniforms, complete with red neckerchiefs or ties with a Lenin pin at the center, and they're all at least a couple of years younger than I am. Since I'm already painting for a living, my school days are probably over. People must be expected to grow up a little faster here.

To judge by the cars and the trains, the technology level seems to be roughly what ours was in the early 1980s. So my parents won't be anywhere near developing Firebird technology of their own. But if they're leading scientists in the Moscowverse, as they are in most worlds, then they'll have access to the kinds of materials Paul will need to build a stabilizer. We can keep this dimension safe.

My apartment building turns out to have been built pre-Revolution. At first I'm happy to see that I live someplace that isn't spitefully drab, even if the paint is flat gray and the original decorations that would have ringed the doors and windows have been chipped or filed away. When it's bright outside, light must stream through the large windows, illuminating the large entryway and wide halls. Then I discover that old doesn't just mean "pretty and full of character"; old also means "stairs." Thank goodness I'm only on the third floor.

As we go through the front door of my apartment, I take off my hat and begin unbuttoning my coat, eager to settle in and explore. The first thing that hits me is that this place is pretty small for me, Mom, and Dad to live in. Josie and I walk into the kitchen, which is tiny, with ancient appliances and no microwave, but it's all in white and pleasantly cozy. The living room is also small, and the walls are painted a deep, vivid green that somehow seems more lively than overpowering. No rug covers the wooden floor. A small table is pushed to one side of the room and covered with a white tablecloth that has red flowers embroidered along the hem. Portraits I've painted of my parents, Josie, people who must be friends, and someone's child are on the walls alongside framed black-and-white photos. A compact, rather faded sofa sits in front of the old-fashioned, boxy TV, which has a screen hardly bigger than a laptop's. Overstuffed bookshelves cover almost all the remaining wall space. Sure enough, tons of science texts crowd the shelves, interspersed with novels and poetry that must be mine. Even though I've never seen this apartment before, on some deep level, it does feel like it could be my home.

A tap on my shoulder makes me jump. Josie is standing right behind me. I'd forgotten I wouldn't hear her walk up. "You're sure you're all right?" Josie cocks her head, studying me. "You'll be okay here by yourself for a while?"

"Definitely." Mom and Dad must still be on their commute back from work. "I'll take a nap. That always helps."

"No doubt you could use one." Josie kisses me on the cheek—another sign of affection she wouldn't show in our own world. "Thank goodness it's not your turn to get Valentina home. You need your rest."

"Don't worry about me. Really." Do we have a third sister in this world? Or maybe Valentina is a coworker I share my commute with from time to time. As long as it's not another clone, I can deal. "Josie, you should head home. Your husband will wonder where you are."

"Yuri's hockey team is playing tonight, remember? But if

I'm going to get to the game, I should hurry." Josie bustles out the door. "See you tomorrow!"

I wave just before she vanishes behind the door, then breathe out a sigh of relief. Yuri. While I have no idea who Yuri is, he isn't Wyatt Conley, and that's good enough for me.

Slipping off my heavy coat, I hang it on one of the wall hooks along with my cap. Then, as I tug off my gloves, I venture into the back of the apartment—which seems to have only one bedroom. That can't be right. Once I'm in the bedroom, I see a pair of men's shoes by the closet, so this is obviously where Mom and Dad sleep. There's one more door though, by the corner in the very back.

I wrinkle my nose. If I remember correctly, neither walk-in closets nor en suite bathrooms were big features of Muscovite life in the Soviet era. Instead, people had to deal with a serious lack of privacy. Can I only get to my bedroom by walking through my parents' bedroom? Wow, the potential for awkward is infinite.

Get used to it, I tell myself, and I open that door.

The first thing I notice is my own left hand on the doorjamb, bare of its glove—with a ring of my own on the fourth finger.

The second: this tiny back room, which is hardly bigger than a closet, contains a baby's crib.

Wait. Whoa. *Wait.*

A light blinks in the corner, startling me. What is that? Then I remember—some deaf people install signals like that to alert them to when the doorbell is ringing or someone opens the door.

Dazed, I go to check, hardly able to look up from my hand until I reach the living room, peer through the opening to the small kitchen, and see Paul standing there with a baby in his arms.

Our baby.

24

world, even holding the baby. With one hand he clumsily signs, "Look, Mama's home."

This must be Valentina—my daughter with Paul.

I sink down heavily onto one of the chairs by the dining table, and Paul frowns in concern. He puts Valentina down on the floor. She's big enough to crawl and happy to do so while he comes to my side. "Are you all right? You look pale."

"I feel faint. Josie walked me home." And now I'm going to pass out from shock. The fate of the Grand Duchess Margarita flashes through my mind. First I find out I'm pregnant, then two weeks later, I have a kid.

Obviously I understand these are different universes, different Marguerites, different babies. But on every emotional

325

level it feels as if I went from conception to delivery in two weeks.

Paul slips off his own gloves and holds one hand to my head before pulling it back to sign, "Do you think you have a fever? It's not the flu, is it?"

"Honestly, I think all I need is sleep." Plus some time to get used to this.

"No wonder. She's been doing so much better, but last night was just like she was six weeks old again, wasn't it? Up every hour." He sighs, and I realize he's tired too. But Paul lays his own weariness aside. "We've got some of the soup left over. I could heat that up, plus the bread and cheese. Does that sound good?"

He wants to make dinner for us, so I can rest. Our daughter is playing on the floor, and this cozy little apartment is ours. At least in one world, it got to be just this simple, this sweet. We fell in love. People marry young here, so we did too. And now we have a family. We share a life.

"Are you crying?" Paul touches my hands before kneeling in front of me.

I shake my head no, even though tears are in my eyes. "I'm fine. Everything is so much better than fine."

He gives me a look, obviously wondering where that came from, but after only a moment he kisses my forehead and goes into the kitchen to get dinner started.

The next couple of hours pass in a blur, a mixture of the mundane and the sublime. For a while, as Paul cooks, I play with Valentina on the floor. In one moment, it feels like babysitting a stranger's child. In the next, it hits me all over again. This is our daughter. Paul's and mine, together.

Will the grand duchess's child look like this? Valentina has big gray eyes like her daddy, but the few wispy curls atop her head tell me she's inherited the lunatic Kovalenka hair. She's beautiful, in the way most babies are beautiful, but the longer I look at her, the more individual she seems. I see a glimmer of my father's smile, then Paul's stubborn chin. In her I recognize parts of most of the people I've loved most in my life.

My parents would call it genetics. To me it seems like alchemy—the luminous space between science and magic.

Even diaper duty isn't enough to make me feel less awed by this. When I scoop Valentina back into my arms afterward and smell her head, a warm little shiver passes through me, and I feel like I could hold her forever.

Once we've eaten, Paul insists on looking after Valentina himself. He settles in with her for yet more block-stacking action as I lie on the couch, when suddenly another small blinking light goes off. Paul winces. "I forgot Mom and Dad were coming by."

"That's okay." I sit up and smile. "I want to see them." What mad scientists will come through the door this time?

But when Paul lets our visitors in, I don't see my parents. I see Leonid Markov and the woman who must be Paul's mother, Olga.

The last time I laid eyes on Leonid Markov, he killed a man in cold blood not three feet from my face. He debated the pros and cons of keeping me alive. And I saw the cruelty and control he used to batter his son into leading a life that would slowly poison Paul's soul. Olga was unknown to me until this moment. All I knew was that she supported her husband's criminal enterprises, and she ostracized Paul for refusing to join the "family business."

Tonight, however, Leonid wears a plain brown overcoat and suit. Olga's hair is piled atop her head in an old-fashioned way, and her dress is a ghastly plaid. But they look, well, normal. They're happy to be here. Most astonishingly, Paul smiles as he lets them in.

"Hello," Olga signs. "Good to see you." Her technique is clumsy, but I can still tell what she means. Obviously she doesn't know much more sign than that, because she then starts speaking to Paul.

He seems used to serving as translator. "Babushka says Valentina grows prettier every day," then signs as he replies to her, so I'll understand too. "Beautiful, but the little tyrant was up all night. Marguerite is exhausted. Tonight isn't good for a long visit."

Leonid nods, smiling. As he talks to his son, Paul signs for me. "The party meeting was tonight, and my parents are tired too. Can they take the baby for a while this weekend instead? It would give you a chance to rest." With a significant look, Paul adds something only for me: "Imagine having hours to ourselves."

I remember the bedroom we share. Oh, I can imagine lots of things. "If it's okay with you," I reply. Paul's smile widens, and he nods as he tells his parents of course, Valentina always loves spending time with her grandparents.

Slowly I begin to put it together. In this world, Leonid isn't a mobster. Instead, he's a loyal member of the Communist Party. Maybe that's what he draws his sense of power from—that gives him the sense of authority he so craves. The USSR prized its top science students and gave them the best of everything, which meant that in the Moscowverse, Leonid supported Paul's ambitions. He's proud to have a scientist son.

I feel sure there's a darker side to this. Leonid Markov is the last person who should ever have authority in a police state, and Paul is intelligent enough to have seen that for himself. But that doesn't change the core fact that in this world, Paul grew up valued, supported, and cared for.

He has no reason to believe he will never be loved, and so, when we met, nothing held him back.

Olga and Leonid coo over Valentina a while longer as Paul serves them a quick cup of tea, but it's not half an hour before they leave and our tiny family is alone again. Valentina fusses a little, and Paul bends down to kiss her head. "She's tired too." He smiles up at me. "No wonder. I'll give her a bath, get her in bed."

"I can help—"

"No, no. Rest." Paul looks skyward. "And hope tonight she decides to sleep."

Although I sneak a peek of him sitting beside the bathtub with her, laughing as she splashes, mostly I explore the front room even more avidly than before. I find a photo album, the kind I remember from my grandparents' house with sticky adhesive pages and old, slightly discolored photographs. Here, though, most of the snapshots are in black and white. This album must have been put together by Olga, then given to us as a wedding gift, because the initial pages show Paul as a little boy—smiling more eagerly than he probably ever did in my own universe. After a few scholastic honors (scarlet ribbons emblazoned with a hammer and sickle, or portraits of Lenin again), the first photo of me shows up. Despite the dowdy school uniform I'm wearing, I grin unabashedly at the camera, both my arms around Paul's waist. It looks like we hooked up here when we were maybe thirteen and fourteen? Maybe even a year younger than that.

A couple of pages later comes the wedding photo. Without a huge commercialized bridal industry to egg them on, brides and grooms keep things simpler here: Paul is wearing a regular suit, and I've got on a knee-length dress with only a couple of flowers in my hair. But there's no mistaking the joy shining from our faces.

I look up from the photo album when Paul walks in carrying Valentina, who is now wrapped in a soft yellow blanket. She yawns, which is insanely cute—her tiny mouth opened wide, her teeny fists. When Paul sees what I'm looking at, he raises his eyebrows—the question he can't ask while his hands are busy holding our daughter. *Why have you pulled that out?*

"I'm feeling sentimental," I tell him.

He sits down in the big chair, cradling Valentina against his chest. At first I think he's talking to her, but as I walk across the room to place the photo album back on the bookshelf, I realize that he's singing.

To my surprise, I haven't actually missed being able to hear since those first few seconds of confusion. Right now, though, I wish I could listen to Paul's lullaby. But maybe it doesn't matter. Maybe it's enough to watch the expression on his face, the complete tenderness, as he sings our daughter to sleep. No song could be sweeter than that.

Then he jumps slightly, enough to startle Valentina for a moment before she yawns again. Paul's eyes widen, and so do mine, when I see the Firebird around his neck. My Paul has caught up with me at last.

He looks at the baby, then up to me, then at the baby again. I pick up a pen and notebook on the table and write one word in huge letters before holding the page up for him to read: *Surprise*.

My world's Paul Markov knows only a handful of signs. The Moscowverse's Paul, despite his fluency, must have learned later in life, because his knowledge isn't ingrained deeply enough for my Paul to access it. I can speak—my voice wasn't affected by the meningitis, and although it's weird to have to deliberately think about how to shape my mouth for each sound and syllable, I can do it. But he can reply only in writing, and the back and forth between his notes and my unheard speech makes the conversation awkward, so it's not long before I stop trying to talk at all. We wind up communicating via a sheet of paper.

Paul writes, *Do you have any idea what your parents do for a living here? What kind of science they specialize in?*

We're sitting on the kitchen floor while Paul sifts through the various cleaning products and medicines, trying to assemble the ingredients for Nightthief. Although being a perfect traveler has involved a lot of danger and drama, I admit I'm not sorry I don't have to inject into my veins any substance more commonly used for unclogging drains. I jot down, *I haven't checked, but if you go through the books on the wall, you'll probably be able to put it together.* I pause before writing the next. *We met when we were lots younger here, so you must have studied with Mom and Dad from an early age.*

Paul stops his chemistry experiment for his next lines. *Do you know where they live?*

Josie and I didn't go to their place, I reply. *You and I have an address book, though, so we can find them in the morning. Once we explain what's going on, they can help us get started.* He nods without ever looking me in the eye. I quickly add, *Why don't you just use the reminders?*

I nearly ran out of charge in the Egyptverse, he replies. If he had, he would've wound up marooned there, unable to awaken or escape. *Not worth the risk. Will we have to call in sick to work, wherever it is we have jobs? Or is tomorrow Saturday?* By this point, my concept of time has been thrown completely out of whack. Probably not a big deal, but even the little complications can sometimes trip things up.

When Paul pours another couple of fluids together, the mixture finally turns the telltale emerald green of Nightthief. *Sometimes the hardest part is finding a needle,* he writes. It's the first thing he's said that is more than strictly necessary. The Triadverse and Home Office actually build small injectors inside their Firebirds. We should do the same.

Don't you feel weird using Nightthief, given how bad it is for people? I write back.

No, Paul writes. *This is a lot like arsenic. People can take small doses without it being toxic. But if you keep exposing the body to arsenic over and over again, eventually it builds up and it becomes deadly. Two or three doses of Nightthief won't have any effects worse than maybe some temporary short-term memory loss because of the inability to dream while on the drug. And those doses are more than enough for what we have to do.*

Two or three doses. Triadverse Theo stayed in our Theo for *months.* But he gave his life to atone for those sins, so somehow I have to learn to let them go.

Paul puts the bottle of green stuff on the counter as he gets up and heads back to the bathroom, hoping no doubt to search the medicine cabinet. Maybe he says something to me as he walks out, forgetting I can't hear, but the feeling of being left behind is too clear. He even had me put Valentina to bed by myself, although I managed it pretty easily, since she'd already been sung half to sleep.

Enough, I decide. I'm not going on like this anymore. I can't make Paul believe—but I can make him listen, even without my voice.

Paul returns with an actual syringe. I walk out of the kitchen as he prepares to inject the stuff, and I take my seat on the sofa with a couple of fresh pieces of paper. Only the slightest tension in his shoulders betrays the moment the needle enters his skin, and he's done with the shot in an instant. Almost as soon as he puts the syringe down, though, he starts to shiver.

I pull him onto the sofa, fearing another full-fledged overdose like Theo had in the Londonverse. But it doesn't get to Paul that badly. He only trembles for a few moments, his pupils dilated, as he attempts to shake it off. I rub his shoulders, stroke his hair.

When the reaction passes, Paul tries to stand up again— but I grip his shoulders and force him back onto the couch beside me. He gives me a look, then writes, *I'm all right now.*

I write back, *I know. But we have to talk. You keep avoiding me, but now you're in a world where we share a home and a bed, so it's time.*

There's nothing else to say. We don't share a destiny. By now we've proved that. One world like this, where we're . . . Paul's hand stills, and I see him glance back toward Valentina's room. Then he starts over again. *One world is only one out-come. It doesn't mean we're fated to be together.*

It doesn't mean we're not. I take his hand as I search for the right words, so he can't move away.

But he takes the pen back first. *You know what the splinter-ing has done to me. Do you think I could go on with you, realizing I'll never be the same?*

Yes! I answer. *So you got hurt. So you've been changed. If you were a danger to me—then yes, I would let you go. Both because I would always protect myself and because I know you'd rather be alone than ever cause me harm. But you aren't a danger to me. You were able to control yourself with Romola, weren't you? You aren't broken. You only have new scars, and I would always love you despite any scars. Wouldn't you love me if I were scarred, or sad, or hurting?*

Paul hesitates. Am I getting through to him? He writes, *Of course I would, but this is different. You won't see that, because you still believe in some mystical fate—*

I snatch the pen from his hands to stop him right there, and so I can say the most important part. *Paul, fate doesn't guarantee us a happy ending. We're not promised to be together no matter what. But in dimension after dimension, world after world, fate gives us a* chance. *Our destiny isn't some kind of mystical prophecy. Our destiny is what we do with that chance.*

I don't dare look up. I don't dare stop writing. It's pouring out of me now, the one thing I feel I've learned for sure.

You said it yourself. Each new quantum reality splits off when someone makes a decision. Every single world we've visited isn't just random—it's the result of countless choices, all of them combining to create a new reality. You and I have been given an infinity of chances, and that's so much more than most people will ever get— but in the end we get to live in only one world, and that's the world we make. I want us to create that world together.

My eyes feel hot. My throat tightens up. When I look over at Paul, I see that he's even closer to the verge than I am.

335

I'm forcing us both to confront the fact that one of our most beautiful dreams was a lie.

We both believed in destiny as a kind of guarantee— a promise from the cosmos that we would have our time together in virtually every world we shared. But now I see that believing only in destiny means giving up responsibility. We fooled ourselves into thinking happiness was a gift we would be given time and time again. It's so much scarier to admit that our lives are in our own flawed, fallible hands. Our futures are not kept safe for us in the cradle of fate. We have to hack them out of stone, dig them out of mud, and build them one messy, imperfect day at a time.

By now my hand is shaking so much that my letters are a mess, but hopefully Paul can still read what I have to say. *You grew up believing nobody could ever love you unconditionally. That you didn't even deserve to be loved. But everyone deserves to be loved, and there's so much waiting for you. You don't need fate to give you a friend like Theo, or mentors like my parents. They chose you. The more they knew you, the more they understood who you really are, the more they loved you. And it took me so long to see you because you hide yourself so well, but I see you now, Paul. I see you and I love you so m—*

The pen falls from my fingers, my words trailing into a scrawl, as Paul pulls me fiercely to him. I slide my arms around his neck and hug him back, willing him not only to understand what I've been saying, but to believe it, too. He kisses my forehead, my cheek, and finally my lips, both of us slowly opening our mouths as we drink each other in.

I swore that I would never make another mistake like I did in the Russiaverse, never again assume what kind of choices one of my other selves might make with her body. But we are within a Paul and Marguerite who share a bed, a life, and a child. What we feel is not so different from what they feel.

We're in our home. We, and this world, are safe. We have the entire night.

I'm the one who gets off the couch, takes Paul's hand, and starts leading him to the bedroom. He's the one who picks me up in his arms to carry me the rest of the way, lays me down on the bed again, and covers my body with his own.

But we each help the other struggle out of our clothes. We each call on our memories of that one night in the dacha. We each reveal ourselves completely, bodies and souls, as we never have before. Paul and I are united in shadow and silence. What we create, we create together.

25

I AWAKEN FROM A DREAM I CAN'T REMEMBER, EXCEPT THAT sounds were a part of it. The seashell roar in my ears jars me only for the first instant. After that, I have more important things to think about.

Paul lies on his side next to me, his gray eyes gentle. How long has he been watching me sleep? I hope I didn't drool or something. Maybe not, because as he sees me blink and stir, a small smile dawns on his face. When I smile back, he traces along my hairline with one finger. His touch warms me like a sunbeam as we lie side by side amid the rumpled white sheets.

We spent one other night together, in the dacha in Russia, but he was Lieutenant Markov then—both my Paul and someone else entirely new. This time, even though we inhabit other bodies, we were no one but ourselves. Despite the tremendous emotion between us then, this is even more intimate. Maybe it's our true beginning.

Or maybe not. Paul's eyes remain sad, his smile wistful. Does he believe in what I wrote last night? Or does he still doubt himself, and believe his splintering will shadow him forever? Does he think destiny is something we can create— or something we've lost?

To ask these questions, or at least get the answers, I'd have to find a pen and a sheet of paper. But maybe it's for the best that communicating isn't as easy between us here. Instead of plunging back into doubt and angst, or having some awkward, irrelevant conversation about anything but what's most on our minds, we simply lie together in this fragile, stolen moment.

Paul startles and turns toward the door in the back of our bedroom, the one that leads to the nursery.

Oh, right. We have a baby, and babies cry.

The rest of the morning is not as romantic.

What else can she want? Paul writes at one point, after the mashed sweet potato becomes the third potential meal Valentina has thrown at us.

I shrug, feeling helpless. My chest is as flat as usual in this universe, so I'm obviously not breastfeeding her. (Which I'm selfishly grateful for, because that would be *deeply weird*.) We changed her. We tried to feed her. We burped her. Now we're trying to feed her again. That's pretty much all there is, right?

Valentina, however, seems positive there is something else we should be doing, parent-wise, that we have shamefully neglected. Tears run down her flushed face as she pushes the rest of the mashed sweet potato away. She looks so miserable that it's impossible to feel angry or annoyed. Instead guilt bears down on me. This little girl needs her mommy. Maybe she senses that's not really me.

Paul must be thinking the exact same thing. As I brush orange mush off the loose white nightgown I tugged on this morning, he writes, *I shouldn't have taken the Nightthief. Then her father could care for her most of the time.*

I shake my head no and take the pen. *We need to get the stabilizer built as fast as possible. The sooner we do that, the sooner she gets her parents back.* Which is all true, and I know it, but I still feel so ashamed as I look at Valentina—

—who says "Milk?"

With her hand, in sign.

"Milk?" I sign back. Valentina brightens, going from looking miserable to hopeful. I open the one small cabinet for dishes and see, on the highest shelf, a collection of bottles and nipples. By the time I turn back around with the fixed bottle of milk, Valentina is already holding out her chubby little hands. When I give it to her, I'm rewarded with the briefest of smiles before she pops it in her mouth.

Of course this Marguerite is teaching her daughter sign language, just like Paul must be teaching her how to speak. The baby is too young to talk, but apparently kids can start signing a little earlier. Paul sags against the small fridge in relief, and I can't help laughing.

An instant later one of the small lights blinks in the corner.

Frowning, Paul goes to open the door, but he smiles when he sees who's come to visit.

"Good morning!" my mother signs to me, then stops as she takes in my nightgown, Paul's T-shirt and boxers, and Valentina's flushed face. Behind her is Dad, who only has eyes for his granddaughter. My parents look basically the same as if they'd come in from our living room back home, if Dad stopped to pick up a really unattractive pair of plastic-rimmed glasses along the way. Mom's idea of dressing up is using bobby pins to hold her bun back instead of pencils. Dad's scarf is a bold shade of blue that probably stood out like a beacon on the streets of Moscow.

I'd be touched by the way my father brushes his hand over Valentina's head if it weren't for what he signs next, which is approximately, "Baby pretty very. Josie said sick you?"

Mom asks, "Sick you also Paul?"

I have to bite the inside of my cheek to keep from laughing. Grammar, in sign language, turns out to be three-dimensional; the meaning and sentence functions of the individual gestures are determined not only by the shape of the fingers or the order they come in, but the positions and movements of the hands, too. Facial expressions matter, as do the sharpness and clarity of finger movement. My parents, the mega-geniuses, have no clue about these parts of signing. Obviously they didn't learn until they were already adults, so they never got very good at it—and as a result, now they talk to me like cavemen.

Well, I got the gist of what they were asking. "I'm fine.

341

Lots better." They don't seem to have come over to check on me, though. Apparently we invited them over for breakfast, or maybe this is just something we do as a family on our days off. "But it took Valentina a long time to decide what she wanted this morning."

Obviously my mom and dad understand sign language better than they can use it themselves. Mom smiles and leans over to kiss the top of her granddaughter's head as Dad tells us, "You clothing we baby storage. Happy to storage."

Storage is as close as they can come to saying *keep*. I beam at Paul, who is staring blankly at the people using sign. "Thanks for keeping Valentina for a little while, Mom and Dad. We'll be right back." With that I take Paul's arm and pull him into the back of our apartment.

We dress in a hurry, making a mess as we go through closets and drawers to figure out where all our stuff is. As I roll thick socks up my legs, Paul pauses buttoning his shirt long enough to write, *We shouldn't tell them about the Firebirds right away.*

I shake my head. *No. I'm done lying to the other universes. In this one, they might even be able to help us!*

This is the USSR, Paul writes. *It's a police state. Friends report on friends, and paranoia reigns. If I come across as an intruder instead of someone offering knowledge, your parents could report me.*

I want to tell him they'd never do that—but Mom and Dad are profoundly shaped by their own worlds. While I think they would never betray me, I can't be sure they'd do the same for Paul.

I could wind up in a gulag, Paul insists. *I need to introduce the topic slowly. So, for a while, they need to think I'm this world's Paul. I can talk to them in Russian—that's the language they said hello to me in—but what if they notice I'm not signing with you?*

Oh, good catch. Let's say you hurt your hand yesterday. Nothing serious, but you need to give it a rest. That ought to work.

Neither of us acknowledges the bed filling our room, its cover and sheets still crumpled, the pillows still softly sloping in where our heads lay. What we did last night, what I said—it almost feels like a dream I had, one I wished into being. Does Paul believe me about our infinite chances, our one world? Or do the scars of his splintering, and his own terrible past, run too deep?

When we emerge, Mom and Dad are standing in the middle of the room, the weirdest expressions on their faces—somewhere between shock, fear, and amusement. Mom is holding Valentina, but at arm's length, like she's something they found unexpectedly. They both startle to see Paul and me, and Mom says something out loud. I don't have any idea what. Lip reading is especially hard when you don't know which language someone is speaking in.

Paul takes a step back, jaw dropping in surprise, which is when I see the glints of metal at my parents' necks. Those are Firebirds. Which means the Mom and Dad from this universe just became my mom and dad, who have traveled through the dimensions at last.

Quickly I grab the pen and paper from last night, flipping over the private things I said to Paul, and write, *This is Moscow. Paul and I live here and that's Valentina. I'm deaf.*

Mom and Dad look stricken, and Mom's hand reaches toward me. Why are they so upset? They recover quickly, though. After a second my father takes the pen and writes, *Is this your baby or ours? I'm not sure which possibility is more terrifying.*

I laugh. *Ours, which is terrifying enough.*

Dad shows this to Mom, and the two of them get this gooey-sweet expression as they look at Valentina—like they're melting inside at the mere sight of their almost-grandchild. Meanwhile Valentina stares at all of us with suspicion. I think she's figured out we're a bunch of impostors.

Mom shifts Valentina onto her hip with practiced ease, and the four of us sit down at the table with the embroidered cloth, paper and pen at the ready to explain what's going on.

My father begins, with his chicken-scratch scrawl, *Once we had enough Firebirds collected from the various dimensions, your mother and I realized we could speed the process up considerably by finally traveling ourselves. Rather than leave P and T to build all stabilizer devices to protect the dimensions, we could handle a few of them in person.*

Theo has taken over communication between the universes for now, Mom writes next, her other arm wrapped around Valentina in her lap. Her handwriting is as delicate and precise as she is. *He's still feeling ill, so Josie's come home to help him out.*

Dad taps the piece of paper, wanting his say: *You can imagine how appalled she was when we told her the Home Office's motivation. She said she'd rather be dead a thousand times over—any version of her would, and I believe her—*

Mom gives Dad a look as she takes the pen back. *Time is*

of the essence. Thanks to data from the other universes, particularly the tracking information from the Warverse, we've determined that the Home Office has changed its plan of attack. They're going after more source vectors now.

I suck in a breath and grab the pen. *You mean, they're willing to kill even more dimensions?*

My parents nod. Paul mutters something that I don't have to lip-read to understand is profanity. The enormity of the Home Office's crimes already stretched almost beyond my ability to comprehend it, and yet they can still become worse. Is there no end to this? How can we ever stop these dark versions of my parents and Wyatt Conley, all of whom are just as smart and several technological steps ahead?

We can't, whispers a traitorous voice in my head, the memory of sound amid the constant rush of white noise.

It's Paul who resumes writing. *Although we should start building the stabilizer for this universe immediately, I have a theory we should explore about using the Firebirds themselves instead. We could link two Firebirds together. If one device were directed to increase the matter-antimatter asymmetry in a dimension, and the other were set to overload*—he pauses writing to mime, on his own Firebird, exactly how that might be done—*the overload might provide as much power as any stabilizer. Meaning two travelers could save a universe, though of course one Firebird would be sacrificed, stranding the traveler there for the time being. But in a worst-case scenario, this option could help us.*

Dad takes the pen next. *Fascinating stuff! But we should stick to what we know works, for now. We can all split up as soon as we're sure things are underway here, and then we'll find out which dimensions to target next. Where can we get the raw materials for the stabilizer?*

Paul responds, *Marguerite and I got here last night, so we haven't had much time to figure out where we study or work.*

I notice the pause between his writing *so* and *we*—the unconscious acknowledgment of what we *did* spend last night doing. Before Mom and Dad can pick up on that, I grab the pen. *Actually, I work as a muralist for the Communist Party. When I got to this dimension, I was painting Paul as a peasant following Lenin to the socialist paradise of the future.* This is amusing, but irrelevant, so I add, *I'm calling this the Moscowverse.*

They start going through their pockets and our mail to see what clues they can pick up. The USSR Academy of Sciences turns out to be not far away, and Dad, Mom, and Paul all have IDs (plain paper, filled out by typewriter, no photos). Before long, Paul and my father have also found a map of Moscow and start trying to figure out how far the university is from here.

As they do so, my mother puts down the wriggling Valentina, who crawls toward her blocks with only one backward glance that clearly means, *I'm onto you people.* Mom watches her, enraptured, only reluctantly turning back to write, *I knew you and Paul might have an extraordinary child, but actually seeing her amazes me.*

She's not ours, Mom. Not even in the very limited way the grand duchess's child is ours—though I actually haven't even

346

told my parents about that yet. Now is so incredibly not the time. *She belongs to the Paul and Marguerite from this universe. Looks like we met about five years ago here. He learned sign language for me.*

I expect Mom to find that almost as adorable as Valentina. My parents have been almost disturbingly enthusiastic cheerleaders for Paul and me since the beginning. Instead she leans back in her chair, wincing as if in pain. Concerned, I touch her arm, but she shakes her head and picks up the pen again. *Was it the meningitis?*

You mean, is that why I'm deaf? I guess so, but I don't know. It must have been a long time ago, here. Besides, it's not as if deaf people walk around with cards saying, This is the specific reason I can't hear you. It's not like I could ask anyone.

Mom shakes her head as she writes back, *It's just so hard to see you like this.*

Why? It doesn't hurt. Honestly, Mom I don't even miss sound that much. I don't need to hear in order to be a painter.

But you can't hear your baby or Paul—the person you are in this universe might not even remember the sounds of our voices.

The weirdest thing about Mom's unhappiness is that, before I came to the Moscowverse, I might have felt just like she does. Now I shake my head no, vehemently, before reclaiming the pen. *That doesn't mean I don't remember you, or feel how much you love me. I mean, it matters—I'm sure this Marguerite has to deal with a lot of problems I haven't even thought of yet—but it's not some massive tragedy. It's just another way to be. That's all.*

I don't think I've convinced my mother, but she lets it go, nodding without writing another word.

So I ask, *Your first trip into another dimension. What do you think?*

It's extraordinary. Mom smiles again, glowing but wistful. *Actually living within another self. Though I would have chosen a locale besides the USSR. This was all we ever wanted from the Firebirds—a chance to see other quantum realities. To explore more of the multiverse. Only to* learn. *Instead, we're trapped chasing the worst versions of ourselves, and for the saddest reason imaginable.*

We're trapped, I think. I imagine the Home Office, what it was like to be there, and wish the sheer force of my loathing could shake the place apart. If only I could return, rip their Firebirds apart with my bare hands . . .

. . . but I could, couldn't I?

The idea of returning to the Home Office has been sneaking around in the back of my mind for a while, but it never emerged as a fully conscious thought. I can't go to a dimension I don't exist in, and Wicked is off on her demonic field trip through the multiverse, so she's not there for me to inhabit . . .

. . . but her body *is* there. Just "not observable."

That's never really occurred to me before. I've never tried going to a dimension with a body that, well, wasn't being used at the time. As I turn the idea over in my mind, more facets become apparent to me, until this isn't just a raw theory I've come up with.

It's an opportunity, one unlike any other we've had.

Coud I leap into Wicked's body while her mind is completely absent? If I did, then her body should become observable again, fully corporeal, the moment I arrive. It's hard to wrap my mind around that. While I know that bodies remain behind, their invisibility and intangibility make it seem as if they go off into the ether somewhere. But they don't.

If I jumped into the Home Office right now, Wicked's body would be right there waiting.

And instead of always being the one on the run, chasing after the Home Office's plans, I could finally take the fight to them.

Normally I'd ask my parents and Paul whether I'm correct about this. But I don't need the physics equations to tell me that this is how it works. After months of traveling through the dimensions, I've got this much down pat. More important, I can't tip them off about my plan. They'd try to stop me. They'd say it was too dangerous.

And it *is* dangerous. Even after days on end of fighting for my life, I know this could be my deadliest journey of all.

But trillions of lives are on the line. That makes it worth the risk.

Dad and Paul remain embroiled in their discussion of Moscow maps. I scoot my chair back and get to my feet. When Mom looks at me, puzzled, I quickly write, *Valentina needs more milk. If I'm going to stay here until you guys have this universe covered, then I should run to the store now, while you can watch her. I think I saw one not far away, yesterday.*

Which is a lie. Last evening I was far too overwhelmed to remember anything like the location of the nearest grocery. But I'm obeying Theo's first law of lying—keep it simple, stupid.

Sure enough, Mom nods. She writes, *Are you sure you'll be able to buy something? There used to be incredibly long lines for goods at Soviet stores.*

I shrug. *We still need milk, so I have to try. I'll be back as fast as I can.*

My coat and gloves from yesterday hang from the hooks I put them on last night. As I bundle up again, then slip a few rubles from my knapsack into my coat pocket, I see my mother explaining to my dad and Paul what I'm doing. My father nods and smiles at me, starts to speak, thinks better of it, and then gives me a little thumbs up. I smile back, trying very hard not to dwell on the danger of what I'm about to do.

Paul looks at me searchingly. Does he suspect where I'm really headed? No—if he did, he'd tackle me to keep me from walking out the door. But he gets to his feet, as if to walk me to the doorway. Valentina chooses this moment to pull at his trouser leg. Even if he's not exactly her daddy, apparently he's close enough, and she wants his attention now. Paul leans down to scoop her back up in his arms.

I watch him studying Valentina, taking in the shape of her face, her eyes. Is he, too, thinking about our child in the Russiaverse, and wondering if this is our glimpse of her? My heart twinges as I realize this is probably the last time I will ever see this little girl that could have been mine.

But she belongs to this Marguerite, this Paul, this world. That's why I have to protect them all, at any cost. I wave goodbye and go through the door, shutting it behind me and never once looking back.

I walk out of the apartment building and move quickly along the sidewalk, taking turn after turn, getting myself as thoroughly lost as possible. I go through my pockets to make sure I don't have any identifying information with my address. Since I left my wallet at home, everything seems to be in the clear. If Wicked leaps into this body, she won't know how to find her home or the people waiting there, and it might take her hours to sort everything out.

This world's Marguerite, though—she'll remember everything. She'll understand why I have to act.

So I know she'll also take a note back to my parents, and Paul.

I reach a small park, which is nearly deserted on this cool, overcast morning. Taking a seat on a bench, I pull out the pen I nabbed from the dining room table and the one piece of paper in this coat pocket. The back is large enough for me to write:

> *Everyone—*
> *I'm sorry I didn't talk this over with all of you, but you would've stopped me, or at least argued with me for a long time. But I have to do this, and I have to do it now.*

We'll never stop the Home Office by chasing after them.
We can only go back to the source. And as long as Wicked
is running through other universes, her body remains in the
Home Office, existing but not observable until she returns.

Or until I do.

I'll have Wicked's body to myself. That could make me
the ultimate weapon or even make her the ultimate hostage.
Could I hold a blade to her neck the way she held one to
mine?

Valentina's face shimmers in my mind, replaced by the
sight of the grand duchess asking Paul what to name their
baby. Her dimension is one of the ones I must save.

Yes. I can do this.

Keep going. Keep saving world after world. Don't wait to
find out what happens, and don't come after me.
I love you all—Marguerite

After a moment, I add at the bottom: *We can make a better*
world.

That's for Paul, only for him. He'll understand that. But
will he believe?

I slide the paper back into my coat pocket for this Marguerite to refer to in a minute. Getting to my feet, I see
St. Basil's and the Kremlin in the distance, vividly colorful
against the wintry grays of the city and the sky. A wave of
nostalgia sweeps through me for this country I've known in

two different guises. One of them showed me the heights of wealth and tragedy; the other cradled me in love and security.

And I'm willing to sacrifice myself for them both.

26

THE SUDDEN PRESSURE OF THE CHAIR BENEATH ME FEELS like an impact, though of course Wicked's body has been sitting here all along. More startling is the silence—real silence—broken by the subtle whirr of the ventilation system and the newly strange sound of my own breath. I grip the armrests and open my eyes to look out on the darkly garish megalopolis stretching out from below Triad headquarters. Small airborne craft dart around the gigantic skyscrapers like fireflies in the night, and in the distance, one of the high-speed monorails shimmers with electricity, a scar of light on a gloomy horizon.

The Home Office. I'm back to the beginning of the conspiracy at last.

I feel subtly different—as if I'd just gone swimming or done yoga, my body pleasantly energized instead of exhausted. Then I realize it's because I'm alone in here. Wicked is off tormenting some other Marguerite somewhere, so I have this body all to myself. The last time I was here, her sorrow and anger weighed me down like an anchor. Now I'm free.

What time is it? To judge by the darkness and the relative stillness of the megalopolis outside, it's the time of night when "very late" turns into "very early." Perfect. The fewer people around to observe me, the better.

I get to my feet and start searching for this universe's version of a computer terminal—a slim black panel that can be found on a table, or a wall, or even on the arm of a chair. If Wicked is Triad's most trusted operative here in the Home Office, then her clearance should allow me to access any information I need. Do I look for a main computer core? For Firebird storage? Any damage I can do to their data would help, but I need to figure out how to maximize my impact—and, preferably, take the Home Office out of the universe-destruction business completely.

My parents would've had a better idea exactly what to target; so would Paul. Biting my lower lip, I wonder whether I should've told them about my plans after all.

The resistance! Memories flash through my mind as bright as victory banners: This world's Paul and Theo, former employees of Triad, living as a band of outlaws on the murky, underpopulated surface of this world. The weapons they held. The mission they all agreed upon—the downfall of Triad.

If I can find them again, they can tell me what to target—and then Wicked's body will become our ultimate weapon.

"Miss Caine?"

I turn to see two men standing in the doorway, both tall and blank-faced as mannequins. Although their monochromatic gray outfits differ only slightly from mine, instinctively I understand these guys are Triad security. Are they here to guard me or to guard against me?

"You sent no advance word of your return to this universe," says the same guy who spoke before—that, or they both have the same dull, monotonous voice. "This activates primary security protocols. What was the color of the Beatles' submarine?"

Not purple. My world is the only one where it's purple. What did Wyatt Conley say about this? In some universes, the Beatles sang about a "Big Green Submarine," but mostly the submarine is yellow. Shouldn't I go with the most common one?

And yet I still can't wrap my mind around the idea of a yellow submarine. So I roll the dice. "Green. The Beatles' submarine was green."

The guard lifts his arm and begins speaking into what must be a communicator bracelet: "All security to level forty-seven. Extra-dimensional intruder detected. Imposter Marguerite Caine reveals knowledge of entity called 'the Beatles.'"

Trick question. Damn! I look around wildly for somewhere to run. A door farther down the hallway opens, and I brace myself for a phalanx of guards rushing in to arrest me—

—and instead I see Romola Harrington, again, wearing

an outfit all in rich royal blue. One lock of her blond hair has escaped from its braid, marring her usual smug, placid expression. As she hurries toward us, she wrings her hands together and says, "You're not supposed to be back yet."

"Intruder," the security guard says. "We're taking her into custody now."

"Indeed not." Romola acts as though the butler asked her whether she wouldn't rather eat her roast pheasant off a paper plate. "The other Marguerite requires level-one interrogation. Leave that to me."

The security guard pauses. "Level one . . ."

Romola draws herself even more rigidly upright. I imagine her spine straightening until it snaps, but no such luck. "You don't have the clearance. I do. If you'll excuse me, gentlemen?"

The other guard, the silent one, hands over what must be a pair of handcuffs—though they're made of plastic. Romola clicks them around my wrists as if she's done this a thousand times before.

But she hasn't, because one of the binders doesn't fully close. It's not locked, which means I can still get out. Despite the surge of triumph I feel, I bow my head as if in defeat and bide my time.

"You'll receive the appropriate credit and commendations," Romola says smoothly to the guards as she guides me toward the nearest elevator, her hand firm around my upper arm. "Please remain here to await further instructions."

The guards nod as we walk into the elevator. I wait until the doors slide shut. As the floor shudders with the tiny jerk-and-give of motion, Romola says, "My goodness, I never thought—"

I don't know what she never thought, and I don't plan to find out, because that's when I punch her in the face.

I've gotten better at hitting people since I started traveling with the Firebird, but it still hurts like hell. The heel of my hand jars against Romola's jaw, sending her staggering backward. She grabs at my sleeve, though, and takes me down with her.

When we hit the floor of the elevator, I grab a fistful of her hair. "Where are my parents?"

"I don't know!"

Romola sounds panicked—but in the very next moment, she clamps both her hands around my free wrist and twists hard enough to make me cry out and let her go. She tries to pin me, but I get one of my knees between us and use it to throw her off.

The security guards can't reach us in here. Nobody's coming to help her. Romola's stronger than she looks, but she won't want to hurt me badly, because this is Wicked's body she'd be breaking. But I'm willing to mess both of them up, which means I'm going to win.

Nobody told Romola that, though. She lunges at me with enough force to send me sprawling onto my back. "What are you doing?" she yells. "Have you gone completely mad?"

"Tell me—where—my parents are!" I grab at her arms,

trying to get her off me—which is when I see that she, too, is wearing a Firebird.

Wait.

She raises an eyebrow. "Catching on at last, are you? Thank goodness. Where are you from?"

"The Berkeleyverse. Where are you from?"

"The Mafiaverse, which by the way is an atrocious name." Romola lets go of me, flops onto her butt, and sighs. "Good lord. Do you think next time you could wait to hit someone until you've checked to find out whether that person is on your side?"

"Probably not, actually. No time to waste." I can't quite wrap my head around this. Romola's on my side this time? My brain rejects the idea, replaying memory after memory of Romola doing me wrong. Getting me wasted so I wouldn't look for Paul on my own, freeing Wicked to continue her mission of destruction, or setting me up to destroy the Romeverse.

But none of those were this Romola. This is the one who met me at the movies in Times Square, watched a goofy comedy, and showed me the glory of mixed M&M's and popcorn. This Romola is my friend, and she traveled through the dimensions to help.

I've been so shaken by finding my one worst self that I never considered how much it might change our fates by finding someone else's best self. Travel through enough dimensions and maybe you'd find the hero and the villain in everyone.

I ask, "How did you even know to come to the Home Office in the first place?"

"We all agreed we needed a pair of eyes 'on the inside,' as it were. I seemed to be the best candidate—the one the Home Office wouldn't suspect." Romola shrugs. "When security signaled about capturing an alternate Marguerite, I knew it could only be you."

"How long have you been here?" I ask as we start to get to our feet.

"Not quite twenty-four hours, I think?" Romola smiles unevenly and reaches out to snap the cuff binders off my wrist for good. "Turns out Triad has employee barracks in this universe. Optional, but rather well-populated. I've found it easier to simply remain in my office."

Do I want to know what employee barracks look like? No, I don't. "I came here to sabotage Triad any way I could, but I don't know what to do—or what to do it to. Any insight?"

"Not in particular. You were looking for your parents?"

I shake my head no. "Not really. They'll realize I'm an imposter. But if I'd had to call on them to get out of a level-one interrogation—"

"Got it." Romola nods once. "I've been trying to study their core computer functions, to look for vulnerabilities, but Triad is so vast in this universe, it's like trying to find the center of the internet."

"The resistance will know what we can do. I managed to find Paul and Theo last time, and maybe I can again." I take a deep breath. "Any idea how I can reach public transit?"

Romola clucks her tongue. "Oh, I can do better than that! I've got access to a company car. That was an unexpected benefit. Triad haven't safeguarded anything against me."

"Because they never saw you coming." Finally it hits me that we've managed to turn one of the Home Office's trickiest weapons to our advantage. I begin to smile. "Thank you for doing this."

"Oh, it was nothing." Romola gives me a PR agent smile, then pauses as it fades. "Actually, given that you're trying to keep my universe from potentially being demolished, it really is the least I can do."

She punches the elevator panel, canceling her last floor request and redirecting us toward the garage. We're this close to escaping into the wider world of the Home Office, finding the resistance, and shutting this down once and for all.

Just one problem.

"What do you mean, it flies?" Romola stands outside her silvery car, which bobs a few inches off its platform on some kind of magnetic field. Dozens more hover all around us, shimmering in the garage bay like Christmas ornaments hung from spindly branches. "It's a *flying* car?"

"Did you not see them outside the windows?"

"Of course I did! But I never thought those were the only kind of automobiles this dimension had."

"Well, they are. The city's been built up so high that almost nobody goes down to ground level anymore." I bite my lower lip, wishing for some way out of this, but there isn't one. "You'll just have to try it."

"Me?" Romola's eyes grow wider. "Why me?"

"I don't even have a driver's license for a regular car yet. Just a permit."

This argument isn't as convincing as I expected. Romola says, "I haven't one either."

"What? You're, like, four or five years older than me."

"I grew up in London and never left until I moved to lower Manhattan! When would I ever have had occasion to drive a bloody car?"

Dad, you really should have let me borrow the car more often. I take a deep breath. "Okay, let's try this thing."

If you think driving in two dimensions can be tricky, you have no idea how terrible it is in three. Disengaging from the magnetic "parking spot" is easy, but everything after that is an exercise in horror.

"Oh, my God." Romola clutches at her seat belt as though it could hold her up on its own as the hovercar wobbles out of the garage, and we see just how many hundreds of feet we are from the ground. "We're going to die."

"Way to think positive, Romola." But when I try to turn, and the car bobs even more precariously, I add, "Keep one hand on your Firebird."

Come on, come on, you can do this, I tell myself. *You haven't come this far just to get taken out by a stupid flying car!*

If only the ground weren't so far beneath us . . .

I take the controls and nudge the car downward. The

slope makes me shift forward until my safety belt is all that's holding me in my seat, and Romola whimpers. But I take it slow, edging us down a bit at a time. When I stop thinking of it as a car in flight, and instead remember it as the submarine from the Oceanverse, steering in three dimensions gets a little easier.

"Heavens, it's dark." Romola peers through the front windows with both trepidation and curiosity. The metal and concrete buildings on either side of us loom overhead like cliffs, and our pathway is a valley. "Are you sure you'll know when we're reaching the ground?"

"The altitude sensor will show us." I point to the gauge that I really, really hope is the altitude sensor.

By the time we reach the ground, the gloom is nearly complete. The only illumination besides our headlights comes from a few squats where the poorest of people live, where we see the glow of lanterns and the flicker of candles. We're probably waking up everyone, which can't be the greatest way to keep the resistance's location secret. But without the headlights, I'll crash this thing for sure.

As we move slowly along, about ten feet above the ground, Romola gapes at the makeshift shanties, the rubble that used to be sidewalks or soil, and the ramshackle gangways and rope bridges that connect the dwellings down here. "It looks like a refugee camp," she whispers. "I suppose it is. Except people haven't run away—they've run downward."

"I guess." By now the car is scanning for the location we input—my parents' home address, from the Triad database—because as late as a couple of weeks ago, the resistance was headquartered not that far away (horizontally speaking, at least). No need for me to navigate: All I have to do is keep nudging the car forward and make sure I don't hit any of the gangways. "So, tell me, what exactly is your deal?"

"I beg your pardon?" Romola's tone turns frosty, and she raises an eyebrow. "My 'deal'?"

"Why are you usually so loyal to Conley? Even when he's normally a gigantic psychopath? I mean, I watched another version of you set up a dimension to be destroyed. You wouldn't have done it on your own, but you did that for him."

"I can't answer for a Romola I haven't met." After a pause she adds, "However, were I to speculate, I'm always a very loyal person to anyone I care about. In my world, Wyatt Conley happens to be an extraordinarily inspiring employer and mentor. In a dimension like this—where money is all that matters, and where people think of their corporations as if they were churches—he must seem like a prophet."

Although I'd like to scoff at that image, I can't. In a world so coldly ambitious that it could turn my parents into killers, Conley would be the ultimate leader.

That doesn't excuse what the other Romola has done. But it makes me capable of seeing this Romola as herself.

I steer over a drooping rope bridge. Its shadow slices through the beams from the car's headlights, making the ragged, broken-down landscape around us look as if it has been torn in half. Romola frowns at one of the screens on the dash. "That shows our location, doesn't it?"

One of her long fingernails taps against the blinking green beacon that says our mark is just ahead.

Parking the car turns out to be the easiest part: Hit the right button and it settles itself onto the ground with barely a thump. Romola reaches for her door handle until I lean across to stop her. "Don't. If the resistance is here, they will have heard us coming. Make sure your Firebird is visible, okay?" I tug mine out over my collar so it will show front and center. "Wait until they come to investigate, then we come out with our hands up."

"Oh! We came here to surrender, then. Jolly good." She does what I told her to do with the Firebird, though.

Sure enough, they appear from the shadows one by one. Their figures are faceless in the darkness, but I can very clearly make out the silhouettes of their weapons. I hold up my hands, nudge for Romola to do the same, and then, after a long few seconds that gives them plenty of time to see, I get out of the car.

Even as I put my hands up again, one of them steps closer. Theo's sneer is exactly as obnoxious as I remember from my last time in the Home Office. He wears the same monochromatic outfit in burnt orange, and his black hair radiates out in spikes that are a cross between the style of Ludwig von Beethoven and an anime character. And his strangely boxy weapon is once again pointed at my heart. "You want us to think you're not from this dimension," he says with a scowl. "So prove it."

"How am I supposed to prove a negative?"

"I don't know, but you'd better figure it out."

"The last time I was here, you were acting like a total ass," I retort.

Theo doesn't flinch. "That doesn't narrow it down much."

"The car!" Romola says. When both of us turn to look at her, she points at the car. "You must've seen what a terrible driver this Marguerite is. Yours would know how to handle a flying car, wouldn't she?"

After a moment, Theo says, "Could've faked it—but you didn't." He lowers the weapon, and I feel like I can breathe again as he adds, "Our Marguerite likes to show off too much. She wouldn't let herself be caught dead doing anything that badly."

"Where's Paul?" I look past Theo into the silhouetted band of fighters that came out here with him. Although I could recognize Paul from his profile, maybe even from the way he stood, I can't spot him. "Is he back in your headquarters? We need to talk."

"I'm here."

I wheel around to look behind me. Paul stands there, silhouetted from behind by lantern-light, almost ghostlike in his pale gray clothes. As he steps closer, I can make out the scar on his jawline, and once again I wonder what happened to Paul in this dimension. Who did that to him?

"What were you thinking, coming here?" His eyes burn with anger so fierce I can see it despite the darkness. "It's dangerous, Marguerite."

I could laugh. "Universes are collapsing all around us. There's no safe place left."

"You were safe in Moscow! If you had told us what you were planning—"

"Wait? Paul?" It's my Paul. Despite my warning, he followed me here. "What are you doing here?"

He lifts his stubborn chin. "Protecting you."

"You were supposed to be protecting the Moscowverse—"

"Sophia and Henry can handle it."

"And what about Valentina?"

"She has her real parents back."

Our argument is interrupted by Theo, who steps between us. "Wait. Little brother—that's not you?"

"It is, Theo. Just a different me." Paul gives Theo a flinty smile, one without any pretense of happiness. But it's honest, and hard, and so obviously, completely my own Paul that I take comfort in it despite his simmering anger.

Theo scowls and leans against the flying car. "I don't like the sound of this."

"Ah, just to be clear—" Romola raises her hand. "This is the Berkeleyverse Paul with us now, yes?"

I nod. "Even though the Home Office Paul could probably help us more at the moment." As much as I love Paul, his protectiveness couldn't have kicked into overdrive at a worse time. "Will you please just let me do this?"

Paul folds his arms in front of his chest. "Not without me."

"We're not alone," Theo announces.

Romola sighs. "How true. We all have other selves, so

even in our own individual person, we can no longer be said to be solitary—"

"No, I mean we're not alone right now." Theo points upward at flickering lights in motion overhead. More flying cars, which doesn't seem like a big deal, until the pink-and-red lights begin to flash and a siren's wail begins to echo in this urban canyon.

My gut drops as if I were on a roller coaster. "The police?"

"Triad security," Theo says, as if it's the same thing. His grin is more vicious than his scowl ever was. "Thanks for dropping by. Looks like you led them straight to us."

Paul and I exchange a stricken look. "And now?" he says.

"We fight for our lives. Or we die. Maybe both." Theo checks his gun's charge and points it upward. "Probably both."

27

CABLES SNAKE DOWN THROUGH THE DARKNESS TO DAN-
gle all around us. Triad's guards begin sliding toward the
ground, flashlight beams streaming from their headsets,
their weapons shadowed against the night—black on black.

"Run!" Theo shouts, and the rest of the resistance scatters. Although some of them are armed, more of them were
caught by surprise. None of them were ready for this fight.

Because you set them up, I tell myself savagely as I dash for
one of the nearby buildings.

The nearest building stretches up so high overhead that
I can't imagine where it ends. Its lower stories, however,
must have been abandoned for a decade or more. The windows are shattered, or simply blank holes covered by ragged
cloths. One of them is open to the air, and I vault through it
as fast as I can. My leap is more acrobatic than my landing,
which sends me sprawling onto the floor of a room empty

except for a few broken-up crates.

Mere seconds later, Paul slides through the window after me, though it's harder for him to get his large frame through. The only illumination comes from the brightening spotlights outside. I duck behind one of the larger, more intact crates, and motion for Paul to join me.

As he kneels by my side, he studies the odd, box-like gun he has in this dimension. "The firing mechanism seems obvious," he mutters. "I'm not as sure about targeting."

"You're not shooting anyone! We didn't come here for that—"

"We didn't come here to get captured, either." Paul takes a deep breath. I see him struggling. This is the splintering at work once more, threatening to shred his self-control at the moment he can least afford to snap. But he's not angry with me, and I realize now that I wasn't really the person he was angry with even before the guards. It's just the unending tension of this chase, and the fear that we're fighting a war we can never win.

"You should go back to the Moscowverse or move on," I whisper as shouting begins outside. "This world's Paul knows how to handle the gun, and he knows where to hide. He'd help me."

Paul looks at me in total incomprehension. "I can't leave you like this."

"You can and you should."

But it's too late. A door I hadn't seen before swings open, and a Triad guard runs in. His weapon is in his hands, and he's aiming it straight at me.

Paul moves so fast he's a blur, launching himself at my attacker. They go down together, but Paul winds up on top. The lights attached to the guard's uniform shine in bright rays straight up toward the ceiling, as though the two of them were fighting in a cage of light. Paul doesn't even bother trying to shoot the guard. Instead he uses his weapon as a bludgeon, smashing the guard's face with it.

"No," I whisper as droplets of blood spatter through the thin beams of light. Paul looks like he's going beat this guy to a pulp—or to death. "Paul, no."

But Paul doesn't hear me. Instead he lifts the gun up, preparing for a more savage or even fatal blow. He's lost to the fever pitch of violence. Truly lost.

Or so I think, until Paul freezes, hand with his bloody gun still over his head.

I watch, wide-eyed, as Paul stares down at his defeated opponent. He's breathing hard, trembling from the sheer rush of adrenaline, but in the faint light I can see his face shifting from a grimace of rage back into the Paul I know. After a long moment, he lowers his hand, then tosses the gun aside.

He did it. Paul took control again. He did it! This isn't like last time, where he spared Romola mostly because he thought she could still fire. He beat the splintering, and he knows he beat it. Despite everything going to hell all around us, I start to smile. Maybe now he can begin to hope again, and that hope can save us both.

Movement flickers at the corner of my eye. My mind supplies only one word: *gun.*

The next guard is firing even as he runs into the room. Paul looks up in the split second before he's hit. His body jerks backward, blood spraying from his chest in a halo of red, and he falls.

My screams seem to belong to someone else. This horrible, agonized sound can't be coming out of my throat; it has to be the whole world shrieking at once. *No no no not Paul that's going to kill them both, this world's Paul and mine unless he can get to the Firebird, or I can—*

I lunge forward, but the guard marching toward Paul shoves me back so hard that I tumble to the ground. Looking over my shoulder through the blur of tears, I see Paul lying on his back, one leg bent under him at an unnatural angle. His hand gropes blindly at his chest—for the Firebird? For the wound? I can't tell. But then the guard fires again, and Paul's body jumps once more before lying still.

He's dead. Paul is dead.

My first thought is to rush the guard again, to make him kill me, too. I want to be dead, to be with Paul, not to feel my heart ripping into a thousand pieces.

Memory takes me back to Russia, to a battlefield of snow and blood, to the side of a cot where Lieutenant Markov lay dying. I imagine his face as he whispered his final words: *Every Marguerite.*

Every Paul, I think as I get my hands under me and prepare to hurl myself at the guard. Every world gives us a chance.

I wish I hadn't blown ours. I wish we'd been able to create a world.

Then the wall caves in.

As the guard skitters backward from the tumbling plaster, I see the flying car that just smashed through the bricks. It's dented and scratched, one window busted out, but it's still operational—and behind the wheel is Theo. He shouts, "Get in!"

I hesitate for only one instant before the memory of my mission wins over my grief. Once I dash for the car, Theo swings open the door—and no sooner has my butt hit the seat than he guns it in reverse. Only grabbing the seat belt keeps me from tumbling out the still-open door to the ground that's now rapidly getting much farther away.

"What happened to Paul?" Theo revs the motor as I tug the door shut, then banks hard, sending us zooming upward through a canyon of high-rise buildings.

I choke back a sob. "He's dead."

Theo swears under his breath. "Yours or mine?"

"Both, I think." As badly as I want to think my Paul was able to use his Firebird and get away, I don't see how he could've had the chance. Roughly I wipe at my cheeks, forcing away the tears. I don't deserve the release. "I never should've come here."

His voice shakes even as he tries to talk tough. "Triad was after us long before you showed up. We knew how it could go." That's as close to absolution as Theo can give me.

The resistance members weren't the only ones I

endangered. "Wait. Where's Romola?"

"The Romola you showed up with?" Theo executes a hairpin turn that sends us careening through a narrow, crooked alleyway. "She went back to her home universe, which is exactly what she should've done. This world's Romola? She's back with the guards, probably bitching about how I stole her car. Let's dent this sucker up, huh? Pay her back for what happened to Paul."

The next five minutes are more like being trapped in some kind of video game than anything resembling real life. It would terrify me if I weren't crushed by grief. Theo zig-zags through the densely packed city as if it were a maze he'd run a thousand times before. Once he even steers the car almost completely vertical, vaulting into the air like a rocket blasting into orbit. But he can't shake the guards pursuing us.

They're going to catch us, and if they were willing to kill Paul, they'll kill Theo, too. My hands can't bear any more blood.

"I can't let this happen." I try to catch Theo's eyes. "I can't let you pay the price for this."

Theo simply accelerates. "C'mon. You ought to know by now that I can handle a car in any dimension."

I remember the wreckage after the fatal crash in Quito, the way it felt to shut Theo's eyes for him. "That doesn't mean you always make it out alive."

He doesn't reply, but he does slow down. Slightly. "I've got this, okay? Just hang on."

We soar out into a broader traffic way. Now that it's dawn,

more people are out and about, which means other flying cars swoop and swerve around us. Theo swiftly steers us out of the main drag, just over a long building that's several dozen stories shorter than average. How far are we above it? Not even ten feet. Probably that's Theo's idea of "lying low."

I see it as an opportunity.

"Good luck, Theo," I say, and I grab the door handle.

"Marguerite—no—"

His voice falls away as I leap from the car. For one split second, there's nothing but rushing air, but I remember to tuck and roll. That doesn't keep it from hurting like hell when I land on the roof, but as I tumble over and over, I remain conscious. Skin is scraped from my arms, and pain tells me where the bruises will be, but my bones don't crack.

But I lie there, motionless, even as the guards' vehicles hover around me to take me into custody. I'm too devastated even to cry. Instead I wonder why I'm not dead. Why our hearts don't stop beating the moment they're broken. It feels like my soul has already left me, and my body is just this weight I'll have to carry forever.

Maybe he got away, I try to tell myself as I walk numbly through the corridors of Triad, my wrists held together with binders, a guard at either shoulder. Paul did reach for his Firebird. He could've jumped out. Maybe.

But I can't make myself believe it.

I'm led into an area of Triad headquarters I haven't seen before—their labs, I'm guessing. The narrow black-panel computer terminals I've glimpsed elsewhere are now enormous panels that nearly cover the walls; their calculations show in faint display of color that shine briefly, then fade, as they continue the long work of determining which dimensions have to die. This complex exceeds our power and sophistication by so great a degree that I can't believe we ever thought we stood a chance. They haven't even bothered taking away my Firebird. That's how little a threat I've ever been to them.

Wyatt Conley isn't anywhere around, which is a small mercy. But my parents wait here, standing near a long, glass-walled chamber in the very center of the lab, as if it were the altar in this cathedral of death. Their expressions remain sorrowful but fond—as if they were about to ground me.

"Sweetheart," my mother says. "I'm sorry this has been so difficult."

They still refuse to acknowledge the truth of what they're doing. "You killed other versions of me. You killed an entire universe. That goes slightly beyond 'difficult.'"

Dad shrugs. "Who said it would be easy to raise someone from the dead?"

"What makes you think you can?" Before they start in with their explanations, I gesture as best I can at my Firebird. "You tore my Paul into four pieces. You splintered his soul. And after that he had to fight as hard as he could to stay in control, maybe even just to stay sane."

Paul won that fight. At least he had that moment of triumph just before the end.

I continue, "What do you think Josie's going to become after you put the thousand pieces of her back together again? If you think she'll be your daughter again, the same girl you lost, you're wrong. She'll be haunted by lives she never lived. Controlled by desires she never felt. Unable to love the people she loved before or to promise that she can keep from hurting anyone who crosses her path. Your version of me called Paul 'Frankenstein's monster,' but really it was Josie she was describing. Josie is the one you're turning into a monster."

Finally, my parents are speechless. It takes Dad a long time to muster the ability to say, "We're close, so close—"

"You're willing to condemn Josie to a living hell just so you don't have to grieve anymore. Oh, wait! You *are* going to keep grieving. Just like I had to mourn my dad months after I knew he hadn't really drowned. Remember how you made me think he'd drowned?" Tears well in my eyes again. "No wonder you don't care if Josie turns into a monster. You're all monsters already."

The silence that follows seems to last for years. I wonder dully whether they'll try again to make me work for them. What else can they do to me? Destroy my dimension, probably. That would be the only way to eliminate me as a risk forever.

For a moment I imagine our home in the Berkeley Hills, with its cozy great room, the potted plants and the rainbow table, the chalkboard wall of equations, and the constant chatter of scientific theories, geeky jokes, and boundless affection. It seems like the house stands for our entire world, the one that's about to be lost.

"Look," Mom finally says, gesturing to the glass chamber. "Marguerite, please, just look."

Look at what? The chamber is empty—or is it?

My jaw drops as I realize that there's a translucent shape at the heart of the chamber, the color of fog, almost invisible. After a few moments, I finally recognize what I'm seeing: Josie. She lies there, hands over her heart, the posture she must have been in when she activated her Firebird for that last fatal jump. The universe or universes Triad have already destroyed sent their splinters back, which is just enough to recreate this much of her—a suggestion, a shade, only a hint of the body they're trying to reanimate.

When they look at old paintings under infrared light, sometimes they see the shadows of figures the artist painted over, or outlines of people they meant to draw but finally chose to leave out. That's what Josie is now, just a blurry shadow that doesn't belong anymore.

"Oh," I say. "Not a monster yet. Only a ghost."

"Marguerite, stop it," Dad snaps. "We can't quit. Not this close to success. Not even if—if—"

Not even if we know it's the right thing to do. That's what he's not saying. Mom and Dad can't lie to themselves any longer, but they also can't turn back. Their maniacal commitment won't let them—and they can't let Josie go, not while they can actually see her lying here, so close to resurrection.

I have to set them free. I have to set Josie free. I have one last chance to stop this, if I act right now.

While my parents stare, transfixed, at my dead sister's face, I bring my bound hands to my chest; I have just enough freedom to wrap my fingers around the Firebird. Leaping away would change nothing, and it would save me only for a few hours or days.

But there's incredible power stored inside this locket—and in Moscow, Paul showed us all how to set it to overload.

I close my eyes. I envision his hands, mimic his movements. Did I get it right? A faint vibration between my fingers tells me that I did.

"Josie would never have wanted this," I say. "Not your version, not mine, not any Josie ever. She said so."

My parents look at each other, more surprised and dismayed than I'd thought they would be. "It doesn't matter how long we have to work with her," Mom finally says. "Or how difficult it is. We will put Josie back together again."

The faintest warmth emanates from the Firebird in my hands, as though I had just ended a journey. In some ways, I guess I have. "That's not what I mean. Josie won't be able to go on, knowing how many people died so she could live. She'll hate herself for every breath. And she'll never feel the same about you, or the other me, or Conley. So you're robbing her of everyone she's ever loved. Some resurrection. You're not bringing her back from heaven. You're making sure Josie's life will be a living hell."

But I can save my sister. I can save my whole world. Everyone but Paul.

The metal against my palms warms even more—becomes hot—

"What's that sound?" Dad, who's been trying to ignore me, jerks around and looks at me. His eyes widen. "Dear God."

As fast as I can, I lift the Firebird over my head and hurl it at the glass. One pane shatters, sending shards flying in every direction. The Firebird itself lands in the middle of Josie's shadowy half-form—the body that is only just becoming observable again—and for a moment it glows red where her heart ought to have been. My mother screams, and I wonder just how big the boom is going to be.

When it blows, the explosion seems to roar through all the dimensions at once.

When I come to, only a few minutes must have passed. Broken bits of glass and metal pepper the floor, and most of the nearby computer panels have gone dully dark, their world-ending calculations concluded for now. I lie on one of the tables, and my hands are no longer bound.

The absence of my Firebird feels so strange. I've become so used to the sensation of that weight on my chest, the metal against my skin. By destroying my Firebird, I stranded myself in this dimension forever—or until they decide to exile me to some other dimension so they can bring Wicked back home. She could return to this body at any time, but I'll own her consciousness as long as I remain. Will they put me back in my own universe to die along with it? Or will they cast me into some random, unfamiliar place to blunder through my last hours alone?

My head doesn't hurt. I don't feel dizzy or nauseated. My blackout doesn't appear to have sprung from a concussion. Maybe a human consciousness tethered to a Firebird reacts this way when the Firebird suddenly ceases to exist.

I hear my parents' voices before I see them. Specifically, I hear my mother as she says, "Delete all data related to Project Eurydice. Permanent deletion; hard destruction of former data storage to follow immediately. Authorization Kovalenka One." I turn my head in time to see a green beam sweep past her eye, checking her retina, before the word comes up on the computer monitor in glowing font: CONFIRMED.

Dad hesitates, then sighs. "Secondary Authorization Caine One." Again the word CONFIRMED comes up.

My mother reaches toward the screen before she catches sight of me. To my astonishment, she smiles. It's the saddest smile I've ever seen. "You're all right, then."

"Um, yeah." I try sitting up. I feel okay, and nobody stops me. Not a single security guard is in the room. "What happened?"

"What happened is you destroyed Josie's chance for resurrection." Dad closes his eyes for a moment, but his tone remains gentle. "Not for revenge—we do understand that. We do." He says it like he has had to work to convince himself. "You felt you were saving the other worlds, and her too. Didn't you?"

I nod. The Firebird's explosion would affect even the

"non-observable" body in this dimension—if it didn't have that power, it couldn't bring us back to our bodies to begin with. When I destroyed that chamber, I destroyed Josie's body forever. They have no reason to collapse any more universes, because the slivers of her soul have no place to return to. Josie can finally rest in peace.

I know I did the right thing. What I can't believe is that my parents seem to understand that too. "And you're not angry I did that?"

"We're angry," Mom says sharply. "Losing Josie will never be anything less than the greatest nightmare we've ever known. But what you said—about how she would feel—"

"We thought about ourselves," Dad adds. "Not her."

My mother continues, "We're angrier with ourselves for starting down this road in the first place. For bringing Josie and then our Marguerite into this. We've been trying to cheat a fate we richly deserve. Did you really do anything we didn't push you to do? Are we suffering any loss we didn't earn?"

"We would never have stopped on our own," Dad admits. "But we understand why you had to stop us."

They can't have given up that easily. They can't. Could they have really heard what I was trying to tell them, before? They love Josie so much . . .

. . . but they love me, too. Maybe, despite the terrible loss they've suffered and the renewal of their grief, they can let Josie go if they still get to keep the daughter they have.

Those mutilated portraits in the Josieverse haunt me still.

If the Home Office versions of my parents can give up their quest, I can try to reconcile them to their surviving daughter, even if it means giving Wicked a happy ending she doesn't deserve.

I remind myself not to use the name Wicked here. "Your Marguerite is willing to do anything to get you guys to notice her. To love her best. But you were telling her all these other people were replaceable, that anybody and everybody in the entire multiverse could go straight to hell as long as you got Josie back again. Of course she thinks she's replaceable too. That she doesn't matter. And she hates herself for not being enough. So she killed all these other Marguerites because it felt like committing suicide, over and over."

"No," my mother insists. "She wanted Josie back too, as badly as we did. You don't know her like we do."

"I don't have to know her. I *am* her. Because each version of us is a unique individual who deserves to be recognized for themselves—but something deep down inside is always the same. That's why I can see inside her when you can't. That's how I know this has been destroying her." I struggle for the words. "When she comes home, you have a lot of work to do."

Slowly, Dad nods. "We'll get her back. One way or another."

As long as I never have to deal with her again, great.

My mother finally turns back to the computer console. "Activate final deletion of all Project Eurydice files on my mark."

They're really doing it. They're really going to end their quest for Josie. It's over.

But why did Paul have to die for this? The unfairness and loss claw at me, tightening my throat again. His death saved so many other lives, I tell myself, but I don't even care. Not now, not yet. At this moment I know why my parents thought destroying universes was a small price to pay for bringing Josie back. I feel like I could do terrible things, tear the whole horrible world apart, if only it meant I could see my Paul again.

I wouldn't. Not ever. But now I know just how bad you have to hurt to feel that way.

With the Firebird, I could always find him, or at least a version of him, I tell myself. It doesn't help. Another version won't do. I want the one who gave up everything to save me, the one I held close in Moscow, my Paul. And he's gone.

Mom hits the console. The computer voice intones, "Initiating Project Eurydice shutdown."

Relief washes over me in a dizzying wave. It's over. It's really over.

The lights in the room go out. After a split second of darkness, one of the screens comes on. Projected in front of us, ten times larger than life, is the face of Wyatt Conley.

"Henry, Sophia, if you're watching this, it's because you tried to end Project Eurydice." Conley seems even sadder than they do. "When I swore to get Josie back, no matter what, I had to consider every potential weakness in our plan. One of those weaknesses was the possibility that you would lose your will to continue. So I put measures in place to make sure even you could never stop me."

This can't be happening. But in the projected glow of Conley's image, I can see how pale and drawn my parents have become.

"I'm not angry," Conley says. "I forgive you. Sometimes hope is even harder to bear than grief. For Josie's sake, one of us had to be strong enough to bear it. Looks like it's me."

My mother ducks down to look at the computer terminal, where data is now flashing past at dizzying speed. She whispers, "Dear God."

Conley brings his hands together in front of his face like a man praying and briefly touches his fingers to his lips before he continues. "I took the precaution of locating some of the single most important source vectors in the multiverse. That information is already programmed into the Firebird, ready for Marguerite to act on at any time."

He means Wicked, not me. Her Firebird has been programmed for destruction from the beginning.

"That signal has already gone out to her, and she'll be taking action immediately. Of course, this increases the damage we've had to do, but I know you'll forgive me when we have our Josie back again." Conley smiles. "Until then."

The screen goes black, leaving us in darkness again, except for the flickering light from the scrolling data on my mom's terminal.

"Bloody hell." Dad actually sounds like himself. "We ought to have anticipated this. *He* certainly did."

"But he can't get Josie back!" I protest. "It's impossible with her body gone."

"Wyatt didn't know that when he set up this failsafe," my mother explains. "He must have done this months ago. Maybe even years."

Dad and Mom both just sit there, slumped, as if in defeat. They still don't care about the other dimensions, not compared to their grief. Although they are no longer actively trying to destroy those worlds, they won't fight to save them either.

But I'm not going to stop fighting. Not now, not ever.

"We have to save them." When my parents stare at me, I continue, "Do you have another Firebird? If you tell me what dimensions to go to, what to do, I can still protect them. Still tell them about the stabilizers, all of that. Just tell me you've got a Firebird!"

Mom seems to awaken from her stupor. She walks to a nearby console and pushes a couple of switches. A console door slides open, revealing a Firebird.

Wait a second. As realization dawns, I whisper, "This is *mine*. The one Romola stole from me in the Romeverse."

"The least we can do is give it back," Dad says with a sad, broken smile.

I nod as I try to snap back into action mode. No time to cry for Paul. I can't even let myself think about him, because I won't be able to bear it. I must hold together long enough to complete the mission he died for.

Then I can finally fall apart.

"Okay, I'm ready." I put the Firebird back on. That heavy chain around my neck has rarely felt so good. "Where should I go first? You can give me the data, can't you?"

My dad shakes his head. "It's not that simple, Marguerite."

Mom gestures at the terminal in front of her. "Conley has plots within plots, plans within plans. The multiverse is infinite, and he has exploited its vulnerability to the fullest. Had I any idea he distrusted us so completely—but that's irrelevant now. Suffice it to say that as long as Conley wants to pursue this path, and our daughter is willing to help him, we can't stop him. Blocking an infinite number of pathways is, by definition, impossible."

"That's it? He wins?" I sit down heavily. It sounds like the only way out would be to convince Conley to change his mind, but I don't think I could do that. I doubt anyone could. At this point it's not only about love for his lost Josie; it's about making sure that nobody ever stops him from doing what he planned. Pride can be as strong as love, and a hell of a lot crueler.

"No, that's not it." My mother straightens. "There's another step we can take. Drastic, even radical. But once it's done, Conley can never threaten another dimension again."

My first reaction is anger. "So why didn't you do that in the first place, instead of doing the shutdown thing that tipped Conley off?"

"Because the solution involves sealing this dimension off from all the others, permanently." Dad puts his hand over Mom's, an unexpectedly tender gesture. "We could turn this into a sort of pocket universe, its own tiny bubble."

"So . . . you wouldn't ever be able to travel out of this universe again. Your Firebirds wouldn't work." I can see why they'd be reluctant to do that. However, the stark misery on my parents' faces tells me this scenario has the potential to become far darker.

"That's the best-case scenario," my mother says. "In the worst-case scenario, the bubble pops. This dimension collapses."

"No." That's a fate I couldn't even wish on the Home Office. "That's too much. All the billions of people who live here—"

"Would be lost." My father gazes into an unseen distance, maybe imagining the death of this world. "But that's still fewer lives than we have already taken. And if Conley continues this, a mere fraction of the total death toll."

"That doesn't mean you have to sacrifice yourselves." For Conley, even for my parents, that would be fair. For all the countless other people who live and have lived in this dimension throughout history, it's unspeakably cruel. Maybe you can say that it's worth sacrificing one life to save a hundred, something like that—but once you're talking about entire dimensions, the scale becomes too enormous for that kind of calculus. Billions of lives can't be squeezed down into the X in the equation. "Are you really going to do this?"

And Mom and Dad wouldn't just die. They'd be obliterated, unmade until the end of time. . . .

"Wait," I say. "If your universe dies, doesn't mine go with

it? You've influenced us, changed us."

"But we didn't create you. So no, your dimension won't collapse." My father looks thoughtful. "However, it will warp. Your actions back to the beginning of our intrusion into your universe will be erased, as will all our influence. Your reality will be reshaped."

"Don't worry about confusion," Mom adds. "You won't remember a thing."

"And Paul—he died here—but he'd be alive again, wouldn't he?" Something like hope stirs inside me.

"If he hadn't died in this universe, I'd say yes, certainly." My father says this like any other theoretical. For him this is only a puzzle piece, not a human life hanging in the balance. "As it is, the question becomes far more complex."

"You don't even know?" That brief hope shatters like porcelain. Maybe Paul will return to life—or maybe we'll be thrown back to where we started, with no idea that we ever knew a Paul Markov, or at least no idea what happened to him. He won't only be dead—he won't even be remembered.

All I have left of Paul are memories. I can't let them go.

And if the Home Office's influence on us is erased, so is our influence on other dimensions. If we didn't go to the Russiaverse, the grand duchess would never have had her baby, even though Lieutenant Markov would probably have died in battle no matter what. She would be trapped in that life she hated and forced to marry a stranger, with no child from her great love.

Mafiaverse Theo wouldn't be shot, and Londonverse

would still be alive. But my mother in the Josieverse would still be lost to near-suicidal depression, and the Warverse wouldn't have leaped forward to the technology it needs to defeat its enemy. The cracks in the multiverse would spread wider and wider, beyond any possible judgment of what is better or worse. No one person could ever understand the full ramifications of this act.

In the end, I find myself thinking of the grand duchess, remembering the way her hand stole across her belly. When I stole her night with Lieutenant Markov, I took something precious away from her. I won't take her baby, too.

Paul would say the exact same thing if he were here, even knowing the cost would be his own life.

My actions have consequences. Everyone else has had to live with the repercussions of the choices I made—now it's my turn.

"Don't do it," I say. "We have to figure something else out. You can start by getting your daughter under control."

"No other way offers a guarantee of success." My mother shrugs. "And there is at least a forty percent probability we will survive."

Forty percent doesn't sound like such great odds to me. "Please, you can't do this. If you won't think about your own world, think about mine! You'd be rewriting history. It's like—like destroying yet another dimension, in a way."

"But it will be over." My father's blue eyes, usually so warm, have become remote, and as pale as a pond icing over. "Finally, truly over."

That's when I realize Mom and Dad aren't valiantly sacrificing themselves for the rest of us. They don't care whether they live or die. Josie's gone. They've lost their purpose. Back when they thought they could do some good by stopping Conley, that sustained them. Now they'd rather die than keep on enduring their grief.

My parents only want to be with Josie again.

Dad quietly says, "You should go home immediately. And—that communication you've set up between the dimensions—very clever, by the by, we only picked up on that yesterday, congratulate the other us for us—"

"Henry." Mom pats his shoulder, her usual hint that he is beginning to run on. Even at this moment of mortal despair, they remain connected.

Dad sighs. "If you could use that system to get a message to our daughter, please, tell her to come home."

"What happens to her if she's not here when this universe gets sealed off? Does she die?" I look from Mom to Dad and back again. "Would she be, like, pulled back automatically?"

"She would become . . ." Mom thinks this over. "A spirit without a body. Possibly she would be free to travel from dimension to dimension, but only within other Marguerites. She could never return here. I suspect that would be the same fate she'd face if our universe collapses, though she might prefer being a ghost to simply perishing with the rest of us."

"But ask her. Please. If you can." Dad's voice cracks. "And tell Josie we love her. Right away. Before you don't remember us any longer."

Only a few minutes ago, I thought I could finally see my parents in these people. Now they terrify me more than they ever have before.

I think of all the others out there who deserve to be protected. The grand duchess and her baby. Vladimir, the tsarevich of all the Russias. Josie talking to me in the middle of her Scottish rafting holiday, alive with enthusiasm. Valentina with her little stubborn chin. New York's version of Romola, with her boundless loyalty. Theo in the Warverse, who has already spent so much of his life fighting to stay alive, and who is so helplessly, completely in love.

My father as tutor to the Russian royal family, hiding the secret that one of the children is his. My mother in a world where she's already lost my father and sister, and where the mere sight of a Firebird gave her the hope to go on.

And Paul. The one who learned sign language as a boy so he could talk to the girl he liked. The one who had been rejected, then betrayed, but who still dashed into a collapsing universe to save me. Lieutenant Markov—who is dead, lost forever, but still remembered in a world where his child will someday be born. My Paul, who may be only a memory but who thought and felt and loved, who deserves to *have been*.

All our fates hang in the balance. All our histories. And there is nothing I can do but run.

28

THE MOMENT I APPEAR IN MY OWN DIMENSION, I KNOW IT'S already gone wrong.

Normally returning to your own body is smooth and soft, like easing into a warm bath. This feels like doing a belly flop into icewater. Pain echoes through my body, every nerve crackles, and at first neither my thoughts nor my eyes will focus.

When I can see again, my hand is clutching a piece of paper that reads: YOU SNEAKED INTO MY HOUSE, SO I SNEAKED INTO YOURS.

My hand drops the paper without my volition, and I know then that I really am back home—but Wicked got here before me.

Nightthief. She's already dosed my body with Nightthief. I'm trapped.

As if she can hear my thoughts, Wicked looks up—into the

mirror over my bedroom dresser—and smiles in triumph.

"Let me out of here!" Josie screams from the hall closet. She's beating on the door so hard that it sounds like she's trying to punch her way through. "Give me back my sister!"

Fresh scratches and bruises ache along my arms and torso. Josie would've fought hard, and she's stronger than I am; Wicked only won because of the element of surprise. But the closet door is thick. For now, Josie's stuck.

Wicked walks from the bedroom into the great room, hardly even glancing at the door where Josie's hammering so desperately. The cozy atmosphere has vanished—no, been destroyed. Houseplants have been knocked over, their roots crinkling feebly around the cylindrical mounds of soil on the floor. Books lie scattered around, and the equations have been erased from the chalkboard wall, replaced by obscene drawings and rude commentary on the relative size of Paul's and Theo's . . . of Paul and Theo.

Far more troubling is the sight of Theo, arms belted behind him, bleeding from the corner of his mouth.

"That Nightthief isn't going to last forever," he shouts, and from the hoarse timbre of his voice, I can tell he's been yelling for a while. "You've used it up, and soon it's going to wear off, and then you're screwed!"

"I don't need forever. I'm done here." Wicked lifts her Firebird, leaving mine hanging around my neck. She turns to the same mirror where she braided my hair, triumph gleaming in her eyes. "Next time you take over my body in my dimension when I'm not around? Someone you love dies."

A jolt—and then I slump against the nearest wall. The aching in my beat-up body sharpens, but I don't care. I'm alone in my own head again.

"Theo? It's me now." I hurry over to the chair and loosen the belt that binds his hands behind his back and to the leg. "Oh, God, what did she do?"

"Thrashed me, basically. For the record, she wouldn't have been able to do that if I weren't still recovering." Theo flexes his shoulders, rubs at the reddish dents the leather carved into his skin as he gets to his feet. "Or if Josie had been here at the time. If Wicked hadn't gotten the jump on her, Josie could've taken her *out*."

I hug Theo quickly. "Is there any way to save the Home Office?"

He gives me a double-take. "Whoa. Why are we trying to save the Home Office? And what from?"

"They're trying to seal themselves off so Wicked can never get out again, but there's a chance that whole dimension will collapse, and if it does our history gets rewritten, completely. That can't happen. Besides—if we can save a dimension, we should. Even if it's the Home Office." My parents and Wyatt Conley are only three people among billions. That world's Theo deserves to survive, him and all the other countless people in that world. "I think they've already started the process. Can we stop it?"

Theo takes that in for a second, then shakes his head. "If

I had a month to work on this, maybe I could figure out exactly how they're doing that and how to prevent a collapse. But not even I'm genius enough to do it in a few minutes."

What's about to happen to all of us? Is the reality I know about to be erased? There's no way for me to know, no way for me to control anything. "So we're just . . . stuck here? Waiting to find out if our memories are about to be rewritten?"

Theo groans. "Looks like it."

"Marguerite, is that you?" Josie calls from the closet, then pounds on the door. "Let me out!" I hurry to free her, which right now feels like the only useful thing I can do.

"What's that?" My dad pokes his head out of my parents' bedroom. I realize they've just jumped back too.

I open the closet door to see Josie tucked between our winter coats. She has the beginnings of a black eye and a fist cocked just in case I've been lying about being the real me. But she relaxes when I let her walk past me into the hallway, where Mom, Dad, and Theo have all gathered.

As I explain the plans to seal off the Home Office in its own bubble and its potential collapse, the physicists in the room become agitated in the way they do when thoughts are flying fast. They know our history could be erased without my having to explain it. Impossible as it is, they're still trying to figure out how to preserve the Home Office in time. Theo even grabs a piece of chalk to jot down some rough equations, though he pauses a moment to grimace at what Wicked wrote on the wall. "Really?" he mutters as he erases the words with his bare forearm. "C'mon. Give a guy some credit."

As the math starts to fly, Mom says, "Where's Paul? He left the Moscowverse to follow you to the Home Office. Did you find each other there?"

Words desert me. How can I bear to tell the others that Paul is dead? I have to—I know this—but it seems as if speaking the words will make them true. As if my silence makes it possible that he might return home to us, safe and sound, like this is all one bad dream.

"Good news," Theo announces, saving me from having to answer.

Josie pauses from repotting the poor houseplants. "What?"

"If we're using the tracking technology from the War-verse correctly, and I think we are, Wicked went right back home, as in the Home Office itself. So that mean's she's done, right? They're going to seal off that world—or destroy it—but either way, she's not coming back. Yes?"

"Yes." Her parents don't need me to deliver the message anymore. The Home Office is about to be sealed off forever. No more dimensions are in danger. It's really all about to be over. My throat tightens with unshed tears, both of relief and the sorrow I can hold back no longer.

"Sweetheart?" Dad steps closer to me, the concern in his blue eyes changing to fear. "Did you say whether you found Paul? Did you see him?"

Theo gets this seasick look on his face. He's seen the truth in my face. "No," he whispers. "No, it can't be—"

Nausea sweeps through me, followed by a rush of dizziness. My shoulder slumps against the wall. My hands brace me to keep me from falling. My mother cries out, thinking that I'm collapsing from grief, and by now the others have realized why I'm grieving—why I can't say what happened to Paul.

But another horror overtakes me, seizing my muscles, my voice, and my will. Once again I am imprisoned in my own body. And two Firebirds hang around my neck.

Wicked's back.

"Did you—did you think . . ." She's having trouble talking. The Nightthief is wearing off. She won't control me much longer. "That I—would let them—kill me?"

She found out about the bubble. She found out about the chance of destruction. And she escaped here.

"Marguerite?" Josie says. She's the only one not freaking out about Paul, at least not so much that she can't tell I'm acting weird. Wicked turns away and covers my face with my hands.

You might live! There's a chance! But the words won't come out of my mouth.

Yet it doesn't matter, because Wicked hears me and answers in a raspy whisper. "I don't—like—the odds."

In this strange twilight of the drug, my consciousness can communicate with hers. Surely I'll get control back any second.

But not soon enough, because Wicked takes her Firebird in hand and begins to turn the controls in a way I've never seen before. I know it, though, even before I recognize a little twist of the thumb I recall from Romola Harrington's trick in the Romeverse.

Wicked's setting up a collapse. She's going to destroy my universe.

No. It's impossible. We can protect ourselves. Can't we? We've done this for so many other worlds—

"You didn't—save yourselves—first. Stupid." She laughs once, a bitter sound I can hardly recognize as coming from my own throat. "Always—look out—for number one."

But you'll die too! If your world and ours both vanish, you'll kill yourself along with the rest of us.

"Fine. So long as I get the rest of you. You talked them into this. You dished it out. So take it."

"Marguerite?" my mother says through tears. "What are you—"

Theo catches on and snarls, "Oh, hell no. Not now!"

The ground trembles. Not that much, nothing out of the ordinary here on the edge of the San Andreas fault. My parents and Josie hardly even react. But I know the truth. It's the beginning of the end.

I want to call Wicked more names. I want to tell her she has the worst life of any Marguerite in the entire multiverse, not because her dimension sucks but because she's chosen to lead the angriest, meanest, most vindictive existence possible. I want to taunt her with the horror of what awaits her, an eternity of parasitic possession where she will never, ever be able to call anything or anyone her own.

399

But my fate is even worse. I will never have been born. My last moments will be spent knowing that everyone I have ever loved is about to be erased along with me. Wicked has doomed us all.

The earth trembles again, stronger this time. Her hands tighten over the Firebird, and with a rush she's gone.

I stagger backward as Theo grabs my shoulders and shakes me. "Get out of her. Get out of her!"

"She's gone! It's me!" I cry. "It's collapsing. The universe is collapsing. Wicked used my Firebird and destroyed us—"

"What?" Theo looks like he might faint. Understanding dawns on my parents' faces, followed by horror.

"Wicked jumped back inside me. She started the chain reaction. I couldn't stop her." A sob rises in my throat. My family, my friends, and my world are all about to die at my hand.

"Damn!" Dad runs for the pile of equipment at the far end of the great room, Mom and Theo just behind him. "We can do this. How long do we have?"

A couple of hours, I want to say. It took that long for the Romeverse to fall. But maybe our world is more fragile, because already the earthquake has returned, this time strong enough to rattle the dishes in the cupboard. The few remaining books on the shelves fall to the floor.

Mom answers my father's question. "Not long enough."

But they all throw themselves at it, grabbing material, trying to get the stabilizer device put together in no time. Josie, blank-eyed, starts taking more things off shelves, putting them on the floor so they won't tumble down and get broken—sensible in an earthquake, irrational here. Not that I can blame her for being terrified to the point of shock. My entire body feels numb.

Then I hear footsteps in the hallway behind me. Who else could be in our house?

Only one person.

I whirl around to see—"Paul!"

Oh, God, he's alive. He made it out after all—

—only to come here and be killed along with the rest of us.

I try to run for him, but the shaking earth nearly topples me. Only slumping against the wall keeps me from pitching onto the floor. Paul catches himself, bracing both hands against the sides of the hallway. As soon as it's steady enough to move, he rushes forward. "What's going on?"

"The universe is collapsing," Theo says. "Bad Marguerite possessed Good Marguerite just long enough to make it happen."

Paul turns to me just as I reach him. His arm is still bandaged along the scar she slashed in his skin. I fling myself into his embrace, as if his strength alone could hold me up while the rest of the world falls. The scent of his skin, the feel of his hands on my back, even the catch in his breath as he pulls me nearer—everything about him is more precious to me than ever before. It is the most beautiful and terrible moment of my life.

Terrible, because I know Paul has been given back to me

just in time for us to die together.

Though pent-up sobs threaten to steal my voice, I manage to say, "Where were you? I thought you were gone."

"There was no time to figure out a new destination. I had to jump backward to the Moscowverse. Then I had to recharge the Firebird and—damn." Paul swears again in Russian at the bleak irony of getting home just in time to die.

Although I know the answer, I have to ask, "We can't escape, can we?"

He kisses my cheek, my forehead, and clutches me even tighter. "No way out. Not one we would ever take."

And he's right. Whatever existence we would have after this would be stolen from other selves, other worlds. Would I rob Valentina of her real parents forever? Or force my War-verse self to give up her life so I could lead it instead? Do we decide whether to take one alternate self for good, or to steal weeks or months from others? Escaping this dimension without any hope of going home would turn us into parasites.

I don't want to die. But I refuse to live if the cost is betraying what I believe, and who I love.

At least I got to see Paul one more time before the end.

He turns to look at the frantic activity on the rainbow table. He makes no move to join them. That's when I know. "Paul, can they build a stabilizer in time?"

"No."

The real quake hits then. We all shriek or yell, and every

one of us falls to the floor except Josie, who was already there. Shouts from outside make me wonder what's happening to the sky, or whether the ground has split apart to reveal another moment of pure hell.

Paul crawls closer, reaching out for me. This is it. We're going to kiss each other goodbye and die in each other's arms.

Instead, he grabs my Firebird, and I remember our one chance.

"Linking the Firebirds!" I shout over the din of falling plates and blaring car alarms outside. Back in the Moscow-verse, he said this might work in an emergency. There's never been a bigger emergency than this. "That's going to save us, isn't it?"

"It might," Paul says as he starts fitting them together.

"Might?"

"I give it a thirty-four percent chance of success."

Oh, God. "Do it."

"It's going to hurt." Paul doesn't say this to give me a chance to back out. Already he's readjusting my Firebird and his, working fast because we both know there's no other choice.

Our ceiling morphs and shimmers, then seems to melt, revealing a storm-cloud sky overhead. Josie begins to scream. And Paul brings our Firebirds together.

It's like a lightning strike. Pure pain boils through me, so anguishing I can't even breathe. I've never felt pain like this—a reminder comes close, but a reminder's over in a second and this goes on and on.

Paul shudders in the same agony. But he pulls me into his arms, hanging on as if I could save him. Tears blur my vision. The whole house is falling apart, or maybe the dimension, and surely this is the end.

"I love you." I hold him even closer, grateful for the chance to say this just one more time.

"I love you, too." He folds me against his heart.

If this is how we end, then let it come.

At that moment, light surrounds us, blazing bright as a sun, and a tremendous shudder of energy passes through my body. It's like the eye of a cyclone at the heart of me, winding tight and pulling me inward. The whirl of it hurts more than all the rest. I cling to Paul even more desperately, willing myself to stay in one piece. To stay with him. To stay alive.

Then everything . . . stops.

The pain vanishes. The shaking subsides. The ceiling's just a ceiling again. For a few long seconds we all lie there, not trusting our own senses.

Hope and despair and confusion collide, blurring my thoughts as I hang on to Paul. He looks as astonished as I do. But the silence endures, and the stillness, until I begin to think they might last forever.

"We made it," I whisper. " . . . Didn't we?"

Theo's expression slowly shifts from bewilderment to a

smile. "Either that or the afterlife is way more mundane than advertised."

Paul breathes out in relief. "We made it."

Josie and Dad both start to laugh with joy—they have the same crazy cackle. I should be laughing too, or cheering, or jumping up and down in crazed glee. But I'm still too stunned to feel anything but astonishment.

Theo slides over to us, a grin on his face. "Little brother, what did you just do? Show me this mad sexy science."

Paul sits up, towing me with him. Now I can see that Mom has already pulled herself back to her feet and is busily working with her own Firebird. I try to sit up on my own, but I'm clumsy and slow; the Nightthief lingers in my system, and my muscles twitch in the aftermath of extreme pain. "Mom? What is it?"

"The Home Office. We have to be sure they won't try again." Mom squints at the readouts.

They wouldn't. Wicked might. "They weren't destroyed, were they? Because our history is the same."

"Exactly," Dad says. "I think they've sealed themselves off. And it looks like your counterpart is sealed in there with them."

She went back. She heard what I said and went back, even knowing she might die. Wicked gets another chance she doesn't deserve. But her ultimate fate is in her own hands. If her life is any good from now on, that's because they found a way to get through to her. If her life's a hell, it's because she's still venomous, bitter, and small. I'll never know which, and honestly, I don't much care. For me, it's enough to know we'll never see her again.

Dad's laptop lies open on the floor, dirt from a capsized fern scattered across its keyboard, but it still works, signaling us that someone is calling via Skype. Paul gets that icy look in his eyes as he staggers to his feet. "There's only one person it could be."

My father grabs the laptop, brushes it off, and sets it on the rainbow table as we gather around. Still trembling, I brace myself against a chair. When he clicks Answer, Wyatt Conley's face appears on the screen. His smug satisfaction has been wiped away, replaced by fear. "Listen—I know we're not on the best terms, but if I'm interpreting these readings correctly, we just—"

"—took care of it." Mom folds her arms. "Our world is safe. Triad as you knew it is over. One of your counterparts is dead, and the other is trapped permanently in a sealed universe."

Dad cuts in. "As of now, Wyatt, you're alone. You're also outnumbered—because we now have several other worlds working with us, every one of which has been warned about you. So I suggest you drop the idea of meddling with inter-dimensional travel ever again."

Josie leans between our parents' shoulders to show her face to the screen. "And also, just for the record? We are *never* going out."

It's like Conley can't take it in. Has he ever been defeated before, even once in his life? He's succeeded over and over again, raking in the money and praise of the entire world, but now all he can do is stare. At last he says, "What happens now?"

I step forward to speak to the screen. Hopefully this is the last time I ever have to look Wyatt Conley in the face. "I suggest you go back to cell phones. That's what you're good at."

With that, I hang up. The screen goes blank.

Theo shakes his head. "If we could put that bastard in jail—expose him, make the world see what's he's done—"

"We can't." Dad's expression is rueful as he flops down on the sofa. "They haven't any laws against this sort of thing yet, have they? We stopped him, Theo. Let that be enough."

"Besides, think of all the research awaiting us." Even amid the wreckage of our house, a brush with death not even ten minutes in our past, Mom's eyes are already starry with the thought of discoveries to come. "The links between the universes, the unlimited potential of the data we can share . . ."

"Mad sexy science." Theo manages to smile.

Josie resumes rescuing the poor plants, putting them back in their pots, and Mom tries to sort the scattered piles of paper back in the order they were in to begin with. Dad and Theo head to the front door. This is supposedly to check on how bad the damage is outside in our neighborhood, but probably Theo also wants to be sure his car made it through okay.

"Marguerite?" Paul's voice is gentle.

I look up at him, struck anew with the wonder of his survival. What's even more beautiful is that he's smiling back at me with just as much joy. Just as much hope.

He takes my hand and says, "Let's make a world."

EPILOGUE

AS FAR AS THE NEWS IS CONCERNED, WHAT HAPPENED that day in San Francisco was an earthquake—one with a strange shock pattern, but not even all that serious. Aside from a couple of minor injuries from fender benders, nobody was even hurt.

A few people on social media mention strange things they saw or thought during the quake, and some conspiracy-theory sites blame "chemtrails." Mostly people write the weirdness off as fear and confusion. Hallucinations caused by panic, maybe. No one realizes just how close our world came to destruction. Already the quake has been almost for-gotten. Life goes on.

Josie invites me down to San Diego for a couple of week-ends, and I go. She teaches me to surf, or tries to, anyway. I never manage to do much more than stand on the board for roughly thirty seconds before I tumble back into the ocean.

It doesn't matter. More important are the evenings we spend walking along the beach in our bikini bottoms and swim shirts, towels draped over our arms, an ice cream cone in each of our hands as we talk about everything and nothing.

We always got along, but it doesn't have to be anger that drives people apart. Time and inattention can separate us just as surely. How far apart might Josie and I have drifted if I hadn't had a chance to see how desolate my life could be without my big sister? If we hadn't consciously decided to carve out more time for each other?

I'm glad we'll never know.

The collaboration between the dimensions continues. Now we're much more likely to simply talk than to visit, and journeys are always checked out in advance. I travel less often than the others now, because the trips are de facto scientific conferences. But I've visited along with my parents or Paul just to see how things are going.

In the Warverse, "our side" of the conflict seems to be turning the tide. While none of us are thrilled that they've used their new knowledge to design weaponry, it's their choice to make, not ours. Their Marguerite writes, and receives, long love letters from Theo at least twice a week. If the Paul from that world is ever going to have a chance, Theo will have to seriously screw up.

The Mafiaverse is making significant strides forward. My parents try to visit on weekends when Josie and Wyatt aren't around. Their version of Wyatt Conley continues to be devoted to my sister, so there's no point in tearing him down. Maybe his Mafiaverse self is his best self—the person he could've been here, if his ego hadn't gotten in the way. Their Theo did lose one leg below the knee, which is terrible. But he's learning to deal with a prosthetic, and his anger is directed at the mobster who shot him. The prospect of discovery engages Theo more than any bitterness about the past.

As for the Russian mob version of Paul, well, he's stopped trying to contact that Marguerite. (Our Paul, of course, never visits that dimension.) The police never found him. He's somewhere in that world leading a very sad life. I hope he finds a way out of it before the poison sinks in too deep and turns him into another version of his father.

The Triadverse went completely silent for a while, until the other versions of my parents finally reached out. Without Conley around, or any interference from the Home Office, they've been able to take control of the Firebird project again. That Paul returned to the US from Ecuador with the other me at his side, both of them relieved to be back home.

The Oceanverse continues to believe we should pay for that submarine. Apparently they're superlitigious over there—that's something I didn't pick up on during my visit. We've told them to take it up with the Triadverse, since it was technically that Theo's fault. But his death leaves them still searching for someone to blame. Thank goodness you can't sue someone in another dimension. Not yet, anyway.

In the Cambridgeverse, my parents have forgiven their version of Paul, at least enough to work with him again on the new discoveries. Apparently my other self forgave him too; they haven't gotten back together, but they're . . . doing better. And she got into film school at USC, which is amazing. She dreams big, too—she's even left out some fashion magazines for me when I've visited, complete with jokey Post-It notes asking me which gown would make the best Oscar dress. I've returned to this dimension more than most of the others, although I admit that's mostly to play with Ringo the pug.

Some worlds I'll never see again. The Spaceverse understands that it wasn't exactly me who sabotaged the *Astraeus*, but I doubt I'd receive a very warm welcome. The Moscowverse doesn't have the technology to join in or the desire to play along. In a police state, inexplicable movements and memory lapses are exponentially more dangerous. They were glad to help us in the end, but just as glad to see us go. And of course any world in which a Marguerite died is cut off from me forever. That futuristic London is lost; so is the chance to explore the tombs in Egypt.

But I've visited the world where Dad and Josie died in the carjacking, to spend more time with that Mom. She doesn't want to come here and see them because she says it would set her back. Still, I've been able to share some of their scientific data with her, and she enjoys just hearing about the others—imagining the lives her husband and older daughter would have led.

I might see the Russiaverse again, someday. The grand duchess sent a message for me with Theo, saying that she appreciated my promise not to return, but that I'm welcome to come back one more time, after September, if I want to see the baby. What she really wants is for me to be able to tell Paul about this child that is partly his, partly mine, and entirely hers. That trip will be difficult, not to mention mind-blowing, but I'll go. It would be worth it just to visit Vladimir, Katya, and Peter again.

But I'll do it even if I don't get to see them. I owe the grand duchess so much. It's the least I can do. And I want to see the baby, too.

"This is extraordinary work." The examiner walks around the room where my portfolio is on display. "You have an exceptional breadth of techniques for a student so young."

I want to jump up and down and make squealing cheerleader noises. Instead I manage to stick with "Thank you."

Although RISD remains willing to admit me in January, in the end I had to go after my dream. The Ruskin School of Fine Art holds portfolio reviews in maybe half a dozen cities around the country, during which dozens of applicants present their work for examination. Impressing the professor on the scene doesn't guarantee admission—other faculty members will look at photos later, before the final vote.

But impressing the professor can't hurt, right?

"Tell me more about this series of sketches." He gestures to the papers I've set out on a table.

"Right. I guess you've seen on the news about my parents—"

The professor's eyes take on a hopeful gleam. All the news media knows is that we've proved dimensional travel is possible, and that some of us have done it. We had actual paparazzi outside our house for about a week, which was hilarious. But the details of the alliance remain under wraps for now. We've learned how easily this technology can be abused, and until my parents can develop some safeguards, we can't share too much. In the absence of hard knowledge, rumors have flown, and apparently this stoic, distinguished art professor from Oxford is dying to learn all about it.

Well, I can tell him a little. "I've gone on several journeys, and this is someone who's close to me in many different worlds. So this series is an exploration of how his portrait has to change to reflect his unique fate in every dimension."

Half a dozen sketches of Paul lie on the table—one angry, with dark lines of tattoo ink visible at the neckline of his shirt. Another in medieval garb, his expression gentler, his sorrow obvious. And in the center is the portrait of Lieutenant Markov. I'm proud of that one, because when I look at it, it's as if I can feel his love for me all over again. Really, though, the emotion of the image comes from my love for him.

"Will you be doing any more work based on your travels?" Apparently that's as close to prying as the professor will allow himself to go.

I nod. "I want to do a series of self-portraits, too. I changed

414

as much as anyone in the different dimensions. I want to dig into the complexity. The strangeness. All of it."

Already I know the hardest portrait to do will be Wicked's, which is why it's the most important one to get right. But I'll paint her image as many times as I have to, until I can discover exactly how to show the ways in which we are different—and the ways in which we are the same.

Theo, meanwhile, will be spending his postdoc year at Yale, which offered him a fellowship he couldn't refuse. He's been tinkering with his muscle car, making sure it's ready for the cross-country drive to come.

He's not completely recovered from his exposure to Nightthief, but he's almost there. Every week, his face takes on a little more color, his laugh gets a little louder, and his energy level rises. Before he leaves, he's determined to show Paul yet more "remedial adolescence"—which mostly means them watching "important" action movies on Netflix, but okay.

Theo hasn't spoken of his feelings for me since our good-bye kiss in the Cloneverse. I'm pretty sure those feelings are already changing. The wistfulness I used to see in him when Paul and I were together—that's all but vanished now. He's at ease around us, happy to hang out or to give us time alone. Theo being Theo, he has his own stuff to do. He's even gone out a couple of times with this girl he met at a Lumineers concert.

"Nothing serious," he says when I ask him about her. "I'm

about to move to the other side of the continent. Kinda gets in the way."

Theo wouldn't even let a bomb come between him and the person he loved. I learned that about him, even if he's only just accepting it about himself. "As long as you're happy. That's the main thing."

He smiles over at me. "I'm getting there."

Neither of us speaks of our counterparts in the Warverse, who are so passionately in love, or how devoted his scientist self has become to the grand duchess, even while she's carrying another man's child. Those worlds prove that we could have been together, that there are dimensions where I am his fate, and he is mine.

But in this world, we have a friendship so deep and powerful that I feel sure it's going to last our entire lives. That's a fate worth having too.

For some reason, the fact that my parents got married in so many dimensions has reminded them that they never got around to making it legal in this one. Mom phoned a cousin of hers who has a cottage in the French countryside, and now my dad is checking next year's academic calendar to find the perfect date for him to whisk the family away for a destination wedding.

"At last," I sigh one night, as we're sitting together on the back deck with Rice Krispie treats. I clasp my hands together in melodramatic gratitude. "Josie and I will be legitimate. No longer children of sin."

"You know we would've married long ago if it bothered you girls, but it never seemed to," Mom explains. The tropical-fish lights glow orange and blue in the night. "We kept waiting to find the time. But there's never enough time for everything you want to do. You have to prioritize. Henry and I have finally prioritized getting married."

"We should've done it years ago." Dad is lying on his back, his head against Mom's knee. "Have you seen how much rings cost these days? Good God."

Mom musses his hair. "Soon, we'll be able to share more of our work with the scientific community at large. Then others will pick up the torch, make discoveries we never imagined. We won't have to live and breathe dimensional travel any longer."

"You know what that gives us time for?" Dad's eyes light up.

Please don't be talking about sex, I think. *Please please please.*

But it's even worse than that. Beaming, they say in unison, "*Time travel.*"

Are they serious? I think they are.

Oh, God.

"I wonder what it'll be like when we get to England," Paul says as I fasten my seat belt on the plane. He gave me the window seat.

"You went to the Londonverse twice."

"I mean, when we get to our England." Just as he has been for the past few weeks, he's torn between anticipation and worry. "Dimensional differences will be profound, not to mention the subtle changes in language use and social behavior—and yes, I'm becoming academic because I'm nervous."

Hearing him diagnose his own nerves makes me smile. Paul's learning how to deal. Even better, he's learning how to be happy.

How to be loved.

Two days after I got my admission letter to the Ruskin School of Fine Art, he accepted Cambridge University's post-doc offer. Oxford's very close to Cambridge, which means we'll be able to see each other every weekend. But we'll still have our own college experiences, our own chances to explore and grow up.

Above all, we have our chance to create our shared destiny, together.

The Firebird was built one equation at a time. My paintings are the result of countless small brushstrokes, each one shaded with a different blend of colors, each one with a single, deliberate purpose. Every moment, every day, we are all making something—whether it's science or art, a relationship or a destiny—building it choice by choice, moment by moment. Our decisions shape other people's worlds as well as our own. We are all the center of our own universe, and all of us in someone else's orbit. It's a paradox, but sometimes paradoxes are where truth begins.

My father would point out that the Beatles told us all of this decades ago. They once sang that in the end, the love we take is equal to the love we make. No, we can never be in complete control of our fates—we're all vulnerable to accidents, to cruelty, and to the random misfortune of life. But I try to think about how much of it is up to us. We decide what emotions serve as our building blocks, which feelings we'll use to shape our universe.

So Paul and I are creating a world, side by side, day by day. We have no idea what our future holds, only that we are making it together.

And we're going to make it beautiful.

The jet engines whirr louder as our plane taxis down the runway. I glance back toward the airport, where I imagine Mom and Dad are still wiping away tears. Paul grips my hand so tightly that I wonder if he's phobic. "You aren't afraid of flying, are you?"

"No. I'm familiar with both safety statistics and the laws of aerodynamics." At first I think Paul has gone back into Spock mode, but then he smiles with so much warmth that it's like stepping into sunlight. "I just wanted to hold on to you."

I squeeze his hand back just as hard. "I'm not letting go."

The plane accelerates, pressing us both back into our seats so firmly that we laugh. As we rush forward, faster and faster, we lift off from the ground and claim the sky.

READ ON FOR A PEEK AT ANOTHER
GREAT BOOK BY CLAUDIA GRAY

SPELLCASTER

1

BEFORE ANYTHING ELSE, NADIA FELT THE CHILL.

She wasn't sure why. Her father already had the car's heat on because of the awful weather. Her little brother, Cole, was too engrossed in his game to have rolled down any of the windows. The only sounds were the *slap-slap* of the windshield wipers, Cole's thumbs tapping on the tablet screen, and Dad's classical music—some piano concerto, notes rippling and rolling over them, not unlike the driving rain outside. It was just like the other countless hours they'd spent in this car today.

There was no reason for the trembling cold that snaked its way along Nadia's skin. No reason for her head to swim as all her senses heightened.

No normal reason anyway.

Nadia straightened in her seat—in the back, next to her brother. The passenger seat in the front was always left empty, as if Mom might suddenly return at the next rest stop. "Dad, where are we?"

"Almost there."

"You said that three states ago," Cole chimed in, never looking up from his game.

"I mean it this time," Dad insisted. "We should get into town any minute now. So hang in there, guys."

"I just mean—my head hurts." Honestly explaining what was wrong was out of the question. Nadia already knew that the strange sensations washing over her weren't physical or emotional.

They were signs of magic.

Dad turned the piano music down to a soft wash. "You okay, sweetheart? There's painkillers in the first-aid kit; we could pull over."

"I'm fine," Nadia said. "If we're almost there, let's not stop now."

Even as she spoke, though, she felt as if she had made a mistake—as if she ought to have said, *Yes, pull over, let's get out of this car as soon as possible.* Everything within her told her that they were traveling closer and closer to a source of magic—unlike any she had known before. But instinct alone told Nadia this magic was . . . primal. Powerful. Potentially overwhelming.

Her eyes flickered over to the empty seat next to her father. Mom would have known what to do—

Well, Mom's not here, Nadia told herself savagely. *She's still back in Chicago, probably off drinking cocktails with some guy she just met. I'll never finish my training. I'll never be able to use magic the way she did.*

But we're headed into something dangerous. I have to do something.

But what?

Nadia glanced sideways at Cole, who remained wrapped up in his game. Like her father, he was oblivious to the forces they were approaching; like all males, they were magic-blind. Quickly she closed her eyes and settled her left wrist in her right hand. On her left wrist she wore what Dad called her charm bracelet—and it did look like one, at a glance.

Even after Mom had left, ruining their lives and all Nadia's hopes, Nadia had kept wearing the bracelet every day. It was too hard to let it go.

Her fingers found the small pendant of ivory, the material she needed to balance her spell.

Silently, she went through the spell for illumination of magical shape. The ingredients came back to her faster than she would have thought.

> *A winter sunrise.*
> *The pain of abandonment.*
> *The knowledge of love.*

She went deep within herself, calling up the ingredients, experiencing each more powerfully than real memory—as if she were living them again—

The sun rising on a sharp, cold morning when the snow was high enough to sink into knee-deep, painting the sky a pale pink, while Nadia shivered on the balcony.

Nadia standing dumbfounded in the door of her parents' bedroom as Mom packed a suitcase and said, "Your father and I think we should live apart for a while."

Waking up in a violent thunderstorm to find Cole curled next to her wearing his footie pajamas, in silent, total confidence that his big sister could protect him.

The emotions and images coursed through her, reverberating through her powers, bouncing off the ivory until Nadia could see—a barrier. They were headed straight toward . . . what was this? . . . Was it meant to keep out any other forms of magic, or warn someone else if magic entered this space?

Nadia's eyes widened. She'd be able to pass through the barrier—limits on magic didn't apply to magic users—but that wasn't her biggest problem.

Oh, no, she thought. *The car.*

In the trunk, in her suitcase, wrapped in her clothes, was her Book of Shadows.

"Dad?" Her voice was tight and high with fear as they came closer to the barrier; she could almost feel it now, like static electricity against her skin. "Dad, can we pull over?"

He'd been too lost in his own thoughts to hear her. "What's that, sweetheart?"

And then—impact.

The road seemed to jerk beneath the wheels of the car, as if the earth were being sheared away beneath them. Nadia slammed into the window as her father struggled for control of the wheel—in vain. She could hear the squeal of brakes and Cole's scream as the world turned over, over again, thrashing her in every direction at once. Something hit her head, and then she couldn't quite see, couldn't quite hear. Yet Cole was still screaming—or was it her? She didn't know anymore—

They crashed to a halt, the impact throwing her forward and backward so hard that her seat belt felt like a club smashing into her chest.

She slammed back into reality, and wished she hadn't.

Nadia cried out as the window beside her—now beneath her—splintered, and mud and water began oozing in. Above her, Cole half dangled from his booster seat, wailing in panic. She reached up with a shaky hand to touch him, comfort him, make sure he wasn't injured. But her head was still reeling.

The Book of Shadows—it hit that barrier, and it was like—like an explosion or something—

"Cole! Nadia!" The inside of the car was almost entirely dark now that the lights were as dead as the engine, but she could make out the shadow of her father trying to clamber into the backseat with them. "Are you all right?"

"We're okay," Nadia managed to gasp.

"The water—"

"I see it!" Already the muck was rising—or was the car sinking? Nadia couldn't tell.

Dad stopped trying to get in the back with them; instead he managed to push open the passenger-side front door and climb out of the car. For one moment, Nadia felt crazy terror stab her—*he's left us, where's Dad, where's Dad?*—but then Cole's door opened and Dad reached inside to pull her little brother free.

"Daddy!" Cole wailed as he clamped his arms around their father's neck. Raindrops fell into the car now, hard and stinging. Nadia managed to undo the straps of his safety seat, so Dad could lift him.

"That's right. Daddy's here. Nadia, I'm going to get Cole out of this ditch and come right back for you. Right back! Hang on!"

Nadia nodded, too quickly, because her whiplash-stung neck ached. She clawed at her seat belt, freeing herself just as the water rose high enough to wash over one of her legs. The seat belt had been keeping her out of the mud, and she tumbled into it. It was cold—so cold the mere touch of it numbed her to the bone. A long scrape along her forearm stung tears into her eyes. She was clumsy now, and even more afraid than before. But it didn't matter as long as she could still climb out.

She braced her feet against the armrest and tried to stand; she was dizzy, but she could do it. Where was her father? Was he all right?

Lightning flashed. In the blaze of that sudden light, Nadia glimpsed someone above her.

He was her age, perhaps. Dark hair, dark eyes, though she could tell nothing else in the night and the rain. But in that flash of lightning, she'd already seen that he was beautiful—so much that she wondered if the crash had dazed her into seeing phantoms, delusions, angels. Thunder rolled.

"Take my hand!" he shouted, reaching into the wreck.

Nadia grabbed his hand. His fingers wrapped around her wrist, and they felt like the only warmth in the world. She let him tow her upward, helping him by climbing as best she could. Rain spattered against her face and hands as she emerged from the wreckage, and her rescuer slung one arm around her waist to pull her away from the car, onto the nearby bank of the ditch they'd crashed into.

As they flopped onto the muddy ground, lightning crashed again, painting his face in eerie blue. He must have seen her more clearly, too, because he whispered, "Oh, my God. It's you."

She drew in a sharp breath. This guy knew her?

How could he know her when she didn't know him?

Next to them were Dad and Cole. "Thank you," her father breathed, clutching one side as if in pain; Nadia only then realized he'd been injured.

"Dad! Are you okay?"

"I'm fine," he said, though his whole body was stiff with pain. "I was able to call 911 while our new friend—what's your name?"

"Mateo."

Nadia turned back to him, but Mateo was already looking away from her, as if unwilling to meet her eyes. He, too, was gasping for breath; the rescue couldn't have been much less frightening for him than the crash had been for her.

But how could he know her? *Did* he know her? Was she imagining things in the aftermath of the wreck?

"While Mateo helped you. We'll—we'll be all right."

"What happened?" Cole sniffled. He clung to his father as if afraid he might fall in the ditch again.

Nadia scooted closer to them so she could take her little brother's hand. "It's okay, buddy. We're okay. We had a wreck, that's all."

"Sometimes cars hydroplane during a storm." Dad breathed in and out through his nose, hand still braced against his ribs. "That means the tires are actually on the water instead of the road. It can be dangerous. I really thought—I thought we were going slow enough to avoid that—"

"You weren't doing anything wrong." Nadia wished she could have told her father not to blame himself, but he could never understand what had just happened to them, or why.

She turned back to see her mysterious rescuer—Mateo— but he was gone. Peering through the rain and gloom, Nadia tried to make out where he might be. He couldn't have gotten far. But she couldn't find him; it was as if he'd vanished.

Her father, distracted with pain and Cole's fear, didn't seem to notice that Mateo had left. "We're okay," he kept repeating, rocking her little brother back and forth. "We're all okay, and nothing else matters."

In the distance, sirens wailed, and she could make out the beat of red-blue lights from a far-off police car or ambulance. Help was on the way, yet Nadia shivered from the cold and the adrenaline and the pent-up fear.

She glanced upward to see that they'd damaged a sign in the wreck. Leaning to one side, rocking back and forth in the wind of the storm, was a placard emblazoned with the words WELCOME TO CAPTIVE'S SOUND.

She's real.

Mateo stood in the woods, his back to a tree, as he watched the police see to the family he'd just helped. An ambulance had pulled up for the father, but there didn't seem to be any particular rush for them to get to the hospital. Nobody was hurt too badly. Good.

Despite the darkness, he could see the girl sitting in the backseat of the police car. A pale blanket had been wrapped around her shoulders. It helped to think of her warm and safe.

Lightning streaked through the sky overhead again, and Mateo remembered dimly that standing next to a large tree was probably not the smartest thing he could be doing right now. But shock had numbed him past the ability to move.

Besides—he knew he wouldn't be killed by lightning tonight.

He *knew*.

All day, he'd tried to ignore the dream he'd had. He'd told himself that it was a nightmare like any other—the vision of the storm, the crash, the beautiful girl trapped in the wreckage. But when the sun had set and the rain had come, Mateo had been unable to ignore the dream any longer.

9

He'd come out here in the hopes of proving to himself that it wasn't true. For hours, he'd stood in the rain, watching and waiting, pissed off at himself for even believing this was possible, yet more hopeful as time ticked on and nothing happened.

And then—right when he'd begun to believe it really was only a dream—everything had happened just as he'd known it would.

She's real, he thought. *If the crash happened like I saw it would, then so will everything else I've seen.*

Shaky and cold with horror, Mateo closed his eyes against the realization that he was doomed.

And if the girl from his dreams didn't stay far away from him—she'd be doomed, too.

2

DESPITE WHIPLASH AND THE BANDAGES ON HER SORE arm, Nadia got to work unpacking right away. Dad couldn't manage much with his ribs broken, Cole was way too young to help with anything besides putting away his toys, and besides—there were certain items she wanted to be positive nobody else saw.

Like, say, her witchcraft supplies.

I could come up with an explanation for the glass jars, like, they were for makeup or something, Nadia mused as she unwrapped them from wads of newspaper. *But the powdered bone? Forget it. Dad would probably think I was on drugs.*

It felt stupid to have kept everything. Without Mom, there was no hope of continuing her training; witchcraft was a closely held secret, passed down between female relatives in the rare bloodlines that had the power. Mom had never revealed the other members of her coven to Nadia—which

11

was just how things were. Nadia wouldn't have expected to learn any of their names until she was a true witch herself and able to join the coven in her own right.

Still, she'd thought one of them might reveal herself after the divorce—come forward and offer to teach Nadia, or at least give some advice—

But nothing. Mom probably hadn't even told them that she'd abandoned her own daughter half-trained, with only enough knowledge to get herself in trouble, not nearly enough to solve any of her problems.

No matter how good a student she'd been, no matter how hard she'd worked her whole life—Nadia would never get to become a witch now. Mom had taken that with her, too.

Even as her throat tightened with unshed tears, Nadia tried to snap herself out of it. *You know enough to do some things. It's still useful, right?*

Useful enough to get us in a car crash. If I'd faced facts and ditched my Book of Shadows—

But no. She could never do that. A Book of Shadows—even one as new as hers—had power. You couldn't leave that lying around. And she didn't have the heart to destroy it.

Despite everything, Nadia didn't have the heart to walk away from the Craft yet.

As she thought of the wreck, the images of that night swept over her so vividly that it was like she was back there in that ditch. The way the storm had crashed and rolled overhead. The terror of feeling herself sliding down into the cold muck, not knowing whether she could escape.

And Mateo's face, outlined by lightning, as he reached in to save her—

Nadia's breath caught in her throat. Who was he? And how had he known her?

But that wasn't the biggest mystery of that night, and Nadia knew it. The biggest mystery was—who had put up that magical barrier around Captive's Sound?

And why?

A THOUSAND LIVES.
A THOUSAND POSSIBILITIES.
ONE FATE.

IS BACK

Author of the *New York Times* bestseller STARGAZER
CLAUDIA GRAY

THE EVERNIGHT STORY continues with a thrilling new chapter. When Balthazar agrees to help Skye Tierney, a human girl who once attended Evernight Academy, he has no idea how dangerous it will be. Skye's newfound psychic powers have caught the attention of Redgrave, the vampire responsible for murdering Balthazar and his family four centuries ago. Balthazar will do whatever it takes to stop Redgrave and exact long-awaited revenge against his killer.

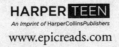

JOIN THE
Epic Reads
COMMUNITY

THE ULTIMATE YA DESTINATION

◀ DISCOVER ▶
your next favorite read

◀ MEET ▶
new authors to love

◀ WIN ▶
free books

◀ SHARE ▶
infographics, playlists, quizzes, and more

◀ WATCH ▶
the latest videos

www.epicreads.com